Praise for the novels of B.J. Daniels

"The new Powder River series is a must for Daniels fans and romantic suspense fans."
—*Fresh Fiction* on *Dark Side of the River*

"Filled with twists, danger, action, secrets, family dynamics, and romance."
—*Comfy Chair Books* on *Her Brand of Justice*

"Daniels is a perennial favorite, and I might go as far as to label her the cowboy whisperer."
—*BookPage*

"Super read by an excellent writer. Recommended!"
—Linda Lael Miller, #1 *New York Times* bestselling author, on *Renegade's Pride*

"B.J. Daniels has [the] unique ability to astound with her mystery and suspense."
—*Under the Covers Book Blog*

Dear Reader,

As I celebrate Harlequin's milestone in history, I'm celebrating my own with them and my readers. My dream at age nine was to write books one day, but life got in the way for a lot of years. I was worried that it would never happen.

I was forty-five when I finally wrote my very first book, *Odd Man Out*—and Harlequin bought it, making my dream come true. But more than that, it set me on an adventure I hadn't even imagined possible.

Thirty years and more than 125 books published later, all I can say is thank you, Harlequin, and my wonderful readers! It's been a wild and wonderful ride! I'm glad we've done it together and I get to share some of your history with my own.

Writing is a solitary lifestyle, just me and my made-up characters hanging out for hours every day. I had no idea when I sold that first book what a world it was opening up to me.

I'd joined the Harlequin family, meeting editors and authors, with many of them becoming good friends over the years.

But the biggest blessing writing for Harlequin is my readers, and I hope I've enriched their lives because they have mine in ways I never dreamed. We've shared so many memories and milestones, and are still making more every day!

Happy anniversary, Harlequin! Here's to seventy-five years—and many more!

B.J. Daniels

RENEGADE WIFE

NEW YORK TIMES BESTSELLING AUTHOR
B.J. DANIELS

FREE STORY BY
CINDI MYERS

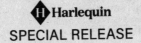
Harlequin
SPECIAL RELEASE

Harlequin®
SPECIAL RELEASE

ISBN-13: 978-1-335-01691-1

Renegade Wife
First published in 2024. This edition published in 2024.
Copyright © 2024 by Barbara Heinlein

Mile High Mystery
First published in 2024. This edition published in 2024.
Copyright © 2024 by Cynthia Myers

For questions and comments about the quality of this book, please contact us at CustomerService@Harlequin.com.

TM and ® are trademarks of Harlequin Enterprises ULC.

 Harlequin Enterprises ULC
22 Adelaide St. West, 41st Floor
Toronto, Ontario M5H 4E3, Canada
www.Harlequin.com

Printed in U.S.A.

CONTENTS

New York Times and *USA TODAY* bestselling author **B.J. Daniels** lives in Montana with her husband, Parker, and three springer spaniels. When not writing, she quilts, boats and plays tennis. Contact her at bjdaniels.com, or on Facebook or X @bjdanielsauthor.

Also by B.J. Daniels

Harlequin Intrigue

Renegade Wife

Silver Stars of Montana

Big Sky Deception

A Colt Brothers Investigation

Dead Man's Hand
Her Brand of Justice
Set Up in the City
Christmas Ransom
Sticking to Her Guns
Murder Gone Cold

Canary Street Press

Powder River

Dark Side of the River
River Strong
River Justice

For additional books by B.J. Daniels,
visit her website, bjdaniels.com.

RENEGADE WIFE

B.J. Daniels

In his youth, my husband spent many hours on the back of a horse working for an outfitter in Cooke City, Montana. I fell in love with him and his stories about that part of his life. After a weekend recently in "Cooke," I also fell in love with the small tourist town nestled at 7,600 feet between Yellowstone National Park and the Beartooth Mountain Range. This book is dedicated to the unique town that inspired this book and helped make my husband the man he is now.

Chapter One

Geneva Carrington Beck pried open her eyes to find herself sprawled face down on the couch. For a moment, she had no idea where she was or how she'd gotten there. She'd awakened with one thought. Something was wrong.

As she blinked, trying to wake, her view was suddenly blocked by a lolling wet pink tongue and a cold black nose. The tongue flicked out to lick her face—and not for the first time she realized as she jerked back, her cheek sticky and wet. She stared down at the large brown eyes set between two floppy ears—one white, one black—as the puppy tried to jump up on the couch with her.

Sitting up abruptly, her head swam. The dog began to bark in little yips that would have been cute if her head wasn't splitting. She glanced from the couch toward the open-concept living-room-dining-room-chef's-grade-kitchen. Silver and white balloons bobbed as if on a breeze along with a banner hanging askew over the massive kitchen island. She strained through her throbbing headache to read the words: Happy Anniv—

Memories shoved their way through the foggy confusion. The new house full of people laughing and talking loudly over the music. The clink and rattle of ice cubes against crystal. An air of excitement all around her as she and Lucian celebrated their first wedding anniversary with the people closest to them. Her handsome husband quieting down the crowd so he could surprise her with her anniversary gift.

"*I would give you the moon and stars if I could,*" he'd said before pulling the wriggling ball of black-and-white fur from a giant box with the flair of a magician. "*But my wife's first puppy is close.*"

The room had erupted into oohs and aahs as she'd hugged the adorable dog to her. She'd been overwhelmed that Lucian had remembered the one thing that had always been missing from her perfect life.

"*You have the most amazing husband,*" her best friend Mitzi had whispered as she'd passed on the way to the bar. "*You've always been so lucky.*" Mitzi had no idea.

The memory, though, made her mouth go dry now.

Turning, she reached down and picked up the puppy, holding her close and getting another lick. As she did, she saw that she was still wearing the expensive green dress Lucian had bought her for the party. The negligee he'd also purchased had been laid out on her bed for after the party. That's when she and Lucian planned to celebrate not just their first anniversary but her thirtieth birthday.

What had happened last night that she'd ended up on the couch alone? She couldn't imagine that she'd drank so much that she'd passed out—let alone why she was having trouble remembering all but random moments from the party.

"Lucian?" With the puppy in her arms, she stood and had to take a minute for the spins to stop. Her head was a whirling maelstrom, and her mouth was Death Valley. She thought she might be sick. "Lucian?" How long had she slept? She could see sunshine streaming into the living room sliders. Beyond the glass doors the Pacific Ocean glistened blue-green as far as the idea could see.

"I love San Diego and this view," Lucian had said the day the Realtor showed them the house. *"I can see us here, Geneva, can't you?"*

She moved to the window now, trying to make sense of why it was early afternoon. Why hadn't Lucian awakened her? It had to be late given the angle of the sun.

She shifted the puppy in her arms to glance down at her wrist, expecting to see the diamond watch her father had given her for her twenty-first birthday. Her wrist was bare except for a small red scratch. She stared at the scratch, her stomach roiling as her gaze flicked to her ring finger. Her beautiful diamond engagement ring was gone, along with her diamond-studded wedding ring.

As she started to panic, she told herself that she might have taken both off last night for some reason. She looked around for her phone. The house was so large that she and Lucian often called one another via cell phone from the different levels.

Her phone wasn't by the couch. Her heart began to pound. That feeling that something was very wrong grew stronger with each step as she checked the lower floor for her phone—and her husband. He wasn't in their joint office or the media room or their gym or in the sauna or the pool outside. Neither was her phone.

At the bottom of the stairs, she looked up with growing trepidation. He could be anywhere in his huge place. Five bedrooms and five baths. She'd argued that it was too large, but Lucian said he wanted lots of room for their family to grow. As an only child, she'd wanted that more than anything.

But after what had happened with her father, she worried about spending too much. *"We deserve this,"* Lucian had said. *"I just want you to be happy."*

She didn't need a house to make her happy, she'd told him. *"You're all I need."*

There were too many places in this house to get lost, she thought as she headed for the primary bedroom with its spa bathroom, his and hers walk-in closets and a sitting space large enough to do cartwheels.

Maybe Lucian had drank too much last night and was still in bed. She recalled him making drinks at the bar downstairs, laughing with their friends. It had been their first party since buying the house. Before that, they'd lived in her apartment for a short time after they'd met because it was larger than where Lucian had been living, but she'd known how unhappy he was there.

"We need a place of our own," he'd said. *"I'm a chef. I want to entertain our friends. I need an amazing kitchen so I can cook for you."*

She thought of him last night when he'd handed her a margarita and whispered something about getting everyone to leave soon so that just the two of them could take the party upstairs. What had happened after that? The party downstairs could have gone on until the wee hours of morning—apparently without her.

As she topped the stairs, she hoped to find her husband still snuggled in their California king-size bed. She pictured the puppy and her climbing into bed with him. But she feared that she wasn't going to find him in the bed. Nor did she expect to find him on the grounds. As huge as the house and property with a view of the Pacific Ocean, she could feel his absence.

Pushing open their bedroom door, her heart fell at the sight of her negligee lying on the bed where she'd left it— the bed covers untouched. But there on her nightstand was her phone. She rushed to it. Lucian would have called. Or sent her a text. He wouldn't have just left.

She saw the time. It was even later than she'd thought, early afternoon. She scanned her phone. No calls. No text from Lucian. She tried his number. It went straight to voicemail. "Where are you? I'm worried. Please call me."

Worry and fear fought for control. Where was he? There had to be a simple explanation, one her befuddled brain couldn't grasp. Maybe he'd told her about his plans last night before she'd passed out on the couch and she forgot the details? That was so unlike her, but what other explanation was there?

She glanced at his bedside table, where he always placed his phone, watch and keys every night. All were gone, sending a fissure of worry through her even as she assured herself that he must have gone out and probably hadn't wanted to wake her.

He'd been talking about trading in his car. He'd probably been up most of the night and decided to go out first thing this morning. She wished he'd left her a note though, but it would be just like him to come back with some amazing car to surprise her. She just hoped he didn't spend too much.

She hurried down the stairs, holding tightly to her puppy as she headed for the oversized four-car garage.

"*We need more cars,*" Lucian had said the moment he'd seen the massive garage. "*Fortunately, I have a couple in mind.*" Her father had encouraged him to wait, telling him it was a bad time to buy a car. He'd agreed, although she'd seen that her father's butting in had annoyed him.

She knew he hadn't quit thinking about trading in his older model Porsche, saying it was too much of a bachelor car. "*I'm a married man now. I need something to drive to show off my beautiful wife in.*"

Geneva reached the entrance to the garage, stopped to shift the puppy in her arms and opened the door. The

Porsche was gone, leaving an oil spot on the concrete floor. But so was her Range Rover. The garage was empty.

Ice ran the length of her spine, and her legs went weak with what she was seeing. She hugged the puppy tighter and closed the door, her baffled mind racing. How could both cars be gone? Maybe he'd had a friend—Mitzi's husband, Hugh—drive the Porsche and Lucian took the Range Rover. She wanted to believe it, almost did, until she looked down at her wrist where her watch had been. That angry scratch told a different story. It looked as if the watch had been ripped from her wrist.

Fear gripped her. What if they had been robbed? What if Lucian had been abducted? She looked at the puppy. "You must know where he went." The dog tilted her head as if considering the question, then let out a single bark and began to wriggle in her arms. She stepped out by the pool to the side yard and put the puppy down to do her business.

Her mind threatened to go to places she refused to consider. That bad feeling she'd awakened with sounding even louder warnings that something was more than just wrong. Once the puppy was finished, she picked her up and hurried back through the house, taking the stairs to the second floor much faster this time. She rushed into their bedroom again, only this time going to her walk-in closet and the safe hidden in the wall. Her fingers shook as she punched in the security numbers. A beep sounded and she pulled open the door.

Empty.

Her jewels, her money, everything. She stared, stunned. How? Only she and Lucian knew the code. For a moment she couldn't move. Lucian would have had to have opened it. At gunpoint? Bile rose in her throat as she closed the safe door.

Putting down the puppy, the two of them went to Lucian's closet. She didn't have to open his safe. The door was standing open. And it wasn't the only thing empty. So was his closet. All his suits, shoes and good clothes were no longer neatly filling the rich cedar-lined space.

The only thing left was one discarded old sweatshirt from college that he'd refused to part with when they'd gotten married a year ago. She picked it up, hugging it to her, breathing in his scent. Her husband was gone. There would be no ransom demand because he hadn't been kidnapped. Nor had he gone to trade in his car. He'd taken everything of value.

And left like a thief in the night.

She dropped his sweatshirt on the floor where the puppy began to chew on one ragged sleeve's wristband.

Chapter Two

Back downstairs, Geneva wandered around zombielike before the puppy began to whine. She looked to see if Lucian had thought to buy dog food. Finding none, she dug out some cold cuts from the refrigerator to pull together a make-shift meal, then took the pup out in the backyard again.

While she watched the puppy frolicking on unsteady chubby legs in the recently manicured yard, Geneva tried to think. But her thoughts circled like vultures. It seemed pretty obvious. Lucian had taken everything and left her without a word.

It made no sense. They'd been so happy, hadn't they? If he was going to leave, why would he insist on buying this house they could barely afford? Because she would be coming into her inheritance on her thirtieth birthday—the same day they would be celebrating their anniversary. The huge party had been Lucian's idea. She'd wanted something small and intimate, but he said their friends all wanted to see the house. Why not accomplish both with one big bash?

She'd gotten caught up in his excitement. After all, he'd bought her an expensive dress for the party and an even more expensive negligee. They'd been spending her inheritance even before she'd gotten it, making her worried. She hadn't even told Lucian or her best friend Mitzi about what she'd gone through with her father.

He'd had a very successful business most of her life. Her mother had died when she was two, and he'd never remarried. Instead, he'd spoiled his daughter, buying her anything her heart desired.

She never suspected that he was in trouble financially. Even when he'd been diagnosed with cancer and had only a short time to live, he'd joked about needing to die before his money ran out. It hadn't been a joke. Her father was broke when he died.

"I'm just thankful that your grandmother left you something," he'd told her on his deathbed. *"I made some bad investments and couldn't pull myself out of debt. I'm so sorry."*

She'd been able to pay the last of his medical bills and for his funeral with the money she had saved from her job at the art gallery in the historic district of San Diego where she worked. It was no wonder that Lucian's spending had worried her. While he'd never said as much, she suspected he'd had limited financial resources growing up. He'd often commented on how lucky she'd been to grow up the way she had.

What was she going to do? The realization of her situation began to settle in as her headache waned. Everywhere she looked, she saw Lucian in this house he'd loved. Standing in the doorway, asking her something, smiling at her, telling her how much he loved her, how much he loved the house, loved their life. It couldn't have all been a lie. It couldn't have.

But if true, why would he leave?

Another woman? Wasn't that usually the case?

But wouldn't he have left a note? A text? Given her some clue?

How could she ever tell anyone about this? Even Mitzi,

her best friend. As desperately as she wanted someone to talk to, she couldn't bear the humiliation right now.

Still stunned, she tried to understand how this had happened. There had been no warning. No lipstick on his collar, no mysterious phone calls or unexplained late-night work excuses. They spent most of their time together when Lucian wasn't at the restaurant where he'd been a chef, until he'd quit to open his own place. They'd been looking together for a building to lease for his restaurant. He'd been so excited, and she had too. She would have noticed if there'd been any red flags, wouldn't she have? He hadn't done anything that cheating husbands did.

Because he was too good at deceit? He'd certainly fooled her, she thought as she stood in her massive bedroom, living in a house she couldn't afford and all alone.

Except for her new dog, she thought with a teary smile. The puppy was asleep on her bed. She started to put the negligee away, but in a fury, wadded it up and stuffed it into the trash. That felt so good that she looked around the room wanting to throw everything away. This house, the furnishings they'd picked out together, all of it had been to accommodate Lucian's tastes. She wanted to burn down the place and walk away—just as he had done.

Hurt and embarrassed, it felt good to be angry. She was down, but she wasn't beaten, she told herself. She still had the money from her grandmother. She would put the house on the market right away. She would be all right.

She stripped down and walked into her spa-like bathroom to take a long hot shower. But her bravado quickly abandoned her—just as her husband had. She had let the man into her heart, into her life, into her bed, and he'd deceived her. She felt weak with shame, the pain of it pushing the anger aside as the racking sobs demanded to be released. How could she have been so naive? Had he targeted her from the beginning, only pretending to love her?

She let the hot water wash away her tears. Her life had been a fairy tale, no bumps in the road. Her loving, wealthy father had seen that she never wanted for anything. After college, where she'd majored in art and art history, she'd traveled with friends who had the freedom and funds to tour Europe to see the world.

And just over a year ago, she'd met Lucian. He'd been working as a chef at a small out-of-the-way restaurant along the beach that her longtime best friend Mitzi had found. She'd introduced them and before long, she and Lucian were inseparable, living a charmed life that her friends all envied, especially Mitzi.

Now, in the blink of an eye, it was gone because it had never been real. Her fairy-tale life had been a lie, her husband was a thief, a liar, a coward and a crook. She couldn't keep pretending that she'd wake up tomorrow and it would all have been a horrible nightmare.

This was her new reality. She couldn't go on pretending Lucian was coming back any moment begging for forgiveness. By the time she came out of the shower, she was angry again. No, she was furious, she thought as she dressed, determined to do something. She would eventually have to tell her friends. She'd never had to deal with a betrayal like this. She could admit that her pampered life thus far had left her ill-equipped to handle this strange situation alone.

She needed to call someone. The police? And tell them what? Everything she and Lucian had owned had been in both of their names when they'd gotten married.

In the past, she would have called her father, but he'd passed not long after she and Lucian had married. Her father had used the last of his money to throw her a wedding he couldn't afford—his idea, not hers. She hadn't known he was insolvent, let alone sick when he walked her down the aisle. She missed him so much. He'd been her hero. Everyone had said how fortunate she was that she had Lucian after losing him. Her father had encouraged her not to marry Lucian so quickly, to take time to get to know him better.

"*Are you sure about this*?" he'd asked her when she'd told him that Lucian Beck had asked her to marry him. "*You barely know him.*"

"*I know I love him.*" She also knew that her father hadn't been well lately. She hadn't known how sick he really was, but she'd worried that if they waited, he might not feel up to walking her down the aisle.

"*At least don't rush into a wedding,*" he'd said. "*Nothing wrong with a long engagement.*" But she hadn't listened. Lucian had been as anxious as she was to tie the knot.

If only she could call her dad. He'd know what to do. He wouldn't say, *I told you so.* He'd take care of her the way he had from the day she was born.

Call Mitzi? She knew she shouldn't feel as ashamed and embarrassed, but she was. She was going to have to tell her best friend at some point. She felt herself start as she realized that Mitzi should have called *her* by now. Her best friend always called after parties to dish about who wore what, who said what, who drank too much, who didn't drink at all. Pulling out her phone, she checked again. No calls. No texts. It was as if Geneva was the only one left in the world, everyone else gone.

Her hand was shaking, and she was fighting tears as she called Mitzi, afraid she would burst out sobbing, but she had to find out if something had happened last night. The phone rang four times. By then, Geneva had made a half dozen excuses for why her friend wasn't picking up before the call was answered, but not by Mitzi. "Hugh?"

"Mitzi must have forgot where she left her phone," he said. "So not like her to take off without it."

"No." It wasn't like her. Geneva swallowed the lump in her throat. Mitzi was already up and gone this morning? That too wasn't like her, she thought until she realized it was afternoon. Mitzi hardly ever got out of bed until noon after a party. Not that she didn't call from bed to dish usually. "Where did she go?"

"I don't know," he said. He sounded like he was walking through the house looking for her. "I'd say she went out jogging early, except she doesn't do early, as you know, and she sure doesn't jog." He chuckled but quickly stopped as he said, "Her car is still here. That's odd." Geneva could hear the concern in his voice growing. "Maybe she went back to bed. Just a minute."

She listened to him breathing as he climbed the stairs. Hugh was thirteen years Mitzi's senior. She joked that she married for money, not realizing that Hugh wasn't going to share it. They lived in a modest house, drove modest vehicles and lived a modest life in El Cajon, to Mitzi's disappointment.

"*I should have been born a Carrington,*" her friend often joked. "*You don't need a husband. You always have Daddy's money and now you have Lucian. Talk about lucky. It's like he was tailor-made for you. Could he be any more perfect?*"

She hadn't told Mitzi that there was no Daddy's money because she felt as if she would be betraying her father's memory. She'd prefer to let everyone believe her father had been successful right to the end. The only one who knew was Lucian, and he hadn't found out until after they were married. He'd been upset that she hadn't told him, saying he didn't want them keeping anything from each other.

"Geneva?" Hugh's voice pulled her back. He sounded worried now, an urgency having crept into his voice. "Mitzi isn't here. I've looked everywhere."

She closed her eyes. The two missing cars in the garage. She knew, heart deep, she just knew. "Did she take some of her things?"

He didn't answer right away. She heard doors opening, hangers being pushed aside. "This is so odd. I don't understand. If she'd planned to take a trip, she would have mentioned it last night."

Geneva knew his confusion, his worry—worse—what Mitzi missing meant. "Lucian is gone too."

"What?" She heard him sit down heavily. "Are you sure? That can't be."

"He took everything, all his clothes, all our cash, including both cars," she said. Now at least she had a pretty good idea of who had driven the second car.

"Have you checked your bank account?" he asked.

She hadn't. They kept quite a bit of cash in the house. She hadn't thought beyond that. "Let me call you back." She disconnected and with trembling fingers called up her account. It took only a few moments.

When she called Hugh back, he said, "Mitzi took everything in the joint account and the savings account I'd set up for her. Thank God I didn't put her name on my business accounts, or I'd be bankrupt right now."

"All of our funds were in joint accounts." Was she telling him this to make him feel better? Or because she felt responsible? She was the one who'd brought Lucian into their lives. "He took every last cent."

She heard something crash and shatter on the other end of the line followed by a string of swear words. Hugh sounded like she felt, shattered more than whatever he'd broken. "I'm so sorry, Hugh. I'm so sorry."

"I need to make some calls," Hugh said and disconnected.

Geneva did the same and had to sit down. Mitzi. Her best friend. Could it have been more clichéd? The puppy had found the dangling cord of the Happy Anniversary banner and was now tugging on it. Geneva didn't have the energy to stop the dog as she found herself ping-ponging between disbelief and devastation. She'd been so happy, so looking forward to the future. Lucian said he'd wanted children, he wanted to fill this house with their laughter. Isn't that why she'd gone along with purchasing this huge house they really couldn't afford?

Geneva stood again, unable to sit still. What was she going to do? If it wasn't for her inheritance from her grandmother, she couldn't even afford the next payment on this house. Her heart began to pound wildly in her chest. She felt faint as she fumbled out her phone again.

Earlier she'd checked their joint checking and savings accounts. She hadn't checked the trust account because she'd been hoping that the money hadn't already gone into it.

But it was, the deposit, the withdrawal. The zero balance. He hadn't let her a dime.

Lucian. He'd taken everything, including her self-esteem and left her with nothing. So where was he now? Somewhere with Mitzi, she reminded herself. Maybe on his way to buy an island.

She glanced out the front window as if she could make him materialize. She desperately wanted to see him coming up their drive, begging her forgiveness, claiming he'd made a terrible mistake.

What she saw instead made her freeze. A large dark

SUV drove slowly toward the house. Unconsciously, she stepped back from the window so she couldn't be seen. The vehicle stopped and after a moment, two large older men got out. They both wore black clothing and jackets that looked bulky.

She saw one man pat his side. Checking for a phone? Or a gun? He had the look of a man who carried a weapon. Cops? She didn't think so. Geneva lost sight of them as they walked up to the front door. She heard the bell ring and held her breath. It rang again, then one of them pounded on the door hard enough to make her chest hurt and the puppy bark. She hugged the dog to her.

A few moments later, one of the men walked across the grass to the attached four-car garage. He cupped his hands to look through the small window in the first garage door, then motioned to the other man. He didn't look any more happy to find the garage completely empty than she had.

All her instincts told her that they were looking for Lucian. She saw them both disappear on the far side of the garage as they headed for the back of the house. The doors were locked, weren't they?

She had gone out to the pool this morning with the puppy, but she always locked the door—unless she'd had too much on her mind earlier. She realized that the security system wasn't armed either. Why would Lucian bother to set it when he left the way he obviously had?

Too late now, she told herself as she moved as stealthily as possible to the guest bedroom with the best view of the pool area. The men came around the corner of the garage and headed for the back of the house. Again she held her breath as they disappeared from view under the awning over the back entrance. Were they in the house?

She reached for her phone, ready to call the police when they stepped away from the back and crossed by the pool.

One of them stopped as if to comment on the pool before they both moved on, disappearing around the house.

Geneva breathed a sigh of relief when she saw them heading for their vehicle. They were leaving. One of them was on his phone. He appeared to be angry, talking fast. Leaving a message for Lucian? She lifted her phone, zoomed in on the two and took a photo, remembering something a friend had done the day before their house was broken into. It had helped the police find the men and get much of what they'd stolen back.

But she didn't think these two had come here to burglarize the house.

Her heart pounded as she watched them drive away. All she could think was *Lucian, what have you done?* Whatever trouble he was in, he'd left her to deal with it. The realization that she hadn't known her husband pierced her heart like a knife blade.

Worse, she couldn't shake the feeling that the two men hadn't given up. They'd be back. Probably once it got dark.

Chapter Three

She had to get out of this house. Rushing to her bedroom, she put the puppy down on the bed and hurried around the end of it, planning to throw a few things into a suitcase. But as she did, she stepped on something halfway buried in the thick carpet.

Reaching down, she picked up what appeared to be a key to a very large padlock.

Geneva stared at it. Had Lucian dropped it in his hurry to get away with his crimes against her before she woke up on the couch downstairs? She suspected he had drugged her. It would explain why she'd slept so late, why her head felt fuzzy and why her stomach was doing somersaults. That and waking up to find out what her husband had done to her—not to mention her best friend's part in it. Either way, she felt sick to her stomach as well as sick in heart to be deceived by people she'd loved and trusted.

As her mind started to clear a little, she studied the key, turning it in her fingers. What had he locked up that he'd kept a secret from her? And where? What if he'd left some of the money there, unable to skip the country with all that cash?

Downstairs in the office, she began to hurriedly go through his desk. He had hardly ever used his office here at home. She found recipes he'd been given by well-meaning people who'd heard he was opening his own restaurant. Was it even true that he'd been the head chef at the restaurant where she'd met him? He certainly hadn't cooked while she was married to him, preferring to go out or order in.

He'd left behind the recipes, no doubt never planning to have to cook ever again, she thought. He could now be a man of leisure, something he must have been planning all along. As she was about to give up, she saw a faded receipt stuffed in the very back of the drawer. It took a moment to pry it out without tearing the thin paper.

Just as she'd thought. It was a receipt for a year's rental of a large storage unit. The date was right before she'd met him, only months before they fell in love and got married. He'd never mentioned having anything in storage, priding himself on never accumulating more than he could load into his Porsche. When she'd met him, he'd been living in a studio apartment, saying it was all he'd needed.

So, what had he valued enough that he'd paid an expensive storage fee all these months?

She pulled out her phone and called an Uber.

As she grabbed her purse and the puppy, Hugh called, sounding both upset and heartbroken. "I always told myself that if something better came along, Mitzi would leave me. I guess I hadn't really wanted to believe it. I wanted to believe that she'd married me for more than my money."

Geneva didn't know what to say since she was going through the same range of emotions. They'd both been duped and dumped, and it felt like a kind of death. The death of the life they'd been living as well as the murder of their illusions about the person they had loved and trusted.

"You think they're still in the city?" he asked, sounding hopeful. She could hear it in his voice that if he found Mitzi, he would beg her to come back. Geneva understood, she thought as she waited for her Uber. But she couldn't imagine taking Lucian back, knowing that she could never trust him again. She thought about her friendship with Mitzi. How could she ever forgive either of them?

"I doubt they'd stay around here," she said. "Hugh, they're gone. Somehow, we have to put it behind us."

"How do we do that?"

She had no idea. Her Uber pulled up out front. She was anxious to get to the storage shed before Lucian realized his mistake in leaving the key behind. He could be sawing off the padlock right now. She had to know what else he'd hidden from her. "I have to go, Hugh. If you hear anything, call."

"I'm just finding this hard to believe. You and Lucian seemed so happy."

Geneva really didn't want to hear this. "It was all a lie, Hugh. He was apparently only waiting for me to get my inheritance from my grandmother when I turned thirty. He planned it right down to the day."

"I'm so sorry, Geneva."

She disconnected and hurried out to the waiting Uber. On the drive to the storage facility, she tried not to get her hopes up. The way her luck was going, the storage unit would be empty. She thought about asking the Uber driver to wait but changed her mind. He let her out at the large storage unit company gate, and she headed for the office. She had no idea how long this might take. The unit could have been emptied out by now.

"Going to need to see some ID," the man behind the desk told her.

"I'm Lucian Beck's wife," she said as she pulled out her ID. "He asked me to pick up something for him." She showed him the key and the receipt as well.

The man glanced at the receipt, then asked, "What's your dog's name?"

She looked over at the puppy in one crook of her free arm. The dog seemed interested in her answer. "I don't know. I haven't decided yet."

"Cute dog." He waved her in.

She walked down the street-like lanes between the units, letting the puppy trot along, until she found number nineteen. The unit was large. What had he hidden that he needed something this size?

Her gaze went to the equally large padlock still on the door. That didn't mean that he hadn't already cleaned out everything he valued, she told herself as she checked to make sure the puppy was close by and pulled out the key.

Nervously, she tried it, afraid Lucian had already been here and replaced the lock. If the key didn't fit, she'd know that he'd realized his mistake in leaving it behind. Her real terror, though, was what she might find once she took off the lock and lifted the huge metal garage door. Her father had been right. She hadn't known Lucian. She'd jumped into marriage just as she'd jumped into buying that ridiculous house. Lucian had conned her, and she'd let him.

The key turned; the padlock fell open. She carefully removed it and reached to lift the door and stopped. With a start, she realized that the storage unit could be full of slowly decaying dead bodies, like that one late night movie she and Lucian had watched. Lucian could have had a secret life much worse than she'd already discovered, and once she opened this door—

She took a deep breath, let it out and pulled. The door rolled up with a clatter. She blinked into the semidarkness of the storage unit, then stared in surprise at one more thing her husband had been hiding from her.

Chapter Four

Geneva squinted at the grill of a shiny black vintage pickup truck. For a moment, she thought she'd opened the wrong storage unit. Until she remembered the framed photograph Lucian had by his bed in his studio apartment when she'd first met him.

It was of teenage Lucian standing next to an old black Chevy truck. At the time, she'd paid more attention to the lanky good-looking teenager than the truck.

"It was my uncle's pickup when he lived in Montana," he'd said admiring the truck in the photo. *"It's vintage. You can't find these anymore—especially ones in such good shape. When I was a boy, I swore that one day I would own one. Just never had the money."*

She realized that she hadn't seen the photo of Lucian and the pickup since that day. Swore he'd own one someday, huh? Just never had the money?

And yet, here was the truck, where it had been for over a year, and with Montana plates on it.

She looked closer. The license plate tags were up to date and wouldn't expire for another six months. What the heck? Why had he kept this from her?

Picking up the puppy now on her heels, she moved along the driver's side to the door and opened it. She put the pup on the bench seat and climbed in, wondering if Lucian ever came out here to visit his truck. She thought she could smell his favorite aftershave.

The keys weren't in the ignition. She checked the glove box, rooting through it. No keys. But there was a paper folder with photographs and negatives in it from a time before cell phones. Pulling it out, she leafed through the photos. She'd half expected the photos to be of Lucian and an old girlfriend.

But that didn't seem to be the case. They were all photos of mountains and wild animals and Lucian and apparently friends. One photo in particular caught her eye. Lucian dressed in the college sweatshirt the puppy had clearly destroyed earlier. He stood in the middle between two other young men, all three grinning at the camera. One of the men was wearing a Montana State University sweatshirt. Lucian's old sweatshirt had been from the University of Alabama. The other man wore a Yellowstone National Park T-shirt.

She didn't recognize the other two men, but from their grins, they appeared to be good friends. Also, Lucian, who hung on to very little, had kept these photos. How was it that he'd never mentioned these men? Why keep the photos in his truck, also something he'd never mentioned? It was clear that the framed photograph by his bed at his studio apartment hadn't been taken in Alabama as she'd been led to believe—but Montana. Why had he kept all of his from her?

Mentally, she smacked her palm against her forehead. The man was a liar. Con artist. A thief. Who knew how many other secrets he'd kept from her? But one thing was clear. Like this pickup, he hadn't wanted her to know about these men or his connection to Montana, where his truck had been licensed.

She looked more closely at the photographs, all of them

apparently taken in the same small mountain town with the same individuals. In one, there were several vehicles with Montana tags.

Quickly looking on her phone, she found that the first two numbers signified what county the plates had been purchased in. Lucian's pickup had Park County plates like some of the others in the photographs. She found the county online and saw that it was right on the edge of Yellowstone National Park.

Looking more closely, she could make out the name of a business behind the men in one of the snapshots. Cooke City Rock Shop? It took only seconds to find the town on her phone. She shoved the photos back into the glove box, along with some papers that had fallen out, suddenly overwhelmed by what she'd learned about her husband and unsure she could handle anything else today.

Why had he hidden the truck and the photos from her? Lucian wouldn't have kept any of this secret unless it was important to him. Earlier, she'd almost hoped that he'd dropped the storage unit key on purpose because he'd wanted her to find it, that he'd left her a clue as to where he'd gone because he wanted her to come find him.

Now she realized how foolish that was. Why would he want her to know anything about him that might help her track him down and get her money back? The thought had its appeal though. She could imagine his face when she showed up in Cooke City, Montana, with his pickup.

On impulse, she checked under the mat at her feet, thinking it was too easy, and let out a cry of pure joy when her fingers closed over a set of keys. Lucian had never been very imaginative.

For a moment, she just sat behind the wheel of the pickup, not sure she was up for what she was thinking of doing. She glanced at the puppy happily inspecting the truck's bench seat. Admittedly, her first thought had been to take a baseball bat to Lucian's beloved truck.

It was the second thought that worried her the most. It was so unlike her to even consider such an impulsive, rash thing. Take off on a quest like this in an old pickup all by herself with a puppy to chase down her cheating, lying, stealing husband.

She put the key in the ignition. The truck started right up. She turned off the engine so she and the puppy didn't get asphyxiated in the large storage unit as she tried to think this out rationally. She could just imagine what her father would have said if he'd even thought she was thinking of going looking for Lucian.

He would have advised her to do nothing of the sort. He'd have wanted to call the police at once, to tell them her brand new Range Rover had been stolen. Foolishly, it too was in both of their names, so it might be one way to find out where he'd gone. At least temporarily. Wasn't there an app they could have set up, but hadn't yet that would allow her to find the car—and Lucian? Too late now.

She saw that her options were few. Broke, except for her credit cards, she realized that it might be only a matter of time before Lucian started using them, and then she would have even fewer options. Where was her husband right now? Somewhere he thought he wouldn't be found.

But he'd be back for his pickup. That much she figured she could count on. Right now he was probably driving her Range Rover with the money from selling his Porsche in his pocket as well as all of hers.

She could wait until he came back for the pickup, she told herself.

Or…she could go after Lucian and everything he'd taken from her. Even if she couldn't find him, she liked the idea of him finding the storage unit empty. She'd rel-

ish his panic when he found it gone and realized that she'd
done something with his pickup. She could actually work
up a smile at the thought.

Or she could stay in the huge house they'd shared with
his ghost, wandering around lost until those scary-looking
men returned tonight.

Back on her phone, she checked the mileage from San
Diego, California, to Cooke City, Montana. "Is that where
you've gone, Lucian?" she asked out loud, knowing it was
a long shot.

The pickup, like the photos he'd held on to, had to mean
something though. She had no idea what, but she really
wanted to find out, because it might also be a clue as to
why her husband had done what he had. She might find the
answers she so desperately needed in Cooke City, Montana. She might find out who she married.

Geneva let out a nervous laugh, her mind made up as
she started the truck and pulled out of the storage unit.
"We're going to Montana," she announced, surprised that
she was actually doing this.

The puppy gave her that cocked-head *Tell me more* look.

"It's a better plan than going back to that house to wait
for those men to return, don't you think?"

The dog barked, the cutest little bark she'd ever heard,
and she laughed. It felt good even though the laugh felt a
little desperate and brought tears to her eyes. "I really do
need to give you a name," she said as she pulled the puppy
close. "Maybe something will come to me once we get to
Montana."

Chapter Five

Calhoun St. Pierre leaned back in his chair perched on the narrow wooden porch in front of his cabin on the main drag of Cooke City, Montana. His feet were propped up on the railing, his Stetson pulled low, the summer sun beating down on him as dust rose from all the traffic on the narrow two-lane road just feet in front of him.

Motorbikes roared past, followed by bumper-to-bumper huge motor homes, pickup campers, vans and every size and color SUV from practically every state in the Union. It was no secret what brought the masses every summer. Cooke City just happened to be surrounded by mountains in one of the most beautiful and remote parts of the state only a hop, skip and a jump from the entrance to Yellowstone National Park.

In the middle of July, the noise alone would have run him out of the busy tiny tourist town since normally he avoided Cooke from Memorial Day to Labor Day. If he wasn't waiting on a delivery, he'd be miles from here right now, high in the mountains where he belonged.

The sound of a vehicle pulling up to park in front of the large red No Parking sign at his cabin made him fume. He told himself that it had better be the delivery he'd been waiting for. Not that he had to even lift the brim of his hat to confirm that the engine he now heard the driver cut wasn't a delivery truck.

He swore under his breath, feeling his irritation rise as he heard the driver get out and slam the vehicle door. Telling himself not to completely lose his temper on a tourist since tourists were his bread and butter, he peered from under the brim of his hat expecting to see a family pouring out of an SUV after completely ignoring him—and his No Parking sign.

What he saw instead made him think he'd seen a ghost. "What the hell?" He shoved back his hat, his boots hitting the worn wooden porch floor as he found his feet, his hands already fisted at his sides as he took in the 1952 black vintage Chevy pickup gleaming in the summer sun.

He knew that truck. He knew its owner. He just never expected Lucian would have the guts to turn up here again—especially in that truck.

Halfway off the porch, he stopped in his tracks as he saw that it wasn't Lucian Beck who'd climbed out from behind the wheel. He frowned. No way. A woman had been driving the pickup? The sight of her made him doubt himself. It was the truck, wasn't it? But Lucian never let anyone drive his truck.

He frowned, telling himself that he couldn't be mistaken. There had to be maybe a dozen of this year's vintage pickups that had been restored like this one. Maybe more. But one this color in this good of shape with that particular license plate...

"Excuse me," the woman said as he walked past her to squint at the small sticker in the corner of the windshield on the passenger side and swore. Like hell, he was mistaken.

Swinging around to face her he demanded, "Where is he?"

She stared at him, clearly taken aback, and he got his

first good look at her. Late twenties to early thirties, pretty with wide blue eyes, heart-shaped face, a nice full mouth and a privileged look in her silk blouse, linen pants and strappy heels that told him Lucian Beck couldn't get a woman like this even in his dreams.

Like most of the tourists, she wasn't dressed for Montana—let alone a town 7,580 feet above sea level where the mountains shot straight up from town. The temperature today might get close to seventy but would drop to below forty once the sun went behind the mountains.

"Where is he?" he demanded, speaking more slowly as he advanced on her. "I'm going to ask you again, where is Lucian, and what are you doing with his truck?"

GENEVA HAD JUST driven over a terrifyingly narrow highway full of switchbacks and breath-stealing drop-offs that had finally led to this mountain town. That was after driving for four long days to get here. Four long days and empty long nights in cheap motels after her husband had taken all of her money, her car and her dignity.

Her chin went up. "I don't think you know who you're dealing with," she said advancing on him.

He stepped back, looking surprised, as if maybe he didn't.

"You have no idea what I've been through to get to this…" she glanced around; it really wasn't much of a town "…town to find you."

"Me?" he said.

She reached into the side pocket of her Prada bag and pulled out the photo and shoved it at him. He took it and looked down at the snapshot as if he didn't recognize it or himself. "That's you, isn't it?" she said jabbing at the man wearing the Montana State University sweatshirt.

Admittedly, the man before her didn't look a whole

lot like the clean-cut, beardless coed in the picture. Fortunately, the first place she'd stopped in the quarter-mile
long town, a store clerk had recognized him as Calhoun St.
Pierre, a local outfitter and pointed her in this direction.

"Where did you get this?" he asked suspiciously.

"I found it in the pickup's glove box." She had to practically yell to be heard over the sound of the traffic. "Is
there possibly a place we could discuss this that isn't so
noisy and dusty?"

He looked from her to the photo, then at the pickup for
a moment before he said with obvious reluctance, "Inside
my cabin." He motioned with his head in the direction of
the small log structure practically built in the road.

"I need to get my dog," she said and turned back to the
pickup to retrieve the small black-and-white springer span-
iel puppy. She held it close as if to protect the dog from
him, which seemed to make his expression appear even
more irritated.

"You live here?" she asked as he crossed the narrow
worn porch and opened the door to a cabin that was smaller
than a playhouse she'd had as a child. He opened the door
for her to enter.

"Live here year-round."

She stepped in tentatively. It was dark as a cave inside,
the log walls covered with a variety of antlered heads,
snowshoes and an old metal sign that warned of bears. A
shovel leaned against the wall by the door next to several
pairs of skis. What windows there were she realized were
covered by rugs that had seen better days.

He stepped past her to turn on a light. It didn't help
much, but in the sudden glare, she took in the narrow
bed, the hot plate, the potbelly woodstove and a recliner
that looked like something a person might find abandoned
beside the road. He must have seen her expression as she

stared at the chair that had so much duct tape applied to it that she wasn't sure what the original material had been. If she'd had to guess, she would have said Naugahyde.

"I got that chair at the dump, but it's pretty comfortable. You'd be surprised what you can find there." He said it almost with pride, then waited for her to sit.

She did so reluctantly, questioning—as she had from the moment she'd awakened from her anniversary party—what was happening to her. This didn't seem like such a good idea after all. But the alternative...

"Now, what are you doing with Lucian's truck?"

"Do you have any water? My dog—"

He said something under his breath she was glad she couldn't make out as he walked over to a sink near the back door. The pipes clanked and rattled for a moment, but the cup of water he handed her looked clear. "It's the best water in the world."

She considered the cup for a moment before she took a tentative sip as he produced a shallow metal bowl. She poured a little of the water in before setting the puppy down on a floor covered with a faded Native American rug. Even worn and not necessarily clean, it looked as if the rug was worth more than this entire cabin.

"What's her name?" he asked motioning to the puppy lapping at the water.

Geneva couldn't help thinking of the morning she'd awakened to the puppy licking her face. It felt like a lifetime ago. "She doesn't have one yet. Lucian gave her to me as a birthday present."

"That right?" he asked leaning against a post at the center of the cabin. She feared it was all that was holding up the structure. "He also gave you his truck?" There was that suspicion in his tone again.

"No." She considered how much to tell him but realized

she had nothing to lose by telling him the truth. "I found it in a storage unit I didn't know he had the day I woke up to find that he'd taken all my money, including my recent inheritance, and my Range Rover, and left without a word."

Calhoun St. Pierre crossed his thick arms. It was the first time she'd noticed how muscular he was or that the tattoos that ran from his wrists to his biceps were actually trees. "That sounds like Lucian," he said. "Can't imagine him leaving behind his truck though. He never let anyone drive it."

"Well, I'm driving it now," she said defensively.

"I can see that. Can't imagine, though, what you're doing here in Cooke."

"When I found the pickup, I found the photos of you and this town. I'd never heard of either. It looked as if you were good friends." He made a rude sound, but she continued. "I thought he might have come here."

He was already shaking his head. "Can't see that happening considering how many people he wronged here before he left over Memorial Day weekend over a year ago."

The timing surprised her. He'd been up here shortly before they'd met. "Unless there was something he left here he had to come back for." She saw that had caught his interest.

He cleared his voice before he asked, "Like what?"

She didn't know. The idea had just come to her. "I thought you might know."

He chuckled at that and almost smiled. "Trust me, he didn't leave anything here but the smell of burning bridges."

She realized even in the dim light this man was nice-looking. His dark hair was too long, his beard needed to be trimmed—if not shaved off—and his general attitude was definitely unpleasant. Mitzi would have called him just a little rough around the edges. But that was Mitzi, who was now with Lucian. The thought brought back an avalanche of pain that swept over her. Betrayed by her husband and her best friend, she was a walking cliché. And now she'd driven all this way to meet his so-called friend, and for what? Nothing.

"So, you haven't seen him?"

He shook his head. "Like I said, he'd be a fool to come back here. He screwed over too many people, myself included."

Geneva realized that she'd put all her hopes on finding Lucian here, straightening out what she hoped was an unfortunate mistake he'd made and putting all of this behind her. If she could fix everything, things could go back like they had been.

Just the thought made her realize how delusional she was. It also made her angry. She'd been living what she'd thought was the perfect life, but she could no longer keep dwelling in that fairy-tale world. Even if she found Lucian and got everything back that he'd taken, she'd never trust herself, let alone Lucian. Maybe not even another man.

The puppy finished drinking and came over to paw at her until she picked up the pooch. She hugged the dog, burying her fingers in the warm fur and fighting tears. She'd been so sure she'd find her husband here.

"Look, I'm sorry," Calhoun said sounding uncomfortable and clearly just wanting her to go. At the sound of a truck's horn directly outside, he said, "That's the delivery I've been waiting for. It's a wall tent. A grizzly tore up the last one. I've got to get this one up to my clients in the mountains. So, I'm sorry, but I can't help you." At the sound of a horn, he added hurriedly, "I have to go take care of this."

Geneva nodded and rose, following him out into the

bright sunshine, noise and dust of the busy town. A large delivery truck was parked in the middle of the street, making the traffic problem worse. She watched as the driver climbed out and walked to the back of his vehicle.

Calhoun followed him, glancing back once. His expression looked regretful, as if he didn't have a clue what else he could say to her as he disappeared from view.

Going to Lucian's pickup, she put the puppy in the carrier she'd bought, strapped it in with the passenger-side seat belt and climbed behind the wheel. She wouldn't be able to get out until the big rig moved. The folly of her latest situation settled over her. This had been a fool's errand. How could she have been so impulsive?

She'd driven a thousand miles over days to get here, and for what? She'd spent money she hadn't had on her credit cards and wasted time because she couldn't accept the truth. Lucian was gone, he wasn't coming back and neither was the life she'd known. She had no idea what she was going to do.

The thought of driving back down the Beartooth Highway's switchbacks was too much for her. She supposed she could go through Yellowstone National Park. She hadn't been there since she was little with friends. Eventually, she would have to go back to San Diego, sell the house and...

But with one look at the traffic heading into Yellowstone National Park, she knew she couldn't drive another mile today. She laid over the steering wheel, trying her best not to cry. She was so exhausted from the emotional roller coaster she'd been on for days. Her only thought had been to reach Cooke City, Montana, find the man in the photograph, find Lucian and get her money back. Had she really thought it was going to be that easy?

At a tap on her side window, Geneva started, sat up and quickly turned toward the sound. Calhoun St. Pierre was standing outside her window looking uncomfortable and possibly angry. She rolled down the glass, biting at her lip as she tried to hide how raw she felt. Disappointment seemed to have filled her insides, making it hard to breathe, let alone move.

"It's late enough that I think you should stay here in town tonight," he said as the large delivery truck parked behind her pulled away. "You didn't happen to book a room at least six months ago, did you?"

She could barely call up a half smile at that.

"Right," he said. "I know a few people. I think I can get you a room for the night. If you get up early, you can avoid most of the traffic in the morning."

She nodded, knowing that if she tried to thank him, she would burst out crying. Kindness, especially from this man, was almost too much to bear.

He seemed to sense how close she was to completely falling apart. "I'll be right back." He disappeared from sight, running between two large motor homes to the other side of the busy street. She caught a glimpse of him down the two-lane highway some distance away before she laid over the steering wheel again and closed her eyes.

Geneva didn't know how long she stayed like that, both she and the puppy having dozed off in the warm cab of the pickup before Calhoun returned. He handed her a key and pointed down the street to a place with small cabins. "You're in number one. It's right on the highway, so it will be noisy, but you look like you won't have any trouble sleeping tonight. There's a café back up that way." He seemed to hesitate. "You have enough money to—"

She nodded, stopping him from going any further. She was humiliated enough about her situation. The last thing she wanted was to take money from this man. Her credit cards were still working, which meant that Lucian hadn't used them, no doubt thinking he could be tracked if he did.

Had her father still been alive, she would have called him. He would have taken over, protecting her the way he always had and making sure she wanted for nothing. There were other friends she could call and pretend everything was fine, that she and Lucian and the puppy had gone on a trip, that he'd gotten mugged—could they send money?

But she had too much pride. She didn't want those friends knowing about Lucian's betrayal even though they would find out soon enough. Not to mention, she wasn't sure how she would be able to pay them back. She'd left a text message for the owner of the gallery where she worked, telling her there'd been an emergency and she'd be gone for possibly a week or two. She had vacation coming and hadn't taken it. Also, the gallery hadn't been that busy lately, so she didn't think she'd be missed.

"You're going to be all right," the outfitter said next to the open pickup window. The air smelled of pine and dust and fried food. She could hear a dog barking from the back of a truck as it roared by. Voices drifted on the summer breeze along with laughter. People came here on vacation to have fun. "It will get better," he said as if he could see that she needed some reassurance.

She could only nod as he touched the brim of his hat and headed for his cabin. He didn't look back as he closed the door behind him.

Starting the pickup, she finally managed to pull into the traffic. Driving down the street to the cabins, she tried not to think about tomorrow. Nothing was going to be all right. It wasn't going to get better. And as for luck…hers had run out.

Once at the cabin, she parked and got the puppy out of her carrier. As an afterthought, she pulled everything from the glove box and stuffed it into her purse. Something Calhoun St. Pierre had said had her wondering if the pickup even belonged to Lucian.

But the moment she and puppy were inside the cabin, she locked the door, fed the dog what was left of some chicken nuggets she had purchased earlier and put the papers from the glove box on the table.

She couldn't face more bad news. She collapsed on the bed, telling herself that things always looked better in the morning.

CALHOUN CURSED HIMSELF as he walked away from the woman. It wasn't the first girlfriend of Lucian's who'd come crying to him. Not that this one had cried, but she'd been damned close.

He told himself that he had too much to do to be worrying about her. He didn't even know her name, which was fine with him. She'd be gone by morning. He'd done all he could for her. She wasn't his responsibility. He thought about other women Lucian had hurt and swore. This wasn't the first disappearing act Lucian had pulled in the years he'd known him.

This woman seemed different from the others though. Definitely not his type. How Lucian had gotten a woman like her in the first place—even temporarily—he couldn't imagine. Well, at least she had his pickup. That made him smile as he imagined what Lucian would think of her driving it.

Standing in the middle of his cabin, he mentally kicked himself for still thinking about her, let alone his former friend. It wasn't his job to clean up after Lucian. He'd done enough of that when they were young.

He needed to get busy loading up so he could head out for the mountains first thing in the morning. Now that his

new wall tent had arrived, there was nothing keeping him
in Cooke. He couldn't wait to get up to his camp. Every
day spent down here, he was losing money, not to mention patience.

But his thoughts kept circling back to that moment when
he'd looked up from his siesta on the porch to see that familiar black pickup. His stomach roiled at the thought that
it could have been Lucian driving it. That, after all this
time, he would have come face-to-face with the bastard.
He fisted both hands even now at the thought.

Calhoun had told himself that he'd put Lucian out of
his mind for good. The last thing he'd needed was a reminder of the hell his once good friend had brought down
on him. Seemed Lucian hadn't changed. One look at the
woman who'd climbed out of that pickup, and he'd known
that she didn't belong here. This was a woman who'd never
roughed it in her life. What had she been thinking coming
here? If she'd arrived a day later, she would have missed
him. Then what? He hated to think.

He made himself pack up what he could before he lay
down on the bed and stared up at the ceiling. This old cabin
meant the world to him because it had been the first thing
he'd ever bought and owned. Also, it gave him a place to
stay on his short visits to town, which weren't often. He
recalled a time when even Lucian had been thankful for
this roof over his head.

What had happened to that young man he'd spent so
many weeks with high in the mountains? That this hadn't
been enough for him made Calhoun angry. This life that
he'd chosen wasn't enough because Lucian had always
thought he deserved more. And look how that had turned
out. Now his former best friend had become a man a lot
of people weren't just looking for—but wanted to kill.

He thought about the woman again, hating that he

couldn't get her off his mind. Did she even know what she was going to do if she found Lucian? He doubted it. Just as he doubted his old friend would come back here.

Unless there was something he left here he had to come back for. Wasn't that what she'd said? Something he had to get before running off to some faraway place to live out the rest of his life in luxury on her money?

He hoped like hell she was wrong about that. But as secretive as Lucian had been acting that Memorial Day weekend when he showed up out of nowhere... The way he'd gone up in the mountains, clearly wanting to go alone. He'd seemed anxious, almost scared. Calhoun swore. What had Lucian been up to?

After he'd come out of the mountains, he'd had to borrow money to get out of town. What he hadn't borrowed, he'd stolen. Was it possible the woman was right, and Lucian was back in Cooke City to collect something he'd left up in the mountains over a year ago?

If so, Lucian would be bringing trouble.

Maybe he already had, Calhoun thought, dwelling on the beautiful out-of-towner.

Chapter Six

Geneva woke the next morning to find the puppy lying on the bed next to her. She had to smile. In a matter of days, the puppy had gone from not being able to get up on the couch to jumping up on her bed. True, the bed was low to the floor, but still it was fun seeing the puppy growing. Had Lucian given her the dog knowing she would need something once he was gone?

Why did she feel the need to see some sign of goodness in the man? She pushed that thought away, just thankful that she felt much better this morning, especially after her bath. She dressed and noticed the things she'd removed from the pickup's glove box last night. What if he didn't own it? That could explain why he kept it hidden in the storage unit. Also, if the truck broke down on the way back to California, she should at least see if there was an owner's manual.

Now she sat down on the end of the bed while the puppy ate her breakfast. The owner's manual was thin, nothing like the ones in cars now. She'd found the registration, relieved it was in Lucian's name. So he hadn't stolen the pickup. That was a relief. She'd hate to think that she was driving a stolen vehicle.

As she started to see what else was in the pile, an envelope fell out. Wrinkled and smeared with dirt, the envelope looked as if it had been wadded up and tossed in the mud, then retrieved, flattened back out and thrown into the glove box.

Intrigued, she leaned down to pick it up and froze. All that was written on the outside of the envelope was one word. Lucian. But she recognized the handwriting and felt her heart drop.

Mitzi. She had written to Lucian? Mitzi had already run away with her husband. But the thought that this had been going on behind her back for some time took her breath away.

Whatever she'd written, it appeared to be several pages given the thickness inside the envelope. Why would Mitzi write him? Too afraid Geneva might stumble onto one of their texts? To keep what was going on a secret?

The foolishness of that thought made her want to throw up. Of course they were keeping their relationship secret. The two of them must have been making plans for their getaway for months. Why wouldn't they correspond in all kinds of ways? Mitzi might have been in this pickup. She might have been the one who'd wadded up the envelope, threw it on the ground, then changed her mind and…and put it in the glove box?

That sounded so ridiculous, and yet Geneva had no idea what had been going on behind her back, did she?

Throw it away. Don't open it. No good will come of seeing what Mitzi sent him. Haven't you already been hurt enough?

All good advice, she thought as she tore into the envelope and dumped out its contents. She already knew that her husband and her best friend were liars, thieves and cheats. Could she really learn anything more about them that could hurt her?

To her surprise, along with what appeared to be some

photocopied sheets of paper, there was only a short note written in Mitzi's handwriting. *Thought you'd want to see this. Talk soon? Mitzi.*

Her first thought was that Mitzi had found an island for them to buy with Geneva's money, now Lucian's. Still, she unfolded the sheets of paper. There were two photocopied pages. The first was a notice of stolen jewelry. There were pinholes in it, as if the sheet had been posted somewhere. A police station?

A light bulb turned on. Or a pawn shop, she thought as she saw the name of the shop written at the bottom. It was Mitzi's favorite pawn shop, where she often went to hock jewelry her husband had given her when she ran out of money before she got what she called her "monthly allowance from the cheap bastard."

Geneva's heart began to beat faster as she saw one of the pieces of stolen jewelry items had been circled in red. She would have recognized the piece even if it hadn't been that long ago that the engagement ring had graced her finger. She quickly found the wedding band, also circled in red.

This couldn't be, but even as she thought it, she knew it was true. Mitzi had seen the notice of the stolen jewelry at the pawn shop. She'd recognized the rings Lucian had given Geneva. But instead of coming to her best friend, she'd made a copy for Lucian?

She flipped to the second photocopied sheet. It was a copy of an article about a jewelry store robbery in Montgomery, Alabama. The jewelry store didn't normally carry one-of-a-kind pieces worth six figures, it said. The shipment had been for a special buyer. Police suspected an inside job since the shipment had only come in that night. A young woman who had worked there was missing.

Geneva pulled out her phone, already knowing what she

would find. None of the robbers had been caught or the jewelry recovered. She looked at the date of the robbery.

Only weeks before she'd met Lucian.

Had she really thought things couldn't get any worse? Her lying, cheating husband was a bigger thief than even she had imagined. And the woman who worked at the jewelry store was still missing? Was he also a murderer?

She felt a chill. Who had she married? And her friend Mitzi… She refolded the papers, her hands shaking with anger and fear as she stuffed everything into her purse. And Mitzi appeared to be a blackmailer? Was this note to Lucian an attempt to get money? It would certainly appear so. Knowing Mitzi, it would be something reckless she would do, not realizing how dangerous Lucian could be.

Was Mitzi even still alive? Geneva couldn't bear to think of what might have happened to her. And all of this had been going on behind her back. She hadn't had a clue, she thought as she looked down at her empty ring finger. There was still an indentation, a pale line where her beautiful engagement and wedding ring had been.

No wonder he'd taken the rings. He'd been found out by Mitzi. He couldn't chance that someone else would recognize them. But he'd also taken her watch, she reminded herself.

All the while, she had worried that Lucian had spent too much money on the rings but hadn't found a way to ask him about it without hurting his feelings. The last thing she'd wanted was for them to live beyond their means.

Geneva couldn't believe how naive she'd been. For a moment, she sat on the bed in the Cooke City cabin unsure what to do next. She'd come here to confront her husband and hopefully get back at least some of what he'd taken from her. Who was she kidding? She'd never get back what he'd stolen—not to even mention the money or valuables.

He'd taken her ability to trust. His behavior forced her into a world that terrified her. She'd driven all this way in his old truck without a thought to her safety. He'd snatched her out of her comfort zone, leaving her disillusioned and the life she'd known destroyed.

What was the point of finding him? Why not do as the outfitter had told her and leave town? Maybe Lucian hadn't come back here. But what if he had? She thought about what Calhoun St. Pierre had said about the last time he saw Lucian in Cooke City. She didn't need to double-check the dates. It would have been right after the jewelry store robbery in Alabama—not long before she'd met Lucian in San Diego.

If Lucian had come back here after the robbery, she had a pretty good idea why. Where better than here to hide the jewelry? Her husband was dangerous. She thought of Mitzi's note, convinced it was a blackmail attempt. Was it possible Mitzi had no idea what kind of man Lucian was? Not just a thief but possibly something far worse? Or had all Mitzi been thinking about was cashing in on what she'd found out?

Geneva's phone rang, making her jump. For just an instant, she thought it might be Lucian. Her hopes soared and just as quickly plummeted back to earth when she saw that it was Hugh calling. Heart dropping, she feared the worst.

"Geneva." The way he said it, she knew something had happened.

"Is it Mitzi?" Silence. "Hugh?"

Fear gripped her before she heard him say, "Mitzi is home."

Relief flooded her. Mitzi had been her best friend for too many years. She'd been terrified that something awful had happened to her after finding the blackmail note. "Is she all right?"

Hugh made a disparaging sound. "She just showed up with some cockamamie story about being abducted by Lucian. When I insisted on calling the police, she broke down and admitted that she'd helped him leave you, but swears she was never romantically involved with him."

Such a Mitzi move, Geneva thought with a shake of her head. "I think she's telling the truth." Hugh scoffed at that. "Did he take all of her money as well?"

"So she says. How can I ever trust her again?"

"You love her. She made a mistake. I'm glad she made it home safely. Like me, I don't think she realized what kind of man Lucian is. I've been worried about her."

Hugh's laugh sounded brittle. "It would be just like you to worry about her even after what she did to you. She helped that man take everything from you and leave you."

"Yes," Geneva said. "But I'm sure he tricked her, just as he did me. She bet on the wrong horse."

"You're taking this much better than I am."

"Let me talk to Mitzi if she's there."

"She's here," Hugh said. "Hold on."

Geneva doubted her friend was going to want to talk to her. Funny how some people's loyalties shifted so easily.

"Hello?" Mitzi sounded timid, not the usually boisterous, confident, funny woman Geneva knew and loved.

"Where is Lucian?" she asked, skipping everything else.

"I don't know." Mitzi began to cry. "I swear. I didn't know—"

"When was the last time you saw him?"

"He told me to sell the Porsche and meet him back at the motel and he'd give me more money for helping him, but when I got there, he was already gone. It turned out that he didn't own the Porsche, so I couldn't—"

Geneva wasn't surprised that Lucian had double-crossed Mitzi. After all, she'd been blackmailing him, both of them just in it for the money. "You should have come to me when you found out about my engagement and wedding rings."

"I know. I know," she said her voice rising. "I just thought—"

"I know what you thought." Mitzi could never have enough money, as if that would make her feel better about herself, her life, her worth. "Did Lucian tell you where he was going?"

"He said he had to pick something up, and then we were going to buy an island," Mitzi said, sniffling. "I *believed* him. I'm such a fool."

Geneva wanted to say something snide about trusting a man who was on the run from a jewelry heist, a man who'd lied about everything and had robbed her best friend and left her heartbroken, but she bit her tongue since she'd been the fool who'd married him.

"I'm so sorry," Mitzi cried.

She knew how sorry Mitzi was and how hard it must have been for her to crawl back to Hugh—let alone come to the phone to talk to the friend she'd betrayed.

"Hugh is a good man," Geneva said. "I assume Lucian found a way to get all of the money you took when you left?" Another sniffle. "Count your blessings that Hugh took you back."

"I don't know if Hugh will ever forgive me," she said. She began to cry again. "Are you ever going to forgive me?"

"I know you, remember? You're lucky you got away from Lucian when you did. There are dangerous men after him, men who he probably ripped off just like he did me, just like he did you. Two of them came by the house before I left."

"You left?"

"It's a long story. Maybe I'll tell you about it someday. I have to go."

"I'm so sorry," Mitzi cried before Geneva could hang up.

"I know." Geneva disconnected, shaking her head. She'd always loved the craziness that came with Mitzi, the high energy, the way the woman could laugh. She told herself that they all had flaws, but she wasn't ready to forgive her. She wasn't sure she ever would be.

Only recently had Geneva become so aware of her own flaws. But she wasn't that naive privileged woman anymore. That woman and the world she'd lived in were gone for good. She had no idea who she would be when this was over or what she would do, but there was no going back to that make-believe place.

She listened to all the traffic noise outside the cabin as she sat, trying to work up anger against her friend, but she couldn't. She knew Mitzi. She understood how desperate she'd been to live a different life. Would she do something that rash again? Probably. But with luck she would realize what a good man she was married to and make it up to Hugh.

She put Mitzi out of her mind, glad her friend was home safe, and turned her thoughts to what she was going to do now. It had been impulsive and foolish to come all this way, chasing after her no-count husband. The smart thing was what Calhoun had said: to leave Cooke City, to put Lucian behind her.

Picking up her puppy, she opened the door, considering what to do with the information she'd found about the jewelry robbery and her suspicion that Lucian had hidden the stolen property somewhere in these mountains. He'd robbed a jewelry store with three other men. The jewelry had never turned up, the robbers never caught. Mitzi had said he had to pick up something, and then they were headed off to buy an island. Pick up the jewelry? Maybe she should let the authorities know. If Lucian had come to Montana, wasn't it possible he had stashed it some-where up here?

Or he could already be out of the country. It wouldn't be that out of character for him to lie about his plans to Mitzi.

As Geneva stepped out on the small deck in front of the cabin, she found three men, all sporting well-worn motor-cycle jackets, standing next to Lucian's pickup.

"Can I help you?" she asked not liking the way they were leaning against the truck, clearly waiting for her with a threatening air about them.

"Where's Lucian?" the larger of the three demanded, trying to see past her into the cabin. There was something familiar about him, but she couldn't put her finger on it for a moment. His appearance had definitely changed from when his photo had been taken with Calhoun and Lucian.

"He isn't with me. I'm looking for him."

"That right?" he asked and took a step closer. "How'd you get his pickup?"

Geneva didn't know how to answer other than to be honest. "I stole it after he took all my money and left me with the help of another woman."

"Damn, that's cold," the man said, but didn't sound in the least bit concerned or sympathetic.

One of the other men turned to his friend and said, "You don't think he's up at the high camp, do you, Ace?"

"I'm sorry, up at the high camp?" She looked from one to the other and back to the largest one standing closest to her. "Where's that?"

Ace shook his head, all of them clamming up. "You sure you don't know where he is?"

"I don't. I'd hoped to find him here." Wasn't that why she'd driven all this way? She still wanted to have him tell her to her face why he'd done what he had to her. She needed to hear it from him. Otherwise, wouldn't she always wonder how much of it had been real—if any of it. Also, if he'd come back here for the jewelry, she'd love to see him get what he deserved—arrested and the jewelry returned to its proper owner.

One of the bikers ran his hand along the hood of the pickup. "What you think the truck's worth, Ace?"

"Not worth what you're thinking of doing," Calhoun said as he came around the side of the cabin.

Chapter Seven

The bikers seemed a little intimidated.

"Calhoun," Ace said, "I see you got a new wall tent yesterday. You goin' up in the mountains lookin' for Lucian?"

"Nope. I'm working. I have clients coming in. Just going up to get ready for 'em."

"Lucian owes me money," Ace said.

"Lucian owes a lot of people."

"You wouldn't hold out on us, would you?"

Calhoun stepped closer to him.

"If I knew where he was right now, I'd tell you."

"And if you go back into the mountains and find him, accidentally?" the biker asked sarcastically.

"Like I said, I'm not looking for him. But if we cross paths, there won't be much of him left for you but slim pickin's. You're wasting your time if you think he has your money. I can tell you without a doubt it's long gone—just like mine is—just like hers is."

"You tellin' me you aren't working for her?" Ace asked.

Calhoun let out a laugh. "Not a chance. Have you ever known me to take a woman back into the mountains?"

"Then you don't mind if we…" He looked over at the truck.

"I wouldn't if I were you," Calhoun warned quietly as one of the bikers kicked at the pickup's tires, walking around it, still considering what the truck might be worth.

"That pickup belongs to this lady now. She needs it to get out of town."

"You don't want to get on the wrong side of this," Ace warned. "Remember who your friends are. If you stumble across Lucian, you let us know."

Calhoun said nothing as the three moved on though, clearly taking their time.

"Thank you," Geneva said when the men were out of earshot. She couldn't believe how relieved she was that he'd shown up. "I was just coming to find you to thank you and buy you breakfast for everything you've done for me."

Calhoun turned to her. She was immediately taken aback by his expression. It took her a moment to realize that the anger she saw there was aimed at her.

"What did I tell you?" he demanded. "It's too dangerous for you here in this town. If I hadn't come along this morning, they would have taken your truck. You need to hit the road. *Now.*"

She was stunned. She'd been nervous during the exchange with the bikers, but apparently, it had been more dangerous than she'd thought. What was maybe more stunning was that the outfitter had been worried about her. Why else had he come to check on her this morning? Clearly, he knew more than she did about the trouble Lucian had left behind here. Just as she suspected, he knew about this high camp the bikers had mentioned where Lucian might have gone.

But did he also know about the jewelry store heist?

Though still shocked by the urgency and anger in his voice, she found his attitude along with this new information had forced her into a decision. "I came here to find Lucian," she said digging in her heels. "You have no idea what it took me to come here. You don't have to tell me that I don't belong here. But if there's even a chance he's hiding out up in the mountains at his high camp, then I'm going up there. Those men seemed to think that Lucian had a cabin up there."

"Not a cabin, a lean-to, which has probably fallen down by now."

"Whatever it is, I'll pay you to take me up there."

He shook his head. "Not happening. I've got a client coming. Like I said, I have a job, and you need to hit the road out of town before there's real trouble." He turned to walk away.

"Is Lucian's cab—lean-to in the direction you're going? I'll pay you to take me along. This is what you do for a living, right? Guide people?"

Calhoun turned back, his words coming out slow but pitched like hardballs. "Even if you could handle riding up into those mountains on horseback, sleeping on the ground, fighting mosquitoes if not bears and other varmints, I'm not taking you." He held up both hands. "Don't make me sorry I helped you."

"Fine. There must be someone in town who will take me. You can't be the only *guide* around here."

He swore again, jerked off his hat and raked a hand through his long dark hair. "I'm begging you. You need to leave here. I'm serious. Lucian isn't here, but there are people who want to get their hands on him. If not him… someone he might care about."

"He doesn't care about me."

"They don't know that. You're driving his pickup. Even if Lucian is up there, your money's gone, I can promise you that. Cut your losses. Go back to wherever you came from."

"San Diego."

"Fine San Diego. Sell that damned truck and put Lucian behind you."

Even if Lucian is up there? He was holding out on her,

she was sure of it. "I saw an outfitter sign on the way in. Maybe he will be more interested in taking my money."

Calhoun looked as if he was gritting his teeth. "You are making a mistake that you're going to regret."

"I already made a mistake that I regret by marrying Lucian."

That stopped him cold. "You *married* him? You're his… *wife*?"

She nodded, surprised by his surprise. He'd thought she was just some girlfriend? "I should have introduced myself. I'm Geneva Carrington Beck. I woke up the night after our first anniversary party to find him gone with everything. Mr. St. Pierre, I've come a long way to find my husband—"

"It's Calhoun."

"—and to get the justice I deserve."

"Justice?" He scoffed. "I thought you wanted to try to get your money back?"

"That too."

He lifted both hands in front of him in surrender. "I warned you. You do what you've got to do. It's none of my business." He turned and walked away cursing.

CALHOUN CURSED HIMSELF all the way back to his cabin. Lucian's *wife*?

He'd had to deal with Lucian's dumped girlfriends in the past, but never a wife. He tried to get his head around it. This woman had *married* Lucian Beck. Was still married to him? Calhoun hadn't noticed the telling white line on her ring finger until she'd said the words. He knew he shouldn't be so shocked. She was driving his truck. She'd said he'd given her a puppy for her birthday.

He swore as he remembered a moment this morning when he'd looked into her eyes. Gazing into all that blue was as blinding as high-altitude sunshine on the surface of a mountain lake. She wasn't just pretty. She was stunning with that long blond hair, those high cheekbones, that heart-shaped face, those bow-shaped lips, those big blue eyes. And unless he missed his guess, she'd had money before she'd crossed paths with Lucian. She had that look, like a woman who had known the better things in life, who'd never wanted for anything. She must have been easy prey for his old friend, he thought with a curse. The woman literally hadn't seen what was coming. Lucian had blindsided her, and she wasn't going down without a fight. It was a fight, though, that she couldn't win.

"Lucian, you damned fool," Calhoun said under his breath, "what were you thinking marrying her for her money, let alone walking away?" What killed him was the fact that she'd been Lucian's wife for a whole damned year. How could he walk away? It had been bad enough when Calhoun had thought that she was one of the women he'd cast aside over the years. But his *wife*?

No way was he taking Lucian's wife into the mountains under any circumstances. She needed to get out of Cooke City and as far away as she possibly could from all the trouble tailing her husband like a bad smell. She needed to put Lucian in her rearview mirror—and quickly.

Except that she wasn't giving up. He'd have thought she would have. Or called her family. Or her lawyer. Or a good friend to come with her. Instead, she'd shown up here alone with a puppy? A cute puppy at that.

He told himself that he'd done all he could do. She wasn't his responsibility. If it hadn't been for a photo taken years ago of him and Lucian and Ace, she wouldn't know about him and Lucian. And coming in that forsaken old pickup, bringing back so many memories, so many regrets, so many questions.

Calhoun couldn't believe Lucian had hung on to the

pickup, he thought as he reached his cabin. He'd told himself after Lucian's last visit to Cooke that nothing meant anything to his once good friend. Lucian had hurt people who'd loved and trusted him, not giving a damn about any of them. And yet he'd hung on to the pickup?

It made no sense. Just as it made no sense that he'd also kept the photos of them taken here in Cooke City. Was it possible there was an ounce of sentiment, one scrap of genuine caring in the man?

Considering what Lucian had done to the woman he married, Calhoun didn't believe it. He'd lived for over a year being angry at the man, convincing himself that if he ever saw him again, he wouldn't be responsible for what happened. Wasn't that what scared him even now? What would he do if he found Lucian up in the mountains at his high camp?

He pushed the thought away since he wasn't going up there, he wasn't going looking for him, he wasn't cleaning up Lucian's messes anymore. He'd been convinced Lucian would never come back here. The one thing his friend had never been was a fool. A crook, a liar, a backstabbing bastard, but no fool. Why would he come back here of all places?

Unless there was something he left here he had to come back for.

He felt a chill. Why had his wife said that? Because she knew more than she'd told him. That thought stopped him cold. Like she'd said, she'd come a long way, counting on Lucian to be here. It had to be because of more than a few photos she'd found in the pickup.

What if she was right and Lucian was here? His former friend knew these mountains. He knew people who would lend him a couple of horses—for the right price up front. He'd also be smart enough not to come into town with so many people just waiting for him, should he return. Maybe he had come back for something he'd left here.

But if true, why had he left his prized pickup behind? Maybe he planned to go back for it once he retrieved whatever he might have left at his camp in the mountains.

Calhoun swore. But why even keep the pickup, let alone those photos? Unless…unless Lucian had left a trail of crumbs for Geneva to follow. If so, that trail had led her not just to Cooke City but to Calhoun himself. What possible motive would Lucian have for doing that?

He shook his head. Lucian was too smart, his survival instincts too sharpened, to come anywhere near Cooke— and people who wanted him dead.

No, he told himself. Lucian was thousands of miles away by now. Why he'd left the pickup he'd held on to all these years was a mystery. Maybe he'd never been sentimental about it or the people in those photos. Surely the man hadn't expected his wife to get in it and come all the way to Montana looking for him.

No one with any sense would take her up into the mountains, Calhoun told himself as he locked up his cabin. His supplies were loaded into the back of the stock truck and trailer, ready for the trip. The horses and a couple of wranglers would be waiting. There was nothing keeping him here in town.

Don't, he warned himself as he climbed behind the wheel. *Don't look for her as you drive out of town.* "Not your rodeo, not your cowgirl."

Yet, as he drove past one of the other outfitters office, he saw her standing outside talking to Max Lander. He recognized the way Max stepped closer, leaned toward her, smiling that bear-eating-huckleberries grin of his.

"Oh, hell no," Calhoun said and hit the brakes.

Chapter Eight

Geneva heard the screech of brakes as a big truck came to a dust-roiling stop beside her. She'd been all over town, which wasn't saying much since the town was so small. She'd also been turned down by the few outfitters she'd talked to. She'd been ready to give up when she had finally found one who said he'd take her. She was just about to hand Max Lander her credit card when a large hand closed on her arm and pulled her back as if she was about to step off a cliff.

"Not a chance," Calhoun said, shaking his head.

"Stay out of this, St. Pierre," the outfitter said. Somewhere in his fifties, Max Lander was a big man, burly with a full beard as round as his belly. "The lady and I have a deal."

"Afraid not, Max. I know the kind of…deals you have with women."

The outfitter's grin broadened as he dropped his arm to finger the sidearm at his hip. "You really need to back off. The lady is capable of making up her own mind. Who's she to you anyway?"

"Damned good question." He met Geneva's gaze. She cocked her head waiting to hear his answer as well. He lowered his voice as he leaned toward her, his breath tickling her ear. "All my instincts are telling me to let go of your arm, get into my truck, drive away and not look back. That this isn't any of my business."

"Sounds like you are getting some sage advice from your instincts," she said. "You're right, this isn't any of your business."

"Can't let you go with this man." He looked as if the words were as painful for him to say as they were for her to hear.

"Excuse me?" He didn't really think he could stop her, did he?

"A moment of your time." He still had a grip on her arm, one he apparently wasn't going to give up. She let him draw her away from the outfitter, figuring this wouldn't take long.

She could see the private battle Calhoun was fighting with himself and didn't stop him. He'd been friends with Lucian. If anyone knew her husband, it was this man. If he agreed to take her up into the mountains to where Lucian used to go to hide out, then he must suspect that her husband was in the area—no matter what he said to the contrary. She remembered the change in his expression when she'd told him that maybe Lucian had left something up in the mountains that he'd come back to get.

"You can't go with Max Lander," Calhoun said finally. "Any other outfitter in town—"

"Max is the only one who said he'd take me up to Lucian's camp."

"Oh, he'll take you all right."

She gave him an indignant look. "If you're worried about me taking care of myself—"

He raised a brow, his gray gaze boring into hers. "Do I really have to mention that you've already been taken for a ride by one man?"

"Thank you so much for pointing that out."

Calhoun sighed. "Have you ever even ridden a horse? Because that's the only way to get from here to where it is you think you need to go."

"Once when I was twelve."

"Great. And, pray tell, what are you planning to do with that dog?"

She held the puppy tighter. "I'm not leaving her behind. Max said I could pay extra for her to come along."

"Oh, did he?" Pulling off his hat, Calhoun raked a hand through his hair. "Lady, you're getting on my last nerve."

"My name is Geneva. Geneva Beck."

"Like I can forget that," he mumbled as his gaze locked with hers. "So, you really did marry him?"

She might have asked why that surprised him, but then again he'd known Lucian a lot longer than she had. Apparently, they'd had a falling-out at some point. Just like the bikers and possibly everyone who'd known her husband. Some apparently wanted to find him for nefarious reasons.

Calhoun rubbed the back of his neck as he swore. "If your no-count husband is up in those mountains, he's going to pay for this, along with everything else."

"You'll have to wait in line," she snapped.

For the first time since she'd laid eyes on the man, Calhoun laughed. His smile eased the hard lines of his face and brought light to those shadowed gray eyes. She realized with a start that he really was quite attractive under all that hair and bad disposition.

She held out her credit card to him. He shook his head. "Put that away." He sighed. "If you're going with me, then you can't go dressed like that, and you can't leave Lucian's pickup parked on the main drag unless you want it used for target practice or stolen."

He was actually taking her?

With a growl, he said, "Let's go."

She turned to apologize to Max Lander, but he'd already gone back inside.

"Come on, don't make me regret this any more than I already do."

Geneva couldn't help being anxious suddenly. She'd made up her mind that she was going up into the mountains looking for her husband. The more Calhoun continued to tell her that she wasn't up to the trip, the more she wanted to prove him wrong.

But now that he'd relented, she realized that he could be right. She didn't really know how to ride a horse, she knew nothing about the wilderness, and worse, she'd be at the mercy of Calhoun St. Pierre. But she'd come this far, and she would see it through if it killed her.

After he dropped her off at the general store and told the elderly clerk what clothes he wanted for her, she and her puppy went into a small dressing room at the back, and she began trying them on. She'd never worn anything like the thick canvas pants, the skin-hugging long johns or the long slicker. It all seemed like overkill given that it was July. She told herself that he was just trying to scare her as she tried on the wool socks and the boots.

"You'll need this too," the elderly woman said, stuffing a wool felt floppy Western hat onto her head, like the one Calhoun was wearing today. Only this one was clean. "I'd tie up that hair of yours. Could be days before you wash it again. Unless you brave the creek. You ever had an ice cream headache? Trust me, dipping your head into a creek this time of year will be much worse."

Geneva thanked the woman and started to change back into the clothes she'd come in wearing, but the clerk shook her head.

"Knowing Calhoun, you'll be heading out right now. I'll bag the clothes you were wearing. You can pick them up on your way out of town." The woman threw in some feminine items and some heavy-duty bug spray, and Geneva paid her bill with her card.

By the time she was finished, Calhoun was waiting impatiently outside the store in the large truck she'd seen earlier. Only she hadn't noticed what looked to her like a horse trailer behind it. He motioned for her to get in.

"What about my suitcase and—"

"I left the suitcase in the truck. Your...cosmetic stuff I already loaded. Now get in. Hand me the dog," he said, his voice a growl.

Her new clothes were stiff. She moved awkwardly, feeling foolish as she handed over the puppy and hoisted herself up into the passenger seat. She saw the look on Calhoun's face before he shifted gears and took off as she was closing her door.

She looked around for a seat belt but didn't see one. She noticed that he was dressed much like she was—only the shine had long been removed from his clothing. They quickly left the town, taking the winding two-lane highway she'd come in on. It was impossible to relax. The truck smelled of dust and horses and something else she didn't want to think about as she pulled her puppy close.

Nor was the ride relaxing sitting on the taped-up cracked seat bumping and rocking down the narrow highway. "I thought you said we'd be riding horses?" She was looking forward to the fresh air. A saddle had to be more comfortable than this truck that seemed to wander of its own accord between the lines, the trailer behind it rattling loudly.

He glanced over at her. "Oh, we will be on horseback soon. For hours. Enjoy the truck ride. It isn't going to get better."

"Could you please quit trying to scare me?"

He chuckled. "By all means. Just understand this. Once

we leave the truck and trailer and go by horseback up into the mountains, there is no turning back. No one is going to come save you if the going gets too rough. You're in it for the long haul until I take you back down to civilization." He shot her a look. "There is no whining, no complaining and, sure as hell, no crying. That understood?"

"Perfectly. Is this what you tell all the women you guide into the mountains?"

"Everyone knows I don't take women. Period. You're the first. And the last," he added under his breath. "And I tell the men the same thing."

"And the men didn't whine, complain or cry, right?"

"Not for long," he said. "The one who wouldn't stop decided to walk out. I made him pay me before he left. Never saw him again. I suspect his body is up there somewhere."

She studied Calhoun for a moment, not believing a word of it. Turning to look out her side window, she watched the pine trees blur past and caught glimpses of a creek, the water clear, the rocks glittering in the depths. They hadn't gone far before he slowed and pulled into a wide spot on his side of the road. "Are those your trucks and horse trailers?"

"Stock trailers," he corrected and nodded.

"So, there are other people up there," she said feeling relieved and no doubt sounding that way because he shot her a look.

"We aren't going where they are. It's not in the direction of Lucian's old camp. Once we hit the trail, it will be just you and me and five horses."

"Five?"

"Two to ride and three for our supplies. There's a reason Ace called Lucian's place 'the high camp.' It's at the top of a peak two days—maybe three—from here, depending on what kind of time we make." He climbed out and she did the same, having to jump down from the running board.

She was surprised they would need that many supplies but wasn't about to question it. "What did you do with Lucian's pickup?" she asked as she followed him around to the back of the stock trailer.

"Step back," he said as he opened the rear door. Inside were saddles and bags and all types of containers.

As he started to unload, two young men came out of the woods. "Got the horses you asked for ready," one of them said.

"Saddle two of them."

The men took the saddles and disappeared back into the trees. Geneva couldn't help her surprise. She'd thought Calhoun's was a one-man operation given the state of his cabin and this truck. It had been so long ago that she'd forgotten that she'd asked about Lucian's truck when he finally got around to answering.

"I hid the truck in an old barn, but I can't promise it will be there when we get back. Word will be out about it and Lucian. Now get out of the way while I pack us up. We're burning daylight."

CALHOUN SAW THE way his two wranglers had looked at Geneva. Like him, they must think he'd lost his mind. Why was he doing this? Certainly not for a woman he didn't know—let alone Lucian's wife. Or was this about some old debt he thought he still owed his former friend? The thought didn't improve his mood.

After getting rid of the pickup, he'd used his satellite phone to call his guide to make sure the other two wranglers were almost to the camp. He'd sent them up ahead of him with the new wall tent so they could have it all set up when these two wranglers brought up the fishing clients. They would be camping and going to the high mountain lakes for the next few days. He'd promised to see them in camp before the wranglers had to leave. This was his business, his livelihood, and he was risking it all for what?

He thought about the professional thugs he'd seen in town a few days ago. They'd been asking around about Lucian, showing locals his photograph. Calhoun had managed to avoid them. But it did make him wonder if Lucian really had come back for something. Why else had the men shown up here now? Why else had Lucian's wife?

Calhoun considered the risk he was taking. Crossing the path of those bad-looking dudes up in the mountains would be more than risky—especially with Lucian's wife along. Yet here he was doing something he said he never would. He wasn't just taking a woman up in the mountains—he was taking her *dog*.

And not just any woman, he reminded himself. One completely ill-prepared for the trip or what they might get into. Worse, she was too good-looking, too vulnerable, too easy as prey once they left behind the last of civilization. That's why he couldn't have let her go with Max.

But was she really any safer with him?

She didn't seem to realize the situation she was putting herself into even now, he thought. Calhoun had an old score to settle with Lucian. No man in his right mind wouldn't be tempted to settle that score with Lucian's wife as payback. After all, Lucian had it coming.

"Two horses saddled," one of the wranglers said as he came out of the pines. "Three ready for the pack saddles. Or want us to catch up to the wrangler who is leading the clients up to camp?"

"Head on up. I've got it. Thanks for sticking around." The two wranglers would get there in time to make sure the horses at the main camp were hobbled, the clients fed, and stoves lit and wood stocked in the wall tents for the night ahead. The temperature dropped considerably in the mountains, even in July, especially near water.

Calhoun had thought about taking at least one of the wranglers with him and Geneva, but he wasn't paying a wrangler to tag along with them. Word would get out soon enough about where they'd gone and why. Better whatever happened up here stay between the two of them—and Lucian—if they found him.

"This is a fool's errand," he said under his breath. He hoped Lucian was too smart to come back here. Once they didn't find him, Calhoun's plan was to head for his own camp, where he'd get one of the wranglers to take Mrs. Beck back to Cooke City so she could return to San Diego, where she belonged.

And if they found Lucian? Or that he'd been there? Then he'd cross that creek when he came to it. But he wasn't anticipating that. He told himself this would be a quick trip and would be over soon. All he had to do was get her up there and back, and all debts were paid in full. Lucian would owe him until the day he died.

"Ready, Mrs. Beck?" he asked. She'd been sitting nearby watching him. Paying attention to how everything was tied on? Or thinking about her no-count husband? He couldn't tell.

She rose and nodded. "But could you please call me Geneva? I no longer consider myself Mrs. Beck."

Maybe she didn't, but he did, and he planned to keep reminding himself of that fact. He tossed her a backpack from the rear of the trailer before he slammed the door. "Put the mutt in there. You can't hold her and control the horse if a grouse flies up and spooks your mare and you both take off." Who was he kidding? They'd both end up in the dust if that happened.

He thought she would put up an argument. Instead, she

took the backpack and slipped the puppy inside. The dog's head popped up, all floppy ears and tongue.

It was official, he'd lost his mind. "Let's get you in the saddle. We have a long ride ahead of us."

Chapter Nine

Henry "Blade" Wallace looked dispassionately at the man being severely beaten by Ricki "The Rat" Morrison and Juice Jensen. "Lucian Beck," Blade repeated, bending forward on his haunches to stare into the bloody face of the biker.

"Told ya," Ace said through swollen, split lips and at least one broken tooth. "Don't know."

Blade sighed and stood. "But you know something you want to tell me though, don't you?" When Ace didn't respond instantly, he started to tell Ricki and Juice to finish him.

"Wait!" the biker cried. He seemed to be choking on his own blood for a moment before he said, "You're right, his truck was seen in town, but he wasn't driving it."

He tilted his head and bent down again. "Don't leave me in suspense. Who was driving it?"

"His wife."

Blade lifted a brow in surprise and stood again. "Lucian got married?" That was so unlikely that he questioned whether Ace knew what he was talking about. "Who told you that?"

"Max Lander, a local outfitter. She tried to hire him. He saw her credit card with her name on it. Geneva Beck. She's got a puppy with her."

He stared at the biker. "A puppy? Somehow you thought that I'd be interested in that?"

"Calhoun St. Pierre took her and the dog up into the mountains. He never takes women, let alone one with some puppy with her."

Blade's eyes narrowed. "When was this?"

"This morning."

Ricki and Juice looked to him for guidance. Blade cleared his throat and said, "I heard you have a beef with Lucian. That tells me that if he was in this godforsaken town, you would know where he was or where he might have gone. But you'd be too smart to keep that from me and my friends, right?" He saw the biker hesitate, only for a second though.

"Lucian had a camp up in the mountains."

"Where?" Blade asked.

Ace shook his head and quickly added, "I can tell you how to get to the area, but only Calhoun St. Pierre knows exactly where. That's probably why he's gone up there."

"With Lucian's wife and a dog?"

The biker nodded. "It's the truth, I swear."

He saw Ace looking at his prison tats, no doubt wondering who Blade and his friends were and why they were looking for Lucian. Ricki and Juice were still waiting. He personally didn't care if this big biker lived or died. But if Ace went missing, worse, if his body was discovered, it would cause him trouble. "Let him go. He's too smart to go to the authorities, let alone get his buddies to come after us. I think he knows who he's dealing with now, right, Ace?"

The biker didn't respond as Ricki and Juice helped him to his feet.

"One more question," Blade said as he pulled out his knife to check himself in the shiny blade. "An interesting tidbit before you go. Want to know how I got the nickname

Blade?" Ace shook his head. "Suit yourself. Then just tell me this. How do we get up in the mountains where Calhoun St. Pierre and Lucian's wife and the dog headed?"

"WHAT DID LUCIAN do to you?" Geneva asked as Calhoun wove his fingers together and instructed her to put her boot sole in his hands so he could lift her into the saddle. "It must have been something pretty unforgiveable given your reaction to his pickup." She stepped into his hand as she reached for the saddle horn and was shot upward. She swung a leg over the saddle, hanging on to the pommel so she didn't keep going over the other side. He worked her boot into the stirrup as she did the same with her other boot. She was shaking and trying not to show it. She didn't remember being so far off the ground the last and only time she'd ridden a horse. It seemed Calhoun wasn't going to answer.

But before he stepped away, he looked up at her, squinting as if there was sun in his eyes. "He slept with my fiancée." With that, he turned and walked to his horse.

She didn't know what to say. Had someone told her that a few weeks ago, she would have argued that Lucian would never have done that to a friend. But back then, she'd thought she'd known her husband. Now, she believed Calhoun. Something told her, though, that there was even more to the story.

When it came to Lucian, she was ready to believe the worst given what he'd done to her. That was the hard part, trying to understand who she'd been married to, she thought as Calhoun hooked up the three packhorses and took the lead, trailing them behind his horse. She followed, bringing up the rear.

He only looked back once to see if she was still there. She was. His expression was grim before he turned back around, making her all the more determined to show him what she was made of. The problem was that she didn't know what that was. She'd never been tried, so she really didn't know if she could do this—especially if it was going to be as strenuous and dangerous as he wanted her to believe.

Geneva settled into the saddle, rocking along, telling herself that this wasn't going to be too bad. She checked on her puppy, who licked the side of her face, but once the horse started moving at a steady gait, the dog curled up in the backpack and slept.

She let her mind wander as the horses plodded along a trail, pines dense on each side. Rays from the sun pierced through the pine branches. She rode in and out of shadows, thinking about the night she first met Lucian back when it had all started.

She'd never seen Lucian before the night she and Mitzi went to a new restaurant her friend had found. They'd barely sat down when he'd come out of the kitchen with his white chef's coat to great Mitzi.

"Glad to see you did come back," he said smiling. *"I hope that means you like my food."*

Mitzi had laughed. *"It was your crepes. I've been dying for them ever since that night."*

He chuckled and looked to Geneva.

"This is my friend Geneva Carrington." He took her hand and gave a little bow. *"Lucian Beck, your chef tonight. A friend of Mitzi's is a friend of mine. I will make something special for you both."*

Had Lucian and Mitzi been in league from the very beginning, she wondered now? She thought about how Lucian hadn't paid any more attention to her than he did Mitzi that first night. Even a few weeks later, at a party at Mitzi's house, Lucian had been casual, polite but not overly interested in her.

"Beware of that one," Mitzi had said. *"He's too good-looking, too charming, too talented, and he knows it."*

Had she been speaking from experience? Or had she already known that Geneva was intrigued by Lucian? They'd been friends for so long, Mitzi would know that Geneva would be attracted to a man who was aloof. Too many knew the Carrington name and that it was synonymous with money. But that was before Geneva had learned of her father's financial misfortune.

Lucian was supposedly new in town. Geneva had believed that he didn't have any idea about the Carrington name. Or about who she was. Her mistake.

The next time they'd crossed paths, Lucian had stopped on the street to talk to her. It had been cool that morning, and he'd suggested they step into the nearby coffee shop. She'd felt his gaze on her, warm like sunshine. She'd been taking his measure, surprised at how nicely he was dressed. The expensive designer clothing fit his lanky body perfectly. He'd grinned as he'd suggested coffee. The smile had made her late for work at the gallery so she could have coffee with him.

That had been the beginning. Geneva, who'd been dating a man off and on, broke that relationship off. Once she began seeing Lucian, he was all she wanted. Lucian fascinated her. He'd been all over the world, had done so many exciting things, worked so many different jobs before training to be a chef. He'd climbed mountains, backpacked in exotic places around the world, swam in water she'd never seen even though she'd done some traveling herself. Now she wondered if any of his stories had been true.

But at the time, she'd been completely taken with him. He was handsome, charming, smart and funny. She'd fallen hard, but fortunately so had he. At least she'd thought so, since it wasn't long before they were practically living together—and he asked her to marry him.

She glanced down at her bare ring finger, thinking of the engagement ring with its beautiful pear-shaped diamond and the matching wedding ring also encrusted with diamonds. "*It's beautiful*," she had cried when he'd put it on her finger.

"*Only the best for you, my princess*," he'd said.

She had felt like a princess—before that morning waking up on the couch alone and knowing something was very wrong. Looking back now, though, with freshly opened eyes, she wondered if calling her his princess wasn't mocking her and her position in life.

Lucian must have seen her as one of the privileged class. She suspected he had always been looking in that window, seeing what he'd wanted, feeling he could never have it. Maybe he thought marriage to her would make him feel like he belonged. Apparently, it hadn't.

She thought back on their year of marriage, starting on her twenty-ninth birthday. Was that when she'd told him about her inheritance when she turned thirty? She couldn't remember. It wasn't something she would have kept from her husband. But had she told him when they were dating?

Geneva didn't want to believe that Lucian had targeted her—maybe even before that night at the restaurant. Had Mitzi set up their first meeting at the restaurant because she knew Geneva would like him? It would be just like Mitzi to tell Lucian that Geneva's father was "loaded." Mitzi could have even told him about her inheritance before Geneva even met him.

She felt bitterness fill her, the sour taste making her stomach roil. The two of them could have set her up. Lucian could have promised to share with Mitzi once they were married. Neither Lucian nor Mitzi had known about her father's financial misfortune.

Greed, she thought with abhorrence. Lucian had taken what money they had, along with her inheritance, but apparently even that wasn't enough. He'd had to take her watch from her father, her car, and left her with nothing, taking it all—and double-crossing Mitzi, who some might say got what she deserved. At least it hadn't cost her her life.

"You okay?" Calhoun called back to her across the three pack animals.

"Great," she said, readjusting herself in the saddle. The puppy was heavier than she would have expected, making her back ache, but she wasn't about to say anything. When they stopped, she would shift the puppy to the front for a while.

If they ever stopped.

ANOTHER TWO HOURS had gone by before Calhoun looked back, almost surprised that Geneva Beck was still there. It wasn't like he'd forgotten about her. In fact, that was all he'd had on his mind. Her and her husband. Especially Lucian.

He hadn't let his former friend clutter his thoughts—until recently when the thugs had shown up asking about him. Right on the heels of that, Lucian's black pickup pulls in front of his cabin? He'd thought he would never see the man again. He sure as the devil didn't expect Lucian's *wife* to climb out.

Reining in, he twisted in the saddle to look back at her, realizing she could probably use a break. He ground-tied his horse and walked back to help her out of the saddle. "Give me the dog," he said and waited while she pulled off the backpack. He could tell that her back was sore and chided himself for letting her bring the pup.

But she was one stubborn woman, and he didn't know anyone who would have taken care of the dog while they rode up into the mountains in search of her husband. Not without having to explain more than he wanted to share with anyone in the small, isolated community of Cooke City.

He set the backpack on the ground and reached for her hand, but as she rose and threw her leg over, he saw how unsteady she was and grabbed her by the waist, lifting her down and setting her on the ground. He could tell that she was saddle sore but was doing her best not to show it.

"Need water?" he asked already moving toward one of the packhorses and turning his back on her. He wanted to give her a minute to get her legs under her again. Normally, he would drink out of the creek, but he wasn't taking any chances with her delicate system. All he needed was for her to get giardia.

By the time he returned with water, she had the puppy out of the backpack. It was waddling around in the tall grass and wildflowers, nose to the ground. Geneva took a drink, stretched and walked around, as if trying to get the kinks out as she pretended to admire the wildflowers. He'd stopped in a small meadow. He didn't want to rush her, but they really needed to get to a spot where they could make camp and get set up before dark.

"If you need to use the facilities…" He pointed to a stand of trees before going to check the packhorses and make sure the loads hadn't shifted.

When he finally looked in her direction again, she and the puppy were coming out of the trees. She looked as if she would survive, but this was only the first day. He grumbled under his breath, mentally kicking himself for weakening. He should never have gotten involved with her. He didn't care where Lucian was. He certainly didn't want to find him. He knew how pointless it was. Closure wasn't all that it was cracked up to be. And that was the best she was going to get from Lucian.

"Ready?" he asked even though she really didn't have a choice. He laced his fingers together and lifted her up into the saddle. As she reached for the backpack, he shook his head. "I'll take the dog for a while." She looked uncertain. "I can handle it," he said, glad he hadn't said, *Trust me.* She'd be a fool to trust him with much more than her dog.

Scooping up the pack and the dog, he headed for his horse, all the time looking up the trail and worrying what might be waiting for them.

GENEVA HURT ALL OVER. The ache had started a few miles up the trail in her legs, her back, her behind. Hours on horseback, and it had all gotten much worse. She'd tried shifting in the saddle, half standing, but it didn't help all that much. Neither did leaning back. Not having the puppy strapped to her back helped though.

She saw that Calhoun hadn't put the dog in the backpack but had put it in front of him on the saddle. As the trail turned and she got a glimpse of the two of them, she saw that the puppy had fallen asleep, head resting on one of his thighs. Who was this man? He could be so gentle and yet such a bear with her.

Not that she could blame him. She'd forced him into taking her up here against his will. Clearly he had his issues with Lucian. But he still must care. Why else would he go against everything, his no women policy and his adamant refusal to take her anywhere up here otherwise?

Geneva was more than curious about his relationship with Lucian. From the photograph she'd found, she'd assumed they'd been good friends. Otherwise, why would her husband have kept the photos? But had Lucian really slept with Calhoun's fiancé? She shook her head. She'd been trying to make sense of all of this for days.

If anything, she was more curious about who her husband had been, the real Lucian Beck—if there had been one. Would they find him up here? And if they did, what was it she hoped to accomplish? She told herself that she just wanted to look him in the eye and—what? Shame him? Demand an explanation? It seemed pretty clear. He'd wanted what she had—her money, her things—just not her.

That, she knew, was what she wanted. She needed the why. It was what kept her awake at night. Why would he give up what they had? Why not divorce her and take half? Why? Because this way, he got it all and didn't have to face her.

She hadn't realized that she'd fallen behind until she looked up and saw that Calhoun had stopped on a pine-covered hillside ahead. They'd been continually climbing for miles now. Surely they were almost to the camp. At least she hoped so. She couldn't ever remember being this physically exhausted. She never dreamed that sitting on a horse would be so painful.

But she would die before she would let Calhoun St. Pierre know.

As she rode up to where he was standing, she saw that he was looking back down the mountainside with a pair of binoculars. She caught his expression as he lowered them.

"What's wrong?" she asked in a whisper.

"We're being followed."

Chapter Ten

Calhoun swore under his breath as he considered what to do. Three men, all on horseback. Not the bikers. Ace hated horses. Could be the out-of-town professional thugs who'd been looking for Lucian earlier in the week. Could be just about anybody.

Whoever it was, they were following him and Lucian's wife. That was disconcerting. The only good news was that they were way behind. Also, they hadn't brought packhorses, which meant they weren't planning to stay in the mountains long—not without supplies.

More important, they didn't seem to know where they were going, or they would have brought supplies—and they wouldn't have been following him and Geneva.

He'd taken a couple of trails he wouldn't have normally taken because they weren't quite as steep due to the inexperience of his…client. Whoever was following them had been following their tracks, taking the same trails. He checked the length of the sun.

It stayed daylight late in this part of the country this time of year. But up here in the mountains, shadows began to fill the pines the moment the sun dropped behind the mountains. The temperature would also drop. He'd planned on building a fire when they camped tonight, but a camp-

fire would lead the men right to them. Unless Calhoun
could get up into the rocks.

"Who do you think they are?" Geneva asked.

"Someone interested in you or your husband or both."

"I wish you wouldn't call him that."

He raised a brow. "Your husband? I'm sorry, did you
get a divorce on the way up this mountain?"

"You know what I mean."

Calhoun did, but he felt he had to keep reminding himself. "I hate to do this, but we're going up the creek. It will
be rougher riding in the creek bed, but it might throw them
off our trail."

She nodded. It wasn't as if she had a choice. Neither
did he. They still had quite a bit of distance between them
and whoever was following them. But not near enough. If
he could trick them…

He and Geneva were almost high enough on the mountain that his crew and camp weren't far off to the north.
The trail cut off from here. It would be easy for the men
following them to mistake that trail and take it, especially
if they lost his and Geneva's tracks when they dropped into
the creek. At least he hoped so.

He had a feeling that whoever the men were, they
weren't trained mountain guides. If they stumbled onto
the large camp with his crew and clients, they might even
turn back since they weren't carrying supplies to go another day or two.

"Come on. Just a little farther." He could see the exhaustion on her face, but there was no helping it. With luck,
they would lose the men—at least for tonight. That was
enough to hope for right now.

Just as Calhoun had said, they rode down a trail for a while,
then dropped into the creek bed. The riding was much

worse, the horses slipping on the rocks under the shallow water and making her hang on for dear life, as her grandmother would have said. The sun disappeared behind the mountain they were climbing. Darkness began to hunker in the trees.

"You said your other wall tent was destroyed by a grizzly bear?" she said when they came out of the creek and stopped for a few moments to eat some jerky and have a drink of water.

He followed her gaze to the deep shadows now settling into the dark pines. "If a grizzly finds an empty camp, they've been known to look around and end up tearing things up."

She couldn't help being nervous. It was so quiet up here. She found herself listening for any sound while she swatted at the swarm of mosquitoes that seemed to like the growing darkness.

"You might want some bug spray. You did buy some, right?"

She nodded, and he went to the last packhorse and returned with her bottle. As she applied it to any skin not covered by clothing, she asked, "Do the bears come into camp when there are people there?" she asked.

"Often enough," was all he said.

She couldn't help thinking about grizzly bears hiding in the woods, jumping out when she least expected it as they rode farther up the mountains. What was she doing up here? She was in a hell of her own making. Why had she insisted on this? As he'd said, Lucian probably wasn't even up here. It had been so easy to demand Calhoun bring her to Lucian's camp when she was standing on the main drag of Cooke City, where it was warm, where she didn't hurt all over, where she had food and a soft bed.

Just when she thought this day would never end, Calhoun rode out of the creek bed. But her hopes that they would now stop were dashed as they continued up one trail, across another and up the side of a mountain. He led them up to a rocky bluff and finally stopped. She fought tears of relief that this might be it for the day. When he swung out of his saddle and began to see to the packhorses, she almost broke down she was so exhausted, so sore, so emotionally and physically worn out.

She feared that if he said anything nice to her—let alone touched her—she wouldn't be able to hold the tears back. She thought about his big hands on her waist earlier, the strength in them at odds with the gentleness, and knew that would be her undoing. Swallowing back the pain and the relief, she swung down out of the saddle, determined that he wouldn't have to help her—only to lose her balance and end up on her butt in the grass.

He walked up to her, seeming to be deciding if she was hurt or not. The puppy lumbered up behind him and charged her, licking her in the face and making her laugh. The laugh was a little too close to a sob, she realized, and was glad when, apparently realizing she wasn't injured, he nodded and said, "I'm going to take care of the horses and set up camp. Think you can collect us some wood for a fire?"

She nodded, having never collected wood for a fire in her life.

As if he realized that, he added, "Just small twigs and branches you find on the ground, none any larger than a foot. We can't have much of a fire."

He started to walk off as she pulled the puppy to her for a much needed hug—not for the dog but for herself. "Did we lose them?" she called after Calhoun.

"For the time being," he said, his back to her.

She buried her face in the puppy's fur for a moment.

Watching him walk away, she wasn't sure she could get up. But she would get firewood, even if it killed her. She had to put the pup down to get to her feet. Her legs trembled as she stood and stretched, and her dog ran after Calhoun. "Figures," she said under her breath.

Patches of darkness had settled deep in the pines. She gathered an armful of wood and carried it up to a spot where someone had made a circle of blackened rocks for a fire near the spot where Calhoun had dropped some of the supplies.

"That should be enough wood," he said. "Here's your bedroll." He tossed it to her. It felt thin, like a rolled-up polyester comforter bound with rope. "Look for a spot not too far from here where it's flat and halfway soft to sleep."

She looked around, unmoving. Her legs ached, her back hurt, and even the slight weight of the bedroll felt too heavy. "There isn't a tent?"

"We'll be breaking camp at first light," he said as if seeing that he was going to have to explain and was irritated by it. "We won't have time to take down a tent."

Geneva nodded, but still didn't move. He expected her to sleep on the ground out in the open where anything could get her? Perfectly reasonable. "What about—"

"You'll want to put the puppy in the sleeping bag with you so something doesn't get her," he said and walked off.

Like something couldn't get them both?

"Don't worry, I won't be far away if…" It had sounded like he was going to say, *if she needed him,* but changed his mind. "If there's trouble." He led the horses into the nearby pines, disappearing from view.

Trouble? She took a deep breath and reminded herself that she had only herself to blame for being here. Calhoun had been right. She wasn't strong enough for this. Why was she putting herself through it?

She thought about her new house with all the luxuries a person could ask for, including a down comforter on the king-size bed and hot running water and walls behind a security system as she looked for a flat soft spot in the tall grass that would be her bed. She thought about her friends all snug in their comfy beds with their luxury high-thread-count sheets. If they could see her now. What she wouldn't give for a nice hot bubble bath for her sore muscles, not to mention something for the rash she felt on her behind and the backs of her thighs. Saddle sores?

Finding a spot not far away, she untied the sleeping bag and unfurled it on the grass. She fought the urge to lie down on it and close her eyes, but she wasn't sure she would be able to get up again if she did.

"Hungry?" Calhoun asked behind her.

Ravenous, she realized. She hadn't had breakfast. The jerky he'd given her the few times they'd stopped for a health break and water had done little to alleviate her hunger. She nodded enthusiastically. "Can I help?"

He eyed her, then chuckled. "You do a lot of cooking, do you?"

Her offer had been out of politeness. "No." He nodded as if that had been the answer he'd expected. "Lucian was a chef." She didn't mention that he never cooked except at work.

"You're joking." She shook her head. "He couldn't boil water. The one time he tried to cook at the cabin, he practically burned the place down and incinerated a couple of damned good elk steaks."

"Apparently he learned how."

Calhoun seemed to think about that, rubbing his beard and looking genuinely perplexed. "Guess you knew a different man than I did. You sure his name was Lucian Beck?"

She'd never considered that the man she married might

have stolen another man's name. Nothing would have surprised her at this point. She started to explain why she'd never learned to cook, but stopped herself. She'd had nannies and cooks growing up. Mostly she and her father ordered in a lot in later years. Where they lived, it was too easy to order any kind of food you could imagine and have it brought right to your door.

"So, what do you do?" he asked as he squatted down and began to unpack the bag he'd dropped by the firepit.

"I work at an art gallery."

He looked up from the small stove he was unfolding to look at her. "Are you an artist?"

She was pretty sure that artists painted or sculpted or did something other than design a few things for her father's company after college. "I studied art and art history."

He gave her a look that was anything but impressed. Her father had hired her after she graduated with degrees in art and art history. She'd never wanted to be a designer.

"I've always wanted to paint," she said, trying to fill the heavy silence as she watched him take out a small pot, pour some water from a bottle into the pan and then dump in what appeared to be a freeze-dried meal.

There was something in those wolf-gray eyes that was waiting for not just more but for honesty. "So, what stopped you?"

She flinched. "Life. Lucian. I was working with him to find a building to open his restaurant." This time the look he gave her was pure disbelief. "I know, in retrospect, that must seem pretty dumb to you."

"Which part? The one where Lucian said he wanted his own restaurant? Or the one where you went along with it?"

His comment hurt, but it was so true that she couldn't think of a response.

"Don't mind me," he said with a shake of his head.

"He conned me too, and I knew better, having grown up with him." He stirred the concoction in the pot and must have seen her expression. "It tastes better than it looks," he added.

"I was hoping we could talk about Lucian," she said as their dinner boiled and bubbled.

"What's there to talk about?" he asked dismissively as he pulled up two large stumps, one apparently for her. "Clearly, I didn't know the man you did, otherwise you would have never married him."

His words shocked her. "I thought you were friends." She sat down on the stump, grateful for a chance to sit down on something that wasn't moving. Her backside was definitely sore, her leg muscles feeling as if they wanted to spasm.

"*Were* being the key word here. It was a long time ago." He pulled out a piece of jerky and gave it to the puppy, who sat chewing happily next to him.

"How long were you friends?" she asked as he pulled the pot from the small stove and began to scoop food onto a tin plate.

He handed her the plate and a spoon from a small box that apparently held the entire kitchen setup. "Since we were kids."

For some reason she'd thought they'd met in college. "What was he like?"

He shrugged as he sat back on the ground, leaning against the tree stump he'd drawn up and stirred his food in the pan. He took a bite and chewed for a few moments as if thinking about it.

Hers was too hot to eat. She scooped up a spoonful and let it cool before taking a tentative bite. He was right. It didn't look very appetizing, but as hungry as she was... "This is delicious."

Calhoun laughed. "You really were hungry." He had a nice smile. She wondered what he would look like without that full beard. There was a shine in his gray eyes that she hadn't seen before as he seemed to take her in. Was there some respect there? Some admiration? She'd gone all day without whining or complaining, and other than a few times of almost crying, she'd done fairly well, in her humble opinion. Not that she expected him to congratulate her.

"Lucian was okay," he said after a moment. "We used to spend a lot of time up here in the mountains. He seemed to love it as much as I did."

"Seemed to love it?"

He smiled at that. "I guess after Lucian betrays you, you start questioning everything. But I don't have to tell you that, do I?"

"What was his family like?"

"Nice people, much nicer than mine. If you're looking for answers as to why Lucian turned out the way he did, you're barking up the wrong tree. I loved his parents. I have no idea why he turned out the way he did, and I knew him for years." Calhoun ate in silence for a moment before he finished all but a little of his meal and put the pan down for the puppy, who stuck her head in and began making slurping sounds.

"When did he change?"

His answer came quickly. "Who says he changed? Maybe he just hid what he was like from all of us. He fooled you, didn't he?"

She looked down at her plate, remembering the handsome, charming man she'd met. He hadn't come on too strong. If anything, he'd seemed unwilling to get involved. Had that been part of the appeal? He'd seem to want nothing from her.

"Why did he go to college in Alabama instead of Montana?" she asked as she watched Calhoun fill the small pot with water, put it back on the stove and collect her plate and spoon to wash the dishes.

"He got a scholarship to play basketball. He was good. Then, like a lot of players, he got hurt and ended up quitting the team and later dropping out just before graduation."

She thought about him not finishing college. "What was he majoring in?"

"Journalism. He always talked about being a foreign correspondent. Was into politics. He wanted to travel. He resented kids whose parents paid for them to go to Europe after high school or let them take off on trips around the US." He began to wash the dishes, putting them into a canvas bag. "He always wanted to go somewhere, so he went to Alabama to school. Far as I know, he didn't get much farther."

She thought about the stories he told of his experiences around the world. Lies? "But he came back to Cooke City?"

The outfitter looked at her as if he wished he hadn't said anything if she was going to keep peppering him with questions. "We'd always spent summers up here. He hadn't been here for a couple of years. Then he showed up Memorial Day weekend just over a year ago."

She couldn't understand why Lucian had given up on his dream. "Did he tell you why he quit college so close to graduation?"

"I never asked." He rose and put away everything from their dinner. "We ride before daybreak. You should get some sleep."

"What if a bear comes into camp?"

He chuckled. "Oh, you'll know, don't worry about that." He took the portable kitchen to one of the packs and came back with a bedroll much like the one he'd given her.

She watched him spread it out before lying down, his back to her. "I can't believe you're just going to sleep. What about the men you said were following us?"

"We lost them for now, and it's dark."

"But once they realize—"

He rolled back over to face her. "They won't attack in the dark, not up here on this cliff, not until daylight. So how about you let me get some sleep until then."

She nodded although that made no sense to her at all. He rolled back over, and within seconds, she heard him snoring.

WHEN HAD LUCIAN CHANGED? The question kept Calhoun awake as he pretended to snore to shut up the man's wife. After Lucian's junior year in college in Alabama, Calhoun had gotten the feeling that he'd fallen in with some rough friends.

The change had been subtle at first. Lucian had always loved Cooke City and the great outdoors, so when he was back the first couple of years for the summer, he seemed almost the same. The area challenged a man with its steep peaks, rough terrain, uncertain weather and wild animals. There was so much up here that could kill you. That's why you had to put any personal problems aside when in the mountains. You had to always be alert for danger.

Calhoun couldn't help seeing an even greater change the last time he'd seen his old friend. Lucian had been nervous, anxious to get up into the mountains. He'd insisted on taking off on his own, something Calhoun had advised him against, and yet Lucian had gone anyway, as if he couldn't wait. Or as if something or someone was after him.

"*Want to tell me what kind of trouble you're in?*" Calhoun remembered asking him.

Lucian had laughed, waving it off, but Calhoun hadn't

been fooled. He'd told himself that he knew the man too well. Lucian was in trouble.

"*If there is anything I can do to help...*" he'd offered.

"*Best to stay as far away from me as you can,*" his friend had said. "*Right now, I'm Typhoid Mary.*"

"*I doubt whatever you have is catching.*"

"*You might be surprised.*"

"*How contagious are we talking?*" he'd asked, afraid of what Lucian had brought to Cooke.

"*Don't worry, I'll be gone before you start seeing any symptoms.*"

Lucian had gone up into the mountains. Calhoun had clients he had to take to a series of high mountain lakes for a five-day fishing and camping trip. By the time he returned to town, his friend was gone, leaving a path of destruction in his wake. In a matter of days, Lucian had burned every bridge, cheating everyone he knew and some he'd just met.

It wasn't until a few weeks later that Calhoun learned what else Lucian had done—this time to his supposedly good friend. Calhoun still couldn't understand why, but in the long run, his old friend had done him a favor by sleeping with his fiancée.

He'd known the moment he walked in the door at her apartment in Billings and saw Dana's face. His expression must have given him away as well, because she had burst into tears, assuming Lucian had told him.

"It just happened," she'd confessed. "Lucian stopped by on his way out of state. He seemed so sad and scared. I felt so bad for him, and I guess I just wanted to…"

He wasn't sure what Dana had wanted to do. He'd never asked. He'd walked out and hadn't looked back. Instead, he'd gone looking for Lucian but hadn't found him, which, looking back, was also a blessing. He feared what he might have done.

That Lucian could betray him like that felt more than personal. His friend had taken a chainsaw to the ties that had bound them for years. It was as if he was sending him a message. Calhoun had gotten it loud and clear. Their friendship was over, smoldering in the ruins that Lucian had left behind.

He'd been convinced that Lucian's treachery against him meant he would never show his face around Cooke City ever again. Calhoun had never dreamed that the painful reminder of Lucian's betrayal would come in the shapely form of Geneva Carrington Beck driving up in her husband's prized pickup.

Calhoun closed his eyes, needing sleep so he didn't spend the dark hours mentally kicking himself for what he'd already done by bringing Geneva up here—and for what he might do before this excursion was over.

Chapter Eleven

Moving her sleeping bag a little closer to his, Geneva spread it out and laid down as he had done. The ground was hard under her, some of the wildflower stems poking her through the thin stuffing. She realized that he'd had her collect firewood, but he'd never built a fire. He'd just been trying to keep her out of his hair.

Grumbling under her breath, she rolled over on her back, telling herself that she would never be able to sleep. She'd never in her life slept outdoors, she thought, listening for bears. All she could hear were mosquitoes buzzing around her. Swarming really, making it hard not to swallow some of them.

Her eyes focused on the star-filled sky through the pine branches and she was struck with awe. She'd never in her life seen a sky like that. The stars looked so close she felt as if she could touch them.

Breathing in the cold night air, she snuggled deeper in the bag, the puppy next to her. The quiet felt intense. She could hear the faint breeze whispering in the tops of the pine boughs and Calhoun softly snoring. One of the horses moved, shuddered and then fell silent again.

Geneva hated to close her eyes, the stars were so magnificent, but she must have because it seemed only moments later that she awoke to Calhoun packing up the horses. A sliver of orange outlined the black of mountains to the east as the sun slowly scaled the backside, harkening daylight. She hurriedly wiggled out of her sleeping bag and rose. Her body ached as if she'd been beaten with a bat. She saw that her puppy was already up. The dog came waddling over to her. Geneva bent down to pet her and got a reassuring lick.

"I fed her," Calhoun said without looking at her.

"Thank you." She stretched, trying to work out the kinks. It was the first time she'd ever slept in all her clothes—except for the night Lucian left her, she corrected.

Calhoun finally turned to look at her. He actually seemed to see her. "Good morning."

Unconsciously, she raked a hand through her hair and quickly tied it up. His greeting surprised her. It was the most pleasant he'd been, especially in the morning.

She needed to pee, but she was also desperate to wash her face and brush her teeth. "May I have my makeup bag, please?"

He made a disgruntled sound. "Make it quick," he added gruffly, and he went to the closest packhorse to pull out her toiletries.

Taking it, she headed for the creek. As she cut through the pines, she looked back, wondering how far she'd have to go to get the privacy she needed. She had to follow the creek a few yards downstream before she could no longer see Calhoun or the horses or the camp.

Stepping away from the creek, she did her business, then had just began to wash her face in the freezing cold water when she heard a rumble in the distance. She looked in the direction it had come from. Thunder?

A thin light had turned the darkness to the east to twilight. But something darker rimmed the peaks. A thunderstorm?

"COME ON, we have to get moving," Calhoun said as she hurriedly returned. He took her makeup bag and stuffed it into one of the panniers on the packhorse. "I'll take the puppy. There's a storm headed this way. We need to try to get to shelter before it hits. We probably won't, so prepare for some cold, wet water."

He tossed her the long yellow coat the clerk had called a slicker. She shrugged into it, feeling his sense of urgency. Was he saying they were going back to town? She had to admit, the idea had its appeal. She still felt the effects of the long horseback ride and sleeping on the ground last night. Her desire to face her duplicitous husband was fading fast at the thought of another long day in the saddle, let alone being caught in a thunderstorm.

"Use that log over there to mount your horse. I might not always be around."

Before she could ask him what that meant, he was scooping up the puppy and heading for his horse.

Geneva led her already saddled horse over to the fallen log he'd indicated and used it to swing up into the saddle. She couldn't help grinning because she'd done it. Still, his words worried her. In case he wasn't around? She really didn't like the sound of that.

She quickly realized that they weren't heading back to Cooke City. Instead, they climbed higher, the trail more rugged and rocky, as the dark, ominous storm clouds gathered in the mountains ahead of them. To her, it appeared they were headed right into the tempest—as if that wasn't what they'd been doing coming up here to begin with. Why had this seemed like a good idea?

Geneva didn't know how long they'd been in the saddle before she felt a large raindrop hit her in the face, then another. She pulled the brim of her hat forward as the sky opened up, dumping icy rain and darkness with a fury of sound like none she'd ever heard. The mountain seemed to shudder under the inundation of pounding rain and thunderous booms. Lightning splintered the darkness in blinding flashes.

Geneva bent over her horse, hanging on in terror that the storm would spook the mare and it would take off, unseating her. She couldn't bear the thought of being bucked off since she feared it would break every bone in her body when she hit the ground.

When Calhoun finally stopped, she felt such a flood of relief that she had to choke back tears. He helped her down from her horse, taking the reins and pointing toward the large boulder above them. She had to lean into him to hear what he was saying. All she caught was the word "cave" before she took the soaked and trembling puppy from him and worked her way up the slippery slope to find shelter back under the rock.

The space provided little head room but was spacious enough that she could have laid down. Something she definitely thought about. She was cold and damp and tired. She hugged the wet puppy, slipping her under her slicker as she tried to warm up the little dog. There was a firepit someone had made with a circle of small rocks and some dry wood, but she had no way of starting a fire. Something else she'd never done. The list just kept getting longer.

Calhoun was gone for so long that she began to fear that he'd left her here to die. She'd never been so happy to see anyone as he ducked into the cave, dragging a large canvas bag behind him. He looked at her huddled over the puppy shivering and quickly began to build a fire. "You're going to have to get out of your wet clothing." It took him only a few moments to get a fire going. The smoke rose to escape through a crack in the rock above them. "Give me the dog."

Reluctantly, she handed over the puppy but hesitated to take off her clothing. The slicker had kept most of the water off of her, but still the pouring rain had soaked her canvas pants and her base-layer top. While the space was large enough for both of them, there was no privacy.

Calhoun looked at her and groaned. "If you think I'm going out in the rain while you change…" He didn't finish as he pulled out what she recognized as long johns and a long-sleeved top. He tossed them to her and shook his head, pulled the puppy close to him and turned his back to her.

Geneva quickly changed out of her wet clothing and put on the way too large long underwear. "Done." She crossed her arms over her chest as she noticed her hard nipples pressed against the fabric. "Thanks."

He shook his head at her as he pulled a woolen vest out of the bag and handed that to her as well. Before she could put it on, he stripped off his wet T-shirt.

There was no place for her to turn away unless she wanted to stare at the stone wall of rock directly behind her. She reached for the puppy, brushing Calhoun's arm as he dropped the wet shirt on the bag he'd brought in. He stopped to peer at her as she quickly averted her eyes from his bare chest.

"What's so funny?" she demanded as he began to laugh.

"You. I'm just trying to imagine you and Lucian together. He must have smoothed off a lot of his rough edges to get you to marry him. Clearly, stripping down in the wilds isn't something the two of you did."

"Excuse me?" There was no reason to argue. She and Lucian hadn't spent any time in the wilds—let alone gotten naked in a cave in the woods. She could hear the thunderstorm moving off, but the rain now fell in a steady curtain just beyond Calhoun. "I'm not a prude."

He lifted an eyebrow at that.

"Because I didn't want to get naked in front of you?"

"Because you'd rather die of hypothermia than change your clothing with me here. Worse, you'd rather I freeze to death than make you uncomfortable by taking off my wet clothes," he said, kicking off his boots. "But princess, that isn't going to happen. You might want to avert your eyes." He stripped off his jeans.

Of course, he went commando. She dropped her gaze to the puppy even as she felt his gaze warm her cheeks. He was enjoying her discomfort. She kept her eyes averted, feeling foolish because some of the heat in her cheeks had nothing to do with embarrassment.

From what she'd inadvertently seen, Calhoun St. Pierre had an amazing body, muscular and quite impressive. She wished she was the kind of woman who could have openly appreciated it and this complicated man. Maybe he was right. Maybe she was a prude. She'd only had a few boyfriends before Lucian, only one of them serious enough that she'd slept with him.

"*I can't believe how inexperienced you are,*" Mitzi had laughed the night the two of them had drank too much and she'd confessed she'd been with only one other man besides Lucian. "*If you tell me that you were saving yourself for marriage—*"

"*I wasn't. I just never met anyone I wanted to get that intimate with,*" Geneva had said.

"*It's just sex,*" Mitzi had said with a laugh.

"*Not for me.*"

"*OMG, you really are a prude.*"

Apparently so, she thought now.

"I'm sorry," the outfitter said.

She looked up as Calhoun sat back down, now dressed in a pair of canvas pants and a long-sleeved T-shirt. He held his hands over the fire before glancing out of the cave. The rain was letting up.

When he turned back, his gaze met hers. "I shouldn't have made fun of you."

"It's okay, you're right. I am a prude."

He shrugged, his gaze still holding hers. "I never thought I'd be jealous of Lucian." He chuckled.

It took her a moment to realize what he'd said. Was that a compliment? She stared into his wolf-like gray eyes, her heart kicking up a beat. The heat from the fire warmed her cheeks. So did the way he was looking at her.

Before she could react, he reached over and brushed a lock of her wet hair back from her cheek. Those gray eyes seemed to pin her to the spot. She couldn't have moved if she wanted to. Nor could she breathe as his thumb found its way to her lips, the callused pad rough, the friction sending heat lightning arcing through her. A new heat raced along her veins to her center.

As he drew his hand back, she swallowed the lump that had risen in her throat. Her nipples were hard, only this time not from the cold. She started to cross her arms again, afraid he'd see her reaction to his touch, to that way he had of looking at her when it wasn't anger he was feeling, and remembered the vest he'd handed her. She quickly put it on.

He cleared his throat, seemingly as uncomfortable as she felt. Uncomfortable and yet drawn to this man in a way that sent goose bumps racing across her skin. "The rain's stopped. We need to get moving," he said, but didn't move.

She looked into his eyes, shocked to realize how badly she wanted him to touch her again. She didn't question her motives, but it had nothing to do with getting back at her no-count husband.

Calhoun broke eye contact with a curse and began putting out the fire. "The sun can dry our clothing on the way.

In the meantime..." He pulled out the second pair of canvas pants he'd made her buy and handed them to her. As he did, his gaze went to her chest. "You can keep the vest on until it warms up."

With that, he turned and ducked out of the cave. Her puppy wiggled out of her arms and went after him. Apparently, she wasn't the only one Calhoun St. Pierre was growing on.

BLADE SHOOK THE rainwater from his hat. They'd lost valuable time being forced to take shelter under a stand of pines to wait out the storm. Not to mention that cold night they'd spent huddled by the fire. He told himself that Lucian wouldn't have been going anywhere in that downpour either. Or in the dark last night. If the man was still up here in these mountains, they would find him.

He could hear Ricki and Juice complaining. They should have brought more clothing, something to eat other than jerky. What did they know about Montana weather in the summer high in the mountains? They were Alabama born and raised and damned proud of it. Blade had thought they would have reached the camp by now, found Lucian, finished their business and be headed back to town a long time ago.

"Juice needs to get warmed up," Ricki said as he rode his horse up to him. "He wants to build a fire and dry out his clothes."

"We're all drenched. There's no time. The sun will have to warm us up." He turned in his saddle to look back at Juice, who was visibly shivering next to his horse. "The sooner we get to the camp, the sooner we can get back to town and have a big Montana steak. Saddle up."

He saw Juice's expression and thought for a minute that the man would argue. Blade figured if he did, he'd shoot him where he stood. He'd had enough of both his and Ricki's complaining. Maybe it was time to end this partnership.

His hand went to the sidearm on his hip as Juice swung up into the saddle. A gunshot would alert Lucian. Also, Blade might need both of them if Lucian put up a fight. He groaned under his breath as he reminded himself that both Juice and Ricki had waited for him to get out of the joint after they'd both been released from prison.

Still, he couldn't help being irritable. They'd been following the outfitter and the woman but had lost them yesterday afternoon. He removed his hand from his gun to swat at the swarm of mosquitoes buzzing around him.

"Let's go get Lucian and what he owes us and then get the hell out of this country."

They hadn't gone far when Blade smelled a campfire. He rode toward the scent along the trail that had them headed north—instead of higher up the mountain. He saw his two companions perk up as the scent of frying bacon and coffee became stronger.

A few minutes later, they cleared the pines to see a large camp with several big wall tents and a couple of smaller tents next to a creek. But as they reined in, he saw only one person.

"Calhoun St. Pierre around?" Blade asked the wrangler making breakfast over an open fire.

"He's with another client, different trip," the wrangler said.

"Do you know where they're headed?" he asked, convinced they were headed for the same place.

The wrangler shook his head.

"How about Lucian Beck's camp. We're going up there to meet him, but I think we got turned around."

For a moment, the wrangler looked as if he were going

to deny knowing where the camp might be. "Nope, you're still on the right trail. I don't know exactly where it is. Just that it's up there." He pointed to the peak in the distance—that matched the description the biker had given them.

"So, you haven't seen St. Pierre and his client?"

When the wrangler shook his head, turning his attention to his cooking, Blade was pretty sure the man was lying. But he let it go when four fisherman came out of one of the larger tents to see what was going on.

"Maybe we'll cross paths," Blade suggested.

"Doubtful," the wrangler said with a laugh. "Not unless you get lost, since they aren't headed in the same direction you are."

Maybe, Blade thought, remembering how they'd lost their trail yesterday. He couldn't help being suspicious. If the outfitter had taken the client Blade heard he had up here, then they were both looking for Lucian.

"Thanks for your help," he said to the wrangler. No matter what the cowboy said, Blade had a feeling he'd be seeing St. Pierre and Lucian's wife soon.

GENEVA FELT AS if she had blisters on her legs and behind. She shifted in the saddle, glad that Calhoun had the puppy. They'd ridden back into the mountains for a couple of hours already. Just when she thought she couldn't take another minute of the pain, they reached the top of a ridge and small open area, and he drew his horse up.

She saw what was left of a lean-to, as Calhoun had called it. Basically, it was a couple of long poles attached to adjacent trees. The old tarp that had once formed a shelter across the top was in tatters. "Is this it?" she asked, glad to be off the saddle as she walked past the packhorses toward Calhoun.

He'd dismounted and was now inspecting the camp in

the towering pines. She stopped next to his horse, watching him as he searched for tracks. If this was Lucian's camp, he obviously wasn't here. Had he been? Or was all of this a waste of time and energy? She tried to see him here and couldn't. Not the man she'd met and married.

Turning, she looked back at the way they'd come. The view was incredible. She realized how far she'd come from the life she'd known with Lucian. If he hadn't destroyed that life, she would never have made this journey. She breathed in the air, turning her face up into the sun and closing her eyes. It felt so good to be off the horse. She reminded herself that she still had to ride all the way back down again. *Thanks, Lucian.*

Strange, but she didn't feel that molten pit of anger she had on the long days driving up here in his pickup. She felt almost at peace until she looked at Calhoun, who was frowning. "What?" she demanded. "This is Lucian's camp, right?"

"No."

"No?"

"It's on up the mountain."

His answer seemed to zap all her strength. She sat down on the nearest fallen tree and stretched out her legs. Had they really come all this way, and they still weren't there? Turning her face up to the sun, she closed her eyes, but not even the morning rays and the high mountain air helped right now. She heard rather than saw Calhoun approach.

"Are you all right?" he asked quietly.

She didn't open her eyes because she might start crying. The sun felt heavenly on her face. She wasn't on a horse. She told herself that she didn't want anything or anyone to spoil this moment not in a saddle—especially Calhoun St. Pierre. "I see why you like it up here."

There was a smile in his voice when he spoke. "Some places just call a person."

She opened her eyes and looked at him. He'd hunkered down next to her and was looking out at the seemingly endless mountains ranges before them. She'd never felt a place call to her. She hadn't been called to where she lived in California; she'd been born there, raised there and still lived there. She'd left for trips but had never thought of moving. But now, she couldn't imagine what had kept her anchored to one place for so long.

"Has Lucian even been here?" she asked.

"Someone has. One person traveling with an extra horse. I can't tell if it was him. Maybe. I can see where the person made a small fire and hobbled the horses."

She opened her eyes to look at him. "He already left?" So why wasn't he more upset? Why wasn't she?

Worse, why was a part of her glad that they'd missed him? She'd been all about facing him, knowing she'd probably never see a cent of her money, but wanting to at least tell him what she thought of him. Right now, she couldn't have cared less. She was too tired and sore.

Her puppy came over and climbed into her lap. She found herself smiling as she looked down at her. The dog was growing, the little chubby legs getting longer and stronger every day.

"If it was Lucian, he didn't stay here long," Calhoun said, pushing to his feet. "He's headed for his high camp farther up. I'm going to take a look around, and then we need to go." With that, he walked off, all long legs and purpose, the puppy jumping off her lap to chase after him.

They were getting out of here to go to Lucian's high camp farther up this mountain? She rose on shaky legs, groaning silently at the pain. "What if he just stepped away for a little while?" She called into the pines where

Calhoun had disappeared to suggest the possibility but
got no answer.

She listened but heard nothing. What if Calhoun ran
into him out in the woods? Or worse, ran into the three
men who he'd said had been following them yesterday?
What if he didn't come back?

She looked around, feeling more alone than she ever had
in her life. With Calhoun close by, she'd felt secure, safe
and protected. But now she couldn't hear Calhoun or the
puppy bustling through the trees. All she could hear was
the wind high in the pine boughs, its sigh almost human.
She felt a chill even though the sun was warm on her face.
Would she even know how to get out of these mountains
by herself? Remembering what Calhoun had said about
her needing to know how to saddle up without him didn't
help her growing concern.

A twig cracked somewhere in the distance. A squir-
rel began to chatter closer. Spotting Calhoun's rifle in the
scabbard on his horse, she quickly moved to it and pulled
it free. She assumed the weapon was loaded. She also assumed she wouldn't have to actually use it if anyone other
than Calhoun came out of those trees.

"Put down the rifle."

She swung around, heart lodged in her throat. Calhoun
stood in the clearing, the puppy in his arms. "Put down
my dog."

Calhoun slowly lowered the puppy to the ground. "What
are you doing?"

What *was* she doing? "I got scared."

He nodded as he walked toward her. "You know how
to fire that?"

"I was hoping I wouldn't have to."

As he reached her, he grabbed the barrel of the gun
and wrenched it from her hands. "Never point a gun at

someone unless you're planning to use it. So let me show you how for next time." Next time? She watched as he patiently showed her how to load it and make sure it was ready to fire.

Her heart was pounding even as she told herself she'd never have to fire the rifle. At least she hoped not. "You could use some target practice, but that would alert anyone interested in us as to where we are. So, if you have to use it, point the sight on the end at the center of the person, take a breath, hold it and pull the trigger. Now, we need to get going." Again he didn't move, his gaze intent on her. Could he tell how terrified she was at the thought of shooting someone? He was right. She wasn't strong enough for this.

Calhoun was standing just inches from her. He smelled of pine and the outdoors. He looked so capable, easily shifting his tone from gentle with the puppy and her to fierce and scary with others when necessary.

When he spoke, his voice was soft. "Can you ride a little farther?"

She nodded, although it was the last thing she wanted to do.

"Then let's go. Come here, pup," he called to the dog. "You really need to give this dog a name. If you don't, I will." Their gazes met. She could feel the power of this man in the intensity of his gaze, she glimpsed a hunger in those eyes that matched her own and felt a shudder move through her. "Damn it, woman."

"That's a terrible name for a puppy," she whispered as he advanced on her.

He grabbed her, wrapping his free arm around her waist and pulled her hard into the solid wall of his chest. His mouth dropped to hers, forcing her head back as he pulled her even closer. Her lips parted as he deepened the kiss, opening her up with his tongue as she surrendered to his passion.

Geneva didn't hear the approaching riders. It was as if all her senses were on his plundering kiss and the rock-solid feel of his body against hers.

He drew back so quickly that she almost fell. Quickly moving away from her, he swung the rifle up into his hands and whispered for her to get the puppy and go into the pines and stay there. She scooped up the dog and, on trembling legs, plunged into the pines to drop behind a huge fallen tree.

A few moments later, two men rode into the camp.

Chapter Twelve

Geneva stayed crouched down where she was. Calhoun's voice floated on the air. She could only make out a few words of the conversation, but it was clear that he knew the men.

"Thanks for letting me know," she heard him say, and listened as the two men rode off before she stood and walked back into the clearing.

Calhoun was putting his rifle into his scabbard on his horse when she came out of the woods. She caught a glimpse of two riders through the pines before they disappeared from view.

"Who were those men?" she asked, sounding breathless from the kiss right before the surprise of horseback riders approaching.

He didn't answer right away. Nothing new there. She still had the taste of him on her lips, or she would have thought she'd dreamed the kiss. "Who were those men?" she asked again.

He stopped what he was doing, let out a sigh and turned. "They work for me. They rode over to tell me about the three men who came through their camp this morning. Now, could we please get moving?" He didn't wait for an answer as he took the puppy from her and swung up into the saddle.

"I guess this means we aren't going to talk about the kiss," she said as she started to walk back to her horse. She smiled to herself as she heard him swear under his breath. She'd gotten under his skin in more ways than one.

But then he'd done the same to her.

As she led her horse over to a stump, she mounted it as if she'd done this a million times. Her body felt as if she had. She touched her tongue to her upper lip, remembering the kiss, remembering the urgency in him as he'd pulled her against him. His arm had locked her in place with a strength that had made her dizzy. That woman he'd kissed and who'd kissed him back felt as if it had been someone else. She barely remembered that *other* Geneva Carrington Beck, the one who was still married to Lucian.

Once in the saddle and trailing up the mountain behind Calhoun, she looked at his broad back astride the horse and warned herself to be careful. She'd never met a man like this one. He wasn't the kind of man a woman dallied with, she told herself. That kiss proved it.

As she rode after him and the packhorses, she realized that whatever his men had told him, it had the outfitter worried and moving faster than he had before.

As Calhoun glanced up toward the mountain ahead, he felt a chill. His men had brought him disturbing news, which he hadn't shared with Geneva. He'd wanted time to think, to make sure he wasn't going off half-cocked before he decided what to do. But he also had to get up this mountain as quickly as possible. Those three men who'd come through his outfitter camp this morning were on the other side of the mountain—not that far away.

Also, there was now no doubt that they were looking for the same thing he was—Lucian Beck. What the wranglers had told him about the three men had been the most disturbing of all. The one who'd done all the talking had a Southern accent and numerous prison tattoos. The others looked of the same ilk. Dangerous men on a dangerous mission. All noticeably armed and apparently determined to get to Lucian's camp.

All looking for Lucian. Or maybe something else. What bothered Calhoun is what they were all doing here looking for Lucian. Why did they think he was here? And if he was, why now? It had been over a year since he'd gone up into the mountains by himself, acting nervous, suspicious, before he'd taken off without saying goodbye. Unless Lucian stopping by and sleeping with Calhoun's fiancée was his idea of saying goodbye.

What really bothered him, though, was that, for some reason, Geneva wasn't the only one who thought Lucian had come back here. The question had always been, Why would Lucian show his face around Cooke City after the mess he'd left more than a year ago?

One reason kept coming up. Because he'd hidden something up here on this mountain, and now he'd come back for it. Geneva had hinted at the possibility. Calhoun had thought she was just clutching at straws in her hopes that she would find Lucian here.

But it would seem that the men after Lucian might be thinking the same thing. Calhoun couldn't see them making this trek up here unless there was more of a payoff than them just settling some old score with Lucian. What worried him was that it might be the same reason Geneva had insisted on coming up here and putting herself through this arduous trip.

Any way Calhoun looked at it, trouble was headed right for them and right now. He wasn't sure who he could trust. He thought of Geneva pointing his rifle at him. She could have shot him if she'd wanted to. What did he know about her motives for wanting to come up here? He knew nothing about this woman other than what she'd told him, which hadn't been much.

Mentally, he kicked himself. What had he been thinking kissing her? He'd wanted to do a whole lot more than that, which worried him. Was this about Lucian? Or had this woman gotten to him?

He shook off the thought and tried to think clearly. From what his men had told him, the three weren't just armed, rough-looking and determined to get to Lucian's camp. One of them had a small collapsible shovel tied to his saddle. For a grave? Or something else?

The fact that the men had an idea where to find Lucian's camp meant that someone in Cooke City had to have told them. Which, given how few people even knew of the camp, Calhoun could narrow it down to one person. Biker William "Ace" Graham knew because he and Lucian had been tight when they were younger.

Calhoun wondered what it had taken for Ace to give up where those men might find Lucian though. He worried that Ace might not still be alive given what his wranglers had told him about the men after Lucian.

Thanks to his wranglers, the three outlaws were headed for Lucian's camp on the longer route around the mountain. With luck, they would reach there after he and Geneva had left.

But then what? Any fool would be able to follow his and Geneva's trail now that the rain had stopped. Even if the three missed them at Lucian's camp, Calhoun knew the men could find them before they got off this mountain. So why was he still headed for Lucian's camp?

There was only one reason. If Lucian was there, Calhoun might have time to warn his old friend—not for Lucian's sake but for his wife's. She thought she wanted justice, but he suspected she was still in love with the man. The problem was, even if Lucian was there, they might not have time to warn him and then clear out before all hell broke loose when the three outlaws showed up.

Calhoun reminded himself that this wasn't his fight. He'd once owed Lucian his life, but that payment was settled before Lucian slept with Calhoun's fiancée. He'd felt no guilt for that until Geneva had shown up and now, realizing that if he didn't try to warn Lucian, he would be letting those men kill him.

The smart option was turning back, walking away from a fight he couldn't win and wasn't his battle in any case. No matter what he might feel for his old friend or this woman who'd grudgingly earned his respect, he didn't owe Lucian his life. Geneva especially didn't deserve this after what Lucian had already done to her.

Calhoun swore under his breath. So why was he trying to beat the men to the camp? To warn his once good friend? Surely he didn't think that he could prevent whatever these men had planned for Lucian once they found him. If not on this mountain, then these men would eventually find him. That kind of trouble would eventually catch up with his old friend—and anyone who got in their way.

He felt a sliver of fear bury itself under his skin. Geneva Beck thought she wanted justice. He doubted she would like what she found—whether Lucian was up there or not. If Lucian was, he'd be lucky to get out of these mountains alive. But now Lucian wasn't the only one.

He realized he was avoiding what was really at stake here. The reason all of them were risking their lives.

Calhoun reined in his horse, dismounted and set down the puppy, who'd been sleeping curled in his lap. The sun lolled in a pristine blue sky overhead. The heat felt good, the smell of pine and creek water filling the high mountain air as he walked back to Lucian's wife, the dog on his heels. This had always been the place that had filled his soul.

Why had he brought Geneva up here? Because he'd thought she would be safer with him than Max. He still would be here now, he thought. He would have gone looking for Lucian without her. True, he shouldn't have kissed her, but he didn't regret it—especially if there was a good chance he might die today.

Admittedly, he'd expected her to give up by now and turn back. He'd planned on it, had it all mapped out, how he would take her over to the main camp and have one of the wranglers return her to town.

But once they crossed this next ridge, they would be in sight of Lucian's camp, and there would be no turning back for either of them. This was between him and his old friend. Geneva didn't realize it yet, but she didn't want any part of what would go down. They'd lost the men trailing them yesterday, but the men knew where he and Geneva were headed. They might even think they were after the same thing.

But what was that? The more Calhoun had thought about it, he knew that the three men were after more than vengeance against Lucian. He hadn't taken it seriously when Geneva had thrown out the idea of Lucian having hidden something back up here that he'd returned to retrieve. Given the interest in the three outlaws headed for Lucian's camp, he had a bad feeling he was the only one who didn't know what was really going on.

But he was about to find out, he thought as he and the puppy trailing after him reached Geneva. She seemed surprised that they had stopped.

"We need to talk," he said as he dragged her off her horse.

"WHAT ARE WE really doing up here?" Calhoun demanded, his fingers gripping her upper arms as he held her just inches from him.

Geneva couldn't have been more shocked by this change in him. She'd seen him angry, but this was different. She'd seen him gentle and almost sweet. She'd kissed this man. But right now, he was scaring her. "I don't know what you mean."

"I think you do. Why would Lucian come back here, let alone go up to his camp? It doesn't make any sense unless, like you said, he'd left something here that he'd come back for. What is it?" She opened her mouth, but nothing came out. His gaze hardened. "You haven't been completely honest with me, but you're going to right now. Tell me."

Geneva thought of Mitzi's blackmail threat to Lucian. So, maybe the two of them really hadn't been lovers. Not that it mattered anymore. She still couldn't be sure that Lucian and Mitzi hadn't been in on taking her for everything from the very beginning. What had made her angry was that she wasn't the one who'd found out Lucian's secret. She was just the naive, trusting woman who'd married him, believing everything he told her.

Calhoun gave her a little shake. "What aren't you telling me?"

"It has nothing to do with any of this," she said lifting her chin in defiance. "Why should you care about my reasons for wanting to go after Lucian?"

"Because my wranglers told me about the three men who had been following us. They're headed to the same place we are. They want Lucian. But I suspect they're after something more, and you know what it is, and we're not going another foot until you tell me."

She looked down at where her engagement and wedding ring had been. She could no longer see the pale imprint where they'd been. Gone as if it had never been there.

"Don't lie to me," Calhoun said in a low growl.

Lucian's betrayal had been enough. She didn't want to tell this man about her best friend's as well. But when she looked into his eyes, she saw something else behind the anger.

"Why did you really bring me up here?" she demanded. He let go of her, drawing back as if in surprise. "You broke your own rule about women. On top of that, you had every reason not to help me given what Lucian had done to you. So, what are we really doing here?"

Surprise gave way to anger that seemed more directed at himself than her now. "That's what I'm telling you. I wish I hadn't. These men who are after Lucian, they will kill us and him too if I'm right and there is more to this than just getting closure from your husband. Who are these men and what do they want? Time is running out. Tell me."

Geneva swallowed. "You didn't tell me why you brought me up here. *Don't lie to me.*"

He actually smiled at his words being thrown back at him. Shaking his head, he said, "Were you always like this?"

"No. I'm terrified of this woman Lucian has made me into."

Calhoun nodded as if she scared him too. "Just tell me this, whatever it is Lucian's neck deep in, were you in on it with him?"

She looked him in the eye. "No. I swear. He blindsided me. If he hadn't forgotten the key to the storage shed..."

"That's where you found the pickup and the photos?"

Geneva hesitated, but only for a moment. He was right. It was time to be completely honest. He needed to know the truth. "There was also a note to Lucian written by someone I considered my best friend," she said. "Lucian didn't leave alone."

"He took off with your best friend?" Calhoun swore, then his eyes narrowed as if realizing that wasn't why they were up here on this mountain.

"I don't know if they were romantically involved or not. I'm pretty sure the note I found was a blackmail threat. Apparently, my friend Mitzi recognized my engagement and wedding ring set as one that was stolen in a jewelry store robbery in Alabama. The four masked thieves were caught on video but never captured—nor was the one-of-a-kind jewelry worth over several million dollars ever found. The notice had been posted in a pawn shop Mitzi frequents when she needs money. Her husband keeps her on a short chain financially. Or at least he did before she took everything she could scrape up and left him as well."

"When was this robbery?" Calhoun demanded.

"Days before the last time you said you saw Lucian in Cooke City," she said.

CALHOUN CLOSED HIS eyes for a moment, everything starting to make sense. Lucian's behavior the last time he saw him. His friend going up to his camp alone. Maybe even him sleeping with Dana. Lucian had been on the run after probably double-crossing the men who'd helped him with the theft of the jewelry.

He looked at the woman standing before him. Betrayed by her husband and her best friend. That would make anyone want to avenge herself. But still he had to ask. "I'm guessing that Lucian ripped off his partners in crime and came back to Montana to hide his ill-gotten gains until the heat died down. So, where do you fit into all of this?"

She shook her head. "I have no idea. I guess he was just killing time until he could get the jewelry and realized he could make enough off me to carry out his plan with my money until he could fence the jewelry or whatever he has planned."

"What I don't understand is why now? If he has all your money, why not forget about the stolen jewelry he hid?"

"Greed? Or maybe married to me, he was hidden from his past. But once he surfaced and started throwing money around, there were other people after him. Several stopped by the house looking for him before I left San Diego."

Did it really matter? This woman wasn't the only one who thought Lucian had come back here. But at least now he knew why. "I've never understood why you wanted to come up here looking for him. Are you sure this isn't about the stolen jewelry?"

Her laugh was brittle with bitterness. "I didn't even know about the jewelry theft until when I discovered the blackmail note from my best friend to my husband hidden with some other papers in the glove box of the pickup. I know it must seem ridiculous to you that I want to face Lucian, look him in the eye and tell him what he did to me."

"Not so ridiculous."

A thought seemed to cross her mind. She eyed him suspiciously. "You really didn't know about it? Lucian didn't tell you about the jewelry heist?"

He let out a string of oaths. "You think I wouldn't have turned him in?"

"I don't know. Had he slept with your fiancée yet?"

Calhoun chuckled. "Good point, but I can tell you one thing. I wouldn't have brought you up here if I'd known."

"But you still would have come."

She knew he would have. That should have bothered him more than it did. While he'd been trying to figure out this woman, she'd been doing the same with him. He rubbed his neck for a moment. He had to decide what to do. Either way, they had to get moving.

He feared it might already be too late to abort. The three outlaws would be traveling fast once they got what they'd come up into these mountains for. Once they'd dealt with Lucian. If they found him but not the jewelry, they might get it into their heads that he and Geneva knew more than they did. After all, they seemed to be after the same thing—both headed for Lucian's camp.

He weighed their options quickly, knowing that time was of the essence. What if they got to Lucian's high camp and he'd already come and gone? What would the men after him do then? He and Geneva would be sitting ducks—especially if they turned around now and headed back to town. The men might think that they had the goods.

They couldn't win for losing, he thought, wishing he could get his hands on Lucian for doing this, not just to him but to Geneva. He wanted to blame her for them being in this spot, but he knew it was his own fault. He'd wanted to protect her and give her closure. But he also wanted it for himself. If Lucian was at his high camp, Calhoun had a few scores of his own he wanted to settle with him.

But that meant getting to the camp before the three men did.

He looked at Geneva. This morning her blue eyes were the exact color of Montana's summer sky. The memory of the kiss made his knees weak. Worse, he wasn't sure he would be able to protect her. The odds weren't good. She had to know what they were up against. This wasn't a decision he could make on his own.

"We're between a rock and a hard place," he said. "Your husband is in a world of trouble. He's ripped off the wrong people. He's probably about to get what he deserves. Quite frankly, I don't think he's worth dying for."

GENEVA SAW IT coming even before he said the words.

"I'm going to take you over to my camp so one of my wranglers can get you back to town. Once there, you can pick up the truck and drive out as quickly as you can."

"Don't I have any say in this?"

He met her gaze. "Haven't you made enough bad decisions lately? What are you doing out here in the wilds with a man you don't even know?"

"I don't think you're that scary."

He laughed at that, shaking his head, before his gaze found hers again. "I hate to mention that you might not be the best judge of men."

"You're not like Lucian."

"I might be worse," he said stepping closer. "You think I haven't thought about settling one old score with my former friend by sleeping with his *wife* the way he slept with my fiancée?" His gray eyes bored into hers. "You have no idea how tempting it is."

"Don't I?"

"Be careful," he whispered, leaning even closer. "There are some impulsive decisions you can't take back."

"Like you sending me back to town while you go on up to Lucian's camp alone?" she asked, standing her ground.

"I don't want to get you killed. Is that so hard to understand?"

"You said yourself there isn't time for you to take me to your camp and then reach Lucian's before the men after him get there. You'd be walking into an ambush." She shook her head. "If Lucian's up there, someone has to warn him."

Calhoun swore. "You sure about that?"

She gave him an impatient look. "You didn't have to bring me up here. You wanted to settle some things with Lucian as much as I did."

"Fair enough, but now that I know what's at stake, I

can't take you to his camp. I won't risk your life. We'll both turn back. I'll take you to town myself."

"How far is Lucian's camp?"

He thought about lying. "Just over the next rise."

"You would make better time alone without me and the packhorses," she said. "Leave me here. Go warn Lucian, then come back."

He stared at her. "You still love him."

"I still love the man I thought I married," she said. "But that man never existed. Can you live with yourself if you don't go warn him? That's what I thought. Go, I'll be all right. I've watched you care for the horses. I can do it." She could feel his gaze measuring her as she picked up her puppy, who'd been playing in the wildflowers at their feet.

Calhoun met her gaze again before he reached down into his boot and pulled out a handgun. "It's point and shoot once you pull this back." He handed it to her, showing her how to hold it in both of her hands, to steady it, to point at her target, put the red dot on the spot, take a breath, hold it and then press the trigger.

"Remember, if you point it at someone, you'd better be ready to shoot." He hesitated. She could see the battle going on inside him. "I don't like leaving you here alone. I'm going to leave my horse and go on foot up to the camp."

Her hand shook as she tucked the gun into the vest pocket. She was no longer in the world she'd grown up in. She felt as if she'd traveled to a foreign land where there were no rules except survival by any means.

She'd known this country up here in the mountains was dangerous. Men carried guns to protect themselves from the wild animals—but apparently also from each other. They knew that once they left the paved roads, they were on their own. Capable men like Calhoun St. Pierre who felt at home up here and yet respected the danger because it was always here.

"You'll be back for me."

"And if I'm not?" he asked holding her gaze.

She smiled at that. "You'll be back."

He handed her what he said was a satellite phone. "If I don't come back, call for help."

CALHOUN HATED LEAVING HER. He wouldn't be able to protect her if he took her with him. He sure as hell wouldn't be able to protect her leaving her alone back there either.

But the truth was that she'd been in danger the moment she met Lucian Beck. If the men after her husband didn't get what they wanted, they would be coming after her. If not on this mountain, then when she returned home. There would be no escaping the hole Lucian had dug for himself—and her.

She was already in jeopardy. Leaving her even for the time it would take to get to Lucian's camp and back, made him more than nervous. He felt as if he'd been left few options. Taking her with him was far more dangerous because, unlike her, he didn't trust Lucian not to kill them both.

Lucian's camp was just over the rise, much closer than he'd wanted Geneva to know. He could feel the three men breathing down his neck. They would be moving fast. They would want this over quickly. They'd taken a longer route, but they too would be anxious to get to Lucian, to get to the jewelry before he absconded with it. With luck Calhoun would beat them to the camp. If Lucian was there…

He realized that all of this might be for nothing. Lucian could be miles from here. He could already be in another country.

Except that Calhoun didn't believe that. Once he'd heard

about the jewelry heist, he knew that Lucian had come back for the loot. Once he had it, he would be gone, leaving the rest of them to deal with the men after him. Leaving Geneva in trouble. It wouldn't take long for the men to find out that she was Lucian's wife once they returned to Cooke City empty-handed. But only if they didn't already know who she was.

That was why Calhoun was making his way up the side of the mountain toward the rim of rock to Lucian's high camp. Not to warn his former friend but to make sure the three men got what they'd come up this mountain for. He planned to end this for Geneva, because she deserved better.

Chapter Thirteen

Calhoun worked his way through the trees. The only sound was the breeze in the branches, but he wasn't fooled. Lucian would have heard him coming. He might have been expecting him. The two of them had spent a lot of years in these mountains. He doubted his old friend would have lost his instincts for survival up here.

The camp sat high on the side of the mountain, butted against a sheer rock cliff and hidden from view by a large boulder. The mountain was steep, but there was a flat spot high on the cliff behind the huge rock. Lucian had stumbled on this spot when they were young, scrambling up the steep mountain to climb the boulder. He'd wanted to see the view from the top of it.

Calhoun thought of him with his arms spread wide, a grin just as broad on his face as he stood there precariously balanced on the top of the boulder. A fall would have killed him. That was Lucian. It wasn't until Calhoun joined him that he saw Lucian was right. It was the perfect place for a camp. A flat space for a lean-to hidden by rocks miles from civilization. The camp was just hard enough to get to.

From that point on, it had been Lucian's high camp, although the two of them had spent many hours up here hunting elk and fishing the high mountain lakes on the other side of it. The view had been amazing, which meant that if Lucian was up here, he might have already spotted him coming up the mountain.

Calhoun battled the memories as he circled around and came in the side of the camp. He wondered which of them had failed the other as longtime friends. He had to admit that he'd lost track of Lucian after college. He hadn't tried to find him, but then Lucian hadn't reached out to him— and Calhoun had been a whole lot easier to find.

He spotted the tracks first. They were fresh. He could see where someone had dug into the dirt at the base of the cliff. He moved to it, not surprised to find a good-sized empty hole. Lucian had been here and retrieved what he'd come back to Montana for.

Checking the rest of the small flat area, he saw tracks where one man had led two horses down the backside of the mountain because it wasn't as steep. That's when he saw that something had been scratched into the large boulder at eye level. It took him a moment to make out the crudely written words.

Sorry I missed you old buddy

Calhoun swore as he stepped to the edge of the mountain and looked out past the top of the huge boulder. Lucian hadn't just been here. He'd known they were behind him, coming for him. He must have spotted them.

But did he know about the three outlaws also coming for him? They would be riding up from the backside of his camp. They might have already found him.

His heart pounded as he started to hurry back to the steep trail he'd come up. If the men hadn't found him, then Lucian might be headed down the mountain. He might stumble across Geneva. Lucian couldn't be that far ahead of him. In fact...

He realized his mistake too late. He heard the rumble of moving rocks. He didn't bother to look behind him at the cliff, he knew at once that Lucian hadn't really left, just as he knew what Lucian had done.

Calhoun threw himself down the mountain, running for his life as the landslide behind him began to career down, crashing into the pines next to him. Calhoun was fast on his feet, but not fast enough to beat an avalanche of rock.

It roared down, stones bouncing all around him as he scrambled for shelter below the massive boulder. One rock struck his leg, another his shoulder. But it was the one that hit him in the side of the head that turned out the lights as he crashed into a pile of dried pine needles.

GENEVA TOOK CARE of the horses, then got something for her and the puppy to eat. The sun beat down on her, forcing her into the shade. She could feel time slipping away and tried not to worry about Calhoun.

He would come back for her. She had to believe that. But what would he find when he reached Lucian's camp? There was already bad blood between him and his former friend. That she had no idea what would happen when the two met again worried her. She didn't have any idea how her husband would react to seeing Calhoun up here—let alone finding out that he'd brought her.

It just made her more aware of how little she'd known Lucian. Look what he'd done to her. What would he do to Calhoun? Or his former friend to him?

She started at a rumbling sound off in the distance and stopped to listen. More thunder? Another storm. It sounded close but ended fairly quickly. She hugged herself against the chill that raced over her flesh. She told herself that Calhoun would be back soon. Her phone was in her bag, but without being able to charge it, even if she could get cell service up here, there was no reason to check it.

Calhoun had left her a gun, food, shelter and a satellite phone to use if he didn't come back. What he hadn't said was that if she got into trouble, no one would be coming to help her in time. She was on her own for the first time in her life in a place that was frightening even without possible killers headed this way.

But to her surprise, she wasn't terrified—not the way she'd been when she'd realized that Lucian had left her and taken all of her money and dignity. That had been a different kind of fear, a different kind of alone. She'd never felt that kind of desperation before.

That she felt stronger surprised her as well. She breathed in the day, listening to the breeze swaying the pine boughs over her head. A kind of peace filled her. From the moment she'd awakened alone after her anniversary party, she'd been consumed with finding Lucian and—what? Making him pay?

Now she wasn't sure what she needed from him. A divorce would be nice. But other than that, she didn't expect much of anything. She was sure that Calhoun was right, and the money was gone. The puppy came over and licked her hand before falling over on her back in the grass and biting at a blue flower bobbing above her head.

Geneva smiled, thankful for the dog. She'd questioned why Lucian had given her such a present. Because he'd known it would make their friends ooh and aah over it. Make people think he was the best husband ever. It made no sense, considering that the next day, everyone would know the truth.

She rubbed the puppy's pink belly, wanting to see this gift as a sign that Lucian wasn't all bad. That maybe a part of him had loved her. That the only reason he'd left was because he was desperate. That it hadn't been easy to walk away from her.

Then she noticed the faint line from the small scratch on her wrist where her watch had been and feared she was wrong. Was that why she wanted to come face-to-face with her husband? To find out the truth about him?

At a sound off in the trees, both she and the puppy froze. Unlike the rumbling sound she'd heard earlier, this one was much closer. She held her breath, waiting to hear it again. Her hand went to the gun in her vest pocket as she scooped up the dog with her free hand and moved to a spot in full sun, feeling a chill.

Had she and the puppy heard Calhoun returning? She tried to measure how much time had passed by the angle of the sun. Maybe it was Calhoun back already. He'd gone to the campsite, hadn't found Lucian and was now back. At least she hoped it was him.

One of the horses let out a whinny. She heard a rustling sound in the opposite direction at the same time the puppy barked, making her jump. She swung around, leading with the gun as a man stepped out of the woods.

Chapter Fourteen

"Lucian." Geneva stared at the man who walked out of the pines toward her. It was just shy of a week since he'd left her, and yet she barely recognized him. He hadn't shaved, his beard scruffy, and his hair, usually always neat with the products he used, was now ruffled in the breeze.

He was dressed much like Calhoun, same type of canvas pants and long-sleeved knit shirt under fleece. He wore cowboy boots, apparently an old pair he'd had hidden somewhere, since they didn't look new.

He also had a gun strapped to his hip. She didn't doubt that it was loaded, and he knew how to shoot it. No wonder she barely recognized him. Even his expression wasn't one she'd seen before. She didn't know this man. No doubt ever had.

He stopped a half dozen yards from her. "What are you doing here?" he asked, his words heavy with what could have been regret. Or anger.

"I found your pickup, your photos and the note from Mitzi," she said hugging the puppy closer. The gun was still in her hand but pointed at the ground. She didn't remember doing that. It was as if seeing Lucian had made her forget that she had the weapon. "Everything I found led me here."

"To Calhoun." He nodded, smiling almost wistfully.

"You always were smarter than me, though I never expected this."

It confirmed what she'd suspected. "So, you didn't leave it for me to find you," she said, disappointed because she'd wanted to believe he'd had some remorse. That he'd left it to give her a chance to—if nothing else—tell him what she thought of him.

"No," he said with a shake of his head. "I wanted to spare you from ever having to see me again."

"How gallant of you."

Lucian looked at the ground. "Go ahead. Tell me what a bastard I am. I deserve it."

She had thought it was something she wanted, but looking at him, she no longer cared. "I assume you've spent all my money."

"Our money," he corrected. "Sorry, but I owed a lot of people who wanted to kill me."

"I can understand the feeling. Why?" she asked. "Why would you marry me and then leave me like you did?"

He shrugged. "I already told you. I owed a lot of people who wanted to kill me."

"Was that your plan from the moment you met me?"

He gave her a sheepish look. "Pretty much."

"Was Mitzi in on it?"

"Not hardly. I know she's your friend, but she proved to be a pain in the neck. I couldn't wait to ditch her." He motioned to the gun in her hand. "You going to shoot me?"

"There are still a lot of people who want that pleasure— like the men on their way up here who think you have the jewelry from the robbery," she said.

He lifted a brow. "Right, so you know about that. The note from Mitzi. I should never have given you those rings, but they were beautiful, and I wanted to impress your father."

"My father? Nice to know you were thinking of him and not me, although it's clear that I was just a mark to you. No surprise after the way things ended. At our anniversary party, no less. If I'm not mistaken, you drugged me and let everyone think I drank too much, right?"

"What can I say? I'm no good, but you've realized that by now," Lucian said. "If it helps, leaving you was one of the hardest things I've ever done. I would have stayed if there was any possible way. I liked the lifestyle you could afford me. But I owed too much money, had too many people looking for me, and I'm greedy. I didn't even want to share it with you."

"Why are you saying these things?"

"What? You don't want to hear the truth?" he asked. "I thought that's why you came up here."

She noticed the protective way he placed his hand over the saddle bag thrown over his shoulder. His other hand hung at his side. Next to the weapon holstered at his hip.

"What now?" she asked. "You fence the jewels, skip the country, buy that island you always wanted?"

"You don't want to know. You shouldn't have come up here."

"You're right. I'm sorry I did."

"Why did you?" He sounded as if he genuinely wanted to know.

"At first, it was about finding you. I wanted to face you, ask why. But at some point, I no longer cared. You're not the man I thought I married. You should get on down the mountain before the men who want to kill you catch up to you."

"I did one thing nice for you." He nodded toward the puppy in her arms. "What did you name her?"

The name came to her in that moment. The puppy had gotten her through the days and nights after Lucian left.

It had made this journey with her. It had given her hope that she wouldn't always hurt the way she had at first. It had shown her even a side of Calhoun St. Pierre that she wouldn't have seen otherwise. She was Geneva's good luck charm.

"Her name's Lucky. She helped me get through this even if you were the one to give her to me."

He laughed, shaking his head. "You always did see a half empty glass and think it was almost full. You were just wrong about me."

She could see that. He lifted his head as if listening. Was he worried that Calhoun would show up at any moment? Or, she realized as her breath caught, her heart dropping, did he know something she didn't—that Calhoun was never coming back?

"Tell me you didn't do anything to Calhoun," she said, her voice breaking.

"Calhoun, is it?" Lucian swore. "I should have known he'd use you to pay me back."

She made a disgusted sound. "You think everyone is like you? Calhoun isn't like that. He went up the mountain to warn you about the men after you. That's the kind of friend he is."

Lucian laughed. "Boy, he sure showed you, but when it comes to men, you really aren't that experienced, are you?" His face sobered. He looked almost sad. "You should have stayed in California. I didn't want it to end like this. That's why I drugged you and left you on the couch. I never dreamed you'd come after me. By the way, where is my truck? I realized too late that I'd misplaced the storage unit key. I hope you didn't mess up my truck. I want it back."

That he wasn't worried about Calhoun answered her greatest fear. He had done something to him. The outfitter wouldn't be showing up here and saving her. She couldn't bear the thought that he might be dead or badly injured back up this mountain. She'd gotten Calhoun into this. He would have never been here if it wasn't for her.

"Some friend you turned out to be," she said, hating the way her voice broke.

"I made a worse husband," he said with a laugh. "Here's the problem, Geneva, we both know you aren't going to let me walk away. The minute you get back to town, you'll call the cops. You can see the problem we have here. I can't let you do that."

She told herself that he wouldn't hurt her, then realized the damage he'd already done to her. But could he kill her? She looked into his handsome face and saw a desperate stranger standing there.

Could she shoot this stranger with Lucian's face? She felt the weight of the weapon in her hand. She wasn't sure she could. The puppy kept wriggling. She couldn't hold on to her much longer since she'd gotten so heavy. She had to put her down on the ground, but as she did, she feared Lucian would take advantage of her movement and go for the weapon at his hip.

Instead, the moment the puppy's feet touched the ground, Lucian called the dog to him. Before she had time to realize her mistake, Lucky raced to him and Lucian snatched up the puppy, tucking her under his arm.

"I think you might have made a mistake naming this dog Lucky." His eyes narrowed as he looked across the space between them. "Throw down your gun, Geneva."

Chapter Fifteen

Calhoun woke in pain and covered with rocks and dirt. He pushed off the larger ones and tried to sit up. His head swam. For a moment, he couldn't remember what had happened. Then it came back in a rush. The rockslide. Lucian.

He swore under his breath as he pushed himself up. One clear thought emerged through the pain. He had to get to Geneva before it was too late. Climbing over the rubble from the slide, he became aware of his injured leg and shoulder. Both hurt like hell, but nothing seemed to be broken, at least he hoped not. He had a hard head, thankfully. He didn't think he had a concussion. At least not a bad one.

He stumbled down the mountain, trying not to make too much noise for fear Lucian would hear him. He didn't know where his old friend was. Maybe he'd set off the rockslide, then gone another way out of the mountains. Or maybe right now he was with his wife.

Calhoun's fear pushed him harder even with his head feeling woozy and his shoulder and leg making every step filled with debilitating pain. Fortunately, he didn't have far to go. He moved down through the pines and over the ridge. All his instincts told him Geneva was all right. He hadn't heard a gunshot. But then again, he couldn't be sure she'd be able to pull the trigger if it was Lucian.

He didn't know how much time he'd been knocked out.

He might not had have heard the gunshot. It might already be too late. He told himself that Lucian wouldn't kill her. Otherwise, Calhoun wouldn't have left her. He'd almost convinced himself that Lucian could have killed her while they were married and taken everything legally and hadn't.

But even as he thought it, he feared he was wrong. Lucian had never been patient. It was amazing that he'd waited this long to come back for the jewelry. Maybe even more amazing that he'd waited a year of marriage to leave Geneva, unless there was another reason he had to wait.

Even as a boy, his friend had wanted what he wanted when he wanted it. There was no waiting with Lucian, which was why he'd been a lousy elk hunter. He couldn't just sit and wait for a perfect shot. It was why he'd had to follow a blood trail for miles sometimes to find his elk and finally kill it.

Calhoun thought about Geneva—and the gun he'd left her. She wouldn't be able to kill Lucian, and that would be her last mistake when it came to the man. She still thought there was good in him. Was she still thinking that there was a chance Lucian could change? That they could be together?

The thought made him grind his teeth. He'd been drawn to her because of her strength—not her misplaced loyalty to the man who'd lied and cheated and left her. He'd seen her as a survivor. She hadn't curled up in a ball crying. She'd gotten in Lucian's pickup and come all the way to Cooke City after him.

On this whole arduous trip up the mountain, she hadn't complained or whined. She'd almost cried a couple of times, but she hadn't. She was strong and more capable than he'd ever suspected—more than even she herself had thought, he figured. Lucian hadn't broken her. Calhoun couldn't let him kill her.

But right now, he had no idea what she would do if Lucian found her. Tell him off? Beg him to come back to her? He shook his head. Whatever it was she needed from her lying, cheating, abandoning husband, Calhoun feared it was going to get her killed. Lucian might have already found her and not bothered to give her a chance to tell him how she felt about him, he thought as he caught a glimpse of the clearing where he'd left her.

BLADE COULD SEE at once that Lucian wasn't here as he rode into the camp. It was exactly as the biker had described it. But what a long ride to get here. He was sick of Ricki and Juice complaining and more than once had wanted to shoot the two of them.

Like his companions, he ached from riding the damned horse. Riding a horse had looked adventurous and exciting in movies. Instead, it was barbaric. Lucian would love putting him and the others through this agonizing experience. It would give him so much satisfaction—just as Blade was sure ripping them off after the heist had.

Dismounting, he couldn't ignore the pain in his legs as he followed the tracks in the still damp ground to the hole at the base of the cliffs where someone had dug.

He knew the jewelry wouldn't be there, but still he had to look. The boot tracks were fresh. Lucian's? Or had the space been empty when whoever this was had walked over to look?

When he'd met Lucian, he hadn't known about his connection to Montana or about this camp high in the mountains. He and his cohorts had come to realize how little Lucian had told them was even true. So much for honor among thieves.

But then again, they'd all met in prison. Probably not the best place to find people you could trust. The thing was, he'd liked Lucian, who appeared to be down on his luck after being arrested for domestic abuse and sentenced to a year in prison. He said his girlfriend had tried to kill him, and all he'd done was defend himself, and his girlfriend had gotten into a fight earlier in a bar brawl.

It was later, when they were all out, that Blade had run into Lucian. Not too surprising it was in a saloon. Lucian had told him that he and his new girlfriend had gotten into a fight. From the black eye and cut lip, Lucian had gotten the worst of it. What Blade had found interesting was that this girlfriend Lucian had been dating worked at a jewelry store.

He bought Lucian a beer. Later that evening, after plying him with liquor, Lucian said the reason they'd fought was because he'd found out about a big hush-hush shipment that was coming in next week. She'd been all cranky and on edge about it. He'd snooped on her phone, thinking she had a man on the side, and found out about the shipment. He wanted to take the entire shipment but said he had no idea how. At least that was his story.

That's where Blade and his little group of criminals came in. Without them, Lucian would have never been able to pull off the heist. That's the part that kept Blade up at night planning his vengeance. He'd promised himself he would find Lucian and then make him pay.

What had surprised him was that the jewelry had never surfaced. He'd taken Lucian for an amateur. He'd thought for sure that the fool would try to pawn the jewelry or try to sell it to a fence who turned out to be an undercover cop. It seemed though that Lucian hadn't done either. Nor had he sold off a piece at a time like an amateur would have.

Blade had tried to find the woman who'd worked at the jewelry store, but she'd disappeared. The cops wanted her for questioning. It looked like a dead end, like Lucian was going to get away with what he'd done to them.

Blade had a friend in law enforcement, had given the cop Lucian's name and said he'd make it worth his while if he let him know if Lucian Beck ever turned up.

After a year, he'd almost given up hope. Then he'd gotten a call that Beck had been pulled over in Red Lodge, Montana, for speeding. It hadn't taken much for Blade to find out where Lucian had been headed. He had no idea what Lucian planned to do once he retrieved the jewelry wherever he'd hidden it, but he suspected someone in Cooke City would know where he could find his back-stabbing cohort.

Blade had been surprised that Lucian had sat on the stolen jewelry all this time, waiting. But for what? He'd asked a few questions around Cooke City, Lucian's old stomping grounds. Once he'd learned about a camp up in the mountains, the pieces had begun to fall into place. He tracked the man through his illicit past to his old friend Calhoun St. Pierre. Unfortunately, the outfitter had already headed for the hills—with Lucian's woman.

Blade had no idea what Lucian had planned. It still wouldn't be easy to turn the jewelry into cash. But it was clear that someone had been here, and now that person had the jewelry. Lucian? Or Calhoun St. Pierre?

So, where is the jewelry now? he asked himself as he studied the tracks in the soft still damp earth.

"He's not here," Juice said. "Maybe he was killed in the rockslide."

"You think?" Blade headed back to his horse. "Maybe he started the rockslide. Sounds more like him. He can't be that far ahead of us. See the tracks? He's got what he came for and is heading out of these mountains. We're going to find him before that happens."

CALHOUN FOLLOWED LUCIAN'S tracks straight to Geneva. He tried to convince himself that his old friend wouldn't hurt her. He had to have felt something for her to marry her and wait a whole year before he left. But the truth was that Lucian had already hurt her.

Worse, Calhoun had left Geneva with a gun that he doubted she would be able to fire at her husband. He just hoped she didn't point it at Lucian, who might just be looking for an excuse to kill her. After all, his old friend had just left him for dead after starting a rockslide he assumed had killed him. It almost had. It wasn't like Lucian had come to check to see if he was still breathing.

He should have known he might be walking into a trap. He just hadn't expected Lucian to try to kill him. Just as Geneva wouldn't either. Calhoun had almost perished because he'd trusted his old friend. Geneva still loved the man. She didn't stand a chance against him.

As Calhoun neared the edge of the clearing, he pulled his weapon. He could hear voices, he realized with a wave of relief. Geneva was still alive. Should he race in guns blazing or try to sneak into camp? Lucian wouldn't be expecting him, thinking he was dead. But every moment he did nothing could cost Geneva her life.

It was a gamble, but one he had to take. He came out of the pines moving fast. He had no idea what he could find. The moment he cleared the pines, he saw something that made his heart drop. Geneva and Lucian in what appeared to be a standoff. In that split second, he saw Geneva, the gun in her hand, her gaze locked with Lucian's. Across from her, her husband held the puppy with one hand, his free hand going for the gun at his hip.

Chapter Sixteen

Geneva hadn't heard Calhoun approach. Her gaze was locked with Lucian's. Her only thought, fear for her puppy.

"Drop the gun, Geneva." Lucian's other hand moved as he went for his weapon. "I swear I'll kill—"

She pulled the trigger as Calhoun had instructed her, terrified that she would hit the puppy. But she couldn't bear watching him hurt Lucky. Her first shot must have been close because Lucian flinched. Her second was more accurate. She thought she heard a third shot but was sure she hadn't fired it.

Lucian dropped Lucky into the tall grass. Her gaze went to the dog, panicked that she might have hit her or the fall had hurt her. But to her relief, the puppy was on her chubby feet and headed in her direction through the grass.

That's when she looked up and saw that Lucian was gone. Not dead. Just…gone. And Calhoun… She hadn't seen him until after she'd fired the second shot. Until Lucian dropped the puppy and her attention had moved to Lucky as the puppy raced toward her.

She scooped the dog up into her arms as Calhoun rushed to her. "Are you hit?" he cried grabbing her shoulders and locking his gaze with hers.

She shook her head, unable to speak for a moment.

"I thought you were dead." She began to cry as Calhoun hugged her and the dog. She looked past him. "Lucian?"

"He got away."

"I didn't kill him?" She remembered seeing Lucian stagger, thought she remembered seeing blood.

"No, you only wounded him."

She felt relieved. She didn't want to kill anyone. "He threatened to hurt Lucky." She looked down at the dog between them.

"Lucky?" Calhoun asked.

"You have to admit, she's one lucky dog." Her face fell. "Lucian was threatening to harm her."

"But you stopped him." He wasn't looking at the puppy. He was looking at her. It was a look she'd glimpsed before in his eyes. Admiration? She didn't feel that what she'd done was admirable in anyway. She could have killed a man. Not just any man, the man she'd married. It made her sick. She began to shake, her teeth chattering.

He pulled her closer. "He would have killed you if you hadn't pulled that trigger. He wouldn't have spared Lucky either."

She nodded, knowing it was true. Lucian had told her he couldn't let her go to the cops. He hadn't left the truck keys because he'd wanted her to come after him. He'd made a mistake. Just as she'd made a mistake when she'd married him and again when she'd come all the way to Montana, expecting some form of remorse from him for what he'd done to her.

Calhoun moved and she saw him wince.

"You're hurt," she cried.

"I'll live."

She saw the blood soaked into his hat. "Calhoun, what happened? Lucian...what did he do? He tried to hurt you, didn't he?"

"No, he tried to kill me. Just as he would have you if you hadn't shot him." He cupped her cheek in his warm hand. "Let's get out of here." He seemed to read her frightened look. "Lucian is headed down the mountain. We'll go to my camp to the northeast."

She realized how hard it must have been for him not to go after Lucian. "You're giving him a chance to get away," she said unable to hide her surprise.

"I wanted to go after him," he said. "But I'm not leaving you alone again. I almost got you killed, and those men after him are still somewhere on this mountain."

CALHOUN SAW THE effect of his words, but by now she had to know who and what they were dealing with. He had desperately wanted to chase Lucian down and end this once and for all, but it was true what he'd told Geneva. It would have meant leaving her alone again. He couldn't do that, even as hard as it was to let the bastard get away.

Those men after Lucian would find the camp empty and follow not only Lucian's tracks but also his own right to them.

"We can't stay here. Lucian left us to deal with his former partners in crime," Calhoun said. As long as Lucian had the jewelry, Geneva was in danger. They all were. He thought about using the satellite phone to call the authorities. But there was no law enforcement in Cooke City, none for miles. There were park rangers right over the border in Yellowstone National Park, but though some were trained just like law enforcement officers, their authority was inside the park—not outside the border.

Calhoun had wanted to end this up here on the mountain, but now that wasn't going to happen. He got the horses ready. He wondered how badly Lucian was injured. If his wound was life-threatening, he might not make it far. Geneva's second shot had wounded him, but Calhoun's had also.

As soon as they reached his camp with his wranglers there to protect Geneva, he would go looking for Lucian—even though it might mean running into the three outlaws also after him.

He saw Geneva carry the puppy over to the spot where Lucian had been standing. She held the dog against her chest as she looked down to where there was blood on the ground. Head wounds tended to bleed—even if the bullet had only grazed Lucian's scalp. The third shot, the one Calhoun had fired, had hit Lucian in the chest as he'd dropped the puppy. It was hard to say which wound would stop him—if either of them could.

"Let's go," he said, hating to see the pain on her face.

"I wanted to kill him."

"I understand," he said. She had no idea how much he understood or how hard pulling that trigger had been for her. He'd had experience with killing after serving for a time in Afghanistan. He had hoped never to have to fire a fatal shot at a man again. He especially hadn't wanted it to be at his former friend.

"I'm glad I didn't kill him."

"I understand that too," he said.

She handed him Lucky and headed for her horse but didn't get far before she stopped and pointed to the clouds that had formed over the mountains to the west. Another squall was headed their way.

He would have loved to have waited it out in a shelter, but there wasn't time. He hadn't noticed how dark this one was until now. All his thoughts had been on Lucian, on finding him, on getting the jewelry and ending this. This squall looked as if it might contain more than rain.

Geneva turned to look back at him. "You think we can reach your camp before it hits?"

He doubted it, but they had to try. Taking shelter was the smart thing to do under normal circumstances. But there was nothing normal about any of this. "We make a run for it. Wear your slicker. Don't worry about Lucky. I have her."

She nodded. "This won't be over—will it?—until the jewelry is returned. Lucian won't stop and neither will the others."

"No, it won't be over."

Tears filled her eyes. He was about to remind her that there was no crying when she said, "Thank you."

He knew she wasn't thanking him for taking care of her dog. He suspected that she'd realized that if he hadn't shown up when he did earlier, Lucian would have fired at her, and, even wounded, he would have killed her.

"I'm so sorry I involved you in all this," she said.

"If you and I hadn't already been headed up into the mountains, those three men after Lucian would have tried to get his location out of me. I might have been foolish enough not to tell them. Old loyalties die hard. So you saved my life."

She smiled at that. "Lucian said I always see a half-filled glass and think it's almost full. Seems you do too."

He returned her smile, but she was wrong. Right now, he couldn't be optimistic about any of this. He knew how much danger they were in and not just from the approaching storm.

THE DRIVING RAIN pelted her as hard as the hail that followed. Geneva ducked her head, glad for the Western hat and the slicker she wore. She kept her head down, her horse following the others through the storm.

She still felt shaken by her encounter with Lucian. Her

emotions felt all over the place. She didn't want to believe that he would have hurt her puppy—let alone have killed her, but she knew soul-deep it was true. Look what the man had already done to her. Why would she think he couldn't kill to get away with it?

Ahead of her, she could barely make out the horse in front of her let alone Calhoun in the hailstorm. She could feel an urgency in the outfitter and knew that once they reached the camp, he would go after Lucian. The thought scared her. Not for Lucian but for Calhoun. Lucian had already tried to kill him, so Calhoun knew what he would be facing. But if he did go after Lucian, Geneva knew he would be doing it for her.

She also knew that the men after Lucian and the jewelry wouldn't rest until they found him and would use anyone who knew him—including her—to get that jewelry. She had every reason to be afraid, but she'd already faced down Lucian today. She'd wanted to kill him if he hurt her puppy. What kind of man would even threaten to do such a thing? He could have killed her and would have if Calhoun hadn't shown up when he did. The thought made her shudder. She'd used up all her adrenaline. Now she just felt cold and wet, tired and saddle sore.

Geneva realized with a start that the horse in front of her had stopped.

A few moments later, a wrangler came out of the storm to help her off her horse. He steered her toward a small wall tent beside the creek. "Calhoun said he'll bring your things in shortly."

She stepped inside, instantly rewarded with a rush of warm air from the woodstove in the corner. While small, she could stand up in the tent. Hail peppered the canvas top, sounding so loud she thought it would break through the fabric, then it fell silent. She could hear the men's voices coming from the larger tent she'd seen. She pulled off her wet slicker and left it and her boots and canvas pants by the door.

Shivering, she was about to strip down to nothing but her skin when the canvas door opened and Calhoun stepped in, his arms full. As he set down her puppy, Lucky came running to her. Calhoun had stopped just inside the tent. He took her in for a few moments before he quickly looked away and put down two bedrolls and a bag with her spare clothing.

"The storm has passed," he said. "There's a kettle of warm water on that stove and soap in this bag. Put on some dry clothing when you're finished and come on over to the larger of the tents. You must be starved."

Her stomach rumbled in answer, and he chuckled. When his gaze returned to her, it was warmer than the woodstove in the corner of the tent. She tried to find words of gratitude. Warm water, soap, dry clothes and food. Civilization.

But all she could think about was this man. She would be going back to Cooke City in the morning with one of the wranglers. She would probably never see Calhoun St. Pierre again. She felt an ache in her chest that made it hard to breathe. The man had saved her life. More than that, he'd gotten under her skin.

"Calhoun?" She turned, uncertain as to what she was about to say. Not that it mattered. She saw that he'd already ducked back out the door, her puppy going with him.

THE SUN HAD sunk behind the mountain, the camp full of long shadows that pooled in the pines as Geneva walked back to the small tent after dinner. The tent sat at the edge of the meadow some distance from the other tents like an afterthought. His wranglers hadn't expected him to join them and need the tent. She realized that he normally would have slept outside under the stars or in the wranglers' tent.

He'd had them set up a tent for her. And him? Calhoun had gone with his men to check on one of the horses that had come up lame. Lucky had gone with him, Calhoun promising to bring her to the tent when he came back.

A soft quiet had fallen over the camp. Several of the clients sat around the campfire talking about their day fishing one of the almost thousand high mountain lakes.

It was so peaceful that she could almost forget why she'd come up here, let alone only hours ago coming face-to-face with Lucian and how that had ended. Who was that woman who'd fired those shots? Not the Geneva Carrington Beck she'd known.

This had changed her, she thought as she stepped into her dark tent. The only light was the glow of the stove in the corner. She could never go back to being the person she was. Unfortunately, she couldn't imagine where that left her. Or what she would do.

Earlier, she'd joined all the men in the large tent around a long portable table. She'd taken the chair she was offered across from Calhoun. He'd given her a reassuring smile when he'd seen her. But he'd also passed a message. No one but his wranglers were aware of what else was happening back up in these mountains. He wanted to keep it that way.

The clients had another two days of fishing, and then they would be headed back to town. They were a merry bunch, joking around about who caught the largest fish, who'd fallen into the freezing water of the lake, who'd panicked when they thought they'd seen a bear that had turned out to be an elk.

It had all felt so normal that she should have been able to relax while she ate. Instead, she'd been too aware of Calhoun sitting across the table from her. In a matter of days, so much had happened, of course it had formed a bond between them. She told herself not to make more of it than it was. This was Calhoun St. Pierre. He didn't take women up into the mountains. But he'd taken her.

She'd thought about the first time she'd laid eyes on him, hat covering most of his face as he'd snoozed on his porch in front of his cabin on Cooke City's main drag. She couldn't have seen where she would end up that afternoon. It hadn't been something she could have imagined.

As she stepped into the tent, she was surprised and pleased to see two cots had been set up close together given what little space there was in the small tent. She crawled up on one and lay staring up at the canvas ceiling. Pine boughs threw dark shadows over the tent, moving to the breeze. She'd dozed off when she was awakened by Lucky. The puppy jumped up on her cot, tongue lolling, tail wagging as if happy to see her. Her gaze had gone to the tent's doorway and the man standing there. Calhoun took off his hat and coat and moved toward the two of them.

"Oh, she smells like horse manure," she cried and put the dog down on the floor after hugging her for a moment.

"We call that road apples," he said grinning.

She looked up at him, happy to see that it seemed he planned to sleep here tonight. "How's the horse?" she asked as she watched him take off his jacket, then go to the woodstove to wash up with the extra water she'd left in the kettle on top.

"Nothing serious." They both fell silent as he climbed onto the adjacent cot. Lucky had curled into a ball over by the stove, seemingly content after her latest adventure.

Geneva realized how late it must be. She couldn't hear the men's voices around the campfire. The night had fallen silent. The only light was from the woodstove. She glanced over and felt a strong pull at heart level and an ache much lower.

Calhoun lay on his back. The air in the tent seemed to spark with electricity she couldn't see but could feel. Regret was a weight on her chest, because she could feel the distance growing between them even before he said, "I probably won't be here in the morning when you wake up."

Rolling up on her elbow, she looked over at him. The tent was so small, their cots were almost touching. He still wasn't looking at her. "One of the wranglers is going to take you back to Cooke. He'll take you to the barn where I left your pickup and then you can—"

"You're planning on going after Lucian, aren't you?" He didn't answer. He didn't have to. "What will you do when we find him?" she asked. He shook his head. "I don't want you to kill him." She feared what it would do to Calhoun.

He finally turned his head to look over at her. "That will depend on Lucian."

"I don't understand you," she said. "You'll carry my dog all the way up into the mountains on your horse, but when it comes to people..."

"I like animals."

"What about people?" She knew what she was really asking, *What about me?* but she couldn't bring herself to say it out loud. He'd made it clear that theirs had been a business arrangement and now it was over.

Her disappointment must have shown in her face because he added, "There's some people I like more than others." His gaze locked with hers.

"But you could kill a person."

"I could also kill an animal if it was threatening to kill me or someone I cared about."

The look in his eyes made her fall silent for a moment. "You are so passionate about so much," she said, finding it hard to breathe when he looked at her like that. "So gentle and caring and capable and yet...so stubborn, so fiercely independent, so...dangerous. I've never known anyone like you."

She was inches from him. Her desire to touch him felt overwhelming. She leaned toward him. The need to touch him so strong that—she hadn't realized that she'd reached for him until she felt his large, callused fingers close over hers gently but firmly.

He shook his head. "Bad idea."

She swallowed, her gaze still locked with his. "Are you sure about that?"

Calhoun let out a chuckle as he pushed up on his elbow so they were face-to-face. So close that their lips were almost touching. "You're scared and not thinking clearly." She shook her head in denial. "You're tempted to walk on the wild side, but you'd regret it." Again she shook her head. His eyes darkened. "You're Lucian's wife."

"All the more reason."

He laughed, shook his head and fell onto his back again. "You think you know me, but you don't." He glanced over at her. "But none of those reasons is why I'm not making love to you right now. When it happens, it won't be one night in a tent. It will be for the right reasons, and you won't be Mrs. Lucian Beck. Now get some sleep or at least let me." He rolled over, giving her his broad back.

She laid back and stared up at the canvas tent overhead trying hard not to cry. "Didn't you mean to say, *if* it happens?" He grunted, but it sounded like a chuckle. She closed her eyes. She could hear the soft crackle of the woodstove. She could smell the soap they'd both used with the kettle of hot water in their tent. Her hair was still a little damp, but she wasn't cold, her desire for this man running hot through her veins. She'd never felt more alive lying here next to him.

GENEVA DIDN'T KNOW how long she'd been asleep or what had awakened her at first. Then she heard Lucky whine over by the tent door. "What is it, girl?" she whispered as she slowly climbed off the end of the cot, careful not to wake Calhoun. He was snoring softly as she moved to the puppy and opened the door to let her out.

Worried that something might get the puppy, Geneva stepped out into the night while Lucky did her business. The night was darker than usual, clouds hiding most of the stars. She hugged herself against the cold even though she was wearing her clothes. She thought of that negligee she'd been planning to wear the night of her anniversary party. How her life had changed. Here she was sleeping in her clothes that smelled of woodsmoke, leather and horses.

The thought made her smile as Lucky came charging to her, busting through the tent door as if anxious to get back to her spot by the fire.

As Geneva started to step back toward the tent, she heard a sound. Before she could turn, she was grabbed from behind. A large hand clamped down over her mouth as she was lifted off her feet. She didn't recognize the harsh whisper at her ear, but she understood the words perfectly.

"Make a sound and I will slit your throat."

Chapter Seventeen

Calhoun woke with a start, coming face-to-face with the puppy. Lucky licked him on the nose, then whined. He sat up, aware of two things instantly. The tent door was partially open, a cold breeze coming in, and the woodstove fire had gone out.

He quickly rolled over to find the cot next to him empty. In an instant, he was on his feet, pulling on his boots. He had no idea what time it was, only that it was still dark outside, but daylight wasn't far off. He told himself that Geneva had just stepped out to pee. She wouldn't go far.

But why hadn't Lucky gone with her?

Trying not to panic, he moved quickly to the door and looked out into the gray darkness. He didn't want to set off an alarm in camp—not until he was sure. "Geneva?" he called quietly. Then a little louder. He could hear the breeze in the pines but nothing else.

Ducking into the tent, he grabbed a flashlight and hurried back outside. He had no idea how long she'd been gone. Worse, why the puppy hadn't gone with her. It didn't take him long to realize that Geneva hadn't just stepped out to pee. He found drag marks in the still damp earth that led from the tent into the pines.

It took a little longer to find the tracks into camp and where the two horses had been tied up not far from their tent. Not the horse Lucian had been riding or the spare horse he'd brought up into the mountains. Calhoun knew those tracks.

No, these had to be the men after Lucian. *But why take Geneva?* he asked himself even as he feared he already knew as he hurried back to the tent to scoop up Lucky. He'd slept in the tent with her because he'd been worried about her, and yet someone had still taken her. He'd thought he could keep her safe. He'd been a fool, telling himself he was taking the high road last night not making love to her. If they had pushed the cots together, he would have been holding her in his arms. He would have awakened when she got up.

Silently berating himself, he carried the dog over to the wranglers' tent, opened the door and awakened his men. "Take care of the dog. Someone's taken Geneva. I'm going after them."

He closed the tent door. It didn't take him long to get his horse saddled, but it had seemed interminable. Once in the saddle, he checked to make sure his rifle and sidearm were loaded, then he began to track the person who'd taken her, knowing that before this was over, he would have to kill—or be killed.

GENEVA TRIED TO BREATHE. The bandana the man gagged her with tasted vile. Worse, he'd tied her hands to the saddle and taken her reins as he'd led her back through the pines away from the camp. The one time she'd tried to scream for help, he'd punched her, almost knocking her out.

"Do that again and I'll leave you here to bleed out," he'd whispered next to her ear as he tightened the rope on her wrists until she let out a muffled cry.

His chuckle told her everything she needed to know about the man who had abducted her. Bound the way she was, she could see no way to escape. Any attempt would be met quickly with a painful response from him. Heart in her throat, she told herself to be careful while hoping for a chance to get away.

Terrified as to what he planned to do to her, she tried to rein in her frantic thoughts. She thought of Calhoun and Lucky and fought tears. She needed to keep her wits about her. This had to be one of the men after Lucian. She couldn't imagine why he would have abducted her otherwise. But where was he taking her? And for what purpose? By now, Lucian would have gotten away with the jewelry. Surely this man didn't think she had it—or anything to do with Lucian, did he? Or even more ridiculous that he could use her to make Lucian give up the jewelry?

Was Lucian even still alive? She remembered all the blood at the spot where he'd been standing. Calhoun said she hadn't killed him. But then again, Calhoun might not have wanted her to know the truth—that her shot had been fatal and that Lucian had died alone out in the woods.

Calhoun. Just the thought of him made her heart ache. He had stirred something in her, making her want not just to move on from her no-count husband and her fake marriage, but also to survive to, as the outfitter had said, take a walk on the wild side with him. She feared that would never happen, but it gave her hope that it still might. If she could get away.

Ahead, she heard a horse whinny. As they rode into a camp, she saw two men huddled on the ground next to a campfire that had burned down to only wisps of smoke.

"I thought you were going after Lucian," one of the men said.

That she'd been right and that this man was one of the three who were also looking for Lucian gave her no satisfaction.

She thought about Calhoun. What would he do when he woke and found her gone? He'd come looking for her. If anyone could find her, it was him. She thought of her puppy but knew he would also take care of Lucky. If he could, he'd take care of her.

But first, he'd have to find her before it was too late.

BLADE WAS GLAD that he'd gagged and tied the woman to the horse. In retrospect, he wished he'd done the same thing to Ricki and Juice, given how quiet this ride had been compared to the ones with his so-called partners. The sun was coming up, turning the sky to the east a bright orange by the time he reached the makeshift camp where he'd left his cohorts. The campfire had burned down, both men had been asleep when he rode up and had let the fire go out.

He swung off his horse next to Ricki on the ground and gave him a swift kick. His yelp woke up Juice. "Get up. We're leaving."

"Can't we wait until the sun is all the way up," Juice whined. "We won't be able to see in the trees. I'm hungry. I can't keep doing this without food."

Blade moved swiftly to the man, his horse's reins in one hand, the knife in his other. Moments before, they'd been one horse short for the trip out of here. He pointed that out to Juice as he plunged the knife into the man's neck.

He heard a sound come from the gagged woman still tied to the horse as Juice dropped to the ground, blood spurting from his neck.

"What the hell, Blade?" Ricki demanded.

He swung around to face him. "You want some of this too?" Ricki took a step back, holding up his hands. "Good. Now let's get moving. You bring up the rear."

Ricki looked skeptical. "What are you planning to do with *her*?"

"She's Lucian's wife."

"What kind of answer is that? I thought we came here for the jewelry."

Blade was sick of answering to these two. He thought about leaving Ricki here as well but realized he still might need him.

"If this is about getting even with Lucian—"

"I don't have to explain myself to you. I'll do whatever I want with her. Now move."

Blade hadn't planned to take her. He'd seen where their tracks had headed back to the camp he and his men had stopped at yesterday. It was Lucian's tracks that had headed down the mountain, then stopped. The storm had hit, and Blade had lost him. They'd waited out the storm and built a fire to warm up.

He'd gotten to thinking that Lucian might have circled back. He was pretty sure that Lucian was wounded. He'd found blood droplets on his trail. Maybe Lucian had gone to that outfitter's camp for help.

But he could find no sign that his back-stabbing former partner had been there. Blade had been contemplating what to do when he'd seen the woman come out of a tent at the edge of the encampment. He'd realized that this had to be Lucian's wife, the woman he'd heard about back in Cooke City. He decided to take her, use her if needed to deal with Lucian—or anyone else who tried to stop them.

"Lucian can't be that far ahead of us," Blade said, hating that he had to spell everything out to Ricki. "That storm had to hold him up just like it did us."

He started to saddle up again, when he caught movement out of the corner of his eye.

The first shot hit with a dull thud in the middle of Ricki's chest. He made an *ooufft* sound and dropped to his knees.

The second shot caught Blake in the leg as he was trying to tell from what direction the gunfire was coming from.

He grabbed his horse and, foot in the stirrup, was pulling himself up when the third shot hit him in his shoulder. He fell back, his boot tangled in the stirrup as his horse reared. The rope was still wound around his saddle horn from the woman's horse. That horse also began to rear as Blade frantically tried to free his boot from the stirrup.

CALHOUN FOLLOWED THE trail the horses had left, using his flashlight. Still the going was slow. Not just that, his light could be seen from a distance. Whoever he was following would know exactly where he was. It would be easy to walk into a trap or, worse, be ambushed before he could get to Geneva.

He knew he had to be getting close. Whoever had taken her couldn't have gotten that much of a lead. He cursed himself for bringing her up here. What had he been thinking? He reminded himself that he hadn't known about the jewelry theft. Nor had he realized how much trouble Lucian was in. He'd gone past having a friend who wanted to punch him for what he'd done or even three bikers who wanted to kick the daylights out of him as well.

Lucian had graduated to the big leagues. Hardened men out of prison who he'd double-crossed no doubt wanted to kill him.

The worst part was that he'd gotten Geneva involved. Tricking her into marriage, deceiving her, taking everything before he left her wasn't bad enough; he had to leave behind his pickup, where she would find his past and track him to Cooke City, Montana. Even if he hadn't meant to, this was all on him.

Last night, he'd planned to go after Lucian at first light. He hadn't wanted to leave Geneva, his mistake. As it was, he'd lost her on his watch. He'd never forgive himself for that. Being caught in the landslide and the rest had left him exhausted and in pain. He'd fallen into a bottomless sleep filled with nightmares and awakened to her gone.

He'd failed her when the last thing she needed was another man she couldn't depend on. Last night it would have been so easy to make love to her. He was thankful now that he hadn't. He was the last thing the woman needed.

At the sound of gunshots, his heart dropped. He spurred his horse, racing toward where he thought the shots had come from, worried why whoever had taken Geneva would give away his location with gunfire.

Chapter Eighteen

Blade was bleeding badly, in horrible pain from the gun-shot to his shoulder, not to mention the one to his free leg. His other leg was twisted to the point of breaking, and if this horse should take off running… He was fighting desperately to get his boot free until he felt a shadow fall over him and reached for the gun at his hip. He got it out, but as he looked up, he saw Lucian an instant before his former cohort stepped on his wrist, leaned down, took the weapon from him and tossed it a few feet away.

"You look like hell," Blade said. Lucian did. The side of his face was covered in dried blood and so was the front of his shirt.

"You should talk," Lucian said. "Give me your knife."

Blade hesitated. He'd already lost his gun. He felt naked without his knife. If Lucian was going to kill him, then he'd just as soon get it over with.

But then again, lying here on the ground, his leg twisted painfully in that damned stirrup, what choice did he have? Lucian would shoot him before he could get his knife out and stab the lying, cheating double-crosser.

He worked the blade out of his scabbard against his wounded leg. The pain of the gunshot wound was excruciating. He promised himself that if he got the chance, he would make Lucian pay for this and everything else with hours of torture.

"Where's the jewelry?" Blade asked as he slowly pulled the knife free.

Lucian only smiled as he stepped on Blade's wrist again, leaned down and carefully pried the knife from his fingers—just as he had the gun. "What are you doing with my wife?"

Blade had forgotten about her. She tried to say something through the gag that he couldn't make out, but it made Lucian smile.

Walking over to her, Lucian cut her free of the horse, but left her hands bound. He dragged her to the ground, grimacing in obvious pain. It was clear that Lucian was hurt worse than he was pretending. Frantically she worked at the gag on her mouth. Clearly, she had something she desperately wanted to say but couldn't get it loose with her hands bound.

"I'd leave that gag where it is," Blade advised as he felt his foot slip a little in his boot. "From the look in her eyes, she doesn't like you any more than me." If he could pull his foot out and free his leg... He kept his eye on Lucian. Just a little more and he'd be free. Then it wouldn't take much to get the gun Lucian had so carelessly tossed aside.

CALHOUN HAD ONLY one thing going for him, he told himself. The element of surprise. He knew the risk. It could just as easily get him killed. Even as he raced toward where he thought the gunshots had come from, he knew he might be too late. Geneva could already be dead. The thought sent a molten fire of anger through his veins. He would kill the bastards.

As he burst through the pines, he had his gun drawn. It took him only a few moments to assess the situation. There were unmoving bodies on the ground. Several horses. One man on the ground.

But his focus was on Lucian. He had Geneva. She was gagged and bound. But she was alive. For the moment.

Lucian raised his gun and fired a shot as Calhoun leaped off his horse a few yards away, taking cover. The bullet missed him but not by much. He saw Geneva try to get away, but Lucian pulled her into a headlock, turning so her body shielded his own.

"Calhoun," he called as he put the gun to her head. "You don't want to get this woman killed, so come on out. Let's talk about this."

"Let her go, Lucian. You've hurt her enough. This is between you and me."

Lucian shook his head. "I feel bad about what I did to you."

"I doubt that."

"Truth is, I always wanted what you had. But you should know that. Now it appears you want what I have. Funny how things work out, isn't it?"

Calhoun wanted to keep Lucian talking until he could get a clear shot. But the man who'd been on the ground was moving, working his way toward one of the bodies nearby. Going after a gun?

He swore under his breath. "That's bull, Lucian. You've stayed in my cabin. You can't have been jealous of what I have."

"You have the life you want. I've never had that. I've finally got a chance now. But only if I get to walk away from here. Only if you help me."

"You don't look good," Calhoun said as he saw the man belly-crawling closer to something on the ground.

"You're the second person who's pointed that out," Lucian said with a chuckle. "I'll tell you what. You come out, hands up, gun on the ground, and I'll let her go. You can both ride out of here. Just let me do the same."

It was a tempting offer, but he didn't believe him for a minute. Nor could he let the other man get to a weapon. The fool would either try to kill him or Lucian. With Lucian holding Geneva the way he was, the man couldn't get a clean shot at Lucian any more than Calhoun could. The difference was the man didn't care if he killed them both. In fact, Calhoun figured his plan was to kill all of them.

Unfortunately, he couldn't get a clear shot through the horses and bodies to stop the man. Any moment, the man would reach the weapon on the ground, roll over and begin firing.

"Your friend is going for a gun," Calhoun said.

Lucian only smiled, his weapon still pointed at him.

Calhoun realized there was only one way he could save Geneva. "I'm coming out," he announced and tossed his gun out. "Let her go." He rose slowly, hands in the air, his gaze on Geneva's terrified expression as Lucian shoved her away, his gun coming up to fire.

Out of the corner of his eye, Calhoun saw the other man reach the weapon, roll to his back, the gun in his hand as he turned the barrel toward Lucian and fired seemingly at the same time as Lucian pulled the trigger.

Calhoun dove for his gun, his gaze drawn away from Lucian and the weapon that had been pointed at his chest. He hit the ground and came up armed again. His gaze going first to where Geneva had been standing. She wasn't there. She was on the ground.

He looked at Lucian, surprised to see him sway on his feet. His gun was still held in front of him, but not pointed at Calhoun. It took a moment to realize what had happened. Lucian hadn't fired at him. He'd shot the other man, but that man had gotten a shot off, and Lucian had taken it in the stomach.

Calhoun rushed to him, afraid Lucian would turn the gun on him or, worse, Geneva. He wrenched the weapon from his former friend without a struggle as Lucian slumped to the ground, his back to a stump.

Calhoun scrambled over to Geneva, still afraid that she'd caught one of the bullets. Her eyes filled with tears when she saw him. "Are you hit?" She shook her head. Still, he checked her over quickly, assuring himself that she hadn't been caught in the crossfire.

He helped her take off the gag, then pulled out his knife and cut her hands free. She threw her arms around him, and he held her for a long moment before she released him, and he rose to make sure the man Lucian had shot was dead.

All three of the men in the camp were dead. He moved to Lucian, seeing at once that his wound was fatal. Had they not been miles back into the mountains and even further from a hospital, Calhoun still doubted he would have made it. There would be no saving him. Geneva must have realized it as well. She sat, arms around her knees, crying softly.

Calhoun crouched down next to him. The side of the mountain had fallen into a deep silence as the sun rose above the peaks. Rays wove through the pines, chasing away the dark shadows.

"You are one stubborn bastard," Lucian said.

"Funny, someone mentioned that recently."

Their gazes locked. "She's too good for you."

Calhoun nodded. He could see Lucian's lifeblood seeping out into the dirt on this mountain range he had once loved. "Where's the jewelry?"

"Does it matter now?"

Probably not, he realized. There were more important questions he wanted to ask. "Did you love her?" What he really wanted to know was if Lucian would have killed both him and Geneva.

"What do you think? I know you'd hoped to see me behind bars. Not going to happen. I'm going to die here. Poetic, huh?"

"You're wrong. I never wanted any of this for you."

Lucian smiled through his pain. "But you want my wife." His laugh was a blood-filled gurgle as he grabbed Calhoun's arm. "Take care of her."

He stared at a man he had loved as a friend and watched the life fade from his eyes, and his grip loosened. Lucian's arm dropped to the ground next to him.

Calhoun sat back for a moment before he closed Lucian's eyes and moved to Geneva.

"Is he…?"

He nodded and pulled her to him. "He saved our lives, you know?" Overhead, he heard a helicopter. His men had called in backup. He tried to breathe, caught between simply being thankful to be alive and wishing it hadn't ended this way. There was so much he had wanted to ask Lucian, starting with why he hadn't killed him when he'd had a second chance. Why he'd married Geneva, then betrayed her. Why he'd asked him to take care of her, the woman who had wanted to believe there was good in Lucian probably to the end. He'd jeopardized their lives, but at the last second, he'd saved them both.

He'd had the jewelry, he was getting away, so why had he come back? All Calhoun knew was that Lucian had died, and he and Geneva were alive because of it.

The chopper touched down in a meadow some yards away. He liked to think that Lucian had realized that no one would be safe as long as his former partners in the heist were alive and that he'd come back to save the woman he'd loved after taking everything from her but her life.

That was the problem with Lucian. It was hard to nail down what he was, other than a walking contradiction. He'd brought violence and death to these mountains that he loved. He'd also ended his lifelong battle within himself here. Calhoun liked to believe that Lucian had finally found peace.

He helped Geneva up from the ground as law enforcement officers rushed toward them.

Chapter Nineteen

Geneva heard the sound of a pickup engine in front of the cabin. She'd gotten up with Lucky, taken her out, fed her, and then they'd both gone back to bed. Yesterday when she'd finally been released from the authorities and allowed to go to the cabin Calhoun had rented for her, all she'd wanted was a shower and to sleep on a bed. She'd thought she could sleep for days.

But her sleep was fraught with real-life nightmares. Awake, she went from numb to dazed to shocked to heartbroken. She couldn't bear to think about Lucian. She had watched him die feeling nothing and yet feeling everything. She'd chased him to Montana, her motives not even clear to her. If her goal had been to find out who she'd married, she'd done that, and yet... Calhoun had said that Lucian saved their lives after putting their lives in danger.

Lucian Beck was a criminal who appeared to be soulless, but he'd saved her and Calhoun up in the mountains. How did she deal with all that knowledge about the man she had loved and married and had never really known?

She had forced herself to rise from bed, shower and dress, knowing that she had to face it all and move on. She would have days on the road with Lucky to deal with her grief, her loss and her regret. She was broke and a widow. Her husband, a known criminal, was dead. She wasn't sure she would ever trust her best friend again. And then there was Calhoun.

At the sound of the truck's engine, she picked up Lucky and walked to the door. Just seeing Calhoun standing next to Lucian's pickup lifted her heart before dropping it again. She would always think of the pickup as Lucian's. Would she always think of Calhoun as Lucian's once good friend and remember the last day in the mountains with pain and heartbreak? It was a reminder she didn't need or want, bringing up the image of Lucian dying before her eyes and Calhoun holding her as if he never wanted to let her go.

Calhoun must have seen her expression. "You can sell the pickup here in Montana and fly back to San Diego with Lucky. I can take care of selling it for you."

Geneva smiled. Sometimes the man seemed to know her better than she knew herself. He had to know that it wasn't just the pickup that was the problem. This man had saved her life. She'd put his in danger. "How are you?"

"I'll live," he said and she could see what the past few days had done to him as well. But his look said he was more worried about her. Lucky squirmed in her arms. The moment she put her down, the dog bound off to him.

Calhoun smiled as Lucky leaped into his arms. Geneva watched him pet the dog, knowing that Lucky would miss him as much as she would. In a matter of days, the man had made his mark on both their lives. Maybe she and Lucky had done the same to him.

Or maybe he would be relieved to see them both gone, taking the bad memories with them. He could now get back to his life. She wondered, though, if he would be haunted by what had happened up in those mountains. She knew she always would. She'd seen the life that her husband had lived, running from trouble, and a part of him knowing it would catch up to him one day. She couldn't imagine what demons he'd lived with without her even knowing.

Calhoun put Lucky into the pickup's front seat and met her gaze. "You must be anxious to go home."

"Yes," she lied, her eyes burning with unshed tears. The first thing she had to do was put the house up for sale. "I still don't feel right about taking the reward money." Unfortunately, everything he'd stolen from her was gone to pay off other people he's cheated who wanted him dead.

"It's what Lucian wanted," he said. "With that and the money from the sale of the truck, will you be all right?"

"I'll be fine. You don't need to worry about me anymore."

His look seemed to say that wasn't possible. Calhoun glanced away for a moment before his eyes returned to hers. "Going to take a while to sort it all out, huh?"

She knew exactly what he was saying. She had so many emotions running rampant right now. She wasn't sure how she felt about anything. Except for Calhoun. That she knew heart deep. "Thank you."

He smiled at that. "For almost getting you killed?"

"For taking me up in the mountains. For saving my life. For…everything." She held his gaze. "I'm sorry I involved you in my mess. I owe you my life."

He shook his head. "I'm sorry about Lucian. At least now you know that he loved you."

"In his way." In the end, Lucian had surprised them both, but his change of heart couldn't save him. "I'll never forget the days I spent up in the mountains with you," she said, her voice breaking.

He had no idea how hard it was to walk away thinking she would never see him again. But now she had to go back and face the past while figuring out what she was going to do in the future. "Thanks for the offer about selling the truck, but I think I need to drive. Lucky and I could use a long road trip right now."

Calhoun held out the pickup keys and she took them. Her fingers brushed his, sending sparks flying. He pulled back, looking uncomfortable. "If you ever get back this way…"

Geneva smiled, feeling tears flood her eyes. She made a quick swipe at them, determined not to cry. She had come here for answers. She'd gotten most of them. She hadn't known Lucian and never would understand why he'd done the things he had. Lucian was dead. So were their dreams.

She was no longer that woman who'd awakened the morning after her anniversary party scared and alone. She would never be that woman again. But she knew it wouldn't be easy going back, facing everything—especially her feelings for Lucian, for Mitzi and most of all, for Calhoun.

Her heart felt as beat up as her body did right now. She wasn't sure she'd ever be able to sort out everything. She and Calhoun had their own histories with Lucian and a few days together in the mountains where they'd both faced their own mortality. Not the kind of bond a person built a relationship on. She figured Calhoun couldn't wait to put the entire experience behind him.

"I would imagine that you're headed back up in the mountains," she said to fill in the suddenly very heavy silence that fell between them.

"I have clients leaving and another batch coming in," he said with a nod, but he didn't sound happy about it.

"Lucky and I should get going. You're burning daylight."

He smiled at that. "I'll never forget you." The words seemed to come out as if against his will. He pulled off his hat and kneaded the brim in his hands for a moment, dropping his gaze to the dog. "If you ever need anything…"

"I know where to find you. You have my number and I have yours."

He nodded and put his hat back on. His look confirmed what she already knew. Neither of them would be calling the other.

"Let me help you with your bags," Calhoun said.

Geneva went back into the cabin and brought out her two small duffels that she'd packed for what she'd thought would be a quick trip. He took them from her and loaded them behind the pickup's bench seat before giving Lucky another hug and closing the door.

"Calhoun—" Her voice broke and she couldn't continue.

He stepped to her, taking her in his arms and holding her against him tightly for a few moments before he stepped back. "Drive careful."

She could only nod, move to the pickup and climb behind the wheel. She tried not to look at him standing there as she worked the key into the ignition and started the engine. She saw that he'd filled it up with gas. She looked up at him and mouthed, "Thank you." Their eyes locked, and she felt a chunk of her heart break off and drop to her feet.

At the sound of motorcycles pulling up, she turned to see Ace and his friends. Ace looked as if his injuries were healing. He gave her a nod, and out of the corner of her eye, she saw Calhoun walk over to talk to them.

Shifting the pickup into Reverse, Geneva backed out, then pulled onto the road at the first break in the traffic. She looked back once to see Cooke City in her rearview mirror. Then she went around a curve, and it was gone.

CALHOUN WATCHED HER drive away and swallowed the lump that had formed in his throat. His chest ached. Hell, his whole body ached. He was still limping a little from the rockslide that had almost killed him. But that pain was nothing like watching Geneva drive out of his life.

"Go after her," Ace said from where he was straddled on his bike.

Calhoun had forgotten the bikers were there. "And say what?" He shook his head, telling himself to get over it. He had work to do. Weeks of clients coming in before the first snowstorm, before the season ended and winter settled over Cooke.

"Tell her that she got under your skin, man, that you don't want her to go."

He glanced over at Ace. "Have you seen my cabin? How about my lifestyle? There's a reason I don't have a woman in my life."

"Or did you adopt this lifestyle to make sure there wasn't a woman in it?" Ace asked. "You were never serious about Dana, and she sure as hell wasn't that serious about you. When you walked away from her, you weren't feeling what you are now, were you?"

Calhoun laughed. "When did you become a life coach?"

"It's pretty obvious that you don't want her to go. We all saw you mooning over her."

"I knew the woman for only a matter of days. No one falls in love that fast. Nor do I have time for this." He started to walk toward his cabin, where his stock truck was parked, already loaded with supplies for his next clients. Truth was, he didn't have to go back up in the mountains with these out-of-state fishermen. His wranglers and assistant guide could more than handle it.

But he knew he couldn't stay here in town. For the first time in his life, there was no place he could go to outrun the way he was feeling.

"You're making a mistake," Ace called after him.

Calhoun stopped to look back at him. "Admit it, you just want the pickup."

"I forgot about that," Ace said, his smile exposing the broken teeth. He hadn't said who'd done the damage to his face, but Calhoun could guess. He'd met Blade.

"She's going to sell it once she gets back to California."

The biker shook his head. "I just like the idea of how much Lucian would have hated me driving it. He's really gone?"

Calhoun nodded. "He saved my life and Geneva's. It cost him his own. I like to think it was as selfless as he'd ever been. But then again, he might have realized that he wasn't going to be able to get away because of his injuries and had nothing more to lose."

"Did you see the jewelry?" Ace asked.

He shook his head. "And before you ask, I didn't get the reward for its return. I saw that Geneva got it. She'd lost everything, almost including her life because of Lucian. He owed her."

Ace snickered and looked to his friends: "Right, Calhoun doesn't care anything about her."

He laughed and walked away shaking his head. The last thing he needed was to be taking romantic advice from Ace. He needed to get back into the mountains, he thought, even as he knew he'd never be able to escape thinking about Geneva. He wouldn't be able to lay out under the stars without looking over to see her lying close by, looking up with that kind of awe that had pried his heart wide open to her.

Chapter Twenty

The days on the road driving back to California had helped. Geneva knew that she'd needed them. The long hours formed a bridge from Cooke City to San Diego, a transition from a life nothing like the one she'd known to what was waiting for her at the place she'd once felt at home.

On the way, she called a Realtor she knew and told her to put the house on the market. She realized that she didn't want the furniture. All she wanted was her belongings, and she could walk away without looking back.

But in the meantime, she had little choice but to go back and face the music, as her father would have said.

It felt as if she'd been gone for months as she parked the pickup in the garage and went inside the house. The place felt different. This time, Lucian really was gone. She didn't see him standing in the kitchen or lying next to her in the huge bed. He came to her in her dreams and only in passing. It was Calhoun who haunted her days and nights. When she ached to be held, it was him she thought of, which made her feel guilty. How could she forget her husband, who she'd been with for over a year, compared to Calhoun, who she knew such a short time?

She'd been back a few days when she heard a vehicle pull into the circular drive and stop. For an instant, she thought of the two men who'd come looking for Lucian.

But when she looked, she saw it was Mitzi. She'd thought about calling her when she'd gotten back, but she hadn't been sure what she wanted to say.

Opening the door, she saw at once how nervous the normally self-confident, devil-may-care Mitzi was standing there, her back to her. At the sound of the door opening, Mitzi swung around. There was so much pain in her expression that Geneva couldn't help herself.

She stepped to her old friend and pulled her into a hug. Mitzi hated crying, especially in front of anyone, so Geneva was surprised when she began to blubber.

"Come on in before the neighbors see you," she joked since there were no close neighbors. Still she knew her friend was embarrassed. She led her into the kitchen. "You still drink coffee?" she asked as she took down Mitzi's favorite mug she always drank out of when she came to visit.

Mitzi made a sniffling sound, grabbed a paper towel and blew her nose before pulling up a stool. Geneva handed her the mug full of coffee and watched her friend cup it in her hands as if needing the warmth. "I know what you must think of me," she said, sounding as if she might start crying again.

Geneva shook her head. "You made a mistake. You went for the brass ring without thinking of the consequences. Remember? I know how convincing Lucian could be. How are things going with Hugh?"

Her friend's face fell. "Not good. He'll never trust me ever again, not that I blame him." She blew her nose again, then added, "He's been better about money. I think things are going to be all right. Eventually. What about you? Did Lucian take everything?"

She nodded. "The house is for sale. I never liked it anyway. It was too big for the two of us, but Lucian loved it." She thought about him saying that they would fill it with children. There were still those painful reminders of the dreams he'd crushed, but they came more seldom and hurt much less as the days went on. "The jewelry was found."

Mitzi's interest peaked, just as Geneva knew it would.

"I have the reward money. It's enough to hold me over until I sell the house, find somewhere small to live and get a job."

"Wait, you got the reward money? I know you said you left, but where did you go?" Mitzi leaned forward, elbows on the kitchen island as she looked at her with a kind of awe.

Geneva topped their coffee before taking a seat at the island next to Mitzi. "I went to Montana." She told her about finding the pickup and clue about a past she also hadn't known about.

"Calhoun St. Pierre," her friend said. "He was some kind of mountain man?"

She smiled to herself. "He's an outfitter. He takes people up into the mountains to fish, hunt, hike, camp. So, yes, I guess he is a mountain man." She told her about riding horses for days on end, sleeping under the stars, eating venison in the main camp with the wranglers and clients.

Mitzi shook her head. "I can't imagine you doing any of that."

"Me neither."

"And you found Lucian and the jewelry."

"I was abducted, gagged, tied to a horse and taken to another camp. Lucian showed up. It was the second time I'd seen him. The first time—" she looked up at her friend "—I shot him."

"What? With what?"

"A gun Calhoun had left with me. I thought Lucian was going to shoot me. I think he planned to. Anyway, Calhoun showed up and Lucian got away that time."

Mitzi was shaking her head. "I can't even imagine what you've been through."

She told her about the three men Lucian had pulled the jewelry heist with and apparently double-crossed since he ended up with all the jewelry. "He hid it in the mountains, I guess, always planning to go back for it. I think his past misdeeds kept catching up to him." Geneva fell silent for a moment. "I was there when Lucian died."

"I'm so sorry. I can't believe what you went through. It's amazing that you survived it."

"It was something I will never forget," she said with a sigh and took a sip of her coffee. "Just being in those mountains, seeing that night sky. The air up there is so... amazing." She shook her head and saw that Mitzi was giving her a look she recognized only too well.

"Calhoun St. Pierre?"

Geneva couldn't help but smile. "I've never met anyone like him. Irascible, impatient, obstinate and yet so gentle, so caring, so capable of just about anything. He saved my life."

"Wow. So, do you think you'll ever see him again?"

She shook her head. "There's no room in his life for a woman. He spends most of his time up in the mountains with horses and clients. I was the only woman client he's ever taken up there, and I'm sure I'll be the last."

Mitzi seemed lost in thought for a few minutes. "Lucian really did love you."

Geneva nodded. "As much as he could love, I agree. In the end, he came back to face the men he'd done the jewelry store heist with as if he'd known they would come after me—which they did. It cost him his life."

Her friend was shaking her head. "I've always envied your life, but never more than I do right now. You were so brave to take off to Montana like that, to go after Lucian into the mountains... You're a lot stronger than me."

"It took a lot of courage for you to go back to Hugh."

"Desperation more than anything, but it was hard to face him after everything I've done. It did change things between us. I love him more than I ever did before." She shrugged and finished her coffee. "I should go. I was worried about you," she said as she got to her feet, studying Geneva as she did. "I'm not worried anymore. You're going to be fine. I just hope you get to see your mountain man again."

"I THOUGHT YOU were going up in the mountains with clients," Ace said as he roared up in front of Calhoun's cabin, climbed off his bike and scaled the ladder leaning against the new structure going up behind the old cabin.

"I changed my mind," Calhoun said. "You know, I've been meaning to build something on the empty lots I own behind the cabin for years."

Ace stood looking out through what would be a bank of windows facing the mountains. "You're going to have one heck of a view."

He'd always planned to build into the hillside, go up a couple of stories so he had a great view, especially of Pilot's Peak, the most distinctive of the mountaintops that could be seen from town.

"Just decided to do this now, huh?" Ace said with a wink. Calhoun ignored him. For years, he'd told himself that he didn't need anything more than his small cabin. Now he found himself racing against time to get the structure he was erecting closed in before winter. "You know, I'm pretty good at wielding a hammer," Ace said.

Within hours, others stopped by to help. The house went up quickly with so many hands. When it was all closed in, roof on, windows and doors in, Calhoun threw a party to thank everyone.

"I have to ask," Ace said. "Did she ever sell that pickup?"

He shrugged. "I would imagine so."

"You haven't talked to her?"

"Nope. Get you another beer?"

Ace swore. "What is wrong with you? We all know why you're building this place. Shouldn't you at least see if she wants to live here?"

"What woman in her right mind would want to live here?" Calhoun said in answer. "This has nothing to do with her. I've always talked about building a place behind the cabin."

"*Talked* being the key word. You know, if I had to pick one person who was fearless, it would have been you. I met those men, remember? I have scars to prove it. But you rode into that camp outnumbered, knowing you might die to save that woman. Don't tell me you don't feel something for her. I don't think I would have done that for a woman I had just met. I know you're a Boy Scout, come on, Calhoun, she got to you big-time." He motioned to the house he'd help build. "Have the guts to go after her and find out how she might feel about all this."

Chapter Twenty-One

"Didn't you tell me that you always wanted to paint?"

Geneva stared at the woman standing on her doorstep, then at her wrist and her new smartwatch. "Mitzi? It isn't even nine in the morning. What are you doing up this early?" she asked as her friend swept past her and into the kitchen.

They'd been spending more time together, Mitzi helping her get the place ready for the open house. Her real estate friend said everything had to be perfect, including when it went on the market as well as the open house.

Geneva had hated that it was taking so long. She'd wanted to be out of it, and yet she hadn't found another place to live that would take a dog. So she and Lucky had settled in for the duration. She just hoped she could get the house sold before she ran out of money.

"I'm not wasting any more of my life," Mitzi announced. "I'm getting up in the morning, fixing breakfast for my husband and then planning my day. I found a painting class for us to take."

"Sounds like you're planning *my* day," Geneva said as she reached for Mitzi's mug and poured them both coffee.

"It's a watercolor class. Then I thought we would go to lunch."

Geneva couldn't help but smile. She loved this new Mitzi,

and she had to admit that she'd enjoyed painting when she was young but hadn't done it for years. She'd always thought she'd do it again once she was settled and had time.

Geneva looked at her friend. "When does the class start? My Realtor is coming by later this afternoon."

"This morning."

She felt herself getting excited and, looking at Mitzi, was glad she'd been able to forgive her. "I'm glad you're my friend."

Mitzi teared up, then quickly finished her coffee. "Pick you up in thirty?" As she passed Geneva, she reached over to squeeze her hand before heading for the door.

CALHOUN KNEW HE could call Geneva. He had her cell number. But it felt as if it had been too long to suddenly call, and he had no idea what he was going to say. It wasn't like he hadn't thought about calling dozens of times. He'd talked himself out of it, telling himself it was better to leave things like they were.

He knew the city where she had lived, San Diego. But he also knew that she'd planned on going back to sell the pickup and the house. He had checked online for Lucian's truck but hadn't found it listed. Maybe she hadn't sold it. Or maybe she hadn't listed it online.

After she'd left Cooke City that morning, he hadn't called to check on her even though he now wished that he had. He'd thought it would be best if he put her behind him and let her put everything behind her as well. He thought that's what she wanted since he hadn't heard from her either.

Now he could admit that he'd been a fool. A day hadn't gone by that he hadn't thought of her with a yearning like none he'd ever felt. In the mountains, he sensed her as if she'd left a part of herself up there with him.

There were so many real estate offices. He began calling them, telling them he was looking for a house owned by Geneva Carrington Beck and that he'd lost the information. Was there going to be an open house? For all he knew, she'd already sold it. Or changed her mind and stayed in it.

After dozens of calls, he was about to give up when he struck gold. As a matter of fact, there was going to be an open house this coming week. He didn't hesitate. He caught a flight out of Billings and headed for San Diego, arriving a day before the open house.

He had no idea what he planned to say to her. In his rental car, he put in the house's address and let the navigation system take him to an exclusive part of the city. "You have now reached your destination." He pulled to the curb and got out. Butterflies were doing cartwheels in his stomach. Was he really doing this? He checked the address again on his phone, stopping just a few yards from the rental car.

Staring at the monstrous house, he suddenly felt sick. What was he doing here? He thought of the three-bedroom house he'd built in Cooke City. It wasn't even finished yet. But even finished, there was no comparison.

He'd known that Geneva had had a pampered life the first time he saw her. Did he really think that a few days in the mountains with him would make her want something else? Would make her want him and his lifestyle?

Geneva had lived here in this mansion with Lucian, and the fool had left her. Calhoun thought again of the house he and his friends had built back in Cooke City. This, he told himself, is why he hadn't contacted her. He never should have listened to Ace. What had he been thinking, flying down here like a madman, to do what?

But as much as he knew he should drive away, he couldn't. Ace thought he was brave. What the biker didn't realize is that this was more terrifying than anything he'd ever done. With Dana, he'd asked her to marry him knowing it probably would never happen. One of them would back out. As it was, she took the easy way out by sleeping with Lucian.

But Geneva... She was so out of his league. Still, he'd come this far. He had to at least see how she was doing.

He'd say hello and catch up, and then he'd go home. Everyone would think she'd turned him down, which was fine with him.

Calhoun realized he was a bigger fool than even he had thought and started to turn back to the rental car. He should never have come here. He was delusional if he thought—

The front door of the house opened and he saw her step out. She stopped. Even from a distance, he could see that she was frowning. He felt his heart thundering in his chest. She didn't recognize him.

A blur of movement caught his eye as a black-and-white dog came barreling out. Lucky stopped just as his mistress had but then began barking. He hadn't noticed until that moment that Geneva was holding a leash in her hands. Had they been going for a walk?

Ace had been right about one thing. Calhoun had been afraid of little. But right now, he fought the urge to rush back to the rental car and drive away as quickly as possible. He could hear Geneva calling the dog back. "Lucky!"

Calhoun was moving toward the car when the dog stopped barking. When he looked up, he saw Lucky racing toward him, all wagging docked tail, floppy ears and lolling tongue. When the dog reached him, Lucky jumped around him in obvious excitement at seeing him again.

He dropped down to hug the dog to him. He'd never been so glad to be remembered—even by a dog. "How have you been, girl? I've missed you."

He felt a shadow fall over him and looked up to see Geneva standing there smiling down at him. He saw her momentary confusion, then surprise. "Calhoun?"

He'd forgotten that he'd shaved and gotten his hair trimmed. He'd also picked up a pair of trousers and a button-down shirt. The only thing he hadn't changed about his attire were his cowboy boots.

She too looked so different from the woman who'd driven up in front of his cabin all those weeks ago. That woman had hollowed eyes, a look that said she'd been beaten down by life and was angry and scared and hurting. This woman looked radiant. There were no dark shadows under her Montana sky blue eyes. Her long hair was pulled up into a ponytail. She looked young. She also looked happy.

He realized he might be bringing all the bad memories back with him. He shouldn't have come. He should have left her alone. He definitely shouldn't have listened to Ace, of all people.

"Calhoun, what are you doing here?" she asked. Her smile was as bright as the sunshine-filled day.

He opened his mouth, almost afraid of what might come out, then Lucky licked him in the face. "She's gotten so big," he said. "I didn't think she would remember me." He met Geneva's gaze. "I figured you wouldn't either."

HE HAD A POINT. Geneva had hardly recognized him. Now, though, she couldn't help staring—or smiling. Calhoun had cut his hair and shaved off his beard. She recalled thinking that he would be more handsome without all that hair. He was gorgeous with or without the long hair and beard. To her surprise, she missed his old look.

She couldn't believe he was here. When she'd first left Montana, she'd thought she might hear from him. She'd left him her number. He'd seemed embarrassed when he'd pocketed it. He hadn't offered his own, instead saying something like, *"You know where to find me."* But she had his number since it was listed online. Still she hadn't called.

Not that she'd expected to ever hear from him again. She'd told herself that he was just glad to have her out of his life. After all, she'd made him break his standing rule of never taking a woman up in the mountains. She'd forced him into taking her and almost gotten them both killed.

"I just assumed you never wanted to see me again," she said, her throat as dry as her mouth.

Calhoun rose slowly to his full height as she attached the leash to Lucky and ordered her to sit. Like her, the dog was too excited. Her own heart was pounding wildly. "What are you doing here?" she asked, still taken aback.

He chuckled and looked around as if unsure. "Now that I'm here?" He shook his head as his gaze came back to hers. "I don't know what to say."

She could see how uncomfortable he was. "Well, I'm glad you're here, and Lucky has already expressed how she feels. Would you like to come inside?" Calhoun glanced toward the house. She saw his expression. "It's ridiculous," she said of the house. "I never wanted it. Lucian…well, he loved it. Or we could go somewhere if you'd prefer."

His gaze came back to her, and she saw the relief in his expression. "I could use a drink if there was some place around here, but Lucky—"

"This is California. There is a bar nearby that allows dogs." She glanced at his car. "That's if you don't mind taking her in your—"

"It's a rental. I'd be honored to have Lucky ride in it." He smiled, lighting up his whole face. She'd seen how nervous, how out of place he'd felt and was glad that he seemed to be trying to relax. He still hadn't said why he was here, but she'd learned a long time ago that Calhoun St. Pierre answered questions when he was darn good and ready.

He put Lucky in the back seat and opened the passenger door for her. She slid in and tried to catch her breath. Her heart was still pounding. Calhoun was here in San Diego. He'd come to see her. She had no idea if he was just passing through town, but she didn't think so.

She looked over at him as he climbed behind the wheel. Had he cut his hair and shaved because of her? "I miss your long hair and beard," she said as he started the car.

He shot her a surprised look and then chuckled as if he didn't know what to think of her and her taste. They fell into a companionable silence for a few moments as she told him how to get to the bar. "I thought traffic was bad in Cooke. I'll never complain about it again."

Geneva couldn't seem to keep the smile off her face. She was so happy to see him. "I'm glad you're here. How have you been?"

"Busy," he said. "Building a house."

"A house?"

"On the property behind the cabin. I always planned to but had never gotten around to building it."

"So, things are going well?"

He met her gaze, and to her surprise shook his head. "I've missed you."

She laughed, seeing how hard that was for him, this man of few words who kept his emotions tied down tighter than the packs on his horses. "I've missed you too."

He smiled then, so much like the old Calhoun that she felt her heart soar.

"You're doing well," he said. She could feel him studying her as he drove.

She met his gaze. "I'm doing okay."

"Do you have a place to live once your house sells?"

"Mitzi, my old friend, has offered me their guesthouse for as long as I need it."

"Really?" He seemed surprised by that. "The one who blackmailed Lucian?"

"That's the one. We'd been friends for too long to let the friendship go." She shrugged. "Life's funny."

"Isn't it?" They'd reached a small out-of-the-way tavern. Because it was early, the place was almost empty. Still, they sat outside under an umbrella, where they were entirely alone.

"Tell me about the house you built," she said, feeling as nervous as he looked. What was he doing here? She hated to get her hopes up and kept tamping them down, but still, him being here kept reaffirming her hope that he'd come to see her for a reason.

"The house isn't anything special. Certainly nothing like you're used to."

The bartender brought out the beers they'd ordered.

"I never wanted that house. It was too big, too much, but Lucian…" She shrugged. "I hope it sells today. That would make me very happy. I put down a large down payment. It would be nice to get that back, and I guess the market is really hot right now. My Realtor thinks the house might go into a bidding war and I'll get more than I paid for it."

"I suppose you have plans for the money, another house?" he asked.

She shook her head and cupped the beer bottle to keep her hands from shaking. "I'm not staying here." She saw his surprise.

"But you have friends here. I thought you've always lived here."

Geneva nodded. "You do realize this is the most I've ever heard you say. I thought all you ever did was grunt and answer questions in monosyllables. What are you doing here, Calhoun?" Sitting under the umbrella outside, drinks in front of them and Lucky curled up at their feet, she asked him again. "Isn't this your hunting season with clients?"

"My hired guide can handle it for a few days," he said, then picked up his drink and took a sip, not looking at her.

Okay, he wasn't ready to tell her. "It doesn't matter, I'm so glad to see you. It's a wonderful surprise."

"Did you sell the pickup?"

"Not yet. Lucky likes it too much." She shrugged, feeling foolish. "It has sentimental value, but not because of Lucian. Maybe despite Lucian. I don't expect anyone to understand, but it's become a sign of my freedom. Without it, I would never have had the courage to go to Montana, I would have never forced you to take me up into the mountains." She held his gaze. "I would have never met you." She saw the effect of her words on him.

He swallowed. "If you're not staying here, what are you planning to do after you sell the house?"

Geneva hoped she knew what he was asking. "I don't know. For the first time in my life—make that the second time in my life—I don't know what I'm going to do."

"I would think you'd buy another place, maybe not as large as the last one."

She shook her head. "I'm not really interested in doing that." A silence fell between them. "I've been taking painting lessons. My friend Mitzi signed me up. It's been fun. I've missed painting."

He raised an eyebrow. She wasn't sure which surprised him the most, her being friends with Mitzi again or painting classes.

"Eventually, you're going to tell me why you're here," she said as they sipped their beers. "Or do you need another beer first?"

Calhoun chuckled. "I keep thinking there is no way you could know me after just a few days in the mountains."

"Those were some few days," she said.

Lucky squirmed on the floor in the middle of a dream where she was running after something. Her legs moved, and a soft cry emitted from her throat. It must have been a good dream. Geneva reached down to pat her, and Lucky fell back into a peaceful sleep.

She felt Calhoun watching her. She'd gotten the feeling that maybe he'd come here to ask her something. Now she thought that maybe he'd changed his mind.

CALHOUN CONSIDERED THE woman across from him. She was right. What had happened between them had been so intense that they had imprinted on each other. At least that's the way Ace had explained it.

"You remember Ace?"

She raised a brow. "Your biker friend?"

"He has a master's in psychology. He tried to explain to me why I've thought about you every day since I met you and in the weeks since you left."

"You've thought about me every day?" she asked with a grin. "Funny, but I've thought about you too."

"Really?" He studied her, telling himself that she really might know him, but he knew her too. At least he knew the woman he'd spent that time with in Cooke City. Seeing her house here in San Diego and her, he'd thought she was a stranger. But she wasn't. Still, she was out of his league even if Ace had been right about there being a connection between them, one that felt strong enough that he was sitting here about to ask her—

"How long are you staying?" she asked.

"I fly back this evening. I know it's a quick trip, but..."

"You almost didn't stay to see me earlier. I was afraid you were leaving without saying a word."

He nodded, embarrassed at how close he'd come to chickening out. "I wasn't even sure you'd want to see me."

They ordered another beer as the sun went down. Calhoun would have to head to the airport soon. He'd booked a return flight for later, telling himself that once Geneva turned him down, the best thing he could do was get home.

"So, tell me more about the house you've been building," she said. "After all, daylight's burning."

He smiled, remembering how many times he'd told her the same thing. "It's a proper house on my property behind the cabin. The cabin will still be where I work out of. Clients like it." He shrugged. "It's…authentic."

"Like you."

He grinned at that and rubbed his jaw, thinking how unauthentic he felt being here dressed the way he was in dress pants and shirt. He hadn't been able to give up his boots though, but he'd left his hat at home.

"So, this house," she said, when he hesitated.

"Three bedrooms, running water, heat and a view I think you'd like," he said, warming to his subject. "A person could live there year-round, but wouldn't have to."

She smiled and nodded. "What would a person do in this house?"

"They could paint, or they could spend the summer and fall in the mountains and leave in the winter. Go somewhere warm. Like…" he glanced toward the window "…like here, I suppose." He shifted his gaze back to her.

"Seems like you've given this some thought," she teased. "Ace help you out with this?"

He laughed, knowing how foolish it sounded. It felt good to laugh though. He could almost breathe, even with his heart still pounding. "Ace did say a few things that made sense. He and a lot of other people in town helped with the house. Full disclosure, it isn't finished. I thought I should get some advice from someone knowledgeable about such things as to how to finish and furnish it."

She leaned closer. "Sounds interesting. Tell me more."

Calhoun felt his mouth go dry. He shook his head and looked away for a moment before he met her gaze again. "I'd say this was the scariest thing I'd ever done, except I've already lived that when I thought I'd gotten you killed. Would you want to…? Hell, I can't believe I'm here, let alone saying this." He looked away. "I've always done okay with women." His gaze came back to her. "But you. You make me feel like the first time I asked a girl I liked to my birthday party back in grade school."

She laughed. "Are you asking me to your birthday party?"

He let out a sigh, his gaze locking with hers. "The problem is that I don't have much to offer a woman like you."

She raised an eyebrow. "A woman like me?"

"You know what I mean." He swore. "I knew this was a mistake. I shouldn't have listened to Ace."

"You're taking advice about me from your biker friend? What did he tell you to do?"

"To come down here and tell you how I feel."

Geneva leaned back and raised both palms up. "How do you feel?"

"Right now? Foolish. You and I, we live such different lives. Ace doesn't know what he's talking about."

"When you aren't feeling foolish and blaming Ace, how do you feel?"

He met her gaze and held it. "You're enjoying my discomfort."

"A little," she admitted. "If it helps, I know how you feel, like this thing between you and me happened too fast, the feelings can't be real, we hardly know each other, and yet…"

He nodded and picked up his beer. "How did this happen?"

She shook her head. "We went through a lot in the days we were together. We got to know each other quickly and rather…intimately because of it."

"We'd be fools to rush into anything," he said. "I mean, even if you wanted to come back with me to Cooke to see if it could work, you might hate it, you might realize you didn't like me anymore than you liked winter there, but to ask you to just come with me…"

"If you're asking if it will take marriage to get me to go with you…" She shook her head, still looking amused by his dilemma. "Here's a thought. Maybe we should at least kiss again. Maybe there isn't any chemistry anymore and your problem is solved."

He chuckled, seeing that she was teasing him. But he did relax a little as he leaned toward her. He'd wanted to kiss her from the moment she'd come out of her house.

Mitzi would have called it the Kiss Test. Only Geneva wasn't worried. This was one test she knew they would pass. She remembered the kiss up on the mountain. It had kept her going from the day she drove away from him until this moment.

Calhoun drew her to him, gazes locked, and then he kissed her, stealing her breath, sending her heart off at a gallop. The chemistry had only grown stronger. It was like lightning high in the mountains. It rattled through her, igniting desire and passion and sending a fiery heat to her center.

When they finally pulled apart, they were both breathing hard. She could tell that Calhoun had felt it as well.

"Looks like we're getting married," she said with a laugh. Before she could tell him she was only kidding, he pulled her to him and kissed her again.

"I'm just afraid you'll be disappointed. In the house. Or in me."

"Don't you realize by now that the only way you could have disappointed me was by not staying to see me today? Trust what you learned about me in Montana, not what you think you see down here in San Diego."

Calhoun took her hand. "I haven't been able to get you off my mind. You're all I've thought about. I've never felt like this. I want to marry you, but don't say anything right now."

"Calhoun—" her voice broke.

"Just listen." He took a breath. "Since the day I met you, I've done things I swore I would never do. What is it about you?" She shook her head. "How can I be saying this? I'm crazy about you. I want to marry you. I want to take you back to the house I'm building and live there with you. But that's my heart talking. My head is telling me it will never work. But I want you so bad. Tell me if I'm completely off my rocker for thinking you and I…"

She shook her head. "That you and I are falling in love?" He kissed her again. The next time they pulled apart, they just looked at each other as if equally shocked by the passionate feelings between them. Her heart was pounding, and she was having trouble catching her breath. "Is this really happening?"

He nodded as if understanding how she was feeling. "I want to make you happy. Is it possible that you could be happy up there with me?"

She cupped his freshly shaven cheek. "I think I could be happy anywhere you were. You love it in Montana. You don't want to live anywhere else."

He nodded, looking miserable. "But I would leave in the winter if it's what you wanted."

"I fell for those mountains even though sometimes they were scary. I fell for your life. I fell for you, Calhoun St. Pierre. I know it seems impossible that it could happen so quickly. But it did. I've thought about you every day since I left. All I could think about was going back, but I didn't think you would want me."

He groaned again and pulled her to him. "Want you? It's all I want and that terrifies me. But I'm here. Tell me what we're going to do about this?"

That was an easy one, she thought. "We're doing this. But I have to tell you, that marriage proposal, if that's what that was?" Geneva shook her head. "I agree we shouldn't jump into this. However, I'm warning you right now. The next time you ask me to marry you, you'll need to work on your pitch."

He laughed and pulled her to him. "I can't wait until you get to Montana."

"I'll come as soon as I sell the house."

"You flying or driving?"

She grinned. "Driving."

"OH, THAT IS so romantic," Mitzi said when she told her about Calhoun's visit. "But you can't be serious about going back to Montana. I looked that town up online. Have you seen it in the winter?"

Geneva chuckled. "I'm looking forward to it. As soon as I sign the papers on the house, it's history." It would be the last of Lucian—at least here in San Diego.

"I can't believe how much money you made on the house," her friend said. "You were so lucky to have sold when you did."

"That's me—'lucky.'"

Mitzi seemed to remember her words at Geneva's anniversary party only months ago. "I know I was jealous of you. I swear I'm not anymore. You'll invite me to your wedding, won't you?"

"We're a long way from that. I'm not jumping into another relationship. Calhoun and I are both going to see how it goes. We're both gun-shy."

"You have to admit, it's so romantic. He built a house for you."

Geneva laughed. "You might change your mind when you see it."

"I doubt that since I know how much you hated Lucian's house. It wasn't you. I'm betting Calhoun knows you better than Lucian ever did."

She liked to think that was true. "Lucky loves him and so do I, although I haven't told him. But there's going to be time."

"You're really driving to Montana in that pickup again?"

"Lucky and I like road trips. Anyway, I can take what few things I'm keeping of mine and pack them in the back. I got a camper shell for the truck. It really feels like mine now." She saw Mitzi's wistful look. "How are things with Hugh?"

"Good. When I told him about your plans, he was happy for you. He suggested we come up to see you. He's never been to Yellowstone National Park. What am I saying? Neither have I. He's suggested maybe we could travel more, something I've always wanted."

"Sounds like things are going well." She was happy for her friend. "Come visit soon." Geneva couldn't wait, knowing that, like the first time she went to Montana, this would be the adventure of her life because it would be with Calhoun.

Epilogue

It had been snowing the day Geneva and Lucky drove into Cooke City. Huge lacy flakes had fallen from the heavens as she'd parked in front of the No Parking sign in front of Calhoun's cabin. As she'd turned off the pickup's engine, she'd been thinking about that first day back in July when she'd seen the cowboy napping with his boots up on the porch railing.

That day, she'd been wondering about what kind of man Calhoun St. Pierre was and whether or not he would help her find Lucian. That day, the town had felt deserted, nothing like it had during the summer with all the traffic. Calhoun had warned her that it would get busy again come winter when snowmobiles would be roaring up and down the road. She'd sat in the pickup excited about winter.

Now, as she watched the snowfall, she smiled to herself. Just as she had that day so long ago, she loved watching it snow. It was warm in the house Calhoun had built for them. She loved the windows that overlooked the town with amazing views of the mountains. This spot was her favorite, just as Calhoun had known it would be.

She heard him come up behind her and leaned back as he nuzzled her neck. His hand went to her swollen belly to wait to feel his daughter move. She felt his contentment, so like her own as he pulled her back against him as they both looked out at the falling snow. The forecast was for two to three feet.

It didn't matter. They weren't going anywhere for a while. Lucky trotted up beside them and rose on her hind legs to rest her feet on the windowsill and look out at the world. Cooke City in the winter was beautiful. Even the buzz of snowmobiles didn't bother Geneva. Every day in the winter felt like Christmas to her. She knew it was because she'd grown up in San Diego, where the weather was much the same every day. Up here, she loved the seasons.

She also loved this house Calhoun had built for them that looked over the town. Soon there would be more of them living in this home they'd made together. She'd loved getting to choose flooring and window coverings, as well as furnishings.

It was where they'd had their first party to welcome her to town. They'd been married here, with Ace as Calhoun's best man and Mitzi as her matron of honor. They'd celebrated almost every major event in this house.

They'd been together for six months when Calhoun had asked her to marry him. It had been right before Memorial Day, right before the town would fill with tourists again for the summer season, and she and Calhoun would be going back into the mountains with clients. She loved the trips, enjoyed his clients and had learned to fly-fish on the lakes. She loved being on horseback now, feeling at home in the saddle.

It was on one of those early trips back into the mountains to check to see if the camp was ready for the first clients that he'd asked her.

The day had been perfect. Blue sky, a cool breeze coming down from the still snowcapped peaks, but warm in the sunshine. They had just ridden up and he'd gotten off his horse to drop to one knee in the new grass.

"Geneva Carrington?" She'd taken her maiden name back, telling herself that her marriage to Lucian Beck hadn't really counted.

She'd smiled at him down on one knee. "Yes?"

"You are the most challenging woman I have ever known. You've made me a better man just knowing you. When I look into those blue eyes of yours, I want to move heaven and earth—whatever it takes to see you smile, to hear you laugh. I love you, Geneva. I want to marry you. Is there any chance you'd marry me after getting to know me for the past six months?"

She'd laughed. "I thought you'd never ask."

He'd picked her up, kissing her soundly and then carrying her into the tent. Two cots had been pushed together, both covered with wildflower petals.

"Better than the first time I asked you to marry me?" he'd asked after they'd spent the afternoon making love.

"It was perfect," she'd told him snuggling against him. His beard had grown back out and so had his hair. He looked like the man she'd first met, the one she'd fallen in love with. Only now, he kept both trimmed.

"I was so afraid I couldn't make you happy here," he'd confessed.

"I've never been happier. I'm excited about opening the art gallery this summer. I had no idea there were so many artists around." She'd been painting, surprised to find a community of like-minded souls in other artists, including writers. Also, she'd been surprised that several of her watercolors had sold down at the local café—Calhoun's idea, since he said they were beautiful and showed real talent, just like her. She'd been pleased but embarrassed when he'd told her what they'd sold for.

As frugal as Calhoun had always lived, she'd been surprised to find out how much money he'd invested from his business over the years. With the money she'd made on her house in San Diego, they were more than comfortable. She loved that he was like her, believed in saving rather than spending.

"I just hope I can give you the only other thing that could make you happier," he'd said that day up in the mountains in the tent after his second proposal.

She'd looked over at him and grinned, suspecting he'd already known the news she'd been waiting to tell him. "Oh, my love, you already have."

His hand had gone to her stomach. Tears welled in his eyes as he'd kissed her. "Let's start with one, but if we get the hang of it…"

"Sure," she'd said laughing. "Maybe we could make a few more."

Now from the baby's room came the sound of crying. It was followed by a second crying child. "I believe your sons are now both awake," Geneva said. Cal was almost three. Will—named after William "Ace" Graham, local biker and friend—was two. Soon, the boys would have a sister.

"We keep this up, we're going to have to add onto this house," Calhoun joked as he went to see to their sons.

Geneva hugged the daughter growing inside her. She loved the idea of filling this house with children. Cal and Will were already riding horses. She figured her daughter would be before long as well.

Never had she imagined that this would be her life. For a moment, she thought of Lucian. She seldom did anymore. But she couldn't help wondering if he was happy for her as if he'd had a hand in this—even though he'd denied leaving the storage unit key for her to find. She knew it was silly to think he had.

Maybe it was just fate, the way she'd met Calhoun St. Pierre.

Or maybe it was destiny.

But she was thankful that she'd had the courage after finding that old black pickup to make this trip north to Montana. Beside her, Lucky leaned against her leg for a hug. Geneva reached down to pet her and looked into those big brown eyes. "What would I have done without you?" she whispered to her faithful companion.

Calhoun came out of the bedroom with a boy in each arm. The three filled the house with laughter as they headed for the kitchen. Lucky went to join them, and Geneva followed them and the enticing scent of the elk roast Calhoun had put in the oven earlier while she had made a salad.

After he sat the boys down at the table, Calhoun turned on music and stopped to dance a few steps with her before he went to see about the roast.

Her heart filled to overflowing as he began to sing along with the music, the boys joining in. Lucky began to howl, making them all laugh.

Outside, snow fell silently. Inside, Geneva watched her family with a kind of awe. This was all she'd ever wanted—and more than she had ever imagined.

Calhoun turned to see her standing there fighting tears and moved to her. They began to dance, hearts beating in time with the music and each other as their children watched in giggles.

Geneva had to laugh. However she'd ended up here, she couldn't have been more thankful. Her father would have approved.

* * * * *

A Q&A with BJ Daniels

What or who inspired you to write?
I grew up in a family of storytellers. I was only weeks old
when my parents took me on my first camping trip all over
the Northwest. I grew up camping. I still love the smell of
a canvas tent because of all the nights I would lie in my
tent and listen to the adults talking around a campfire, telling stories that always got my imagination going. I knew
early on that I wanted to be a writer. I had stories going
in my head all the time—and thought everyone else did,
too. It was a shock to find out that they didn't.

What is your daily writing routine?
I write every day even if it is only a few pages. It keeps
the story going that way. My office is four blocks from
my house in the original phone company building—one
of the first buildings in our small Montana town. I love it
because it has big glass block windows so it's really light
inside. I get there, I pour myself a Coke Zero (yes, I bought
myself an ice machine), then I turn on my computer and
go to work.

I break for lunch with my husband and our two springer
spaniels, Dot and Ace, and then it's back to work for a few
hours.

My husband has become the chef at our house so when I

get home, dinner is ready. I am very spoiled. But years ago when we met, he encouraged me to write, seeming to think I could do this. Because of him, I do.

So that's my writing routine.

Where do your story ideas come from?

Everywhere. I swear, I can be at the grocery store and overhear a conversation that sparks an idea. It's like people say what I need to hear. During my life, I've met a wide variety of people. All my experiences, all my dreams, all my mistakes in life and all the people who have touched my life contribute to my stories.

Do you have a favorite travel destination?

I fell in love with Palm Springs years ago when I was a kid. My parents were the original snowbirds. We would go south every winter. My father was a masonry contractor who worked down south until it was warm enough to go back to Montana. I love the desert. There is nothing like the winter nights down there.

What is your most treasured possession?

That's a tough one. Since we can't possess the people we love, it has to be our cabin on the lake. My father loved lakes and passed it on to me. I grew up on a lake and now have a small cabin on Fort Peck where we spend the summer. My husband and I have sixteen grandchildren that we love to share the cabin, boats, paddle boards and just the lake life with.

My father always had to have the fastest boat on the lake. I got some of that from him too. There is nothing like being on water. I think of him often when I'm there because he would have loved it—and he was my first big fan. He told me I could be anything I wanted and to not let anything keep me from it. Thanks, Dad.

What is your favorite movie?

I am a sucker for *Sweet Home Alabama*. Part of it is the music. But I also love the sense of community in the heroine's old hometown, and the friends that were there for her even when she tried to put them in her past. I love stories about lovers who find their way back to each other.

How did you meet your current love?

He was my annoying deskmate and one of my editors at the newspaper where we both worked. As annoying as he could be, I noticed how generous he was. If he brought three cookies to work, he'd share them and have none for himself. Over time, we became good friends, went out for lunch, played miniature golf. It was much later that we admitted the spark between us. That was thirty years ago. We now have sixteen grandkids between us and a wonderful life that neither of us could have dreamed.

What characteristic do you most value in your friends?

My best friend Susie is the kindest person I've ever known. She makes me a better person. She's always thinking of others. I'm fortunate to have found a bunch of super creative friends who tell their stories through the quilts they piece. They too are generous, giving of their time and their quilts.

How did you celebrate or treat yourself when you got your first book deal?

When I sold my first book, we were so broke, there was no money for a big celebration. My soon-to-be husband made me dinner that night in a beautiful condo at Big Sky that a friend had offered us. Whenever I smell garlic sizzling in a pan, I remember that night and the pasta dish he made. It was cheap but delicious. I just remember how excited he was for me, and proud. He made that night special.

Will you share your favorite reader response?
Years ago when I was writing short stories for *Woman's World*, I got a note from a woman who told me that she loved my story and thought I should write a book. It was my first fan letter.

But when it comes to an amazing response, it has to be from the woman who wrote to say her mother had died. Because her mother loved my books so much, the daughter told me that she'd buried some of my books with her mom. What an honor. To have touched someone's life with my stories is such a blessing.

Cindi Myers is the author of more than seventy-five novels. When she's not plotting new romance storylines, she enjoys skiing, gardening, cooking, crafting and daydreaming. A lover of small-town life, she lives with her husband and two spoiled dogs in the Colorado mountains.

Also by Cindi Myers

Harlequin Intrigue

Eagle Mountain: Criminal History

Mile High Mystery

Eagle Mountain: Critical Response

Deception at Dixon Pass
Pursuit at Panther Point
Killer on Kestrel Trail
Secrets of Silverpeak Mine

Eagle Mountain Search and Rescue

Eagle Mountain Cliffhanger
Canyon Kidnapping
Mountain Terror
Close Call in Colorado

Eagle Mountain: Search for Suspects

Disappearance at Dakota Ridge
Conspiracy in the Rockies
Missing at Full Moon Mine
Grizzly Creek Standoff

Visit the Author Profile page at Harlequin.com.

MILE HIGH MYSTERY

Cindi Myers

For Jim. Always.

Chapter One

The storm-swelled creek roared like a jet engine readying for takeoff as it rushed through the narrow canyon. The normally shallow trickle of water was now a torrent, tearing great chunks of earth and rocks from its banks and carrying broken branches and whole trees along in its wake. On the other side of the cataract, a group of campers clustered around several vehicles, cut off from escape by the rushing water.

Zach Gregory stopped at the edge of the water, alongside his fellow Eagle Mountain Search and Rescue members, and studied the situation. They had to find a way to get the stranded campers to this side of the swollen creek, even as rain continued to pour. He counted at least six adults, several children and three dogs. All of them were drenched. Even in rain gear, Zach felt cold and damp, rain lashing his face and seeping past his collar and down the back of his neck. He moved up alongside fellow SAR volunteer Caleb Garrison. "How are we supposed to get over to the camp?" he shouted to be heard above the din of the water.

Caleb pointed downstream. Zach followed his gaze and leaned forward to get a better look. The creek channel widened into an open area, the water forming a wide pool, the current much less swift. Newly elected SAR captain

Danny Irwin motioned for the group to move toward this pool, and they set out, splashing through puddles and slipping in mud and on slick rock as they shouldered the rescue gear they had carried from the nearest road. The main route to the campground was washed out, and the weather had been deemed too bad to risk bringing in a helicopter to airlift the stranded campers. With conditions only expected to worsen, the forest service, Rayford County Sheriff's Department and Eagle Mountain Search and Rescue had decided to attempt a land evacuation.

Away from the swiftest water, the roar dulled enough to make conversation possible. "We're going to shoot a line across to that group of trees over there." Danny indicated the clump of piñons up the bank. "We'll attach instructions for someone on the other side to secure the line. Then we'll send a group over to assess everyone and send them back across, one at a time."

Someone unpacked the chunky, red line-throwing gun, which used compressed air to propel a coil of strong cable across a chasm. Volunteer Ryan Welch handled firing the gun. A crowd had gathered on the opposite bank, and two men ran to retrieve the other end of the line as soon as it hit the trees. They unwrapped the note and sent a thumbs-up signal across, then began fastening their end to the trees, while Ryan and Eldon Ramsey secured the cable on this side.

"Think it will hold?" Ryan asked Danny when the line was secure.

"Only one way to find out." Danny looked around. "Any volunteers to go first?"

Silence as they contemplated the turbulent gray water rushing beneath the thin line. Fall into that, and even with a life jacket, you could be in trouble.

"I'll go." Zach stepped forward.

Danny looked him up and down. "I guess if the line will hold you, it will hold anyone," he said. "Get suited up, and we'll give it a try."

Five minutes later, fitted with a helmet and personal flotation device, Zach slipped a harness over his hips, clipped onto the line and grabbed hold of the strap attached to a pulley on the line. Tony Meisner clapped him on the back. "Ready?"

Zach barely had time to nod before Tony pushed him and he was sliding down the line across the water. The cable sagged beneath his weight, and he felt spray from the churning water splash onto his legs as he skimmed over the creek. But the cable held. If not for the driving rain and heavy pack on his back, it might have been a fun trip, like riding a zip line on vacation.

Two men rushed to greet him as he landed on the opposite shore and helped him off the line. The radio attached to his shoulder crackled. "I'm sending Hannah and Sheri over next, so get ready," Danny said.

Paramedic Hannah Richards and former captain Sheri Stevens arrived in quick succession. They were greeted by a growing crowd as additional campers gathered beside the creek. Zach followed Sheri and Hannah into a chaos of wet and anxious campers. Dogs barked, children cried and everyone seemed to be talking at once. Everyone was muddy, wet and frightened. "We woke up, and there was water running through our tent," one man told Zach. "My oldest boy left the tent to go pee, and he almost fell in the river."

"There's a tree down on an RV at the back of the campground," another man said. "I think someone might be hurt."

"My husband was hurt by a falling branch," a woman said. She hefted a toddler on her hip. The child—a girl, judging by the pink barrettes in her hair—stared at Zach, her thumb in her mouth. "He's over by our trailer, but someone needs to look at him."

Hannah keyed her radio. "We've got some terrified kids over here," she said. "And some of the adults aren't in much better shape. Apparently, a tree came down on an RV, and there may be injuries or people trapped inside. We've got other injuries from falling trees. We need people over here to administer first aid. And a couple of people to ride with the kids back across wouldn't hurt."

"I'll send people over, and we'll start the process of getting people over to this side," Danny said.

"Zach, start gathering people who are ready to get out of here," Sheri said. "Make sure they know they've got to ride across that line, so only a small backpack or a bag they can carry in one hand can go with them. Everything else has to stay here."

"I can't leave my dogs," one woman wailed.

"We'll get the dogs out, too," Sheri said.

Ten minutes later, Zach was sending the first of the campers back across the line. As the woman started across the water, Hannah approached Zach, carrying a blanket-wrapped small child. "This is Micah," she said. "He's three, and he's suffering from hypothermia. I've tucked some hot packs in around him, but he needs to get to someplace warm and dry ASAP. I'm sending his mom right behind you." She put the child into Zach's arms.

Zach stared down into a pair of frightened brown eyes. Micah had his thumb stuffed into his mouth and said nothing, though tears—or maybe raindrops—slid down his flushed cheeks.

"It's okay, baby." A petite woman, dark hair plastered to her head, stood on tiptoe and stroked Micah's face. Then she looked up at Zach. "Don't drop him," she said.

Zach tightened his grip on the child. "I won't."

Traveling back across the river was much slower than the original traverse, since it required being towed uphill by volunteers on the other side. Halfway across, Micah began to squirm and wail. Zach held tight and tried to talk soothingly, though he was terrified he would drop the squirming child, despite them being clipped into safety lines He sagged with relief when fellow team member Carrie Andrews stepped forward to take the boy from him, then he stepped to one side a few moments later to allow Micah's mom to reunite with her son.

The next hour was a blur of traveling back and forth across the flooded creek. The rain stopped and the sun came out, and Zach began to sweat in the heavy rain gear, but it was too much trouble to divest himself of pack, life vest and harness, so he left everything on and focused on the work. He carried another child across, transported medical gear and escorted a frantic, snapping golden retriever who was determined not to be harnessed to anything. Zach was only able to get the dog to cooperate when someone produced a packet of beef jerky, which Zach fed, bit by bit, to the trembling dog all the way back across the water.

After the dog, there were only two more adults to get back across, and they didn't need Zach's help. He shed the harness and layers of gear and drank a bottle of water someone handed him. A tall blonde woman he hadn't seen before, one of the campers, he supposed, moved through the volunteers. "Thank you so much," she said to each one. When she got to Zach, she took his hand. "You were amazing."

"I was happy to do it," Zach said. It felt good to help other people, to make a difference.

She smiled, showing dimples. "I'm Janie. What's your name?"

"Zach. Zach Gregory."

"Well, Zach Gregory, you and the other volunteers are real heroes," she said, then surprised him with a hug.

He stepped back, a little embarrassed but also pleased. He hadn't joined Search and Rescue for the adulation, but who didn't like to feel they had done something good for someone else?

"How is it you rate a hug and all I get is a handshake?" Caleb grinned at Zach after the woman had moved away.

"I guess I'm just lucky."

"Right. I'm sure that's all it was." Caleb punched him in the shoulder, then moved on to help gather up their gear.

Zach bent and picked up his harness, helmet and rain gear. At six foot four and 230 pounds, he was used to attracting attention, and women seemed to like his looks, but he preferred to stay in the background.

"You did great out there today," Sheri said as she joined him in collecting gear. "You stayed calm, and you kept everyone else calm."

"Thanks." This was the kind of praise Zach preferred— for the job he did, not for how he looked.

"Uh-oh." He and Sheri both turned at this exclamation from Ryan. Across the river, Hannah, Eldon, Deputy Jake Gwynn and Forest Ranger Nate Hall stood around a fifth figure on the ground.

"Jake and Nate went to search the RV that was damaged by the fallen tree," Sheri said. "They must have found someone hurt."

They hurried to join Danny, who was on the radio. "We'll send a litter over," Danny said. "Secure the body, and we'll bring it over."

"Is there a fatality?" Sheri asked when Danny ended the transmission.

He nodded. "I don't have any details. Jake and Nate found her near a van hit by a fallen tree."

While some team members prepared to bring the body to this side of the creek, Zach and the others gathered their gear and escorted the rest of the civilians up the trail to the road, where sheriff's deputies and Forest Service employees, along with a few of the campers' relatives and friends, waited to drive them back to the town of Eagle Mountain.

They were packing up to leave when a solemn procession came up the trail—Ranger Hall, followed by Jake, Eldon, Hannah and Danny with the litter bearing a wrapped body. They stopped beside the Search and Rescue vehicle and lowered their burden. Sheriff Travis Walker, in muck boots and a yellow slicker over his khaki uniform, came to meet them. "What have you got?" he asked.

"Her ID says her name is Claire Watson, from Maryland," Jake, who was a sheriff's deputy as well as a Search and Rescue volunteer, said. "None of the other campers seem to know her. We found her under a tree just outside of a rental van. She was probably trying to get away when the tree caught and pinned her." He folded back the blanket covering her. "You can see she was hit pretty hard in the back of the head."

Zach started to look away, but something about the woman's thick brown hair and high white forehead made him look again. He shuddered and went cold all over. "Cammie!"

He didn't realize he'd said the name out loud until the sheriff put a hand on his shoulder. "Do you know her?" Travis asked.

Zach took a step closer and stood over the body. This couldn't be real. He put out a hand as if to touch her, but Travis grabbed his arm and held it. "Zach," he said, his voice firm. "Zach, do you know this woman?"

Zach sucked in a breath, trying to pull himself together. He nodded, then said, "Yes," though the word came out as more of a croak. He was vaguely aware of the other team members gathered around, staring at him.

"How do you know her?" Travis asked.

Instead of answering the sheriff, Zach looked at Jake. "Could I see her arm?" he asked. "Her left arm."

Jake glanced at Travis, who nodded. Jake bent and peeled back the blanket enough to untuck the dead woman's arm. She was wearing a long-sleeved fleece top, blue with white trim. Zach swallowed hard. "Is there a tattoo?" he asked. "Just above her left wrist?"

Jake pushed up the sleeve, and suddenly Zach couldn't breathe. He stared at the blue-and-green butterfly tat, no larger than a dollar coin, the name Laney in script beneath it. He closed his eyes, and Travis gripped his shoulder, steadying him. "Do you know her?" Travis asked again.

Jake nodded and opened his eyes. "That's my sister," he said. "That's Camille. Camille Gregory."

"When was the last time you saw your sister?" Travis asked.

Zach choked back a moan. This couldn't be happening. How could it possibly be happening? Travis repeated the question. Zach forced himself to look at the sheriff. "Four years ago," he said. "At her funeral." Then, to make sure Travis understood, "My sister, Camille, died four years ago."

Chapter Two

Zach sat in the gray-walled interview room at the sheriff's department, gaze fixed on the unopened bottle of water in front of him, but all he saw was Camille. Not the pale, dead woman who had lain on that litter, but Camille as she had been in life—smiling, quick-witted, so smart it took his breath away. Losing her had been the worst thing that had ever happened to him. Was it true that she had been alive all this time and he hadn't known it? That she had died again so close to him and he hadn't been aware that she was here?

The door to the interview room opened, and Sheriff Walker and his brother, Sergeant Gage Walker, entered. "How are you holding up?" Gage asked. A little taller than his brother, the more outgoing of the two, Gage rested a comforting hand on Zach's shoulder. "Do you want some coffee or something?"

Zach shook his head. "No thanks." He looked to Travis. "Can you tell me what's going on?"

Travis slid out a chair across from Zach and sat, while Gage leaned against the wall behind him. "Maybe you can help us fill in some gaps," the sheriff said. "You say your sister's name was Camille?"

"That's right. Camille Louise Gregory."

"How old was she?" Travis asked.

"She was two years older than me," Zach said. "She was twenty-six when we buried her."

"The driver's license we found says this woman was thirty," Travis said.

"That's how old Camille would have been now." Zach massaged his forehead, trying to subdue the pain pounding there. "I don't understand any of this. What was she doing at that campground? And you said she was in a van?"

"The driver's license in her purse identified her as Claire Watson," Travis said. "Does that name mean anything to you?"

"No. I've never heard it before."

"You said you last saw your sister four years ago. At her funeral. So you saw her actual body?"

"No. It was a closed casket. The officers…" He swallowed past the knot in his throat. "The officers who found her body, and the funeral home people, said it would be better that way. But they were sure it was Camille. And my parents identified the body."

"How did your sister die?" Gage asked.

"She was murdered."

The brothers exchanged a look he couldn't decipher. "Who murdered her?" Travis asked.

Zach took a deep breath, though it was hard, as if someone sat on his chest. "The case is officially unsolved, but she was probably killed by one of the Chalk brothers or someone they hired." At the sheriff's puzzled look, he added, "They're a family in Houston, where we're from. Wealthy businessmen, but they're crooks. You can check with the FBI. They have a file on the Chalk family."

"Why would they kill your sister?" Gage asked.

"She had agreed to testify against them. Two of the brothers—Charlie and Christopher—were charged in the murder of a district court judge. Camille was there that night, at the restaurant where it happened. She testified about what she saw, but the brothers were acquitted." He shook his head. That whole ordeal had been a blur, and time hadn't clarified his memory.

"And you think the Chalk brothers were responsible for your sister's death?"

"That's what the FBI told us they suspected, though there was no evidence they could use to convict the brothers of the crime. They said she was gunned down leaving work—another restaurant job. My parents went to identify the body, and we had the funeral—so how did she turn up here, in Colorado, four years later?"

"You're sure this woman is your sister?" Travis asked. "You couldn't have made a mistake?"

"Camille had a tattoo like that—the butterfly with the name Laney. What are the odds that another woman would have that same tattoo in the same location?"

"Who was Laney?" Gage asked.

"Our sister. Camille's twin. She died when the girls were eleven. Meningitis."

Both brothers were still looking at him like they didn't believe him. "Check with the FBI," Zach said. "I'm sure every bit of this is in Camille's file."

"Does the name Carla Drinkwater mean anything to you?" Travis asked.

"No. Who is she?"

"The van this woman was driving was rented under the name Carla Drinkwater. She had a second driver's license in that name."

He felt dizzy again, like he was falling. He grabbed the bottle of water, twisted off the lid and drank. When he set the bottle down again, his head was a little clearer. "How did she die?" he asked. "I heard something about a tree falling on the van."

"We were waiting to hear back from the medical examiner's preliminary exam," Travis said. "Apparently this woman—Carla or Claire or Camille—was stabbed in the chest. She had been dead several hours by the time that tree fell. I've got deputies out talking to as many of the campers who were in that area as we can find, to try to determine if any of them saw anyone else near her campsite."

"None of this makes sense," Zach said. "You're telling me my sister was murdered—twice?"

"We're still not certain this woman was your sister," Travis said. "How could she be, if your sister died four years ago?"

"I don't know the answer to that," Zach said. "But I'm sure this was Camille. I know my own sister. Can't you get dental records? Or DNA? You can compare it to my DNA. Or my parents—" He stopped. "Have you contacted my parents?"

"Where are your parents?" Gage asked.

"They live in Junction. They came here not long after Camille…after we thought we had buried her. To make a fresh start."

"But you've only been here a few months," Travis said.

They must have checked out his background. Or maybe one of his fellow SAR volunteers had mentioned he was new to the group. "Nine months. I moved around a little before I came here to be closer to my parents." He should have stayed with them all along, but he had been so torn up about Camille. It had been a long time before he had been able to think straight and realize he had a duty to look after his parents. He was all they had left. "You need to let me break this to them," he said. "But not until we figure out what's going on."

"Until we have a positive identification, we don't see the need to involve anyone else," Travis said.

"Good." Zach nodded. "They've been through enough." Losing Laney had crushed them. Losing Camille fifteen years later had almost destroyed them.

"Is there anything else you can tell us about your sister that might help us identify her or her killer?" Travis asked. "Do you have any idea why she was in Eagle Mountain?"

"I don't know," he said. "Unless she was here to see me." He swallowed again, fighting a surge of emotion. "Camille and I were close. Especially after Laney died." After her funeral, he had struggled to accept that she was gone from his life.

He had told himself at the time he was indulging in wishful thinking. But apparently, he hadn't been entirely wrong. Camille hadn't been dead then. So was she really gone now?

SPECIAL AGENT SHELBY DRYDEN's first thought upon meeting Camille's brother at his home in Eagle Mountain was that the photograph in Zachary Gregory's file did not do him justice. She knew all the particulars by heart—six foot four, broad shoulders, dark hair, dark eyes. But the file—and the grainy photo that accompanied it—hadn't conveyed the man's brooding nature, the sensual quality of his lips or the heavy-lidded gaze that lent a seductive air to his expression, though she was certain that was not what he had in mind. If anything, Zach Gregory looked thoroughly upset with her. And she couldn't really blame him. Five minutes ago, he hadn't known she existed.

Rather than prolong the inevitable, as soon as he opened his door and she introduced herself and showed him her credentials, she had announced that the woman found dead in that Forest Service campground that morning was indeed his sister, Camille Gregory, aka Claire Watson, that she had been in the Witness Security Program for the past four years and that she had disappeared from her home in Maryland five days ago.

"I understand why you're angry, Mr. Gregory," she said, keeping her voice low in case any of the neighbors in the townhomes around them were eavesdropping. She had driven to Zach's home immediately after confirming Camille's death with the local sheriff's department. She had taken the first flight available from Houston to Junction after the sheriff's department had contacted the FBI with news of Camille's death. Apparently, Zach had been on the scene when Camille's body had been found—not at all what Shelby or anyone else involved would have wanted. Now it was up to her to try to calm him down and find out how much he knew. "As terrible as this was for you and your family, we had to make you believe Camille had died. It was for your own protection. And for hers."

"You didn't do a very good job of protecting her if she's dead now," he said. "If she's really dead this time."

"Yes, she's really dead this time." Shelby glanced to either side. "Could I please come in and talk about this?"

He stepped aside, and she moved past him into the townhome's front room, aware of his bulk looming over her. Camille had referred to her brother as a gentle bear of a man, but Shelby sensed none of that gentleness now. She was used to people being angry with her, but they were usually people who had broken the law or failed to cooperate in an investigation. Zach Gregory was the first she had encountered whose anger she understood. In his shoes, she might have wanted to break someone in half.

He closed the door and turned to face her again. "Let me see your ID again."

She held up her Bureau-issued identification. He peered at it, then at her, and she felt his gaze to her core. Weighing her. Judging whether or not he could trust her. "Shelby Dryden. I don't remember you from the trial."

"If you mean the Chalk brothers trial, I wasn't there." She tucked the ID back into her pocket. "I met your sister after she went into witness security."

"They told us she had been murdered, gunned down by an unknown shooter on her way home from work. They said she had refused a security detail, and that they had no suspects in her death. They said they were very sorry." His mouth was grim, but his eyes had the bottomless look of someone who was beyond exhaustion.

She wanted to take his hand. To try to comfort him. But there wasn't any way to make this whole ugly mess better. Instead, she looked toward the sofa and chairs arranged in front of a fireplace on one side of the large, open living room. "Let's sit down," she said. "And I'll try to answer all your questions."

He followed her and dropped onto the sofa, while she sat on the edge of a low-backed, upholstered armchair on his left. All the furniture looked new, which fit with the information she had, that he had lived in Eagle Mountain less than a year. His home was neat, but as impersonal as a hotel, with no photographs or art on the walls, no books or magazines on the coffee or end tables. The only sign that anyone really lived here was a half glass of water and a half-eaten sandwich on a paper napkin on the table beside the sofa. She must have interrupted him eating dinner.

"Tell me what's going on," he said. "The truth, this time."

She nodded and smoothed her palms down her thighs. "Just know that your sister wasn't forced into anything," she said. "Going into witness security was her choice, as was the decision to fake her death and not tell her family. She felt doing anything else would put you all in too much danger, and we had to agree."

"And she went where? To Maryland?"

"Yes. She started a new life there. She had a town-house in a nice neighborhood and a job as office manager of a small insurance agency. She made friends. She had a good life."

His expression didn't soften. "She didn't have her family."

"No. And I know she missed you all. She talked about you sometimes." She especially talked about Zach. How she worried her death would send her little brother off course. Camille had blamed herself for putting him in danger, though Shelby had tried to convince her this wasn't the case.

"So what happened?" Zach asked. "Why is she dead now? And why was she even here? Why was she camping?"

"Maybe she thought camping was a good way to hide out. I think she was trying to reach you," Shelby said. "I think she wanted to tell you something. Or warn you about something."

"Warn me about what?"

"I don't know. But looking back on conversations we had before she disappeared, I think she believed the Chalk brothers had learned something that put you in danger. She wanted to warn you to be careful."

"So the Chalk brothers killed her?"

"Probably someone who worked for them, but yes, that's what we believe."

"But you don't have proof." He shook his head. "There's never any proof. Or enough proof. My sister put her life on the line. She sat in that courtroom and told them everything she saw that night at the restaurant. She saw that judge die, and the Chalk brothers were the only ones there, but it wasn't enough to put them behind bars."

"She didn't see the shots fired," Shelby said.

"She heard them!" he protested.

"She couldn't swear there wasn't anyone else there that night. The defense team took advantage of that."

"You know they killed that judge."

She nodded. "Yes. We believe they lured the judge to the restaurant that night. Possibly they offered him money. Instead, they killed him. But knowing isn't enough. We have to have proof."

He leaned forward, elbows on his knees, face buried in his hands. He wore jeans and a blue plaid flannel shirt open over a gray T-shirt. The muscles of his back and arms strained the shirt. He looked like a mountain man. Someone strong and capable, not the baby brother Camille had worried about so much. Shelby waited, giving him time. The house was so silent, not even traffic noises coming from outside.

At last, he raised his head. His eyes were red rimmed, but he looked less angry now. "What are you doing here?" he asked. "Doesn't the US Marshals Service handle witness protection? Or witness security—whatever you call it? Why is the FBI involved?"

"The US Marshals Service is in charge of witness security," she said. "But the FBI is still actively investigating the Chalk brothers. And we will investigate your sister's murder."

"So you drew the short straw and had to talk to me?"

"I volunteered for that." She leaned forward a little more. "Camille was my friend. I know how much you meant to her. Talking to you was something I could do for her."

The grief that flashed across his face was so raw her own eyes stung with tears. He looked away, the skin along his jaw white as he clenched his teeth, his throat convulsing as he swallowed.

She stood and retrieved the glass of water and handed it to him. He took it and drank, then froze and stared at her. "What about my parents? Did you send someone to talk to them, too?" He stood. "I should be there with them. I was waiting until we knew more about what had happened before I talked to them."

"I was planning on talking to them after I visited with you," she said. "We can go together."

He didn't sit back down but rubbed a hand over his face. "Are they safe? Will whoever killed Camille go after them next?"

He wasn't worried about his own safety, only his parents'. That fit with everything Camille had told her. "Junction Police have been alerted to keep an eye on them, but we don't believe they're in any danger." Zach might be a different story, if Camille's suspicions were true. "Sit down and talk to me," Shelby said. "I have some questions I need to ask you, then we'll visit your parents."

He sat, perched on the edge of the sofa, as if prepared to spring up again at any second. "What about my questions? Are you going to tell me what really happened?"

"I'll tell you as much as I can."

He didn't look happy with that answer but pushed on. "You say she disappeared? What do you mean? Was she, like, monitored or something?"

"She had a team with the Marshals Service who kept an eye on her. Not exactly bodyguards, but they watched for anything unusual that might pose a threat, and we— the FBI and the Marshals—tried to stay alert to any developments with the Chalk brothers that might indicate they had located her. And she and I talked every few days."

"Because you were her friend?"

"Yes. And because I'm still involved in the case. She would share anything she remembered about the Chalk brothers in general and that night at the restaurant in particular."

He stilled, as if suddenly transformed into a statue. "Zach?" she asked.

He shook his head, as if to clear it. "Did she tell you anything new?" he asked.

"Nothing big. But sometimes she would remember little details that hadn't come out at the trial. Like she had seen the brothers in the restaurant two weeks before the judge's murder, with a third man. We haven't been able to identify that man, but we're working on it. I stopped by her townhouse four days ago to show her some photographs, to see if she recognized anyone in them, and realized she was gone."

"How did you know she was gone?"

"She had a cat. A gray tabby she named Peter. She had given it to her boss's daughter at the insurance agency. She told the girl she couldn't keep it anymore." Sadness threatened to overwhelm her, and she looked away.

"Camille always loved cats," he said.

Shelby nodded. "I knew if she had given Peter away, that meant she didn't think she would be coming back."

"Where did you think she had gone?"

"I thought at first she had decided to strike out on her own. It happens. People get tired of being watched and protected. Or they believe they'll be safer. They move somewhere else—overseas, out West, to Alaska. They take a new name and start a new life. Most of them know a lot about how to do that because they've been in the program. Some of them are even successful. Some of them return to the program after a while."

"And some of them die," he said.

"Yes. People enter witness security because their life is in danger. If that threat hasn't gone away, they are always vulnerable to being discovered and eliminated."

"And you think that's what happened to Camille? She was...eliminated?"

"We're still piecing together exactly what happened, but people who get in the Chalk brothers' way usually end up dead."

"And no one is stopping them."

"We're trying," she said. "That's why I'm here now."

"Showing up after Camille is dead doesn't really help anything."

The words hurt. He probably meant them, too. But she was good at hiding her feelings. It was practically a requirement in the Bureau. No one wanted the reputation of being too soft—especially not a woman. "I already told you, I believe Camille was near Eagle Mountain because she wanted to see you," she said. "She was worried you were in danger."

"So she came here to warn me. But why would I be in danger?"

She met his gaze. "I don't know. She wouldn't tell me. I was hoping you had some idea. Do you know something that would upset the Chalk brothers? Maybe something you haven't mentioned before."

"No. And it's been four years since their trial. Why come after me now?"

"If the Chalk brothers thought you knew something about the judge's murder that hasn't come out yet, they might go after you. Maybe something Camille told you that she forgot."

"The Chalk brothers were already acquitted of that murder," he said. "It wouldn't matter if there was new evidence or not, would it?"

"Only if the evidence implicated someone else," she said.

"Then the Chalk brothers ought to be giving the person who could provide that evidence a medal, not trying to kill them. Their whole case was built on the idea that some mysterious third person stepped out of nowhere to kill the judge and they were innocent bystanders." His face twisted in disgust.

"So you're positive your sister never contacted you. Maybe on social media? She might have used a false name—Claire or Carla, or even Gladys."

"Gladys?" That surprised a harsh laugh from him.

Shelby forced herself not to squirm. "She had a couple of social media accounts under that name. She never posted, but she read other people's posts. Maybe she read yours."

"I don't do social media," he said.

"Never?"

He met her gaze again, his expression hard. "Having the FBI questioning me about every aspect of my life for the year before the Chalk brothers trial made me value my privacy." He stood and stared down at her.

She rose also, though she still felt small beside him. "I'm probably going to have more questions," she said. "I need you to answer them to help me find whoever killed Camille."

"It doesn't matter if you find them if you don't have the right proof," he said. "That's what it came down to with the Chalk brothers before, isn't it? We all know they murdered that judge, but they got away with it. And they probably killed Camille, too. Do you really think you're going to make any difference this time?"

"I'm going to try."

He shook his head. "Go for it, then. Just don't expect me to be any help." He scooped up his keys from the table by the door. "I'm going to see my parents now. You don't have to come."

"I can answer questions for them that you can't." She

followed him out the door. "And I'm required to be the one to officially notify them."

"Suit yourself."

She followed him to his truck. When he unlocked it, she opened the passenger door and slid inside. He frowned at her. "You can follow me in your vehicle," he said.

"It's better this way." She fastened her seat belt. She had made the trip from Junction once today. The hour-long drive would give her time to study him and get to know him better.

She felt sorry for Zach, losing his sister not once but twice. But she couldn't let pity get in the way of doing her job. And she was convinced he was lying to her about something. He wasn't going to get rid of her until she found out the truth.

Chapter Three

Zach tried to focus on the dark highway and the terrible task ahead of him—informing his parents that everything they thought they knew about Camille's death was wrong, but that she was more lost to them now than ever. But the woman beside him drew his attention away from these thoughts. He couldn't see her well in the darkness, but every nerve tingled with awareness of her—the vanilla-and-flowers scent of her perfume or lotion, subtle and sexy. Though why anything about an FBI agent should be sexy to him, he couldn't fathom. The agents who had dogged his family every waking hour after Camille agreed to testify against the Chalk brothers had been nothing but annoying.

None of them had been women. None of them had spoken to the family with Shelby Dryden's warmth or compassion. As much as he wanted to resent her for her part in keeping Camille's existence from him, he had a hard time holding on to his anger. Shelby had known Camille in her new life. She said she had been Camille's friend.

He believed that. He could see similarities between Agent Dryden and his sister. Not physical similarities, but they both had the ability to connect with others. Camille had been a great restaurant server, always pulling in big tips because she had a talent for zeroing in on the best way to put a customer at ease. People would confide all kinds of personal secrets to her, then thank her for listening to them. They seemed to sense that Camille truly did care about the lives of everyone she met.

He felt that in Shelby Dryden, too. When she said she was sorry for his loss, the words didn't come across as a rote platitude. She really did care. And he thought she mourned Camille's death and maybe even took her murder personally.

"Thanks for agreeing to take me to your parents," she said, breaking the silence between them. "I think it will be easier for them than having some unknown FBI agent show up on their doorstep."

"You didn't really give me much choice. But yeah, it probably is better this way." He turned onto Eagle Mountain's main street and headed toward the highway.

"I need to ask them some of the same questions I asked you—had they heard from Camille at all? Have they seen anyone suspicious hanging around?"

"No to both questions," he said. "They would have told me if they had. They still talk about Camille all the time." Some of those conversations were painful, but they were comforting, too, keeping the memory of his sister alive. "And they would have told me if they were worried about anyone or anything."

"Do you think they would? Parents often try to protect their children from things like that."

"I'm not some little kid. And I'm supposed to protect them." His knuckles whitened as he gripped the steering wheel with more force.

They turned onto the highway and headed toward more open country. "Tell me about your mom and dad," she said. "I know what our file says, but the file only contains facts—not a lot about their personalities or emotions."

"They're very strong people," he said. Despite losing two

children under tragic circumstances, they still remained invested in life, active and involved, with many friends.

"They would have to be, to have gone through what they have."

"My dad is more outgoing, like Camille," Zach said. "He manages a hardware store and knows all the regular customers. He volunteers with the local parks board and is on the library board." Tightness pulled at his chest. "If someone wanted to find him, it would be easy enough to do."

"What about your mother?"

"She's quieter, like me. She works at home, doing accounting for small businesses. She had a really hard time during the trial. When they told us Camille had been shot, she fell apart for a while. She's been better lately, but…"

"But you worry about her," Shelby said.

He glanced at her, then back at the road. "Would you tell me if they were in any danger?"

"They're not in any danger that I'm aware of," she said. "I want to check in with them and find out if they've noticed anything we haven't."

"You didn't answer my question."

"I would tell you what I could." She paused, then added, "I have to balance an individual's desire to know with the big picture of whatever case I'm working on. Some cases require more secrecy than others."

He made a sound of disgust, low in his throat, but said nothing. Silence made a wall between them. She shifted in her seat, the fabric of her suit making a rustling sound. "Camille didn't talk about your parents much," she said after a moment. "I think it was too painful for her to do so. But she talked about you quite a bit."

A long silence. But he couldn't shut her out completely.

Not when she was his only connection to Camille. "What did she say?" he asked, finally.

"She mostly talked about good times the two of you had together. She mentioned a trip to Cancun—just the two of you. You took a taxi out to Tulum, and when you had finished sightseeing, you discovered all the taxis were gone and you had to talk your way onto a tour bus headed back to the city center."

"She did the talking," he said. "I pretty much just followed her lead."

"She had a powerful personality," Shelby said. "When someone like that dies, it leaves a big hole."

He cleared his throat. "Do you have any brothers or sisters?" he asked.

"No, I'm an only child. My father is a symphony conductor, and my mother is first chair violin in the same symphony. Our lives revolved around rehearsals and performances."

Her answer surprised him. It didn't seem like the kind of background a law enforcement officer, especially an FBI agent, would have. "Do you play an instrument?" he asked.

"Not a note. To their everlasting dismay, I have a tin ear and can't carry a tune. I'm so unlike either of them that I think sometimes they wondered if I had been switched at birth. They still don't know quite what to make of me."

"My parents don't know what to make of me, either." He ran his hands along the steering wheel, surprised by this urge to confide in her. But he felt compelled to continue. "I kind of fell apart for a while, after Camille's funeral. I moved around, never held a job for long. I know it worried my folks."

"But you're here with them now."

"I'm trying," he said. "But I'm not Camille. I'm not Laney." Those two had been the perfect kids, the shining stars. The sunny, outgoing, smart kids, loved by everyone. He was just himself. Too big and too quiet and awkward.

She made a small noise he interpreted as an expression of sympathy, but when he glanced over at her, he saw she was sitting up straight, staring into the side mirror. "What's wrong?" he asked.

"That white Toyota behind us. I'm sure I saw the same vehicle in Eagle Mountain." She leaned toward the mirror, squinting. "I think it's following us."

Her words were so startling and unexpected Zach couldn't make sense of them at first. He glanced in the rearview mirror. There were headlights in the distance, but there was nothing unusual about that. "How can you tell anything in the dark?" This wasn't like the city. Once they were away from town, the darkness engulfed them, only a sliver of moon and stars like broken glass scattered overhead.

"I've been watching it for a while now. It slows down when we slow down and speeds up when we speed up. And it's staying just far enough back that I can't see it too clearly. But I got a better look at it when we passed through that lighted crossroads a few miles back. I'm sure it's the same car I saw near your townhouse in Eagle Mountain."

"Just because you saw the car in Eagle Mountain doesn't mean it's following us," he protested. "It's probably just someone headed to Junction to shop or go to the movies," he said. "It's the closest larger town, so people from Eagle Mountain go there all the time."

"It doesn't have a front license plate," she said. "That's very convenient for a vehicle tailing another."

"Maybe it's from out of state," he said. "And there are a lot of white Toyotas around. Are you sure it's the same one?"

"I'm pretty sure. I can't make out the driver very well. Like I said, it's keeping too far back."

"I don't think we're being followed," he said. "It's just someone else going to Junction."

She settled back in the passenger seat, but tension radiated from her. "You're probably right," she said, without the least conviction in her voice.

She was beginning to freak him out, though he didn't want to show it. "I guess you're trained to notice things like that," he said.

"Yes." She glanced over her shoulder, crouching down a little, as if she didn't want the driver of the vehicle behind them to see her.

"What should I do?" he asked.

"Just drive normally."

He tried to relax and do as she asked, though his gaze returned repeatedly to the lights visible in his rearview mirror. She was right—the vehicle wasn't getting any closer, or any farther away.

They reached Junction, and Zach signaled a right turn. The vehicle that had been following them sped past, continuing straight on the highway. "Guess they weren't following us after all," Zach said.

"I guess not," she said. "Though a skilled driver might go up a block and circle back, if they wanted to throw off suspicion."

By the time he reached his parents' house, his neck ached with tension, but he hadn't seen the Toyota—or any other vehicle—since. He parked at the curb in front of his parents' house and checked the time. It was after nine. "I should have called ahead," he said. "But I didn't want to tell them about Camille over the phone."

"We'll tell them together," she said and opened the passenger door.

Zach's parents lived in a blue-and-white ranch house in a neighborhood full of homes mostly dating from the seventies and eighties, judging by the architecture. Zach led the way to the front door, Shelby just behind him. She looked around, her attitude wary. Was she searching for signs of trouble or the person she thought had followed them here?

He rang the bell and had to wait a long minute before he heard the door unlocking. His father peered out. "Zach!" he said, then looked past him to Shelby. "Is everything okay?"

"Can we come in and talk to you and Mom?" he asked.

By way of an answer, his father stepped aside. Zach moved past him into the living room, Shelby on his heels. Zach's mother looked up from the sofa, where she was reading, dressed in blue-striped pajamas. While Zach's dad had his son's coloring and facial features, on a much smaller frame, his mother was the image of Camille, older and softer. She looked to Shelby. "Hello?" she asked, a question in her voice.

"Mom, Dad, this is Special Agent Shelby Dryden," Zach said.

His mom's expression changed to one of alarm at the words *special agent*. His father moved to sit beside his wife. "What's this about? Has something happened?"

Zach sat across from his mother. Shelby took the chair beside him. Zach had tried to think of how to break this news to his parents, but there was no easy way. "You've heard of the Witness Protection Program, right?" he asked.

"Oh, Zach." His mother covered her mouth with one hand. "What's happened that you have to go into witness protection?"

"Not me, Mom." He sent a desperate look to his dad, then added, "It's Camille. All this time we thought Camille was dead, she was in witness protection. Or witness security, they call it. In Maryland."

"Camille's alive?" The hope in his mother's eyes was like a knife to the gut.

"No, Mom, Camille isn't alive," he said. "Not anymore."

Shelby leaned forward. "I'm very sorry. I know this is beyond horrible, but Camille died this morning. She was in Eagle Mountain, under an assumed name. Someone killed her."

Shelby continued from there, laying out the story as simply as possible and answering his parents' questions. He watched his mother as the story unfolded. She seemed to get smaller as she absorbed the words, folding in on herself, her face crumpling. He started to go to her, but Shelby got there first. She clasped her hand and led her to the sofa, murmuring to her. Whatever she said must have been the right thing—his mother straightened and filled out again, more herself.

"I can't believe she was alive all this time," her father said after the whole story had come out. "And you say she was happy?"

"Yes," Shelby said. "She had a job she enjoyed, a house she loved, friends and a cat. She missed all of you. But she was happy."

"Why did she leave all of that to come to Eagle Mountain?" Zach's dad asked. "What was so important she jeopardized her safety?"

"We're not sure, but we believe she might have intended to contact Zach." Shelby glanced at him. "Some things she had heard from friends back in Houston—friends who didn't realize she was reading their social media posts—made her believe Zach might be in danger."

"From the Chalk brothers?" his dad asked.

"Yes. Though we haven't found any evidence that any of you are in danger."

"Except that Camille is dead," his dad said.

"Yes," Shelby said. "She may have been the only target, but we can't be sure. Which is one reason we're working with local law enforcement to have extra patrols in this neighborhood. And if either of you see anything suspicious—a person who looks out of place or anything threatening—you should call 911 immediately."

His mom nodded, her face pinched. "I haven't noticed anything," she said.

Zach squeezed her hand. "There's probably nothing to worry about," he said. "Everybody is just being extra careful." He didn't mention the possibility that they had been followed tonight. Shelby didn't either.

It was after ten thirty when Zach finally stood. His parents looked tired, and he was going to need to stop for coffee if he had any hope of staying awake for the drive home. "If you have any questions, or if you see anything suspicious, call me," Shelby said, and handed them a business card. "I'll be in the area a few more days, and I'm happy to stop by anytime."

"Thank you." Zach's mom embraced her. "It's so much to take in, but it was good to meet someone who knew Camille."

"She was my friend," Shelby said. "And I'm going to do my best to find out who killed her."

Neither of them said anything else until they were in Zach's truck again. "I need coffee," he said.

"Yeah," she agreed, sounding as drained as he was.

ZACH FOUND AN open coffee shop on the route they had taken in to town, and they placed an order in the drive-through. Then they headed back out of town. "Thanks for coming with me," he said after a while. "That would have been a lot harder without you there."

"I'm glad I could help." That wasn't the first time she

had had to notify someone that their loved one was dead, but it was the only time the people in question had to hear the news twice, four years apart. "Your parents are wonderful people," she said. "I would completely understand if they were bitter, but they weren't at all."

"Yeah. I don't know how they manage to stay so strong."

"I told your mom that Camille was one of the bravest, strongest people I knew and that she always said she got those strengths from her parents." She sank back in the seat and sipped her coffee, telling herself she needed to relax. The worst of this day was over. But a flash in the side mirror distracted her, and she glanced over, then sat up straight.

"What is it?" Zach asked, his voice sharp.

Her stomach tightened. Maybe she was wrong, but she didn't think so. "That Toyota is back," she said.

Zach started to turn his head. "Don't look back," she said. "Don't let them know we've spotted them."

He checked his mirrors. "Even if that is the same car, it doesn't mean they're following us," he said.

"No." She forced herself to settle back against the seat. To look relaxed, even if she was anything but. "Don't signal, but make a sharp right up ahead, then another right to go back one block."

He did as she asked, braking at the last moment and swinging hard into the turn. She heard the squeal of tires as the Toyota followed. "Can you tell who's driving?" he asked.

"No. I still can't see anything. Take the next left."

He turned the corner, which led to a neighborhood of narrow, curving streets. He headed up a hill and pulled into the parking lot of a church. "What are you doing?" she asked, alarmed.

"If they're following us, I'm going to confront them."

She grabbed his arm. "That is a very bad idea." She unfastened her seat belt and drew her weapon. Whoever was in that car might spray them with bullets before she had a chance to return fire, but she wasn't going to confront them unarmed.

Chapter Four

They waited in the church parking lot for fifteen minutes, but there was no sign of the Toyota. Was the vehicle parked somewhere on the street, waiting for them to exit? "Should we call 911 or something?" Zach asked.

"We could," she said. And then what? Would the local cops even believe they were being followed? She wasn't sure Zach believed it. "Pull out and see if anyone follows," she said.

Zach blew out a breath. "I feel ridiculous," he said. He started the engine and pulled out of the lot onto the street. No one followed. There was little traffic on the highway, and the vehicles she did see behaved normally, passing them or turning off or receding into the distance.

Neither of them spoke. Was Zach annoyed with her? No, he was probably simply processing his grief and the terrible way this day had turned out.

He parked in front of his townhouse, but didn't get out right away. She waited, sure he would eventually say whatever was on his mind. "Do you really think someone was following us tonight?" he asked.

"I do."

He turned to look at her. The parking lot security light cast a harsh glow across one side of his face, turning it into a macabre mask, all dark, hollowed eyes and downturned mouth. "Why?"

"You may be the only one who can answer that," she said. "What do you know that the Chalk brothers would kill to keep quiet?"

"Nothing!"

The word rang loud in the nighttime stillness. Was he telling the truth? "Maybe it's something you've forgotten about," she said, her voice softer. "Or something you don't think is important. Whatever it is, you need to tell me, so that I can help you."

He shook his head. "I don't think anyone can help me. Camille is dead." He blew out a breath. "And the worst thing is, she died for nothing. All she wanted was to make a difference. To bring the Chalk brothers to justice. But that didn't happen. She's dead, and they're still walking free."

"She didn't die for nothing," Shelby said.

He looked at her, the trick of light exaggerating the dark hollowness of his eyes. But she felt that same hollowness in her chest. Like him, she wanted the sacrifice Camille had made to matter. But that depended on her now. She needed to prove Camille hadn't died in vain. But she didn't know if she was up to the task.

She opened the truck door and slid out. "Good night, Zach," she said. "I'll talk to you tomorrow."

He didn't answer. She walked to her rental car and got in, but she waited until he climbed out of his truck and went inside his townhouse before she started the engine and left the lot. No sign of a white Toyota. No sign of any threat to him, but she couldn't shake the feeling one was there.

INSIDE THE TOWNHOUSE, Zach lay back on the sofa and closed his eyes, battered by warring emotions. After four years, he had thought he was mostly done grieving for his sister, only to learn she had been alive all that time, only to be snatched away from him again when she had been almost in reach. The cruelty of that reality burned in his chest, along with anger that he and his parents, and all of Camille's friends, had been duped.

Yet he knew Camille wasn't cruel. If anything, she was too compassionate, going out of her way to make other people comfortable, even at her own expense. At her funeral, those who had attended had spoken over and over about how generous and considerate she was. Knowing this, Zach could believe she would do anything to protect her family, even if it meant letting them think she was dead and never seeing them again.

And then she had come back here. Maybe she had only wanted to check on him, to make sure he was okay, but he didn't think so. Agent Dryden had been right when she said Camille had come to warn him.

The idea made him sick with guilt, and he forced his mind to think about something else. Agent Shelby Dryden. She was pretty—not beautiful, but with a rounded face and full cheeks and blue eyes that looked right into him, as if she was searching for all his secrets. She looked younger than she probably was. She looked delicate and gentle, but didn't back down from a difficult task. She had to be tough to face down the kind of criminals the FBI investigated, not to mention her fellow agents, who, from what Zach had experienced, were a hard bunch.

So Agent Dryden could be hard, too. But she had also been gentle with his parents. She had told them everything they wanted to hear about Camille—all the good things to make them believe she had been happy. But how could she have been happy without her family, when they had always meant so much to her?

Zach thought of the car Shelby Dryden had said was following them tonight. A white Toyota. He didn't know anyone with a white Toyota, but there must be hundreds of them in the county. And it seemed odd that someone would follow his truck but never do anything. They hadn't tried to run him off the road or fire any shots or anything.

The idea that someone had been following him, that the Chalk brothers might want to kill him, ought to terrify him. But he didn't feel fear. All he felt was numb. That was pretty much all he had felt for the past four years. Call it a coping mechanism or the aftereffects of grief. Zach couldn't seem to feel the things he told himself he ought to feel.

Five years ago

"GOOD NIGHT, BENNIE! Have a great time this weekend, Amy! Thanks for everything, Oliver!" Camille waved to the last of the night shift at Britannia Pub as they left the restaurant. Parked across the street, Zach watched the trio of friends pass in and out of the glow of the security lights as they walked to their vehicles at the back of the parking lot. Camille turned the keys in the trio of locks on the back door to the restaurant, then slipped the key ring into her purse and headed down the sidewalk, toward the bus stop.

He started the truck and drove until he was even with Camille. She glanced over and a smile lit her face. "Hey!" He stopped and she pulled open the passenger door. "What are you doing here?"

"I didn't like the idea of you taking the bus while your car is in the shop, so I came to give you a ride home."

"You didn't have to do that," she said, even as she settled into the passenger seat. "But I'm glad you did. Devon says he'll have my car ready Friday. The new ignition module is supposed to be in tomorrow."

"No problem," Zach said. He turned the key in the ignition and checked the mirrors. Unlike during daylight hours, when the downtown Houston streets hummed with pedestrian and vehicle traffic, this time of night—almost three o'clock—he had no trouble pulling into the street. Traffic still eased down the streets, but the cars were spaced farther apart, and the only other people on the sidewalk were a couple of men leaning against the wall outside the Salvation Army mission and a man in a chef's checkered pants and clogs hurrying toward the transit station.

They were scarcely a block away from the restaurant when Camille swore. "What is it?" Zach asked, surprised at the outburst from his normally easygoing sister.

"I left my wallet at the restaurant," she said. "I got it out of my locker on my break to pay Bennie the ten dollars he loaned me to cover lunch the other day, and instead of putting it away afterward I tucked it into the little cubby under the hostess stand." She looked up at him, expression pleading. "I know it's late, but I really need to go back and get it."

"It's okay." He turned left at the next street, went around the block and coasted back to his previous parking spot across the street. "Do you want me to go with you?" he asked.

"No. I'll just run in and get it. It won't take me a second." She unfastened her seat belt and slid out of the truck, then jogged across the street. She stood for a moment opening the locks, then disappeared inside.

Zach rested his wrists on top of the steering wheel and looked toward the corner of the restaurant, which was also the corner of the street. Britannia's front entrance opened onto the cross street, and the red neon of its sign on the side of the building cast a reflection onto the street. The traffic light turned green. By the time it turned red again, he was wondering what was taking Camille so long. He looked toward the alley and the back door of the restaurant, but all was still. He jumped as a loud report echoed down the empty street. Like a car backfiring or firecrackers, maybe over on the next block.

Or a gunshot? Downtown was pretty safe these days, but there was always crime in a city this size. He glanced back toward the corner, and a man ran into the intersection. The solitary figure froze for a moment, lit by the streetlight—a young man in dark pants and a white shirt, his face very pale. He had a prominent nose and chin, his eyes dark hollows in the bright light, his expression one of terror. The young man turned toward him, and instinct sent Zach diving under the dash.

Then the door of the truck wrenched open, and Camille shoved inside. "Go!" she shouted. "We have to get out of here."

Zach straightened. The man in the intersection was gone, and the light was green again. He put the truck in gear and lurched into the street. He drove wildly, in the middle of the street, running at least one red light, but there was no one around to see him do it.

"There! Turn right there!" Camille pointed and Zach wrenched the steering wheel to the right. He sped past a line of parked cars, then slammed on his brakes as he met a concrete barrier. "It's okay." Camille put a hand on his arm. "We'll be okay now. This is a police station."

Zach blinked. Now he saw that the line of cars he had passed were Houston Police cruisers. He looked up and saw the lit sign Police. "What happened?" he asked.

Camille was pale, but she looked so much calmer than he felt. "Someone was in the restaurant when I went inside," she said. "They must have come in after I left the first time."

"How did they get in?" he asked. "I saw you lock the door."

"They must have come in the front door," she said. "They had a key."

"What do you mean they had a key?"

She wet her lips. "If I tell you, you can't say anything to anyone," she said. "Not even the police. Especially not the police. Whatever they ask you, you weren't there, all right?"

"Why can't I tell the police? Cammie, what is going on?"

She leaned closer and gripped his arm. "Charlie and Christopher Chalk own the Britannia Pub," she said. "You know who the Chalk brothers are, right?"

"Of course." Anyone who lived in Houston and watched the news or read a newspaper knew the Chalk brothers. They owned a lot of real estate. Restaurants and bars, apartment buildings, strip clubs, convenience stores. They were rumored to have connections to the mob or to drug cartels or to illegal gambling and prostitution. Maybe they had spent time in prison. Maybe they had murdered people. How much was truth and how much sensationalism, Zach didn't know or care.

"Christopher and Charlie were in the pub when I got there. With another man. Do you know Judge Hennessey?"

"No. How do you know him?"

"Don't you watch the news?" she asked. "He's the judge who got in trouble for not recusing himself from that money laundering trial that ended last week."

"What money laundering trial? And I don't have time to watch the news. I have a life."

"I was having a drink with Diane last week, and they had the TV on over the bar and I saw the story," she said. "Judge Hennessey was accused of taking a bribe, and word was he was going to confess who had paid him."

"Did the Chalk brothers pay him?" Zach asked.

"I don't know," Camille said. "But one of them killed him."

"What?"

"I had retrieved my wallet from the hostess stand and was getting ready to leave when I heard a gunshot. I turned to look, and there was the judge, lying on the floor bleeding, with Charlie and Christopher standing over him. I ran as fast as I could and got back to you. I don't think they know I was there."

"I heard the shot," Zach said. "I thought it was a car backfiring. And there was a guy…"

"What guy?" She grabbed his arm again. "What are you talking about?"

"Just a guy in the street. He ran from the direction of the restaurant. A guy about my age. Dark hair, dark pants, white shirt. Big nose and chin."

She stared at him, eyes wide. "That doesn't sound like Charlie or Christopher. They're both pretty big guys. Charlie must be at least forty. Christopher is a little younger, but he's fat."

"This guy wasn't fat. But he was terrified."

"Did he see you?"

"I don't think so. When he turned toward me, I ducked down."

She gripped his arm tighter, fingers digging in. "You can't tell anyone about this, Zach."

"Why not?"

"The Chalk brothers are terrible people. If they think you saw anything, they will kill you."

"So you're saying we both just keep this a secret?"

"Not both of us," she said. "I'll tell the police what I saw. They don't even have to know you were there."

"Wait a minute—you're saying I should keep quiet because the Chalk brothers will kill me, but it's okay for you to talk? In what world does that make sense?"

"I was in the building when Judge Hennessey was killed," she said. "I was practically in the same room. All you saw was some guy run down the street. He could have come from anywhere. You would risk your life for nothing. And our parents! It's going to be bad enough for them, having me involved in this mess. If you're in it, too, it could be too much for them. You need to be able to focus on taking care of them."

"Who's going to take care of you?" he asked.

"I'll ask for police protection, and I'll get it. I was an eyewitness to murder, and I can help law enforcement convict criminals they've been after for years." Her color returned as she spoke, and her eyes lit with excitement.

"Camille—" He tried to interrupt her, but she rushed on.

"This will work, Zach. You don't have to get involved." She opened the truck door. "Let me out here and drive straight home. I'll tell the cops I ran here from the restaurant. It's not that far."

"I can't just leave you here."

"You have to, Zach. Now go." She slid out of the truck and slammed the door behind her. Then she took off across the parking lot. Within seconds, she had disappeared into the building.

He sat for a long while, gripping the steering wheel, waiting for Camille to return then thinking he should go inside after her. He thought about the man in the street. Zach had seen him for such a brief moment. Was Camille right? Would he be opening himself up to danger for no reason? It could have been someone walking home after a late night, or a street person, terrified by the sound of gunfire nearby.

He texted Camille half a dozen times, but she never answered. Finally, at four in the morning, he headed home. He woke several hours later to a phone call from Camille. "Turn on the TV!" she said. "It's really happening!"

Still groggy, he turned on the television and scrolled through the channels until he came to footage of two men in suits being led away in handcuffs, flanked by half a dozen police officers. He turned up the sound. "…eyewitness statement led to the arrest of the Chalk brothers for the murder of Judge Andrew Hennessey."

"Where are you now?" Zach asked.

"I'm in a safe house. Trust me—I'm being taken very good care of. And so are you and Mom and Dad. If you see more cops that usual, it's because they've promised to keep an eye on you. Just in case the Chalks decide to go after one of you to get to me."

"Mom and Dad are in danger?"

"No. I don't think so. You're all going to be fine."

"What about you? Can they really keep you safe?"

"Don't worry about me. I'll have to lie low for a few months, until the Chalks are safely behind bars, but it will be so worth it. You can't imagine how I feel right now. I've gone from being a server to a crime-fighting hero. I'm thinking I want to go into law enforcement after this is all over. This could be the best thing that ever happened to me!"

"I should tell the cops what I saw," he said.

"No! Don't you dare. You'll just confuse things and put yourself in danger. Promise me you won't do it, Zach. Promise!"

He rubbed his temples, which throbbed from stress and lack of sleep. "You don't think they need to know?"

"They don't. I've told them everything they need. You look after Mom and Dad and root for me from the sidelines. It's all going to be great. You'll see."

Chapter Five

Shelby sat at a table in a small interview room at the Rayford County Sheriff's Department. Next to her, Sheriff Travis Walker listened to the statement of a witness from the campground where Camille Gregory's body had been found. The sheriff had the most perfect poker face Shelby had ever seen. Tall, dark-haired, looking more like an actor hired to play the part of a county sheriff than an actual law enforcement officer, Sheriff Walker had agreed to let Shelby sit in on the interview. Actually, he had said, "Suit yourself," when she had asked to be present for the interview, and then led the way to the interview room.

Brent Baker shifted in the hard metal chair across from them. He tapped his fingers on the table, tilted his neck back and forth, yawned, then smoothed his hands down his thighs. He reminded her of addicts she had seen, jonesing for a hit, except that Baker looked too healthy to have a drug habit. He wore a tight T-shirt that showed sculpted pecs and abs and moved like an athlete. "I camped out there for three nights, rode some of the backcountry trails," he said in answer to the sheriff's question about what he was doing at the campground. "I ran into Carla, and we started talking." He frowned and scooted his chair forward a couple of inches. "She introduced herself as Carla, though I heard later her name is really Camille?"

Travis didn't deny or confirm this. "What did the two of you talk about?" he asked.

Brent scratched his cheek. "Oh, you know, just what a pretty day it was and what a nice campground. She said she had rented the van and was traveling around, seeing the country. I asked if she biked, and she said no, but she was hoping to do some hiking while she was in the area." Another frown. "I prefer biking to hiking, but I asked her if she wanted to go hiking with me."

"Why did you do that?" Travis asked. A legitimate question, maybe, though it made Shelby want to wince. Brent the Biker was clearly flirting with Carla/Camille and wanted an excuse to spend more time with her.

"I thought she was hot," he said. "I was hoping maybe we could hook up." He glanced at Shelby. "No disrespect meant, ma'am."

She nodded. "I appreciate your honesty."

"Did Carla say anything about where she had traveled from or where she was headed?" Travis asked.

"No. She just said she'd been traveling around. She asked if I lived in Eagle Mountain. I told her I was from Lake City, but I'd spent plenty of time around here."

"Did she act nervous, or afraid of anyone?" Travis asked.

"No. She was pretty relaxed. Friendly." The chair squeaked as Brent shifted again. "She turned me down on the hike, though. Said she would probably leave the next day. Then we started talking about the weather. It was clouding up and the wind picked up, and I told her I had seen a forecast that called for rain. She didn't like that much."

"Did you see her talking to anyone else at the campground?" Travis asked. "Other campers or anyone else?"

Brent cracked his knuckles and scuffed one toe on the

floor. "That's why I'm here, right? Right when it first started raining, I came out of my tent to throw a cover over my bike. I looked toward Carla's van and saw this guy running down the road, away from her campsite. I mentioned it to the cop who came around interviewing everybody, and he said I needed to come in and talk to you." He spread his hands wide. "And here I am."

"What did the man look like?" Shelby asked before the sheriff could.

"He was about six feet tall. Kind of thin. He was wearing black pants and a black rain shell with the hood up, so I really couldn't see his face."

"How did he run?" Shelby asked.

Both men stared at her, and she forced herself not to squirm. "Did he have an easy lope, like a practiced runner?" she asked. "Did he do a sort of walk-run thing of someone who's hurrying but doesn't like to run? Or did he run like someone in a hurry to get away?"

Brent nodded. "I get you. He ran like a runner. Long strides, kind of fluid."

"But you're sure he came from Carla's campsite?" Travis asked.

Brent squinted and rubbed the back of his neck. "I'm pretty sure. But maybe he was just out for a jog and stopped by her van to tie his shoe. I mean, it was raining, and I just glanced over." He shrugged.

"Had you seen this man at the campground before?"

"I don't think so. But like I said, he had the hood of his jacket pulled up, and he was running away from me."

"Did he have anything in his hands?" Shelby asked.

"Like what?" Brent asked.

"Anything. A knife?"

Brent's eyes widened. "Is that what killed Carla? We

all thought it must have been the tree that hit her van, but the article I saw online said she was murdered."

"Did you see anything in the running man's hands?" Shelby pressed.

"No."

"The man ran away, then what happened?" Travis asked.

"I thought I'd go over and talk to Carla again. It was raining a lot harder, and all I had was a tent, and she was in that nice van, so I thought maybe I could talk her into taking pity and letting me in." He smiled in a way Shelby thought might be intended as charming but reminded her too much of the boyish types who hit on her in bars. As if the way into a woman's bed was to make her feel sorry for you. "I was headed over there when a guy drove in and said I should think about packing up and clearing out because there was a flash-flood warning, and if the creek across the road into camp rose, we'd be cut off. Then some other people came over, and we were all debating the issue. Then the first guy said he would go around and warn the other campers, and I went to take down my tent and get everything into my truck."

"Do you know if the first man talked to Carla?" Travis asked.

"I don't know."

"What was the man's name?" Travis asked.

"Sorry, I don't know that either."

"You only saw the running man one time—is that correct?" Travis asked.

Brent nodded. "Just the one time."

"Did you see Carla at all after you saw him?" Shelby asked.

"No. And I never did get around to talking to her again. Then I saw the tree on her van." He grew still, the sudden cessation of movement striking. "I should have gone over and helped her. Maybe if I'd gotten to her soon enough she would still be alive."

"Or maybe not," Travis said.

After a few more questions that established that Brent had no more information to offer, Travis thanked him, and a deputy escorted him out. Travis turned to Shelby. "I read the file you sent over, and I know the basics about why Camille Gregory was in witness security," he said. "Do you think the Chalk brothers found her and had her killed?"

"That is the most likely scenario," she said. "But we can't be sure."

"Maybe some other guy flirted with her, didn't take no for an answer, then stabbed her and ran away," Travis said.

"Maybe," Shelby said. "She wouldn't be the first woman traveling alone who was murdered. But I don't think so. Camille was very aware of her surroundings. She was in good physical condition, and she knew how to protect herself. She had taken self-defense classes, and she knew that as soon as she moved out of our circle of protection, she was a potential target. She wasn't naive."

"And you think she came to Eagle Mountain to see her brother, Zach?"

"She was worried about him," Shelby said.

"Why was she worried?"

"She learned through social media that a man who said he worked for the Chalk brothers came back to the pub six months ago and talked to a woman Camille had worked with. He wanted to know if Zach was with Camille that night. Camille said he wasn't, but she was afraid the Chalk brothers didn't believe that, and they might hurt Zach."

"Did the FBI follow up on this?" Travis asked.

Shelby gave him a look that let him know what she thought of the question. It wasn't as if she didn't know how to do her job. "We looked into it. We found the guy, but he swore he didn't know the Chalk brothers. He said he was a freelance writer, following a theory he had. It turned out to be nothing."

"Maybe he was lying," Travis said.

"Maybe he was." Fear that he was right made her throat tight, so she had to force the words out. "I told Camille what we had learned, and I thought she was calmer, but then she disappeared. She left a note saying she needed to see her parents, but that she would be back soon, and to please not come after her."

"But you did go after her."

"Of course we did. But we went to her parents'. There was no sign she had ever been there."

"What do you know about Zach Gregory?" Travis asked.

"Not a lot. He's two years younger than Camille, but the two of them were close. Her death—or what he thought was her death—hit him hard. He drifted around a lot after her funeral, dropped out of college, took a series of dead-end jobs. Lately, he seems to have turned things around. He started working at Zenith Mine and joined Search and Rescue."

"You kept tabs on him?"

She flushed. "We kept track of all her family, in case any threats to them surfaced. And it made Camille feel better to know they were all right. Despite what some people might think, witness security isn't about depriving people of their liberty or making them miserable. We do what we can to help people adjust."

"If you had a good idea where Camille was headed when she left WITSEC, why didn't you come after her?" Travis asked.

Shelby wanted to snap that she wasn't an idiot, but reminded herself that in his boots, she would have asked the same question. "She misled us. She left things that made it appear she had gone to see her parents. By the time we realized we had been duped and headed here, it was too late." She would never forgive herself for that. No matter what her bosses said about not getting personally involved with witnesses or victims, Shelby and Camille were friends. And Shelby would never stop feeling she had let her friend down.

"Do we need to be worried about these men, the Chalk brothers, causing trouble in Eagle Mountain?" Travis asked.

"I don't know. It depends if Camille was right and her brother had become a target. If they were only after her, you don't have anything to worry about." She hesitated, then added, "I went with Zach to see his parents in Junction last night. I thought a car followed us from Eagle Mountain—a white Toyota. I thought I saw the same car again on the way home, but they turned off and there was never any trouble, so maybe I was wrong. It wouldn't hurt to keep an eye on Zach for a few days, at least."

If he was displeased to hear this, his expression didn't show it. "What are your plans?" he asked.

"The FBI is conducting its own investigation into the murder. I appreciate you sharing the information you've already uncovered. I'll need to talk to more people who might have come into contact with Camille or her murderer. And I'll stay in town long enough to determine if Zach Gregory is in real danger. If he is a target, we'll do our best to protect him." She owed Camille at least that much.

"Hey, Zach. I'm really sorry about your sister."

Zach looked up from the ropes he was coiling and saw

Sheri Stevens, one of the Search and Rescue veterans who was helping train rookies like him. He hadn't known how to handle these expressions of sympathy the first time Camille died. Four years hadn't made him any better at it. "Thanks," he said and went back to helping to pack the climbing ropes. He braced himself for the onslaught of questions he was sure would come—about his sister, about her murder, about the judge's murder. They had caught him off guard the first time, before and after the trial. Everyone he met back then, from neighbors to news reporters, wanted some scrap of detail from him that would bring the tragedy closer. Why couldn't they understand this wasn't something he wanted to share with anyone?

But Sheri didn't ask any questions, and neither did any of the other members of the team, though several of them asked how he was doing and said they were sorry for his loss. After a while, he began to relax and accept their condolences as sincere.

"Are you up for this?" Danny asked as they prepared to leave for a callout to an ATV accident on one of the Jeep trails.

"I'm good," Zach said.

Danny nodded. "Then let's get after it."

The network of dirt roads that wound through the mountains above town attracted adventurers on dirt bikes and in Jeeps and all manner of four-wheel drive vehicles, but invariably some of them weren't prepared for the steep terrain, tight turns and rough conditions. Zach had already learned that, next to traffic accidents on the highway that led out of town, calls from the Jeep trails were the second most common crises Search and Rescue responded to each summer.

This accident involved a single rental ATV that had rolled on its side. Zach and the others arrived to find half a dozen other drivers and riders gathered around a lanky man with blond hair to his shoulders and a scruffy goatee, who sat on a boulder a few yards from his overturned vehicle. Blood, already drying, trickled from a cut on his forehead, and the right sleeve of his shirt was in tatters where he had evidently scraped it on the rocks. Danny, a nurse, knelt beside the man. "I'm Danny, with Eagle Mountain Search and Rescue," he introduced himself. "What's your name?"

The blond lifted his head to take in the circle of volunteers around him. "Todd," he said. "Todd Arniston. That's *Todd* with two Ds."

"Let's take a look at that head wound, Todd." Danny, who had already donned nitrile gloves, gently probed the cut on the young man's forehead. "This doesn't look too bad," he said and began to clean the wound. "How are you feeling? Any headache? Dizziness?"

While Danny and volunteer Christine Mercer tended to Todd, Zach and some of the others examined the overturned ATV. An older man wearing an All Who Wander Are Not Lost T-shirt joined them. "I saw the whole thing," he said. "I was waiting my turn to navigate this narrow, rocky section of the trail when he came tearing around the corner. He took that curve on two wheels, and he was going too fast to stay in control when he saw the backup of vehicles here. He lost control in the gravel and went over on his side and skid a long way." The man shook his head. "The whole point of being up here in this beautiful country is to take your time and enjoy the scenery—not race around recklessly."

Eldon Ramsey, one of the group's best climbers, circled the ATV. He looked over at Zach. "This doesn't look too banged up, really," he said. "I bet the two of us could get it upright." Eldon, originally from Hawaii, was as tall as Zach and even more muscular.

"Sure," Zach said. "Let's give it a try."

The others stepped back as Zach joined Eldon on the other side of the ATV. "On three," Eldon said. "One... two...three!" They heaved, and with a groan of springs and metal, the ATV bounced onto its tires. Eldon leaned in and set the brake, then slid into the driver's seat and turned the key. The engine coughed, then growled to life. He shut it off and climbed out.

Todd, on his feet now, walked over to them. Danny had cleaned and bandaged the cut on his forehead and the scrape on his forearm. "Thanks." He shook hands with Eldon then Zach. "What are your names?" he asked. "I want to remember you two." He had a pronounced Southern accent, like someone from Georgia or Alabama, Zach thought.

They introduced themselves. "I can't believe there are people who just volunteer to help others way up here like this," Todd said. "I can't thank you all enough."

Danny shouldered his pack and joined them. "It's a good idea to wear a helmet on these rough roads," he said. "Those side-by-sides will tip over easier than most people think."

"And you need to slow down," the older man who had witnessed the accident said. "You could kill yourself or somebody else."

Todd looked sheepish. "I think I've learned my lesson," he said. "I'll take it a lot slower." He moved toward the vehicle. "I'm just glad I can get this down the mountain without having to pay to have someone haul it."

"Are you sure you're up to driving?" Christine asked.

"Y'all said I didn't have any sign of concussion, and I feel fine now." Todd slid into the driver's seat. "I'll take it nice and slow from here on," he said. "I promise." He nodded to Zach and the others. "It was nice to meet you all. Maybe we'll run into each other in town, and I can buy you a beer." He turned the key in the ignition then gave them a thumbs-up. They all moved back as he guided the ATV onto the trail and puttered down the road.

"Should we have let him leave on his own?" Christine asked as they headed back to the Search and Rescue vehicle.

"I can make medical recommendations, but we can't stop him," Danny said. He stowed his pack in the back of the specially outfitted Jeep used by Search and Rescue. "He'll probably be okay. That knock he took on the head wasn't nearly as bad as it might have been. I told him he should check with his doctor to make sure there's no internal damage, but he probably won't."

"If he does run into trouble, there are plenty of people around who can call for help again," Eldon said. He hoisted himself into the driver's seat. "If it was me, I'd have probably driven down. He'll lose his damage deposit on the rental, but that's probably less than the cost of getting someone up here to retrieve the thing."

"That's the first call I've been on with only minor injuries," Zach said.

"We don't get many like that." Danny settled in the passenger seat, and Christine, Zach, Sheri and Caleb piled in the back. "We see a lot of serious injuries on these trails and more than a few fatalities."

"Were you here when that Jeep exploded?" Christine asked. "I still hear people in town talk about that one."

"That was right after I started." Danny looked grim. "The vehicle rolled three times then exploded. There were five people in it, two adults and three children. Two of the children lived, though it was touch-and-go for them for a while." He shook his head. "The organization paid for a counselor to come in and work with us for a while after that one," he said. "I still think of it every time we come up here."

Zach hadn't responded to a fatality yet. Except for Camille, and she hadn't been the victim of an accident or anything. Seeing her lying on that litter had been surreal. He had thought of her as dead for so long that he still hadn't come to terms with the idea that she had lived another life in the past four years, with a different name, a different job and friends he had never met.

"Dealing with the dead is one of the toughest parts of search and rescue work," Danny said. "But we have resources to help. And if you decide you can't handle that part of it, there's no shame in stepping aside. For me, helping the live victims outweighs the sadness from those we couldn't save."

They murmured agreement. Zach didn't think he'd have trouble dealing with dead strangers, but he wouldn't mind if he had to wait until he had more experience with search and rescue work before he found out.

His phone buzzed with a text message as they pulled into Search and Rescue headquarters.

I need to talk to you. When can we meet? Shelby

He frowned. She had signed her name *Shelby*. Not *Special Agent Dryden*. As if the two of them were pals. She had said she and Camille had been friends, but was that true? Shelby Dryden was investigating the Chalk brothers, and Camille had been a witness to a murder where the brothers were present—and probably responsible. The FBI wanted to know everything Camille knew. How could Shelby interrogate his sister and be her friend?

Had Camille told Shelby that Zach was with her that night at the restaurant? Not inside with her, but waiting outside? Had she confided that Zach had seen a man run away from the direction of the restaurant?

Four years ago, Camille had convinced Zach that what he had seen didn't matter. He had managed to believe that right up until the end of the trial, when the Chalk brothers were acquitted of murder. But even then, Camille had pleaded with him not to say anything. "It doesn't make any difference now," she had said. "And if you speak up, they'll kill you. Promise me you'll keep silent. You have to promise me."

So he had promised. He told himself he did it for Camille. So that she wouldn't worry about him. And for his parents, so that they would have at least one child safe and with them. But all this time another thought had festered inside him—the knowledge that as much as he had wanted to protect his sister, he wanted to protect himself more. He was afraid of the Chalk brothers. After Camille had died the first time, supposedly murdered by the Chalks, he had been even more afraid. He had told himself Camille had been right—that his story about the man in the street wouldn't make any difference.

But now Camille had died again—for real this time. Shelby said she had left the safety of her new life to come and talk to him. Someone had found her and killed her. If Zach had found the courage to speak up, would his sister be alive now?

He didn't know how to live with that kind of guilt, but he was going to have to figure it out. He deleted the text message. He didn't want to talk to Agent Dryden. He didn't want to have anything to do with her.

Chapter Six

Eighteen months ago

Shelby tried not to have expectations about the witnesses she interviewed. She wanted to listen to their testimony without any pre-judgment. But she already knew a lot about Camille Gregory—now Claire Watson—before she knocked on the modest bungalow in a quiet Bethesda neighborhood. She had watched the available video of the Chalk brothers trial and Camille Gregory's testimony against them. Camille was the same age as Shelby—twenty-six at the time of the trial—but she had the confidence and composure of someone much older. On the witness stand, she had sat up tall, chin lifted, and spoken clearly, convincingly. She almost looked as if she was enjoying the experience. The prosecution couldn't have asked for a better witness.

But the Chalk brothers had better lawyers, and their own brand of arrogance that had impressed—or perhaps intimidated—the jurors. The chief defense attorney had emphasized over and over that Miss Gregory had not seen either of the brothers shoot Judge Hennessey. She hadn't even seen them holding a gun. She had turned and run before she had seen much of anything at all.

The woman who answered Shelby's knock was smaller

than she had looked in those videos—thin, but not fragile. She examined Shelby's credentials and smiled with genuine warmth. "It'll be nice to talk to a woman for a change," she said. "Come on in."

Shelby was prepared for Camille to balk at answering questions she had already been asked over and over in the two and a half years since the night Judge Hennessey was murdered. She knew how to tease out information from reticent witnesses and how to use emotion—anger, sadness, regret—to elicit information they might not have revealed before. She was very good at her job.

But interviewing Camille required none of that. The young woman was open, happy to talk about that night and everything that had followed, as if she hadn't told the same story over and over. What she said matched what was already in her file. She didn't embellish the way so many witnesses did over time, perhaps in an attempt to make their story, or themselves, more interesting. Camille knew she was interesting, the way some people accept that they are beautiful or powerful.

After the first hour, Shelby felt as if she was talking with a girlfriend. Camille had brought out flavored seltzer and popcorn, and they snacked and chatted as if they had known each other for years. Camille really came alive when she talked about her family—her parents, her deceased sister, Laney, and especially her brother, Zach.

"I wish you could meet Zach," she said. "I think you would really like him."

"Is he a lot like you?" Shelby asked.

"He's not like me." Camille tossed a kernel of popcorn into her mouth and tilted her head, considering. "Zach is quieter. More thoughtful. I mean, he really thinks about things before he says anything or makes up his mind. When we were kids, people sometimes thought he was slow, but he's actually really smart. He just takes his time making decisions. Me, I think on my feet. I size things up very quickly. Sometimes, he accused me of being rash, but it was never like that. I just made up my mind fast and stuck to my decision. That night at the restaurant, I knew what I had to do right away."

"Does Zach look like you?" Shelby asked.

Camille ate more popcorn. "We have the same dark hair and eyes, but Zach is taller and just, well, bigger." She held her hands out to her sides. "Not fat, just tall and broad-shouldered and muscular. But to go along with all that brawn, he is almost pretty. Those big, dark eyes and long lashes. I would kill for lashes like that, you know. And he has this mole right at the side of his mouth." She touched her own face to indicate the position. "A perfect beauty mark. When he was little, kids sometimes teased him about it, but then he outgrew most of them and the teasing stopped." She shrugged. "He was always my little brother, no matter how big he got. And I always tried to look out for him."

"You didn't think he could take care of himself?" Shelby asked, fascinated by this picture of the beautiful giant who needed protecting by a woman who was all of five feet six inches tall and weighed maybe 125 pounds.

"Yes and no. Zach was so quiet and easygoing. Too easygoing. I don't think he ever understood how danger-ous people could be. How dangerous the Chalk brothers could be." Her expression grew troubled. "When I told him I needed police protection, I think he saw it as me being dramatic." She grinned, showing white, perfect teeth. "Not that I don't occasionally channel my inner drama queen. When it suits me."

Shelby returned to that night at the restaurant, trying to ferret out any detail they might have missed before, but coming up with nothing new. "I know the Chalk brothers can't be tried again for the judge's murder," Camille said. "So what else do you hope to accomplish?"

"I'm reviewing everything in their files, trying to find some detail we've missed that might link them to other crimes," Shelby said.

"I wish I could help you," Camille said. "But I really have told you everything I know."

Shelby gathered her belongings and prepared to leave. "If you think of anything, no matter how trivial, call me," she said and handed Camille her card.

Shelby studied the card, then slipped it into the pocket of her jeans. "Could I call you just to talk? Or go shopping or to lunch or something?"

Shelby blinked. "Uh, sure."

"It's just that I really enjoyed hanging out with you," Camille said. "I think the two of us could be friends. It would be nice to have someone I didn't have to pretend with, you know?"

Shelby nodded. She didn't know, but she could imagine. No matter who else Camille grew close to from now on, there would always be her other, secret life between them. "Call me anytime," she said. "Just to talk or hang out. A person can't have too many friends."

Camille surprised her again at the door by giving her a hug. She felt the other woman's loneliness in that gesture, and a longing that mirrored her own. Being an FBI agent, especially one of the few women in her office, was lonely, too. She and Camille had more in common than Shelby had imagined.

TWO DAYS AFTER arriving in Eagle Mountain, Shelby stood on the doorstep of Zach's townhouse once more, frowning at the smooth black paint of the front door. He hadn't answered her ring, or the knocking that followed. He might not be home—or he might be inside, refusing to talk to her. She had tried his workplace earlier, and a woman there had informed her Zach was out on bereavement leave. She might take her inability to contact him as bad timing, except that he refused to answer her texts or call her back. She understood he was probably still angry about the role the FBI had played in deceiving his family into believing Camille was dead. Frankly, that whole scenario made her uncomfortable, too.

But she hadn't been part of that deception. She hadn't even been with the Bureau back then. All she wanted now was for the two of them to work together to try to figure out who had killed his sister and her friend. She wasn't his enemy.

She walked back to her car, trying to decide what to do next. Before joining the Bureau, she had worked as a sheriff's deputy. The east Texas town she had worked for had been a little larger than Eagle Mountain and not as scenic, but she had investigated her share of crimes. It was one of those crimes—a kidnapping and multiple murder—that had brought her to the attention of the Bureau.

She needed to put herself back into the role of an investigator. Local law enforcement was being as cooperative as any of them ever were when the Bureau swooped in to take over a case on their turf. They had promised to share any information they uncovered about the crime, but that wasn't enough. This was Shelby's case, so she needed to investigate it herself.

She consulted the report she had received from Sheriff Walker, then pulled up a map of the area on her phone, plugged some coordinates into her GPS and began to drive.

Twenty minutes later, she eased her rental car down a rutted, rocky road toward the Piñon Creek campground.

The car's springs groaned in protest as she sank into a pot-hole, and she winced at the screech of metal on rock as she climbed up out of the hole. Mud spattered the sides of the vehicle and spotted the windshield when she splashed through water running over the road—the last remnants of the flood three days ago.

At last, she spotted the sign marking the entrance to the campground and turned in. A kiosk had a list of the rules and a map showing the layout of all the campsites. The sheriff's report said Camille's body had been found in site number 47, near the back of the campground.

She drove slowly along the dirt road. Only half a dozen sites were occupied, and she saw no people at any of them. Were they away for the day, hiking and Jeeping and fishing and whatever else people came here for? Or were they hiding inside their campers and vans, suspicious of the stranger who was clearly not a camper, moving into their midst?

Even if she hadn't noted the number of the site where Camille had been found, she would have known which one it was by the yellow crime-scene tape that still fluttered from the stunted piñon trees. She parked in site 46, across from 47, and walked over.

Tracks in the mud showed where a wrecker had towed the rental van away. The trunk and branches of a mostly dead tree lay next to the tracks, its stump like a broken molar jutting from the red-brown dirt. The other campers, seeing Camille's body on the ground beneath the tree, had assumed it had fallen on her. But Shelby doubted the impact from this half-rotted trunk could have killed her. And, of course, it hadn't. Had her killer pushed the tree over or managed to arrange for it to fall in order to hide his handiwork a little longer and allow him time to escape?

She searched for other tracks in the mud—shoe impressions or tire or bicycle tracks—but the prints of first responders and other campers, and the flood itself, had wiped out anything that was likely to lead to Camille's killer. She paused to study the deep treads of a man's hiking boots, overlaying the van's tracks where it had been pulled from the campsite. Of course, the crime-scene tape would draw other campers to look. Who didn't love a good mystery?

"What are you doing here?"

She whirled to find Zach Gregory stalking toward her. She forced herself not to flinch or step back. He was a big man. Intimidating. And despite all the stories Camille had told her about her smart, funny, kind brother, Shelby didn't really know him. Grief changed people, and not always for the better. For all she knew, Zach Gregory had a violent streak his sister had never seen. "I'm trying to find out everything I can about Camille's death," she said, keeping her voice calm. "Is that why you're here?" She should have thought of that before. Maybe Zach hoped to feel closer to his sister by revisiting the place where she had died.

He came to stand beside her. Uncomfortably close. She caught the scent of pine, perhaps from where he had brushed against the piñon branches, and heard the heaviness of his breathing, as if he was struggling to control his emotions. "I looked around," he said. "I didn't see anything."

"I was wondering about that tree." She nodded toward the broken trunk. "You probably know more about these things than I do. Do you think it just fell, or did the killer push it over or do something to make it fall?"

The question surprised him; she could tell. He glanced at her, then walked over to the trunk. "It looks pretty rotten," he said. He kicked at it, and bark flaked off. He bent closer and she did also, her face close to his. He had a scar by his left eye from where he had fallen on his bicycle when he was eight and had to have stitches. There was something so intimate about knowing that story, especially when he knew nothing of her childhood.

"You can see where it broke." He pointed to the jagged surface of the stump, the wood in the center dry and crumbling. "And it looks like there was a hole here." He pointed to a vacant area just above the roots on one side. "Maybe an animal dug this out to use as a den. That would have weakened the tree on this side."

"So maybe the killer saw that and shoved the tree over?" Heart beating a little faster, she moved over to the trunk. "Where would he have pushed, do you think?"

Zach joined her in examining the trunk. He stepped over it, then rolled it toward her slightly. "The hole I was talking about is right here." He pointed to the broken end of the trunk, the smoothed edge of a hole clearly visible. He stepped back over the trunk to stand beside her, then carefully tipped that side up.

"Is it heavy?" she asked.

"Not very."

He was several inches taller and more muscular than the man Brent Baker had described seeing leaving Camille's camp. "Could a smaller man, one not in as good shape, have pushed it?" she asked.

He straightened, and his gaze burned into her. "You have a suspect?"

"We have a description of a man who was seen leaving Camille's campsite about the time she probably died," she said. "We don't have a name or any definite identification."

"What's the description? Who saw him?"

"One of the other campers saw him. And the description isn't much—about six feet tall, on the thin side. He wore dark clothing and a rain shell with the hood pulled up, so we have no idea of his hair color or what his face looked like. He moved like a runner."

Zach looked back toward the tree. "If the guy was in decent shape, he probably could have pushed over this rotten tree."

Shelby bent to examine the tree trunk once more, estimating where the killer might have put his hands. "If you were doing something like that, how would you do it?" she asked.

"What do you mean?"

"I mean, would you put your hands on the trunk and shove, or find a big branch and whack the trunk?"

"I'd put my shoulder to it and give a big shove," he said. "Get some leg strength into it, as well as upper body strength."

She visually measured the trunk again. "So his shoulder would have been about here." She touched the tip of her fingers to a spot on the trunk.

Zach bent to examine the spot. "Up about six inches, I think."

She brushed her hands up six inches, studying the rough bark. Then she stilled, holding her breath. "Is that a hair?" Zach asked.

The single hair, perhaps six inches long, glinted in the sunlight, then disappeared as she straightened enough to reach into her jacket and pull out her phone. She snapped several photos, hoping they would show the hair in place. Then she tucked the phone away and pulled out her keys. "Go to my car and open the trunk. There's a small duffel bag in there. Inside the duffel is another smaller, black zippered pouch. Bring that to me, please." She kept her hand on the trunk, afraid if she moved, she would never find the hair again.

Zach took the keys and loped away. He was back a few moments later. She unzipped the pouch and took out a plastic evidence pouch. "Hold this." She handed the pouch to

Zach, then felt in another pocket of the pouch for a small case, from which she withdrew a pair of tweezers. She used the tweezers to ease the hair from where it was caught in the bark. She carefully inserted the hair into the pouch, then sealed it. She labeled it with the date, time and location where it was collected, then signed across the seal.

"Can I see?" Zach asked.

She held the pouch up to the light so they could both look. The single hair, a light brown or dark blond, glinted in the light. She said a silent prayer of thanks that the hair was not dark, like hers and Zach's. She didn't have to worry that one of them had inadvertently deposited their own hair on the log in the process of examining it. "Do you think that belongs to the killer?" Zach asked.

"I don't know." She tucked the bag into the pouch and zipped it closed. "It could belong to another camper who stayed here. But if we do find a good suspect for the murder, DNA might help prove he was here in the camp, and that could go a long way toward a conviction, depending on what other evidence we have."

"They had an eyewitness statement for Judge Hennessey's murder," he said. "That wasn't enough to get a conviction."

"We'll need to do better next time."

"Do you think there will be a next time?" he asked. "From what I understand, law enforcement has been after the Chalk brothers for years, and they've yet to make anything stick."

"We're not going to stop trying," she said. "They're going to make a mistake."

"That was one of the hardest things when we thought she died right after the trial," he said. "That she had sacrificed everything to testify against those crooks, and it meant nothing."

"It didn't mean nothing." She gripped his arm, not even realizing she had done so in her desire to make him understand that Camille's sacrifice hadn't been foolish or useless. "We weren't able to put the Chalk brothers behind bars, but we're still investigating them. They have committed other crimes—we're sure of it. And I wish I could make you understand the way testifying at that trial transformed Camille."

"What do you mean?" He didn't look at her as he asked the question, but down at her hand around his arm.

She released her hold on him and took a step back. "I didn't know her before the trial," she said. "But when I spoke to her about it, she spoke with such pride about what she had done. She told me she had spent years feeling guilty that she wasn't doing more with her life. She wanted to make a difference in the world, but she didn't have money or power, and she hadn't excelled in school or in sports. Her life was so ordinary, and then she had decided to speak up about what she saw in the restaurant that night. She had power over Charlie and Christopher Chalk in those moments, and she had the influence to show others that they could speak up, too. Though she was working at an insurance agency as part of her new identity, she was taking college courses, too. She wanted to work as a victim advocate, and she was so excited about everything ahead of her."

"But she threw all that away to come see me."

"I don't think she thought of it that way," Shelby said. "I think she intended to talk to you, then to come back. We had protected her for four years. I believe she trusted us."

"She didn't trust you enough to tell you whatever it was she wanted me to know."

Hearing him say what she had thought so many times hurt more than she had anticipated. "No, she didn't," she said. "But I'm doing what I can now to try to make that up to her." She turned away. "Let's look around a little bit more and see what we can find."

But all they found was a site swept clean of any other evidence. She consulted the sheriff's report again. Deputies had collected half a dozen soggy cigarette butts, a faded and bent beer can, two bottle caps, a gum wrapper and half a plastic water bottle, none of which were likely related to either Camille or her killer.

"Who was this camper who saw this guy with Camille?" Zach asked when they were back at Shelby's car and she was stowing the evidence bag in the trunk.

"I'm not going to tell you his name," she said. "You don't need to talk to him."

He shoved his hands in his pockets. "Maybe he would tell me something he wouldn't tell the cops."

"Or he might feel threatened and accuse you of intimidating a witness." At his thunderous look, she rested a hand on his arm again. "I know you want to do something to help, but there really isn't anything. I promise I'm going to pursue every lead. Camille was my friend, and finding the person who killed her is important to me."

"Were you even going to tell me about this man?"

"I was if you had ever returned my calls or texts."

He flushed and looked away. "I didn't feel like talking to anyone."

"I need you to talk to me," she said. "I especially need you to tell me if you see anything or anyone suspicious. You know this town better than I do. You would recognize someone who was out of place when I might not."

"Lots of tourists visit here, especially in summer," he said.

"Has anyone been paying unusual attention to you?" she

asked. "Have you noticed anyone following you or hanging around your townhouse?"

He shook his head. "There isn't anyone. I think that car the other night was just a coincidence, not someone following us."

Maybe. But maybe not. "I need you to help me," she said.

"With what? You just said there isn't anything I can do."

"Maybe I was wrong." She considered him. Hurt etched every line of his face and every angle of his body. He looked so vulnerable, despite his powerful physique. "Tell me, why do you think Camille came here, to this campground? I mean, why do that instead of going straight to you? Eagle Mountain is a small town. If she knew you were here, she wouldn't have much trouble finding you."

He frowned, but she could see he was seriously considering the question. "Maybe she wanted to make sure no one was watching her," he said. "No one she might inadvertently lead to me."

"So she was cautious like that?"

He shook his head. "Not cautious. She was always pretty daring. But not rash. She made quick decisions, but they were almost always the right ones. She was smart. It was true she didn't do that well in school, but that was because classes bored her. She always wanted to be active. Like you said, she wanted to make a difference."

"Most people aren't like that," Shelby said. "Most people wouldn't risk so much to tell the truth."

"I think it had a lot to do with Laney dying," he said. "When she got that tattoo, she told me it was to remind her that she was living for two people now."

"That helps me," she said. "Knowing what motivated her. Can I come talk to you again about her?"

"Yeah. Sure." His eyes met hers, and the depth of that

gaze, the openness, made her unsteady. "It would help me, too," he said. "Talking about her, to someone else who knew her."

"Then it's a deal." She got into her car before she did something wildly inappropriate like throw her arms around him. He looked like he needed a hug, but she probably wasn't the right person to give it. She was already in trouble with her supervisors for getting too personally involved with witnesses in her cases. She was well aware that they hadn't sent her to Eagle Mountain because they expected actual results. They thought exiling her to this remote mountain town for a week or two might teach her a lesson about what it took to get ahead in the Bureau. They didn't seem to understand that for her, getting ahead wasn't nearly as important as getting the job right.

Chapter Seven

Four and a half years ago

Zach stood at the window of his childhood bedroom and peered through the blinds at the reporters lined up on the sidewalk in front of his parents' house. News vans, white satellite dishes angled toward the sky, crowded curbs and blocked the neighbors' driveways. Ever since someone had leaked Camille's name to the media as the key witness in the upcoming Chalk brothers trial, it had been like this. Zach and his parents had to run a gauntlet every time they left the house.

Zach had moved back home shortly after Camille had been relocated to a safe house to await the trial. At first, it hadn't been so bad. His parents were shaken, but they were strong people, and they were proud of their daughter for taking this stand.

But then the media attention had focused on them. Unwilling to allow his parents to face the constant presence of the reporters alone, Zach had asked for leave from his job. When that had been refused, he had resigned. At least he was big enough to intimidate all but the most forward reporters when he went out to buy groceries or run other errands.

A flash winked—someone taking yet another picture

of their house. He stepped back from the window, and his cell phone vibrated. He didn't recognize the number. This was probably a reporter, too, so he silenced the call. Seconds later, his voicemail alert chirped. Bracing himself for yet another appeal to "just answer a few questions" he called into his mailbox.

"Zach, it's me! I have a new number." Camille's excitement carried through the phone. He pictured her pacing, the way she often did when she was on a call, as if she had too much energy to remain still. "Top secret and super secure and all that. Call me."

He hit the call back button, and she answered right away. "What do you think you're doing, ignoring me, you goof?" she demanded.

"I thought you were a reporter," he said. "Those are the only calls I get these days. That, and the occasional stranger who wants to share his conspiracy theory related to the Chalk brothers."

"I'm sorry about that. The feds are still trying to figure out who leaked my name to the press. But I don't think it matters, really. I mean, my name was bound to get out there when I testify at the trial next week."

"How are you doing?" he asked. *Where are you? When can I see you?* But he had learned not to ask those questions since that information, too, was top-secret. He accepted this was for her protection, but he hated not being able to see her. This was the longest they had been apart in their lives. Even when they had each gone away to college, they had come home for holidays and had visited each other's schools.

"I'm great," she said. "Everyone has been so nice, and this place where I'm staying is super posh. Some rich guy must be lending it to the government. Anything I want, they're bending over backward to give me. I feel like some pampered celebrity. I guess the cops have worked so long to try to get something on the Chalk brothers, and I'm giving it to them, so they can't do enough for me."

"Are you nervous about the trial?" He certainly was.

"No. I've been working with the prosecution on my testimony. They want to prepare me so the defense team doesn't rattle me. I feel really prepared, and I'm excited, really."

"Why is that?" Why be excited about facing a couple of murderers who probably wanted her dead? His stomach turned at the thought.

"I feel so strong!" Camille said. "Ever since Laney died, I've been trying to figure out what I should do with my life. I mean, we were identical twins. Exactly alike, except that she got sick and I didn't. Why was I spared, unless it was to do something important? I think this is it."

"I don't know if I believe life works like that," he said.

"I never went back to work after I left for the night before," she said. "Yet that one night—the night Judge Hennessey was murdered—I left my wallet and had to go back. If that hadn't happened—something that had never happened before—I wouldn't have been there and heard that shot and seen the Chalk brothers standing over him. And I wouldn't be here now."

No. She would be home with the rest of them. Safe. "I was there, too," he said.

"Don't say that. You weren't there. You didn't see anything."

He wanted to argue, but he didn't. Presumably, she was talking on a phone supplied to her by the FBI. They might have the phone bugged. Maybe they were listening in right now. "I want to do whatever I can to help," he said.

"You're doing it by staying with Mom and Dad. How are they?"

"Okay. They're really proud of you."

"I'm trying to make them proud. I was talking to a couple of the agents, and I think after the trial I might enroll in the law enforcement academy. Either that or law school. I haven't decided. But I really think I'm meant to help bring bad people to justice."

"When you were thirteen, you thought your destiny was to open an animal sanctuary." She had been raising a litter of abandoned puppies at the time.

"I'm an adult now. And this is serious. I could never do this—give up my job and my friends and you and Mom and Dad—if I didn't believe this was really important."

"I know. But we miss you."

"Once the trial is over and the Chalk brothers are behind bars for good, I'll be able to come home. We'll have a big party or something."

"I feel like a coward, letting you take all the heat." There, he said it. Any feds listening in could make of that what they would.

"You're not a coward," she said. "But I'm the one with the information the prosecutors need. If anything else came up right now, with the trial so close, it would only muddy the waters. Your job is to take care of Mom and Dad. We're still a team—we just have different roles to play."

Camille was the star in this production, and she was loving it. She would never say so, but she had always had a flair for drama and a desire for attention. Maybe it really was because her twin had been taken from her. She was missing that part of herself, and this was a way to fill that void.

He didn't know. He wasn't a psychologist, and he didn't really care what motivated Camille. He only wanted her safe and home again. If she thought that would happen faster if he kept his mouth shut and his head down, he would do that. No matter how much it hurt to think about. "I love you," he said.

"I love you, too. And don't worry. Everything is going to be fine."

SATURDAY WAS A training day for Search and Rescue volunteers who had been with the organization for less than a year. Veteran volunteers Eldon Ramsey and Ryan Welch taught the class, which focused on climbing skills with an introduction to rigging ropes for various rescue scenarios. "Don't worry about memorizing all of this now," Eldon said. "Just focus on the idea that every situation is unique. Learn the basics, and you'll begin to see how to apply things like anchor points and leverage to the various scenarios you might encounter."

"Being in good shape and building strength will make everything easier for you," Ryan added. "But the right rigging allows us to safely lift an accident victim or another rescuer from a dicey situation without having to rely solely on brute force."

"But being strong doesn't hurt," Eldon said, and nodded at Zach. The two of them were easily the biggest team members.

They practiced working with the various brake bars, pulleys and other equipment for rigging, discussed safety precautions and things to avoid, then left with the assignment to spend at least one evening in the next week at the local climbing park, working on their climbing skills.

Afterward, Zach approached Eldon. "I always thought I was too big to be much of a climber," he said. "All the rock climbers I see are smaller and lighter."

"Not all of us are string beans." Eldon set aside the gear he had been packing away and faced Zach. "A lot of climbing is about using your legs to push you up. When things get really vertical, we have to haul more mass up with our arms and shoulders than the wiry, lighter guys, but we also have more muscle to rely on, so it evens out. I'd say the only real disadvantage is in tight spaces."

Zach nodded. "I guess I just need to get out there and try it."

"We should get together after work one day this week," Eldon said. "I can show you a few tips."

"I'd forgotten that you work for Zenith, too," Zach said.

"You want to head out to Caspar Canyon Wednesday after work?" Eldon asked.

Zach had never been to the popular climbing area, so why not make his first visit with an expert? "Sure. That would be great."

Eldon turned back to the duffel bag of gear. It clanked as he slipped the strap onto his shoulder. "Don't stress too much about the climbing," he said. "It's important to know the basics, but we don't all have to excel in every area. And big guys like us can always contribute."

Zach nodded. His size had always made him stand out in a crowd, but working search and rescue was the first time he had seen that as an advantage. He left the meeting feeling good about the progress he was making. He was fitting in well with the team, and he was even making a friend in Eldon. He hadn't really had a friend since Camille had disappeared from his life after the Chalk brothers' acquittal. He had told himself he didn't want to be close to anyone, but lately, he'd begun to feel differently.

That afternoon, the morning's discussion of the need to stay in shape still on his mind, he decided to go for a run. He didn't much like running, but at least around here there were trails that offered more scenery than a high-school track. He parked at a local trailhead and set out. He hadn't gone far before he heard someone coming up behind him. He slowed and looked back and was startled to see Shelby Dryden.

Dressed in black leggings and a formfitting black-and-purple Lycra top, a wide headband holding her dark hair back from her face and dark glasses blocking the sun's glare, she didn't look much like an FBI agent. She slowed as she neared him, and grinned. "I didn't know you were a runner, Zach," she said.

"I'm not, really." He turned and began to jog again, the fine grit of the trail crunching beneath his feet. "But I have to stay in shape for search and rescue work. Some of our rescues require hiking, and sometimes running, for miles."

She easily kept pace with him. "I have to pass a physical every year with the Bureau," she said.

"Have you ever had to run down a bad guy?" he asked.

"Not with the Bureau, but once when I was a sheriff's deputy, I chased a shoplifter two blocks and tackled him."

"I'll bet you were a hero for that," he said.

"Not exactly." She grimaced. "I was reprimanded because it made a bad impression for the public to see me tackle someone on the sidewalk."

"How did you end up with the FBI?" he asked.

"There was a case in our town, a multiple murder and a kidnapping. The suspected murderer was wanted on federal charges, so the FBI got involved. They had already given up the woman who was kidnapped for dead, but I kept digging and figured out where she probably was. I was right, and that got the attention of the special agent assigned to the case. He suggested I take a course at Quantico." She shrugged. "The sheriff I was working under wasn't very happy about being shown up by a woman—his words—so I decided maybe there was more opportunity for me with the Bureau."

"How long have you been a federal agent?" he asked.

"Three years. I met your sister not long after I graduated from the Academy. I was just supposed to interview her to update our file on the Chalk brothers, but the two of us really hit it off."

Zach nodded. He was getting winded, making it harder to talk, though Shelby was scarcely breathing hard, despite the higher altitude and steep climb.

"Camille and I used to run together," she said.

"Seriously? She was never one for working out or sports or anything."

"She told me one of her first WITSEC handlers was a runner and she would go out with him. It was something she could do that made her feel safe. That was before she moved to Maryland and was given her new identity. That first six months or so, before people settle into their new lives, is tough on everyone. They don't have jobs or friends, they're cut off from their families and they're not supposed to go anywhere alone. A lot of people can't stick it out, but Camille did."

"She was always stubborn." And independent. She had been determined to testify against the Chalk brothers. Just her, by herself. She would bring them down alone. She had made Zach believe she didn't need his help.

"I have her laptop."

He stumbled, then stopped and stared at her. She stopped also and turned back to him. "The sheriff's department recovered it from the rental van at the campsite."

Camille's laptop. Something personal that she had touched. "What's on it?" he asked.

"I haven't looked at it yet."

"Can I see it?" he asked.

She frowned. "I don't know if that's a good idea."

"There might be things on there—things she's written that you don't understand that I would. I mean, we grew up together. We were close. I know how her mind works." Or he used to. Camille had literally become a different person in the past four years. One he hadn't known.

"Let me see what I find first," she said. "If I think you can help me, I'll let you know."

"I want to see it," he said. "I mean, a laptop. That's personal, you know? If she's written things in files on there or searched particular websites or even downloaded certain games, it would help me know what was going through her head these past few years." He stared at the ground, wishing he was better at expressing himself. "It would make what happened seem more real, I think."

"I can't make promises," she said. "But I'll see what I can do."

It wasn't the answer he wanted, but it was better than he could have expected from most people. Most agents. He had thought from the first that Shelby wasn't like those unemotional, by-the-book agents his family had dealt with before and during the Chalk brothers trial. Maybe it was because Shelby had known Camille. The two of them had been friends. He liked knowing Camille had had a friend in her new life without him.

"Come on," she said. "Let's finish our run."

They set out again, Shelby taking the lead again. Zach didn't mind. She made an attractive picture, pounding up the trail ahead of him. She wore a small black pack—he wondered if it contained a gun. Probably. It must be a strange life, to believe you had to go everywhere armed.

"Did Camille date anyone in Maryland?" he asked.

Shelby slowed her pace a little to drop back and jog beside him. "Why do you want to know?"

"I'm trying to imagine what her life was like. She had a job and I assume an apartment or a house. Did she have a boyfriend? Someone more serious?"

"She had a house. A little bungalow near the park where we jogged. And she dated a few guys. One of the only complaints I ever heard her make was that she felt she couldn't have a real relationship with a man because she could never tell him the truth about the past."

"Do people do that—I mean, do they get married and have kids and stuff and their spouse never knows the truth?"

"I think some of them do. Others choose to tell the truth, and then the spouse has to be sworn to secrecy. But they make it work. Relationships are full of compromises. I guess this is just one more. But you would have to be really certain about the other person before you revealed that you were in witness security. Your life could depend on it."

"It makes me sad, knowing she felt she couldn't really be close to someone."

"She had one serious relationship," Shelby said. "With that first WITSEC handler—the guy she used to jog with. His bosses figured out he was developing feelings for her and reassigned him somewhere across the country."

He stopped again. "Wait a minute. They already took everything else away from her—they took that, too?"

"It's not a good idea for marshals and the people they're supposed to protect to get involved," she said. She pushed her hair back and readjusted the headband. "But yeah, it was pretty awful. But probably for the best."

"Because everybody has to play by the rules?"

"Because if he had really wanted to be with her, he could have found out where she was resettled. He would have had access to that information or known someone within the Marshals Service who did. It might not have been easy to uncover, but if he really loved her, he could have found out. But he didn't. Which tells me that once he was away from her, his feelings cooled."

They started running again. Zach focused on keeping an even pace, on breathing and on the trail. Anything but his sister and what must have been a lonely life so far from the people who loved her most.

They reached the top of the trail and began to run along a ridge. Zach caught his breath and his pace became easier. "What about you?" Shelby asked. "Are you involved with anyone in Eagle Mountain?"

"Isn't the answer to that question already in my file?"

"It isn't," she said. "There's no personal information at all."

"Huh." He looked away. "Then why bother keeping a file?"

"We kept track of your whereabouts in case there was any threat to your safety from the Chalk brothers."

"And is there?"

"Not that we've been able to ascertain."

"But you said Camille came here because she thought I was in danger."

"That was what she thought, but we never found any evidence to prove that. Which is one of the most frustrating things about her disappearance. If she had stayed put, both of you would be safe now."

He heard the anger in her voice—and the grief. "Maybe whatever she was worried about is somewhere on her laptop," he said.

She nodded. "Maybe so."

"Will you tell me if it is?"

She pushed the sunglasses to the top of her head and looked him in the eye. "If you're in danger, I'll tell you," she said. "Even if I'm not supposed to."

She didn't wait for his reaction, but turned and took off down the trail, running hard, putting distance between them.

Chapter Eight

"Do you have any suspects?" Shelby's supervisor, Special Agent in Charge Donald Lester, got straight to the point when he contacted her Monday afternoon. Though she had been sending regular reports of her activities in Eagle Mountain, this was the first time they had spoken since her arrival.

"Not yet," she replied. "I'm hoping we can get DNA results from the hair I submitted—"

"What about the brother?" Lester interrupted.

"Zach?"

"He was in town. Maybe his sister contacted him and arranged to meet. He was upset, felt betrayed—whatever. They argued, and he killed her."

"Zach Gregory was one of the first responders on scene when Camille's body was discovered," Shelby said. "He was genuinely shocked."

"You weren't there," Lester said. "Maybe he's a good actor. He could have killed her, then returned to the scene with Search and Rescue and faked his surprise."

Zach? Kill his sister? "Sir, I don't think—"

"Find out where Zach Gregory was at the time his sister was murdered," Lester said. "Don't rule him out until you have proof."

"Yes, sir." Even though part of her resisted the idea that

Zach had anything to do with Camille's death, she saw the sense in ruling him out.

"If Gregory isn't responsible, do you have any reason to believe Camille Gregory's killer is still in the area?" he asked.

"I doubt it, sir," Shelby said. "If this was someone hired by the Chalk brothers, he wouldn't be likely to stick around."

"Then you won't accomplish anything by staying there longer," Lester said. "Focus on the brother, and if you can clear him, I'll reassign you."

She tightened her grip on the phone. "I'm getting closer to discovering what sent Camille to Eagle Mountain in the first place," she said. "She believed her brother was in danger, and if we found out why, that could point us to new charges against the Chalk brothers."

"We know they've committed plenty of crimes," Lester said. "Finding enough proof to put them behind bars has been a problem."

"I'm looking for that proof, sir. I have the laptop recovered from Camille's rental van. I'm hoping it will have something useful on it."

"You can analyze a laptop here in Houston," Lester said.

"Yes, sir. But I want to dig deeper into the brother. He may know something he's not saying."

"Do you think Camille contacted him before she was killed?"

Shelby considered this. "I don't think so. He was truly shocked when I told him about her time in witness security. But Camille had some reason for believing he was in danger. I want to find out why." She *needed* to find out what had led Camille to flee the safety of her new life in Maryland. Whatever it had been, she hadn't felt comfortable confiding it to Shelby, and that hurt, though she would never admit it to Agent Lester. She had worked to keep her friendship with Camille a secret, fearful of being accused of being too personally involved with the witness and transferred off the case.

"Have you found any evidence that the brother really is in danger?"

"No, sir," she admitted. She had tried to keep an eye on Zach and had questioned him and those around him and had uncovered no threat. Which cast a lot of doubt on Camille's motivation to come to Eagle Mountain. Maybe she had just missed her family. "But I'm hoping something on the laptop will clear things up."

"I would have expected her killer to take or destroy the laptop," Lester said.

"Maybe they didn't have time. There were a lot of people at the campground. We have a witness who saw someone suspicious near Camille's van shortly before she died, but the floodwaters were threatening to cut off the camp. He may have decided he needed to leave before he was trapped."

"I read the report," Lester said. "Not a lot of detail to go on." The sound of shuffling papers signaled that Lester had either turned his attention to something else or was growing restless. "I'll give you three more days," he said.

"Thank you, sir." With luck, she would find enough to persuade him to let her stay a week. Her instincts told her the key to this mystery was in Eagle Mountain.

"What's the brother like?" he asked. "The file makes him out to be a drifter. Interesting, considering Camille's degree of focus." Lester had worked the case from the first. He had been one of the agents on the scene immediately after the judge's murder. He had been the first to interview Camille after the Houston Police had contacted the FBI.

"He was grieving his sister's death," she said. "I think

he was restless and reluctant to get close to anyone. That seems to have changed here in Eagle Mountain. He has a good job with a mine and is part of the local Search and Rescue team. That takes a lot of commitment."

"Good for him. But is he going to help us bring down the Chalk brothers? Don't lose sight of the mission, Agent Dryden."

"I won't, sir."

"Good. Do what you have to, but wrap things up as soon as you can," he said. "You have plenty of work to do here."

"Yes, sir." She ended the call and sat back on the bed in the plain hotel room that was her headquarters in Eagle Mountain. She had promised Agent Lester that she wouldn't lose sight of her reason for being here. He thought that was to gather as much dirt as she could on the Chalk brothers and their possible connection to Camille's murder.

But Shelby had another mission in mind. She couldn't shake the idea that she had let Camille down. Looking back on her last few conversations with Camille, she could see that her friend had given her hints about what was going on. "I can't stop thinking about Zach," she had said. "I worry about him." Another time, she had asked Shelby what the Chalk brothers would do if a new witness to the judge's murder turned up—say, someone who had been passing by on the street. Would that person be in danger, given that the Chalks had already been acquitted of the murder?

"I think the Chalk brothers wouldn't want to leave anyone out there who could potentially harm them," Shelby had answered. "They might worry prosecutors would come up with new charges. Or the judge's family might file a civil suit. Do you know of another witness? Did you see someone on the street that night?" Shelby searched her friend's face for some sign that Camille was telling the truth or holding back.

"No. I was just playing around with possibilities," Camille said. "I didn't know if the case could go back to trial if a new witness came forward."

"Not if they've been acquitted," Shelby said. "No double jeopardy."

After that, Camille had switched the conversation to talk of a new television series they had both been watching. Only after Camille had vanished did Shelby replay that conversation and berate herself for not digging deeper. Were Camille's renewed worries for her brother and her mention of a potential new witness that night related at all? Was that what got her killed, or was the murder only payback for testifying against the Chalks in the first place?

Objectively, Shelby knew there were plenty of dead ends in investigative work, and many crimes went unsolved for years. But she was determined to do everything she could to discover the reason for Camille's fears about her brother's safety. She hadn't paid enough attention before, and let Camille slip away to face death alone. She didn't want to make that mistake again.

ON TUESDAY AFTERNOON, Zach was called into the human resources office at work. The HR director, Kathleen, was an efficient woman in her mid-forties with a British accent and long, highly polished nails, her brown hair pulled back in a tight chignon. "Zach, how are you doing?" she asked when he settled into the chair across from her desk.

"I'm okay. What did you need to see me about?"

"I was surprised to see you only took three days bereavement leave," she said. "I wanted to make sure you knew you're entitled to longer time off if you feel the need."

He rubbed the back of his neck. "I'm okay," he repeated. "I'd just as soon be at work. Staying busy helps."

Kathleen nodded, though she continued to stare at him as if prepared to dodge out of the way if he suddenly exploded. "If there's anything we can do to help, with navigating the arrangements for your sister's services, or if you need to travel to be with family..."

"We haven't decided anything for certain. I'll let you know." Was all this concern normal, or merely nosiness? "I'd really rather not talk about it," he added.

"Of course." She pressed her lips together. "I am a bit concerned," she said.

"About what?"

"An FBI agent visited this morning. She said she needed to confirm your whereabouts last Monday. I verified that you worked until noon, when you received a call that you were needed to assist Search and Rescue with evacuating a flooded campground, at which time you were excused from your duties here."

He stiffened. "Who was the agent?"

"A woman." She glanced down at the desk, and for the first time, he noticed the business card on the blotter in front of her. "Special Agent Shelby Dryden."

Why was Shelby checking up on him? "What did she say when you told her I was at work?"

"She thanked me and left." Kathleen leaned forward. "What is this about? Are you in trouble with the FBI?"

"No, I'm not in trouble." He gripped the arms of the chair. "Agent Dryden is investigating my sister's death."

Kathleen nodded. "If you need anything, be sure to let us know."

"Thanks." He stood and moved to the door. Instead of returning to his desk, he went out a side door that opened into the parking lot. Sun beat down, the warmth soothing after the air-conditioned chill of the HR office.

He paced, replaying the conversation with Kathleen. Shelby had been at his job? Why?

He pulled out his phone and found the history of her calls to him—calls he hadn't answered. He hit the call back button and she answered after only two rings. "Zach? Is everything all right?"

"No," he said. "I just got called into the HR office and was told that an FBI agent stopped by to verify my whereabouts the day Camille was killed. What was that about?"

"It's just a formality, Zach," she said. "I know you had nothing to do with Camille's death, but I had to eliminate you on paper, that's all."

"I didn't even know Camille was alive!"

"I know, Zach. I'm just dotting all the *i*'s and crossing the *t*'s. When we do find the killer, a good lawyer is going to immediately try to detract attention from their client by pointing the finger at family. Eliminating that possibility up front saves us all trouble in the long run."

He forced himself to breathe more evenly. "One of the Chalk brothers' defense attorneys tried to say Camille killed the judge." He remembered almost coming out of his chair at that moment in the trial. His father had pulled him down.

"No one ever believed that, but it's a way of planting doubt in jurors' minds."

He nodded, even though Shelby couldn't see him. "I would never have hurt Camille," he said. "Never. If only she had contacted me. She could have been safe with me, instead of at that campground."

"Or the person who killed her might have killed you both." Shelby spoke quietly, but he felt the impact of her words. "I'm sorry this happened, Zach," she continued.

"Everything about this is ugly. But you and I are on the same side here. We both want justice for Camille."

"Okay." He felt foolish now, blowing up at her. He wasn't one to put his emotions on display. "I have to get back to work now."

"So do I. But call me anytime, even if it's only to complain." He heard the smile behind the words and pictured her pretty, expressive face. "I'm tough. I can take it."

She didn't look tough, but he figured she had to be. Whereas everyone who saw him thought he was strong. They didn't know how wrong they could be.

SHELBY UNDERSTOOD ZACH was annoyed with her for checking his alibi. But she didn't want him to stay annoyed. It was important that he trusted her. She waited until she thought he would be home from work Tuesday and drove to his townhouse. He was just closing the front door behind him when she arrived. "I can't talk now," he said when she approached. "I was just leaving."

"Where are you going?"

He looked for a moment as if he might not answer. Maybe he'd tell her his destination was none of her business. It wasn't as if she hadn't been rebuffed before. "I'm going to pick up dinner," he said.

"Could I come with you?" Before he could object, she continued, "I need to eat, too, and I have information for you about Camille's belongings." Someone with the Marshals Service was already in the process of packing everything to ship to his parents, but she could let him know that was happening. Maybe the thought of having her things would be comforting.

He hesitated, then nodded. "All right."

She could see more of his truck in daytime—the interior cluttered with the belongings of someone who spent a lot of time in his vehicle—an extra jacket, a pack, a water bottle, coffee cups and gas receipts strewn about like confetti. "Where are you staying?" he asked as he turned out of the parking lot.

"I'm at the Ranch Motel."

"I would have thought the feds would spring for something a little more upscale."

"We're on a tight budget, like everyone else these days. But it's not bad. It's clean." She glanced in the side mirror but saw no one behind them.

"No one's following us," he said. "Don't be so paranoid."

Instead of arguing the point, she asked, "What did you order for dinner?"

"Special of the day at the Cakewalk Café—meatloaf, mashed potatoes and green beans."

"Just like Mom used to make?"

"Don't tell my mom, but this is even better."

He parked in front of the neat brick building with white lace curtains showing behind the mullioned windows. Inside, the older woman behind the counter greeted him with a smile. "Hello, Zach. Your order will be out in a few seconds." Then she fixed a questioning smile on Shelby.

"I'd like to get an order to go," she said. "Could I see a menu?"

"Of course." The woman handed over a menu, then left.

She opened the menu, and Zach looked over her shoulder. "It's all good," he said. "They do a great burger."

The woman returned. "Here you are, Zach," she said, and handed a bag over.

Shelby returned the menu. "I'll have the Cobb salad," she said.

"Sure thing. You can have a seat over there to wait." She nodded to a pair of chairs by the door.

She sat, and Zach settled beside her, the bag with his dinner in his lap. "Your food's going to get cold," she said.

He shrugged. "It's all right."

The door opened, and a woman entered. She was tall, her long blond hair in a single braid draped over one shoulder. She looked around and focused on Zach. "Well, hello there," she said, full lips curved in a smile. She moved closer and rested one hand on his shoulder. "It's so good to see you again."

"Oh, hey." He stood and set the bag with his dinner aside. "It's good to see you, too. How are you?"

"I'm well." Her gaze shifted to Shelby, blue eyes sharp and heavily lined with black liner. Shelby met the gaze but said nothing, even though there was no mistaking the woman's curiosity.

"Your order's ready."

The woman behind the counter summoned Shelby. She paid and collected her order. When she turned around, the blonde was even closer to Zach. "I'll see you later," she said, squeezed his arm and left.

"She didn't stay to eat?" Shelby asked.

Zach stared after her, looking a little dazed. "I guess not."

"Who is she?" Shelby asked.

"A woman I met on a rescue." He picked up his dinner and held the door for Shelby.

"What's her name?" Shelby asked when they were on the sidewalk.

"Janie."

"Janie what?"

"I don't know." He glared at her. "What difference does it make?"

"Where was the rescue?"

"It was that day at the flooded campground. She was one of the campers."

"The day Camille was killed." She still felt a chill at the words. Maybe she always would. "What was she doing here?"

"I don't know. Maybe she saw me through the window and came in to say hello. It was no big deal." He pulled his key fob from his pocket. "Let's go."

"She acted like the two of you were best friends."

"She did not."

"She couldn't stop touching you."

"Some people are like that. You're making a big deal out of nothing."

Maybe she was, but seeing Zach with the blonde had unnerved her. "I'm trying to be careful," she said. "You need to be careful, too."

"You're too suspicious," he said. "I can't live like that."

"You need to be more suspicious if the Chalk brothers are after you."

"Why would they come after me when all this time has passed?"

"You aren't worried that the person who killed your sister will come after you?"

He put the truck in gear and backed out of his parking space. "They don't have any reason to come after me."

"They don't need a reason. Maybe it's enough that your last name is Gregory." How could she make him understand that there were people in this world who were mean for the sake of meanness? They operated by their own code, and her job was to keep them from running over everyone who didn't live by the same code.

He said nothing else on the short drive back to his townhouse. His silence had the weight of anger behind it. The fact that he still didn't trust her hurt, but she couldn't let that interfere with the job she had to do. She slid out of the truck and stood beside him. "You may not want to believe it, but you could be in real danger," she said. "You have to be careful."

"I'll be careful," he said. "But I'm not going to spend my life hiding in my room. And I can't treat everyone I meet as if they're dangerous." Not waiting for an answer, he stalked away, toward his townhouse.

She didn't try to stop him. He wasn't in the mood to listen to anything she had to say. But she needed to make him understand that no matter how much he was used to trusting people, some of them *were* dangerous. And they didn't always reveal that dangerous side until it was too late. She wanted him to believe this, but how could he? He hadn't had her training. In spite of what had happened to Camille, he was still trusting. That was probably a good thing, but it meant she was going to have to work even harder to protect him.

Chapter Nine

Two months ago

The agents who had been around for the Chalk brothers murder trial talked about how cool Camille Gregory had been under pressure. The lead defense attorney, a beefy guy who had gotten as close to the witness box as he could and bellowed his questions, trying to intimidate Camille, got only cool scorn from the state's star witness. "What I want to know, Ms. Gregory, is what someone like you—a waitress—has to gain from testifying against powerful men like my clients. Who put you up to this?"

"I've always had a strong sense of justice," Camille said, looking him in the eye and not blinking. "But maybe you missed that class when you went to law school."

The courtroom came apart at that, and the judge had to pound his gavel and admonish the witness to stick to answering the question. But Camille wasn't cowed. "Was that a question?" she asked. "It sounded to me like an accusation."

The media had loved her. Countless articles referred to her as a "brave young woman." If she was losing sleep under the strain of the trial, she never showed it, those veteran agents told Shelby when she was first assigned to question Camille.

But Shelby had seen a softer side of her friend. One who confided that she spent more than one break during her testimony in the ladies' room throwing up from the stress of it all. And even though she had been upset that the Chalk brothers had gotten away with murder, part of her was relieved to have that ordeal past her. She had focused on building a new life for herself and doing all she could to protect her family.

So when Shelby visited Camille one Saturday afternoon for a "girls' night" of wine and videos and noticed the circles under Camille's eyes and the chips in her manicure, Shelby knew something was up. "What's wrong?" she asked as she watched Camille fumbling to open a wine bottle.

"Nothing's wrong." Camille tried to smile but couldn't force the expression into her eyes.

Shelby snagged one hand and pointed to the mangled manicure. "Has someone else been picking at your nails, then?"

Camille pulled her hand away. "It's nothing."

"If you're upset, it's something."

"I don't want to get into trouble." She wrestled the cap off the wine and filled two glasses.

"Tell me, and we'll figure it out together."

Camille set aside the bottle but didn't pick up her wine glass. Shelby waited, the silence stretched between them. She was better at this game than Camille and knew it.

"I know I'm not supposed to go on social media," Camille began.

Again, Shelby said nothing. She sipped the wine, gaze fixed on Camille.

"I opened an account. Not under my own name. And I never post. I'm just on Facebook and Insta and a few other places, to see what my old friends are up to."

Shelby wasn't surprised. She hadn't worked much with

witness security, but she couldn't imagine Camille was the first person to break the no-social-media rule. "What name are you under?" she asked.

"Gladys Grunch." Camille wrinkled her nose.

Shelby pulled out her phone, opened the Instagram app and found the account. No posts, as Camille had said. She checked Facebook. Same. "This doesn't look bad," she said. "The cybersecurity people will want to take a look. They can set it up so the account can't be traced back to you."

Camille picked up her wine glass. "Okay."

Shelby laid aside her phone. "What's the problem?" she asked. "What has you upset?"

"A woman I worked with at Britannia—Amy—posted the other day that a man came into the restaurant, asking about the night Judge Hennessey was murdered. At first, she thought maybe he was a reporter and told him she didn't want to talk about it. Then he said he wasn't a reporter, that he worked for the Chalk brothers. He said they had hired him to find out what had really happened that night. He said the Chalk brothers wanted to clear their name."

"Maybe they did hire someone," Shelby said. "We can look into it."

"That's not what upset me," Camille said. "It's that he told her the Chalk brothers believe someone else was at the pub that night, with me. They found out my car was in the shop that night and thought maybe my brother gave me a lift to work and picked me up, so he might have seen something." She set the wine glass down hard enough that some of the liquid sloshed onto the counter. "Zach wasn't there. I took the bus that night. But if the Chalk brothers believe he was, they might hurt him."

"We'll check out this guy and see what we can find

out," Shelby said. "And we'll alert local law enforcement to keep an eye on Zach."

Camille nodded and picked up the wine again. "This place Zach is living—Eagle Mountain. Have you ever been there?"

"No."

"I looked it up online," Shelby said. "It's pretty. Really small, in the mountains. They don't have a traffic light or a single chain store. Hard to imagine."

"I would think it would be harder for a stranger to blend in, in a place like that," Shelby said. "And easier for the local cops to make sure Zach is all right."

"I guess it's silly for me to worry after all this time," Camille said. "I mean, Zach doesn't have anything to do with the Chalk brothers or Judge Hennessey's murder or anything. He's moved on with his life and probably doesn't even think about me."

"Your family hasn't forgotten you," Shelby said. "How could they?"

Camille shrugged and drained her glass. "It's hard," she whispered.

"Hard to be without them," Shelby said.

"That. But it's harder to know I can't protect them. Before, during the trial, I could still keep an eye on them, and there were cops everywhere to look out for them. Then, when it came time for me to leave, I knew that staying away from them was the best way to protect them. Knowing that what I was doing was helping them kept me going those first difficult months. But when I read Amy's post online, I realized how vulnerable they still are. And how helpless I am." Her eyes met Shelby's, shiny with unshed tears. "They shouldn't have to suffer for what I did," she said. "That was never what I wanted."

Shelby put her hand on her friend's. "I know," she said. "I promise, we're still looking out for them."

Camille looked down into her empty glass. "Zach looks tough, but he has such a soft heart," she said. "He could never have stood up to what the Chalk brothers put me through. I think to deal with really bad people like that you have to be a little bad yourself."

"You're not bad," Shelby said.

"Only when I have to be." She smiled, and some of the sadness lifted. "I feel better now, talking to you. Now let's pick out a movie. I'm in the mood for something sappy and romantic. How about you?"

Shelby would have liked to talk more, but she knew when to surrender to Camille. The moment of vulnerability had passed, and the impervious Camille was back in charge. The woman who had made up her mind and wouldn't back down.

ELDON AND ZACH met in the Zenith Mine parking lot after work on Wednesday and drove together in Zach's truck to Caspar Canyon. With the summer solstice approaching, the days were long enough to allow plenty of hours of good light for climbing the many designated routes on the canyon's granite walls. They shouldered their gear, and Eldon led the way into the canyon. They passed other climbers along the way, many of whom called out to Eldon in greeting. "Do you know everybody?" Zach asked after the sixth time they stopped to chat with another climber.

"This is a small town," Eldon said. "Sooner or later you do feel like you know everyone. But the climbing community is especially close."

"How long have you lived here?" Zach asked.

"A little over two years. How about you?"

"Nine months," Zach said.

"You'll be an old-timer in no time." They stopped beside an empty section of canyon wall that towered thirty feet overhead. Smooth rock in shades of caramel, red, gold and cream reminded Zach of melted candle wax—and looked almost as slick. "This is a good beginner pitch," Eldon said. "Let's get our gear set up."

Zach studied the wall again. It wasn't perfectly vertical, but almost, and while permanent pins studded the wall like cloves in a ham, nothing about this said "beginner" to him. "I really haven't climbed much at all," he said as he unfolded his harness. "Just a couple of times during SAR training."

"That's all you need for this pitch," Eldon said. "Trust me."

Helmets and harnesses in place, Eldon reviewed the basics. Then he turned to the wall. "I'd start right there. See that handhold? Grab hold of that, then you can put your foot right there. See where the rock juts out a little. Perfect step. From there, you should be able to reach that little lip to the left. See it?"

Zach looked closer, and he began to notice not smooth wall, but dozens of little divots and protrusions. Enough for a hand-or foothold. Still, he had to be strong enough to make his way up the wall without losing his balance. "What if I miss a hold or lean back too far?" he asked.

"The rope will catch you." He indicated the belay ropes stretched out between them. "I'll climb up first and set this, then you come up after. Don't worry. It will be just like walking up a ladder."

Eldon went up first, without a rope. He easily scaled the wall, moving so quickly Zach didn't have time to make note of every place he put his hands or feet. He anchored the rope and tossed the end down to Zach, who fastened it to his harness as he had learned in SAR training. Then he rubbed his hands together, took a deep breath. "You can do this," he muttered, and started up.

Eldon had lied, he decided after he had hauled himself up the first few feet. This wasn't as easy as climbing a ladder. But it wasn't impossible. And as long as he avoided looking down and focused on carefully choosing his next handhold or his next step up, he could do this. His muscles protested and shook with strain by the time he reached the top, but he didn't freeze or freak out. He was grinning by the time he stood beside Eldon at the canyon rim.

"That was great." Eldon slapped him on the back. "How did it feel?"

"It felt good." He rolled his shoulders. "I felt…strong."

"Didn't I tell you? You may have more bulk to haul up here, but you have the muscle to do it. Did you play football in high school?"

"Left tackle." Ages ago.

"Same here," Eldon said. "Climbing beats crashing into people on the field any day, in my book."

They spent the next two hours climbing in a couple of different areas. In between climbs, they discovered surprisingly similar backgrounds. Eldon was from Hawaii, but like Zach, he had grown up with one sister. She was married with kids in Hawaii. "My whole family can't understand why I would ever leave the islands," he said. "I miss them all, but I'm happier here. I just fit in better here, you know?"

Zach nodded. He was beginning to feel that way, too. He loved his parents, but he was glad they had moved away from Houston. That city held too many reminders of Camille. Here in the mountains they could all start fresh.

Had Camille felt that when she moved to Maryland? She had truly started over, with a new name, a new backstory. Had she gotten to choose the details herself, or had the Marshals Service assigned her a role? Either way, she would have relished playing this new part. She had always enjoyed being the life of the party or the star of the show.

The sun was setting when they packed up their gear and headed back to Zach's truck. They were loading up when someone hailed them from across the parking lot. "Hey!"

They turned and saw a tall blond loping toward them. "Remember me?" the man asked. "Todd. You two were part of the Search and Rescue team that took care of me when I rolled my ATV last week."

"Todd with two Ds," Eldon said. "How are you doing?"

"I'm good." He pointed to the fading cut on the side of his head. "This is almost healed up." He nodded toward their gear bags. "So you guys been doing some climbing?"

No, we just carry this stuff around to look good, Zach thought. Instead, he said, "Do you climb?"

"I've been thinking about getting into it. I just came out here to watch. Say, I owe you guys a beer. Want to go somewhere and grab a drink?"

Eldon looked at Zach. "Sound okay to you?"

Zach shrugged. "Sure, why not?" He wasn't going to turn down a free beer, and it wasn't as if he had anything else planned for that evening.

"You can follow us to Mo's Pub," Eldon said. "Do you know where that is?"

Todd grinned. "It's my new favorite place. Let me help you with your gear." He bent and picked up Zach's gear bag, grunting with the effort.

"I'll get it." Zach stepped in and took the bag from Todd.

Todd slapped him on the back. "Guess I'd better leave the heavy lifting to the real mountain man." He followed them to the parking area, then waved. "See you at Mo's," he said, and loped toward a white sedan.

"You don't mind having a drink or two with this guy,

do you?" Eldon asked when he and Zach were alone in Zach's truck.

"It's okay," Zach said. "He seems nice enough."

"He'll probably want to hear search and rescue stories," Eldon said. "He had that look. But we only have to stay for one drink if he's too much."

"I'm good," Zach said. Normally, he wouldn't spend time with someone he didn't know, but he was trying to be more sociable since moving to Eagle Mountain. He wanted to stay here awhile, and that meant fitting in with the community.

Mo's Pub was busy with a midweek crowd. Drinkers filled the stools around the L-shaped bar, a baseball game showing on the TVs overhead. The three men found a booth along one side and ordered beers. "So what brings you to Eagle Mountain?" Eldon asked Todd.

"Oh, you know, the scenery. The outdoors. I live in Denver and wanted to get away from the city for a few days. I'd never been here before and thought I'd take a look." He turned to Zach. "What about you guys? Have you lived here long?"

"A little while," Zach said.

"I can see why someone would want to settle down here," Todd said. "I really like the vibe of the place. Are there any good jobs? Where do you work?" He glanced at Eldon, then focused on Zach once more. His laser focus made Zach uncomfortable. Why was this guy asking so many questions?

"We work at the Zenith gold mine," Eldon said.

"A gold mine? No kidding? What do you do there?"

"Nothing exciting," Zach said before Eldon could answer. They were never going to see this guy again, so there was no need to tell their life stories.

"Zach Gregory." Todd said the name as if trying it out.

"Are you related to that woman who was killed during the flood at that campground early last week?"

"How did you know about that?" Zach asked.

"I read about it in the paper. Was she a relative of yours?"

"She was my sister." He kept his voice flat, hoping Todd would get the message that this wasn't something Zach wanted to discuss.

"Hey, I didn't know. I'm sorry." Todd shook his head. "That must have been rough. What happened to her? The paper said a tree fell on her van."

Zach met Todd's eyes with a hard stare. Apparently, this guy couldn't take a hint. "I don't want to talk about it," he said.

"Yeah, I get it." Todd nodded, then opened his mouth, as if to ask another nosy question.

"What happened with your rental ATV?" Eldon asked, and Zach was grateful to him for changing the subject. "They didn't ding you too much for the damage, did they?"

"Three hundred bucks." Todd winced. "But I guess it's going to cost that much to knock out the dents. That's what I get for going too fast on those rough trails." He turned back to Zach. "My sister died a few years ago," he said. "So I know how you feel."

I doubt it, Zach thought. "I'm sorry to hear that," he said.

"Yeah. She was shot in a drive-by shooting. They never did find out who killed her. That's hard, you know? No closure."

Zach stared. Was this guy telling the truth? How much did he know about Camille's death? Zach hadn't read the article in the paper, so he didn't know how much it said. Maybe he should find a copy and read it. Or he could ask Shelby.

"Zach!"

He jerked his head up to see a familiar woman working her way through the crowd toward them. More than one man's head turned to watch her as she passed. The tall blonde wore formfitting jeans and a black, low-cut sleeveless top that showed off an impressive figure. Zach stood as she approached the booth. "Hey, Janie," he said, aware of Eldon and Todd staring.

"Hey, there," she said, and leaned in to give him a big hug.

When they separated, Eldon was grinning, and Todd was frowning. "I don't mean to intrude," she said, "but I've been looking all over town for you." She kept one hand on his arm, her hip brushing the top of his thigh. She was tall for a woman, close to six feet, and he felt less like a giant next to her. "I wanted to say thank you again." She looked at the vacant seat next to Zach.

"Sit down," he said, moving over to make room.

"I'd better go," Todd said. "It was good to see you guys again." He slid out of the booth and hurried away.

"I didn't mean to scare off your friend," Janie said as she slid into the booth next to Zach. She sat close, almost touching him.

"It's okay," Zach said. "Um, Eldon, this is Janie. She was one of the campers we evacuated from the Piñon Creek campground."

"I remember." Eldon was still grinning.

"It's nice to see you again, too." She offered him her hand. Her nails were painted pale blue, and her bare arms were tanned, as if she'd spent a week at the beach.

They shook hands. "Where are you from?" he asked.

"I'm from a little town outside of Houston," she said.

"I'm from Houston," Zach said.

He felt the impact of her smile again, heating him up from the inside. "It's a small world, isn't it?" she said.

Houston was a big city, and lots of people from Texas visited Colorado, so it wasn't so surprising he should run into someone from near his hometown. Still, it was a little connection between them. "Would you like a drink?" Zach asked.

"Oh, just a Diet Coke." She hit him with the full force of her smile—white teeth, generous pink lips and brilliant blue eyes that sparkled.

The server arrived, and she ordered a Diet Coke, while he and Eldon asked for two more beers. "Did our friend pick up the tab for the first round?" Eldon asked.

"'Fraid not," said their server, a redhead named Kiki.

"I figured," Eldon said.

"Some friend," Kiki said, and sauntered away.

"You should let me pay," Janie said. "Since I sort of ran him off."

"Don't worry about it," Zach said.

"Are you camping by yourself?" Eldon asked. "Or with friends? A boyfriend?" He smirked at Zach.

"Just some friends." She smiled at Kiki as the server set a glass of Diet Coke in front of her, along with Zach's and Eldon's beers. "Thanks." She sipped the drink, then added, "Actually, they left today to head out to Moab. I decided to stick around a few more days." She moved her leg so that she brushed against Zach. "I was hoping I'd run into you again."

"Uh, yeah. It's good to see you again, too." He sipped his beer, aware of her still touching him. He was flattered by her attention, but why was she coming on so strong? She didn't know anything about him. And all he knew about her was that she was gorgeous and not at all shy.

"How long have you two volunteered with Search and Rescue?" she asked, including Eldon in the conversation.

"A couple of years," Eldon said. "Zach is still a rookie."

"It's really amazing that you give so much of your time and energy to helping others," she said.

"It's a pretty amazing group," Eldon said.

Janie was still looking at Eldon, but her hand was stroking Zach's thigh. Maybe this wasn't even happening. Maybe it was a dream. Any minute now, firefighters would rush in and start spraying him down with a fire hose, or the server would show up with a live duck on a silver tray, or some other bizarre thing would occur to let him know that he definitely wasn't in the real world anymore.

"Now this is interesting," Eldon said. He was looking over Zach's shoulder.

Zach turned his head to see Shelby striding toward them. Like Janie, she was dressed in jeans, but she also wore a light jacket and a grim expression. She stopped beside the table, and her gaze flicked over Eldon and Janie before settling on Zach. "We need to talk," she said.

"Zach's a little busy right now," Janie said. Her voice was pleasant enough, but Zach still flinched at the look she directed at Shelby. He half expected to smell singed hair.

"Janie, this is Shelby," Zach said. "Shelby, this is Janie."

"Agent Shelby Dryden, FBI," Shelby said.

Janie laughed. "Oh, that's funny," she said. "I thought maybe you were Zach's ex-girlfriend or something." She turned to Zach. "But what does a fed want with you?"

"Zach is a potential witness in an investigation I'm involved in," Shelby said. She looked less sure of herself now. She turned to Zach. "I didn't mean to interrupt. But get in touch with me as soon as you can. I may have found something."

"Really? On Camille's laptop?"

She frowned and shook her head. "We'll talk later." With another glance at Janie, she pivoted and left.

Janie leaned in even closer to Zach. "Now that was interesting! You helping the feds? What was that all about? Who's Camille?"

"It's a long story." What had Shelby found that she needed him to see? Was it a clue as to who had killed Camille, or something else?

"I'm gonna call it a night." Eldon pulled out a wallet and tossed a twenty on the table. "That ought to cover my half of the tab."

"I need to go, too," Zach said. He forced a smile and turned to Janie. "It was good seeing you again."

"You don't have to say goodbye yet." She looped her arm in his. "Maybe we could go back to my place?"

Eldon made a choking sound, as if he was trying—and failing—to hold back laughter, either over Janie's heavy-handed seduction or Zach's obvious discomfort. Zach freed his arm. "Thanks, but I really do need to go."

She pouted, but it was such a put-on look he couldn't take it seriously. He saw Kiki headed their way and raised his hand. "We need to settle up," he said.

They paid their bill, and Janie reluctantly moved over and let Zach out of the booth. "I'm sure we'll see each other again," she said, and threw her arms around him. He froze, and when she stretched up as if to kiss him, he turned his head so that her lips brushed his cheek. He mumbled goodbye, then moved past her and out of the restaurant.

Outside, he remembered that Eldon had ridden with him. He waited until his friend emerged from the restaurant. "I was half afraid you were going to drive off without me," Eldon said as he slid into the passenger seat. "You were in a hurry to get out of there."

"Sorry," Zach said. "I wanted to get away from Janie."

"That wasn't what I expected when we decided to stop off for a beer," Eldon said.

"All I did was help with a rescue. I don't know why she was coming on so strong."

"She obviously has the hots for you," Eldon said. "But you can't complain about having two good looking women pursuing you."

"Agent Dryden's 'pursuit' isn't exactly the kind most people want," Zach said. "And Janie is gorgeous, but she's a little over-the-top, don't you think?"

"Over-the-top can be good," Eldon said. "But I know what you mean. She came across as kind of fake. The attitude, anyway. I don't know about the rest of her."

Zach nodded and blew out a breath. "I don't have the energy to deal with her right now."

"What about Agent Dryden?" Eldon asked.

"I'll call her when I get back to my place. She's here investigating my sister's murder. Maybe she's found something."

"That's got to be rough," Eldon said. "I couldn't believe Todd kept going on about that, even after you let him know you didn't want to talk about it."

"Some people are just socially awkward," Zach said. "I don't think he meant any harm. Does that happen often? People you rescue glomming onto you afterward?"

"I've never run into it personally, though I've heard stories about Search and Rescue groupies who pursue volunteers. But most people are just grateful and not pushy. I had a guy buy my dinner once when he saw me in a restaurant, but it was all very low-key. He didn't try to be my new best friend or learn my life story. And I never had a woman come on to me the way Janie did you."

"A groupie, huh?" He shrugged. "I don't get it, but whatever." He glanced at Eldon. "Are you seeing anyone?"

"Yeah. May is a local artist. We met when she worked at the coffee shop. Kind of an ordinary way to meet, I guess."

"Ordinary is good," Zach said. Ordinary wasn't something he had had much of in his life since Camille had returned to the restaurant that night. How could life be ordinary again, when he had a sister who had died twice and a file with the FBI with his name on it?

Chapter Ten

Shelby paced back and forth in the small space between the bed and the door in her hotel room. She had handled this evening with Zach all wrong. When she had spotted the message on Camille's laptop, she had been so anxious to figure out what it meant that she had contacted him right away. But his phone had gone to voicemail, and he hadn't answered her texts. She had started to drive to his townhouse, but when she passed Mo's Pub, she saw his truck parked at the curb and decided to go inside.

That was wrong move number one. Number two was marching up to the booth where he sat with the big Hawaiian dude from Search and Rescue and that blonde beauty queen who practically had blue fire shooting out of her eyes when Shelby had dared to talk to Zach. Where had she come from? Though Zach had never answered her question about whether or not he was involved with someone, her own discreet checking had indicated he was still pretty much a loner. And though he and the blonde—Janie—had been sitting very close together, she had sensed that Zach wasn't all that happy about it. But maybe she had been reading him wrong, and what he was really unhappy about was her intruding on his evening.

Mistake number three was giving Zach the chance to say anything about Camille or the laptop in public. She would have been smarter to wait until he returned her call or text and arrange a meeting at a later date and time. Now she just felt foolish and out of sorts.

Who was that woman? There was nothing in Zach's file about anyone named Janie. He said he had met her at the campground the day Camille died, but was that true? And now she was back in Eagle Mountain, cozying up to him in that booth at Mo's.

As soon as Camille had mentioned she was worried about her brother, Shelby had begun gathering as much information as possible about Zach, and she hadn't run into any mention of Janie or any other woman in his life. She had told herself she was doing it in order to reassure Camille that he was safe, but as weeks passed, Shelby had to admit she became more and more interested in the "big bear," as Camille referred to him. The information she had been able to glean had formed a picture of a quiet, intelligent, hurting man who was struggling to recover from the trauma of losing his sister and rebuild his life.

He was struggling, but he was winning the struggle, she had told Camille. Some people never got over tragedy in their lives, but Zach was stronger than most, physically as well as mentally. Shelby had found herself silently rooting for him when she realized he was staying put in Eagle Mountain longer than any other place he had lived in the past four years. He was part of a community here. He had friends. He was going to be all right.

She ought to be happy he was dating again. Camille would have been. But seeing him with that woman, who was crowding him in the booth as if she wanted to keep him from running away, had unsettled her. Why?

A knock on the door startled her. She froze. Who would be knocking on her door this time of night? The knock came again. "Shelby, are you in there? It's me, Zach."

She let out a breath, then checked the security peep. Zach stood in front of the door, hands shoved in the pockets of his jeans, bouncing on the balls of his feet like a boxer in the ring before the bell sounded. She unfastened the chain and the dead bolt and opened the door. "How did you know which room was mine?" she asked.

"I didn't. I knocked on all the doors on this floor until a guy told me you were in this room."

So much for security. She opened the door wider and let him in. "You didn't have to break off your date," she said. "This could have waited until morning."

"It wasn't a date," he said.

"Oh?"

"Eldon and I went climbing and stopped by Mo's for a beer and ran into Janie. You remember, I told you she was one of the people we helped evacuate from the flood last week." He froze, then swore. "She was at the campground with Camille. I should have asked her if she saw Camille. Maybe she spoke to her. Or maybe she saw someone with her…"

"The sheriff's deputies interviewed all the other campers," Shelby said. "Camille kept to herself and didn't speak to any of them except one man who made a point of speaking to her. He was the only one who saw anyone near her camp."

He still looked stricken. "Still, I should have asked. I was so taken aback by the way she was coming on to me." He flushed.

"She was coming on to you?" Shelby's conscience told her this was none of her business, but this information—and Zach's obvious distress—intrigued her.

"She was just…really grateful," he said.

"Does that happen very often?" she asked. "Grateful women throwing themselves at you?"

He laughed, though there was no mirth in the sound. "Never. And Eldon says it's never happened to him."

"She was very pretty." *In an overdone kind of way*, Shelby silently added. Was that catty of her? Maybe.

"I don't even know her." He straightened his shoulders. "I guess I prefer it if a woman lets me do at least a little pursuing. Or at least if the attraction leads to something mutual."

"You're not one for a one-night stand?"

Again the flush. It made him look boyish. "Let's just say I like to know a woman longer than ten minutes before we decide to go home together."

"I shouldn't have interrupted you," she said. "I apologize."

"No. It's okay. What did you need to talk to me about?"

She looked around for somewhere for them both to sit. The room contained only one chair and a table so small they would have difficulty both sitting at it. She settled for the end of the bed. She sat and indicated the spot beside her. "I want you to take a look at something on Camille's laptop."

The mattress dipped beneath his weight as he settled beside her, and she braced one foot on the floor to keep from sliding into him. Why did the fact that they were sitting on a bed and not a sofa feel so much more intimate? She pushed aside the thought and booted up the laptop.

"Our forensic experts will take a look at this more closely when I send it in," she said. "I'm just doing a quick scan to see if there's anything that seems significant right away. What I'm going to show you caught my attention, but I don't know if it means anything." The password screen opened, and she typed in *CMONKEY1016*, and the home screen loaded.

"How did you know her password?" he asked.

"The background of her password screen is of sea monkeys," she said. "October 16 is the night Judge Hennessey was murdered."

"The night that changed her life," he said. "Still, I probably wouldn't have figured out her password."

"The two of us spent a lot of time together. I knew how she thought." About some things, anyway. She hadn't realized Camille planned to leave WITSEC and head to Colorado until it was too late.

She opened a file labeled MeOhMy. "This was the first thing that caught my attention." She angled the computer so Zach could read the screen. "She's keeping kind of a journal here. This first entry explains her intentions. Read it, then I'll take you to the entry I need your help with."

She reread the entry along with Zach: *I'm starting this journal as a place to write down my thoughts and maybe make sense of some things. I figure it's better to put it here than on paper. If I write for long, my hand cramps, and if I need to, I can easily erase this file and even destroy the whole computer. Phillip showed me how to do that, in a way that no data can be discovered.*

"Who's Phillip?" Zach asked.

"He was the marshal she was involved with. None of the entries are dated, but move to the third entry."

He scrolled down to the entry in question: *I watched an interview online with Charlie Chalk. It was an old one, filmed not long after his and Christopher's trial ended, but I had never seen it before. Something he said made my blood freeze. He said, "There were other people involved that night, and they're the ones who will pay."*

I kept running the video back to replay that part. Maybe he was trying to imply that someone else—a third person— killed Judge Hennessey. That's what his defense team said all along. But Charlie knows that isn't true. So maybe he meant someone else was there that night. And the Chalk brothers are the ones who will make that person pay.

Claude, are you safe? Do you even know how to be safe? I've learned so much in the past four years. Mostly what I've learned is how naive I was before. I thought I had taken care of everything, but maybe I was wrong.

"Who is Claude?" she asked.

He shook his head. "I don't know."

But he wouldn't meet her gaze, and his face had lost most of its color. She carefully set the laptop aside and angled toward him. "Don't lie to me, Zach. I'm being honest with you. I didn't have to share any of this with you, but I did. All I ask is the same consideration in turn."

He stood, everything in his body language telling her he wanted to flee. "She didn't have any friends or coworkers named Claude." He shoved his hands in his jeans pockets and stared at the floor.

"There are other entries in here where the names have obviously been changed," Shelby said. She struggled to keep her voice even, though she wanted to shout at him that she wasn't oblivious—and that he was a terrible liar. "I think *Claude* is a code name, or maybe a nickname. And I think you know who she's talking about. Whose safety is she so worried about, and why?"

He stiffened, hands knotted in fists, jaw tightening, doing battle with himself. She waited, silently willing him to trust her with the truth. After a long, tense moment, he blew out a breath. "She called me Claude sometimes," he said. "There's a bear at the Houston Zoo with that name, and she teased me that I looked like him. But I don't know why she was worried about me."

"That's a sweet story, not an embarrassing one," she said. "Thank you for telling me."

He still looked miserable. Out of proportion for what

had been a pretty innocuous revelation. "What about the other stuff she wrote?" he asked. "Do the Chalk brothers think someone else was at the restaurant the night Judge Hennessey was killed? Are they telling the truth about a third man who was the actual murderer?"

"We've looked into the theory and found nothing to support it." She stood and went to face him. She needed to ask the question she should have asked long before now. "We know Shelby's car was in the shop for repairs the night Judge Hennessey was murdered," she said. "One of her coworkers said that you sometimes picked her up from work when her car wasn't available."

"She took the bus," he said. "She told you that."

"That's what she told us, but is it true? Did you pick her up from Britannia that night? Were you there? Did you see what happened? Is that why Camille was so worried about you? She heard the Chalk brothers were saying someone else was there that night and vowing to make that person pay? Were you that person?"

He grimaced as if in physical pain. "I didn't see the murder," he said. "I was waiting for her outside."

Some part of her had known this would be his answer. "All those times Camille insisted that she was alone at Britannia that night never rang all the way true for me," she said. "She put such emphasis on that one fact—she was by herself, she was alone, she was the only one to hear that gunshot—it was too much. But at the time of the initial investigation, before my time with the Bureau, no one ever doubted her or bothered to collect evidence to prove or disprove her assertion."

"She insisted that since hers was the only testimony needed to prove the Chalk brothers had murdered Judge Hennessey, there was no point putting myself in danger," he said. "She said our parents didn't need two children involved in that kind of danger. And…and I guess it was easier for me to agree with her." He looked away. "She was the brave one. I was a coward, letting her face that alone."

His pain pierced her. She took hold of his arm. "Camille wanted to do it alone," she said. "She may have wanted to protect you and her parents, too, but I think at least part of her didn't want to share the attention."

His gaze met hers, and the gratitude that burned there washed over her. "You really did know her, didn't you?"

"Yes." She told herself she ought to let go of him, but the physical connection between them felt too good to relinquish. "Camille liked the attention and praise she got for testifying against the Chalk brothers. I don't blame her for that. What she did was important and good. But I don't think she wanted to share that spotlight."

"Would it have made any difference if I had testified that I sat outside in my truck and waited for her?" he asked.

"I don't think so."

He put his hand over hers on his arm. He touched her hand, but she felt the sensation all through her body, warming her. Making her feel more alive. The contact only lasted a second but seemed much longer as she stared into his eyes.

Then he lifted her hand away and stepped back, breaking the contact. "I'd better go," he said.

She nodded. She didn't want him to leave, but he was right. Nothing good would come of him staying. "Thank you for telling me the truth," she said.

"I'm sorry I didn't say something before. Maybe if I had, Camille would still be alive."

"You can't know that. She liked taking risks. Maybe she was growing bored in WITSEC. If she hadn't decided to leave protection to see you, she might have found some other excuse. She wouldn't be the first person to take that kind of risk simply for the thrill. When you've been at the center of such intense excitement for years, a normal life must seem very dull."

She couldn't tell from his expression whether he believed her or not. "Good night," he said, and walked out.

She locked the door behind him, then pressed her forehead to the cool metal of the door. Her hand was still warm where he had touched her. That one moment of intense chemistry had been such a rush. She shouldn't have let it happen, but she could never regret it. Camille wasn't the only person in this mess who liked to live dangerously.

Four years ago

"WE FIND THE defendants not guilty."

Zach didn't hear the next words. Not because the crowd erupted into shouts, the judge slamming down his gavel to restore order. Zach didn't hear because the white noise of confusion filled his head. How could this be happening? Camille had been inside the Britannia Pub the night Judge Andrew Hennessey was murdered. She had heard the shot and looked into the dining room to see Charlie and Christopher Chalk standing over the dying man. She had testified to everything she had seen, not wavering when the Chalk brothers' lawyer tried to bully her and practically accused her of lying.

He had never been more proud than he had been when seeing his sister seated in the witness box, head up and back straight, telling her story with no sign of fear, though the dark eyes of the Chalk brothers bored into her.

But something had gone wrong. The Chalk brothers weren't going to prison for the rest of their lives. They were going to walk away from the courthouse as free men.

"What went wrong?" He lunged forward and grabbed

the arm of the lead prosecutor as the man turned to leave the courtroom.

The man glared and shook him off. "No comment," he said, and walked away.

Zach looked around the room for his parents, from whom he had become separated in the chaos after the verdict was announced. He spotted the back of his father's head amid a sea of reporters wielding microphones and cameras, and bulled his way through the crowd to him. "How do you feel, knowing your daughter risked her life for nothing?" a man in a stylish blue suit and dark glasses asked as he thrust a microphone in Zach's mother's face.

Zach leaned forward and shoved the microphone away, then put his arm around his mother. "Come on, Mom," he said. "Let's get out of here."

The surrounding reporters raised their voices, firing more questions. "No comment!" Zach all but shouted, then steered his parents away.

Two FBI agents emerged out of nowhere and herded Zach and his parents into an elevator and upstairs. "Where are you taking us?" Zach's mother asked, but neither of the feds answered—two men in identical dark blue suits, with identical grim expressions.

They led the way to a door and opened it. Zach filed in after his parents, and Camille embraced them. She was pale, her eyes swollen and reddened, as if she had been crying. The prosecutor was there, too, looking less grim than before.

"What happened?" The question came from Zach's dad now. His father, who was only fifty, was looking ten years older, his shoulders stooped, his hair thinning at the back.

"The defense team planted enough doubt that the jury failed to convict," the prosecutor—a man named Zable—said.

"But I was there," Camille said. "I saw the Chalk brothers standing over the judge's body seconds after that gun-shot."

"But you didn't see the gun or see them pull the trigger."

Zach had heard the defense team make the argument that because Camille hadn't witnessed the moment the bullet was fired, the jury couldn't say with 100 percent certainty that the Chalk brothers had killed the judge. Their contention was that someone else had run in and fired that fatal shot while the Chalk brothers were meeting with the judge. Zach hadn't thought anyone would believe that theory.

"Can you appeal?" he asked. "Ask for a new trial?"

"Not on a murder charge," the prosecutor said. "Once a person is declared not guilty of murder, they can't be tried again. Our constitution prohibits double jeopardy."

Zach's dad stood with his arm around his daughter. "What happens now?" he asked.

The prosecutor and the two agents looked at Camille. She eased away from her father. "It's going to be okay, Dad," she said. "I'm going to have police protection for a little while longer, just to make sure I'm okay."

"Is she going to be okay?" His father addressed the agents. "These men are killers. Thugs. They know who Camille is and that she testified against them. What's to keep them from going after her?"

"We have a lot of experience protecting witnesses," one of the agents—the one with the grayer hair—said. "You don't need to worry." He turned to Camille. "You need to say goodbye so that we can leave."

She blinked rapidly, as if fighting tears, then moved over to Zach and hugged him tightly. "Don't say anything to anyone," she whispered. "Promise me."

"I already promised," he said.

"Promise me again."

He said nothing. "What's going on? What's really going to happen?"

"I have to lie low for a little bit, that's all." She forced a smile, but her eyes were bleak. She stepped back. "I'll be okay. You look after Mom and Dad and remember what we talked about."

You weren't there. You didn't see anything. Except he had. He agreed with Camille that what he had seen probably didn't mean anything and wouldn't have made a difference in the outcome of the trial. But he hated that he had let her talk him into silence. She thought she knew what was best, but what if she was wrong?

"We have to go," someone said.

Camille straightened her shoulders and fixed her smile more firmly in place. "I love you all," she said. "Don't worry about me. I'll be fine."

The door opened, and she left the room, though Zach could scarcely see her in the crowd of men who surrounded her. He caught a glimpse of pink from the dress she wore, showing in the midst of a wall of dark suits.

He didn't know that would be the last time he would see his sister alive. Or that four years later, what had happened at the Britannia Pub would still be tearing at him.

ZACH DROVE WITH the windows open, letting the cool night air help clear his muddled thinking. Shelby had thanked him for telling her the truth, but he hadn't told her everything. He hadn't mentioned the man who ran into the street shortly before Camille exited the building. He knew he should have said something, but so many years of keeping secrets made it hard to get the words out. It was almost as if he thought he would be dishonoring his sister by revealing what he had promised to keep secret. The Chalk brothers wanted Judge Hennessey dead. They had killed him. Whoever that third man was, he didn't have anything to do with the crime. He was probably some street person, running from the sound of gunfire.

At least Shelby knew part of his secret. She knew he had been waiting for Camille the night of the murder. Even revealing that bit of truth had felt good, like letting off the pressure of a too tight tourniquet. That had to explain his response to her, that moment of electricity when he had fought not to pull her close.

The intensity of the moment had caught him off-guard, though he had been aware of a sexual tension between them from the moment he walked into her hotel room. He had put it down to the aftereffects of Janie's attempted seduction. Shelby was an attractive woman, but she was also an FBI agent who was investigating his sister's murder. She wasn't interested in Zach as a man. Still, he had spent the hour or so he was in that room breathing in the soft floral scent of her perfume, noticing the way her hair curled around her cheek and the softness of her arm as she brushed against him as she typed on the keyboard.

And then she took hold of his arm, and he felt the connection. He had wanted that touch and more. Whether it was frustration or relief or simple loneliness, it had taken everything in him to turn away from her.

He pulled into his parking spot and headed toward his townhouse, but when he dug in his pocket for the door key, he couldn't find it. He checked his other pockets, then retraced his steps to his car, thinking he might have dropped the key. But it was gone. Had he left it at Shelby's hotel room? Frustrated, he grabbed the door knob, wondering if he could force the door open. To his surprise, it turned easily in his hand.

Goose bumps rose along his arm as he stared into the

front room. "Hello?" he called, then felt foolish. If some-one was inside, were they really going to answer him?

He reached inside and flipped on the light. The room looked undisturbed. Exactly as he left it. He stepped inside. Nothing was out of place. Had he simply forgotten to lock the door when he left for work this morning? He had never done that before, but he had a lot on his mind right now. He went to the bedroom and took his wallet from his pocket and set it on the dresser and checked again for the house key. No, it definitely wasn't in any of his pockets.

He started to unbutton his shirt and turned toward the bathroom and froze. He stared at the small stuffed bear nestled between the pillows at the head of his bed. The kind of thing someone might buy for a child. What was it doing here?

Frowning, he moved closer. The bear, about ten inches tall, stared back at him with amber glass eyes. Was this someone's idea of a joke? Angry now, he leaned forward and snatched up the bear. The head lolled to one side, stuffing spilling from the neck opening. Zach stared, cold all over. Someone had sliced through the neck so that the bear's head hung by a thread.

Chapter Eleven

Shelby reread the last entry in Camille's online journal, trying to find some clue she had missed before about Camille's intentions. But the brief paragraph of an unspecified day's activities was innocuous. *Ran three miles this morning, rewarded myself with an iced mocha. Flirted with Dave, but neither of us is serious about it. Sasha was late again. Sushi for dinner, third time this week. I might be addicted!*

Had she written about such mundane matters to throw Shelby and others like her off the track? There was nothing in the entry about threats or being followed or any suspicion that she might be in danger. That led Shelby to believe that whoever had killed Camille must have picked up her trail after she left her new life in Maryland. Had the Chalk brothers sent someone to watch for any activity near Zach or her parents? Or had they discovered her new identity and merely waited until she was alone and unprotected to strike?

Her phone rang, and she grabbed it up and stared at the screen. "Zach?" She glanced at the clock beside the bed. He had left the motel thirty minutes ago.

He cleared his throat. "Did I happen to leave my house key in your room?" he asked. "I got home and can't find it."

"I haven't seen it. Let me look." Still holding the phone, she stood and scanned the carpet between the bed and the door, then looked all around the furniture. "I don't see it," she said. "Do you think it could be at Mo's?"

"Maybe."

Something in his voice alarmed her. "Is everything okay? You sound…upset."

A long silence. "Zach?"

"The thing is, when I tried the door, it was unlocked," he said. "I never forget to lock the door."

"Is everything inside okay? Do you want me to come over?"

"Everything is okay. Except…"

That silence again. It felt weighted. And wrong. "Zach, what is it?"

"Someone's been here," he said. "They left a stuffed animal on my bed. A bear. And, well, its head's been cut almost off."

Her stomach dipped, then rose. "Don't touch anything. I'm on my way over."

She hung up before he could protest that he didn't need her to come over. She shut down Camille's laptop and locked it in her suitcase and took it with her when she left the room. She locked the case in the trunk, then drove to Zach's, heart racing, even as she forced herself to stay only a few miles over the speed limit. Zach was all right. Whoever had done this thing hadn't hurt him.

Yet.

She parked beside Zach's truck and scanned the parking lot. No one was visible this time of night, and nothing looked out of place. She slid out of the driver's seat and closed the door softly behind her, not locking it in case she needed to leave suddenly, perhaps with Zach in tow. Then she walked to Zach's door, checking all around her for anything suspicious.

The door itself looked undisturbed. No sign of forced

entry. She rang the bell, and within seconds, the door opened. "I'm okay," Zach said before she could speak. "I'm just a little confused."

"Show me," she said.

She followed him into the townhouse, through the living room and down a short hall to the bedroom. Her first impression was of a comfortable room with a king-size bed, a dresser and a bedside table. She focused on the object in the middle of the comforter. A brown stuffed bear, head lolling to one side. It was just a child's toy, but the sight of it, disfigured that way, made her sick to her stomach. "That would freak anyone out," she told Zach, assuming an attitude of calm she didn't really feel. "Where was it, exactly, when you found it?"

"Sitting up between the two pillows at the head of the bed." He gestured toward the pillows. "I picked it up, and the head almost fell off."

"And you're sure the bear wasn't here before?"

He let out a hoarse laugh. "I'm a little old to sleep with a teddy bear."

She shook her head. "Have you seen it—or one like it—before?"

"No."

She pulled out her phone.

"Who are you calling?" His voice rose with alarm.

"The sheriff's department."

"No!" He held out his hands. "I'm okay. Nothing happened. It's just a sick joke."

"You said you lost your house key, right?"

"Yeah."

"And you haven't found it?"

"No. But I probably dropped it—"

"Whoever got in here did it with your key," she said.

"That means they took it from you. Who could have done that?"

"No one. The key was in my pocket. I would have noticed if someone had tried to take it."

"Not if the person was good at picking pockets." She studied him. "What about Janie? She was sitting very close to you when I saw you two together at Mo's."

He paled. "When I left, she hugged me."

"She could have taken the key then."

"But why would she? And why do this?"

"I don't know. But we need to find out. The sheriff can help with that."

She made the call. The dispatcher agreed to send a deputy. That settled, she took Zach into the kitchen and got a glass of water for him and one for herself. "Who else was close enough to you today to pick your pocket?" she asked.

"I don't know. Eldon and I climbed together this afternoon. But he wouldn't do something like this."

She could have argued that anyone might do something terrible with the right motivation, but didn't bother. "Anyone else?"

"There was this guy, Todd. We met him in Caspar Canyon, and he tried to help me with my gear. We had a beer with him at Mo's before Janie showed up."

"Is Todd another friend?"

"No. He wrecked an ATV in the high country last week, and Search and Rescue responded to the call."

"So you don't really know anything about him."

"No." He looked miserable.

The doorbell summoned them, and Zach ushered in a sheriff's deputy. "Deputy Declan Owen," he introduced himself. "I understand you had a break-in. What happened?"

Zach explained about losing his key and finding the

door open, then showed Deputy Owen the mutilated bear. "Nothing else was disturbed," he said. "It's really strange. And unsettling."

"I noticed the front door didn't look forced," Owen said. "Is there any other way for someone to get in?"

"I didn't think of that." Zach looked to Shelby.

"We should check," she said, wishing she had thought of that before.

They followed Owen through the townhouse, but the back door and all the windows were still secure. "I think someone stole Zach's key and used it to get in," Shelby said.

"Any idea who?" Owen asked Zach.

"I had a couple of strangers approach me this afternoon," Zach said. "Both people I had helped on Search and Rescue calls. I guess one of them might have taken the key, though I don't know why."

Owen wrote down the information on Todd and Janie, then bagged the bear as evidence. "Any idea who might want to frighten you?" he asked Zach.

Zach shook his head. "No."

"Zach's sister was in witness security after she testified against Charlie and Christopher Chalk in Houston," Shelby said. "Her murderer may have worked for the Chalks. There's the possibility they're targeting Zach now."

"I don't believe it," Zach said. "They don't have any reason to go after me."

"I used to work for the Marshals Service," Owen said. "I know about your sister's case. I'm sorry for your loss."

"Did you know Camille?" Zach asked.

"I met her once, before she was relocated. She had a good reputation in the office—smart and just a really nice person."

Zach nodded. "That was Camille."

"Why did you leave the Marshals Service?" Shelby asked.

"This is a better fit for me," he said. He nodded to Zach. "We'll be in touch. Call us right away if anything else happens that seems off or threatening."

He left. Zach dropped onto the sofa and rested his elbows on his knees. He looked exhausted. "I'll need to change the locks tomorrow," he said.

Shelby sat beside him. "You shouldn't stay here tonight."

"I'll be okay." He glanced to the door. "I'll wedge a chair under the door knob or something."

"If you have a pillow and some blankets, I'll make up a bed here on the sofa," she said.

He straightened. "You don't have to do that."

"I'm not going to leave you alone."

"It was just a stuffed bear," he said. "Sick, but..."

"It was a threat," she said. "Or a warning."

"You really think the Chalk brothers sent someone after me? Why?"

"Maybe killing Camille wasn't enough for them," she said. "Maybe they want to take out her whole family."

He stood. "My parents!"

She put a hand on his arm. "While you and Deputy Owen were in the bedroom, I called my office, and they're sending someone to watch over your parents. I told them I'd look after you."

He sat again. "This is unreal. You really think I'm in danger?"

"You said Janie was at the campground the day Camille was murdered. She has long blond hair."

"Wait. I thought a man killed Camille."

"A tall, thin figure dressed in a hooded raincoat and jeans was seen leaving her campsite. How tall is Janie?"

"Tall," he said. "Almost six feet." He looked stunned. "You really think she murdered Camille?"

"I don't know. What about Todd? What does he look like?"

"He's tall, too. And thin. And he has blond hair." Zach looked as if he might be sick.

"Was he at the campground that day?"

"I don't remember seeing him. But there were a lot of people there. And everyone was wet and bundled up in coats and rain gear."

"I'll work with the sheriff's department to find out where both of them were after they left you yesterday," she said. "In the meantime, I'll stay here tonight."

He stiffened, and she knew he wanted to protest that he could look after himself, but the memory of that almost beheaded bear must have stopped him. "I'll find you some bedding," he said and left the room.

When he was gone, Shelby took out her pistol and laid it on the coffee table, within easy reach of the sofa. She didn't believe what had happened here tonight was a harmless prank or a sick joke. The person who left that bear wanted to frighten Zach. Fear had a way of wearing people down. Of making them more vulnerable. But she wasn't going to let them get close enough to Zach to harm him. She had failed Camille. She wouldn't fail Zach.

Zach didn't sleep that night. Every time he closed his eyes, he saw that mutilated bear and heard Shelby telling him the Chalk brothers might have decided to come after him. Because they hated Camille so much?

Or because they knew he hadn't told everything he had seen that night in front of the Britannia Pub?

He tossed and turned, then listened as Shelby moved around in the front room. He thought about going out to talk to her. Or to do more than talk. He hadn't forgotten the brief physical connection they had shared in her motel room earlier that evening. How wonderful would it be to focus on exploring that instead of being afraid? To escape for a while in a different kind of emotion?

But that wouldn't be a good idea. And Shelby didn't strike him as the type to get distracted when she had a job to do. So he turned over again and stayed in bed, finally slipping into a troubled sleep full of swirling waters, a blond figure running away from him and a real bear that roared at him from the underbrush.

He went through the next day on autopilot, half expecting his coworkers to ask what was wrong. But everyone was busy in the run-up to the opening of a new mine shaft, and no one questioned the dark circles beneath his eyes or his distracted air.

At four o'clock, Deputy Owen called. "Could you stop by the sheriff's office when you get off work?" he asked.

"Sure. Did you find something?"

"We just have a few more questions to ask you."

Shelby was waiting in the room with Sheriff Walker and Deputy Owen when the office manager, Adelaide Kinkaid, escorted Zach inside a little over an hour later. "Thanks for stopping by," Sheriff Walker said. He nodded to the lone empty chair. "Sit down."

He sat and glanced at Shelby, who looked at him in a way that was probably meant to be reassuring, but only made him brace himself for worse news. "What have you found out about the break-in at my place last night?" he asked.

"None of your neighbors saw anyone suspicious," the sheriff said. "But that's not too surprising, if someone with a key walked up and opened the door and went inside. Most people wouldn't look twice. And the way the townhomes are arranged, your front door faces the street. None of your neighbors could see it from inside their homes."

"Did you talk to Todd or Janie?" he asked.

"Without a last name, we're having trouble locating Janie," the sheriff said. "You say she was at the campground the day Search and Rescue helped evacuate flooded campers?"

"Yes. She came up and hugged me and thanked me for helping out."

"And later at Mo's, she thanked you again?"

"Yes." He frowned.

"You don't remember a last name?" Deputy Owen asked.

"I'm sure she never said. You could ask Eldon Ramsey. He was there, too. And he saw her at the campground."

The sheriff made a note. "What else do you know about her?"

"She said she was camping with friends, but that they left to go to Moab while she stayed in town a few more days."

"What was your impression of her?"

"If you mean, did I think she was the type to steal my key and leave a slashed-up stuffed animal in my townhouse, I sure didn't think that."

"Special Agent Dryden tells us Janie was coming on pretty strong at Mo's."

He didn't look at Shelby, and his cheeks felt hot. "She was flirting."

"There was no one named Janie, and no one who matched that description among the campers we interviewed about your sister," Walker said.

"But I thought you talked to everyone?" Zach asked.

"We were able to match the names of the people we did interview with every occupied site," Walker said.

"Maybe she didn't register," Zach said. "It happens. People occupy a site but don't pay. It's all on the honor system."

"Maybe. Or maybe she wasn't camping there at all." The sheriff glanced at his notes. "We did interview Todd Arniston. Do you remember seeing him at the campground that day?"

"No! He was there? He never said."

"We have a statement from him. But he says he never saw your sister or anyone suspicious."

"I went back out to the campground afterward," Zach said. "It had reopened, but I didn't see Todd there."

"He's moved into town. He's staying at the Nugget Inn. But he was out when a deputy stopped by. The deputy left a card, asking Mr. Arniston to call us."

"If the threat left at your townhouse does have any connection to the Chalk brothers, it might not be a bad idea for you to leave town for a few days," Walker said.

"I can't just leave," he said. "I have a job, and Search and Rescue commitments. And my parents. I can't abandon them."

"I received confirmation this morning that the FBI has a protection detail with your parents," Shelby said.

"Have they been threatened, too?" He needed to call them. He should have called last night, but he hadn't wanted to upset them.

"No. And we haven't told them anything about what happened to you," she said. "They think we're being extra cautious in the aftermath of Camille's death."

He nodded. That was alarming enough, but it was a story his parents would accept. Like him, they would find it difficult to believe they were in any real danger. Not after so much time had passed. Even in the run-up to the trial, when Shelby and her potential testimony had filled the news, Zach and his parents had never felt threatened. All of the focus was on Shelby. As horrible as her death had been, knowing she was gone had made them all believe the Chalk brothers would forget about them.

"I need to stay here," he said. "I'll be careful, but I can't run away."

Shelby pressed her lips together, and he wondered if she was biting her tongue, too, to keep from arguing with him. Her eyes telegraphed her disagreement with this decision, but she apparently knew him well enough now—or realized he was enough like Camille in this regard—that she didn't waste her words.

Zach stood. "Can I go now?"

Sheriff Walker nodded.

Zach left, Shelby on his heels. "You don't have to babysit me," he said. "I got the locks changed, and I promise to dial 911 if anything at all unusual happens."

"By then it could be too late."

"Look, if Janie or Todd really wanted me dead, wouldn't they have killed me by now? They've had plenty of opportunities. You don't think Camille had days and days of warnings, do you?"

She probably wouldn't appreciate it if he told her she looked cute when she frowned like that. Something about her intensity really got to him. "You shouldn't be alone," she said.

"You can't stay with me," he said.

"Why not?"

"You're too distracting." He met and held her gaze. The faintest blush of pink colored her cheeks.

"I... I'm sure we can get past that," she stammered.

Did he really want to "get past" his feelings for her? He shook his head. "I'll stay in touch."

She let him walk away, though he felt the effort it took.

Once he was in his truck, he looked back. She was still frowning at him, lips pressed tightly together. What did it say about him that in spite of everything else, all he wanted to do was kiss her?

Chapter Twelve

"There's been a new development." Shelby sat up straight and kept her expression neutral, just as if she was seated across from Special Agent in Charge Lester, instead of speaking to him on the phone. "A threat has been made against Camille Gregory's brother, and I've identified two suspects in her murder. I need to stay in Eagle Mountain a little longer."

"Who are the suspects?" Lester asked.

"A man calling himself Todd Arniston and a woman named Janie. Both names could be aliases. They were known to be in the same area as Camille at the time of her murder, and they have both shown an unusual interest in Zach Gregory. His townhouse was broken into the other night after his house key was taken, and both of them had the opportunity to take the key."

"Have the local authorities brought them in for questioning?"

"After the break-in at Zach's, they've disappeared, though I believe they are still in the area." She had no proof of this, merely a strong hunch.

"How was Gregory threatened?"

She explained about the mutilated bear. "Camille often referred to her brother as a 'bear of a man' or a 'teddy bear of a man,'" she added.

"This doesn't sound like the Chalk brothers," Lester said. "They don't play games with the people they kill. They assassinate them, and they don't leave evidence behind."

"If Todd or Janie are working for the Chalk brothers, they haven't shown up on our radar before," she admitted. "But Camille definitely believed her brother was in danger. I think that's why she came to Eagle Mountain."

"If she believed that, she should have shared her fears with the Marshals Service and the FBI and allowed us to investigate," Lester said.

"Yes, sir." Shelby thought she knew why Camille hadn't done so. She hadn't trusted law enforcement to act on her suspicions. Or she hadn't believed they would act in time. Testimony at the Chalk brothers trial had shown that the FBI was aware of the threat to Judge Hennessey weeks before he was murdered, and they had failed to act. Camille hadn't wanted to take a chance that her brother would meet the same fate.

"We have the DNA results on the hair you sent from Camille's campsite," Lester said. "There's no match in any database we've consulted."

"So this could be someone the Chalks haven't used before."

"Or someone unrelated to the Chalk brothers. Camille was a single woman, camping alone. She could have been killed by someone random who saw her and decided to kill her, or because she refused someone's advances, or because they wanted her campsite. As much as we'd like to prove the Chalk brothers are guilty of some crime, not everything necessarily relates back to them."

"Yes, sir. But we need to prove that before we move on. I'd like to stay a little longer and continue to look for Todd and Janie. Questioning them might clear up everything."

"All right. We'll take it day by day."

She ended the call and stood. She might not have much time left in town, so she needed to get to work.

She started at the front desk of the Ranch Motel. No registration for anyone who fit Janie's description. She moved on to the Nugget Inn, a sprawling new property in the center of town. The sheriff's department had said Arniston was registered here, but the clerk confirmed that he had checked out the previous afternoon.

"Do you have a woman named Janie registered here?" she asked.

"Do you have a last name?" the clerk, a middle-aged woman with short, tightly curled hair, looked suspicious of this snooping.

"I don't." Shelby pulled out her credentials and watched the woman's eyes widen as she took in the official Federal Bureau of Investigation logo. "But I'd like to speak to her if she's here."

The woman shook her head. "We don't have anyone named Janie here."

"She's in her late twenties to early thirties, blond hair and very tall—almost six feet."

"She sounds like a model," the clerk said.

She had looked like one, too. "Do you have anyone who fits that description staying here?" Shelby asked.

"No. I'm sure I'd remember someone like that."

"Are there any other motels or hotels in town? Other than this one and the Ranch Motel?"

"There's the Alpiner—that's a bed-and-breakfast inn. And there are a lot of private rentals."

A pleasant older woman at the Alpiner confirmed that neither Janie nor Todd was staying with them. Shelby left the inn and sat in her car, trying to decide what to do next.

She phoned Zach. He answered on the fourth ring, the sound of heavy equipment in the background. "Hello?"

"It's me, Shelby," she said. "How are you doing?"

"I'm at work. And I'm kind of busy."

He sounded annoyed. He was probably still upset with her. Because she was being overprotective? Or because she distracted him? She had wanted him to explain exactly how she distracted him, but was a little afraid of the answer. Maybe she had only imagined that he had wanted to kiss her that night in her motel room. And maybe she was the only one who tossed and turned later that same night at his townhouse, aware of him occupying the bed in the next room. He was a good-looking man, and through his sister she had come to know him better and care about him. Her attraction to him was natural, not unprofessional. But acting on it would be, and it would be downright embarrassing if she had misjudged his feelings. Maybe she distracted him because she reminded him of what had happened to his sister, or the way that the FBI and Witness Security had inadvertently ruined his family's lives.

Too bad. She was going to look out for him whether he thought he needed her or not. For one thing, if Camille's killer was hanging around intending to take out Zach, Shelby's best chance of catching the murderer might be to intercept him on the way to Zach. Two, she owed it to Camille to protect what was left of her family. There were other agents watching Zach's parents, but she was all he had. "What are you doing after work?" she asked.

"Going back to my place."

"I'll come over."

"You don't have to do that."

"I don't have to stay, but I want to talk to you."

She wasn't sure if the silence that followed was because

he was debating the question or due to an interruption. "I'll bring pizza," she added.

"All right," he said. "You can come over around six. And I like pepperoni and sausage. No mushrooms."

He ended the call before she could say anything else. She smiled. Zach might be put out with her, but he wasn't shutting her out altogether. She counted that a small victory, at least.

ZACH REMINDED HIMSELF again that inviting Shelby over was probably a bad idea, but he hadn't been able to say no. Around her, he didn't have to pretend nothing was wrong. No one at work or among his friends knew about his stolen house key and the sinister stuffed bear. And unlike the FBI agents he had dealt with before and after the Chalk brothers trial, he thought Shelby would tell him if she learned anything about Camille's murderer or whoever had threatened him.

But when he opened his door and found her standing there in cropped jeans and a sleeveless black top that showed off toned arms, her hair loose about her shoulders, he questioned the wisdom of letting her inside. She didn't look like an FBI agent right now. She looked like a woman he wanted to date.

"Let me in before this pizza gets cold," she said, hefting the large pizza box she carried in both hands.

"Sure." He looked away as she brushed past him, but her floral perfume teased him over the scent of pepperoni.

He moved past her. "Come on into the kitchen."

She followed him, and he took plates and glasses from the cabinet. He didn't ask what she was doing here. "What would you like to drink?" he asked. "I've got beer and water."

"Water is fine."

"Are you saying that because you're on duty?"

"I'm saying it because I don't really like beer. But you go ahead."

He took a pale ale from the refrigerator and filled a glass with ice and water for her. She opened the pizza box. He studied the pizza before him. "Are those mushrooms?" he asked.

"Only on half the pizza. Your half doesn't have any."

"You didn't think I could eat more than half?"

"If you do, you'll have to pick off the mushrooms." She popped a bite of the topping in question into her mouth. "I love them."

He kind of liked that she didn't back down or try to cater to him. Or pretend that she didn't like mushrooms either—he had encountered women like that before, who tried too hard to please. Shelby clearly wasn't trying to please him at all. How perverse was it that it made him like her more?

They sat and began to eat. For a while, neither of them spoke. Hunger sated, he began to feel a little better. "Any new developments?" he asked.

"Todd checked out of his hotel yesterday afternoon. No one seems to have seen or heard of Janie."

"Do you think they've left town?"

"I don't know. But I'm operating on the assumption that they haven't." She plucked a mushroom from her slice of pizza and popped it into her mouth. She wasn't wearing any lipstick that he could tell, but her lips were a natural pink. They looked soft.

At the thought, he looked away again. "If they have left," he said, "it blows away your theory that I'm in danger."

"Maybe not in danger from them. But whoever killed Camille is still out there."

Right. Sobering thought. "Have you found out anything more?"

"No. Has anything else happened to raise your suspicions? Have you seen anyone following you? Have you received any threats you haven't told me about?"

The way she fired the questions reminded him that she was a law enforcement officer with a job to do. Not his friend, or date. "No. Honest."

"I believe you."

They finished eating. She slid the last piece of pizza toward him. "You can have this one. I picked all the fungi off it for you."

The way she said it, with a sneer of sarcasm, made him laugh out loud. He ate the pizza, then stood to carry the box to the trash. "Thanks for dinner," he said.

She rose also.

"You said you wanted to talk to me," he said.

"Let's go into the other room."

They moved to the living room, and he settled on the sofa, her in a chair across from him, hands on her knees. "The results of the DNA test on the hair we found at Camille's campsite didn't find a match in our database," she said. "That doesn't mean the hair doesn't belong to her killer, only that the killer might not be someone known to us."

"Someone associated with the Chalk brothers, you mean?"

"They have a big organization. We have files on most of the principals, but it's always possible they've brought in someone new. It's also possible that Camille's killing has nothing to do with the Chalk brothers. And it's possible that the threat to you isn't connected to Camille."

He stared. "Are you saying my sister dies and someone steals my key and plants a mutilated stuffed animal in my bed and those are just two random things? Bad luck?"

"I'm saying I don't know." She moved to the edge of the chair. "Who knew that Camille nicknamed you after a bear?"

"I don't know. I guess anyone who knew her. It wasn't a secret."

"She told me you were a bear of a man and a big teddy bear. Did she tell other people that?"

"Maybe. I don't know."

"Does anyone in Eagle Mountain know about it?"

He shook his head. "No. I never talk about Camille with people." Only with Shelby. He looked away, trying to control his emotions. "I miss her," he said. "I thought maybe after a while I wouldn't miss her so much, but I still do." He didn't think of calling her every day, the way he had for a while, but there was still an emptiness inside his chest when he thought of her.

"I do, too." Her eyes met his, and he saw his own pain reflected there.

He couldn't keep looking at her this way. It made him too unsettled, wanting things he shouldn't. He stood, and she rose also. "Was she really happy there, in Maryland?" he asked.

"I think so. I mean, none of us are happy all the time, but she had a job she enjoyed and friends, a nice house. I thought she was pretty well settled."

"How did the two of you become friends? I know you said you questioned her about the Chalk brothers, but it sounds like you stayed in touch after that."

"We just really hit it off," Shelby said. "We were about the same age, and she was easy to talk to. She was so smart and thoughtful, and she was a risk-taker. I guess we had that in common."

"I guess you don't get into law enforcement if you're the type who always wants to play it safe." He glanced at her again, and she was looking at him, head tilted to one side, as if she was studying a painting or statue. What was she seeing? Was he Camille's brother to her? A potential witness who could contribute to her case? A guy who had lost his sister, someone she felt sorry for? A man she wanted to know better?

"She talked about you a lot," Shelby said. "She said people underestimated you because you were such a big guy. They sometimes treated you like a dumb jock, when you were really smart."

He shook his head. What she said wasn't a lie, but it wasn't like he was a genius or anything.

"She said you were really funny, too, with this dry sense of humor and a deadpan delivery. She told me so many stories. I felt like I knew you even before I met you."

Camille could have told her some stories, all right. "She probably told you all my most embarrassing moments."

"Only the endearing ones. She never told me anything bad."

"I let her take all the heat from the Chalk brothers," he said. "I never admitted I was waiting for her that night at the pub."

"You did it for your parents. And for her."

"Maybe. But it was also easier not to get involved. When I saw what the prosecution put her through on the stand, I was glad that wasn't me up there being cross-examined."

"I read the trial transcripts," Shelby said. "She did a great job."

"She did. And then afterward…" The familiar vise squeezed his chest. He would never forget the FBI agent telling them that Camille was dead. That moment still replayed itself in his nightmares. His sister had vanished from his life at that moment, even if her real death had occurred four years later.

Shelby rose and put her hand on his arm. She had small hands, and her touch was delicate, but he felt the heat of her seeping into him. "I'm sorry," she said. "I'm sorry we put you through that pain. Not once, but twice."

He shrugged. "Camille agreed to it." Maybe later he would wrestle more with that idea—that Camille had played a part in deceiving him and his parents. She had always thought she knew what was best, but had she, really?

"She agreed," Shelby said, "but I don't believe it was easy for her. She wanted to protect you all."

"And it cost her everything."

He met her gaze again, and she moved closer, until they were almost touching. Her hand was still on his arm, and she brought her other hand up to grip the other arm, as if she might shake him. Maybe she was going to tell him to snap out of it, to quit moping and get on with his life. Other people had said as much.

But instead of scolding him, she pulled him close and laid her head on his chest. He slid his arms around her and returned the embrace, the intensity of the moment almost overwhelming—sadness and regret and a rush of desire a confusing cocktail surging through him. The perfume of her hair, gently floral, surrounded him, and her breasts, soft and rounded, pressed against him. He slid his hand along her spine, tracing the fine bones, down to the dip above the curve of her backside. She must be feeling how much he wanted her, and he expected her to pull away at any moment.

Instead, she tilted her head to look up at him again, her eyes half closed, her lips soft and parted in invitation.

He kissed her, pausing when his lips met hers, giving her time to pull away. Instead, she returned the caress and brought one hand up to cradle the back of his neck, urging him closer still.

SHELBY HAD WANTED this from the first day she had met Zach Gregory. She had told herself her desire was inappropriate and would never be returned. She was used to the men she encountered on the job seeing her as an agent first and a woman second. That was how she wanted to be seen 99 percent of the time.

But Zach... Zach wasn't just any man. Everything Camille had told her had built up the image of this strong, thoughtful, sexy man. The kind of man she had longed for in her life. And then she had met him in person, and he had turned out to be so much more.

He deepened the kiss, and she arched her body to his. He shaped his hands to her backside and slid one thigh between her legs, tucking her in closer still, and she gasped at the sensation. He slid his tongue into her opened mouth, and she gave up all pretense of holding back, sliding her hands beneath his shirt to caress his muscled back.

Two sharp, loud reports that sounded as if they came from right outside the door made them freeze. Heart hammering hard in her chest, she pushed away from him. "That sounded like gunfire," she said. Hours spent at the firing range had drilled that particular percussive echo into her brain. She raced to the kitchen and retrieved her own weapon from her purse, then moved to the door, Zach right behind her.

"Maybe it's just a car backfiring," he said, his last words almost drowned out by the piercing squeal of brakes and the growl of tires on gravel.

Shelby wrenched open the door and peered out in time to see the red glow of disappearing headlights. The silence that followed fell heavy as a blanket. "I don't see anyone," Zach said. He stood over her, also looking out the door.

She waited another long minute, then opened the door a little wider. Zach's neighbor emerged from his door. "What was that?" he asked when he saw the two of them look-ing out.

Shelby tucked the gun in the back of her jeans and pulled her shirt down over it. "I don't know," she said. "Did you see anyone?"

The neighbor shook his head. "Maybe it was a car back-firing."

Still wary, Shelby stepped outside, but Zach pushed past her. "Your car," he said, and pointed at the rental Shelby had picked up in Junction. The sedan leaned sharply to one side. She followed Zach over to the vehicle and looked down at the flat tires on the passenger side. The tread on the nearest tire had clearly been shredded by the impact of a bullet.

The neighbor had followed them out. The young, stocky man, dressed in gray joggers and a T-shirt that didn't quite cover his belly, let out a low whistle. "Someone doesn't like you," he said.

Shelby suppressed a shudder. She was used to people not liking her, or at least not liking the job she had to do. But maybe this attack wasn't really about her. Maybe who-ever had done this had known she was inside with Zach, and he was the real target.

Chapter Thirteen

For the second time in as many nights, Zach stood in the parking lot in front of his townhouse with a sheriff's deputy. Shelby was talking to the wrecker driver who had come to tow her rental car to his shop, where he had promised he would replace her destroyed tires in the morning.

"Do you think the same person who shot out her tires broke into my townhouse last night?" Zach asked.

Deputy Owen turned from his contemplation of the car to meet Zach's gaze. "I don't know," he said. "Do you?"

"Maybe whoever did this thought that was my car." He looked past her to his truck, parked just a few spaces down.

"Maybe," Owen said. "Or maybe they knew the car belonged to an FBI agent and were making some kind of statement."

Zach nodded. In the almost two weeks Shelby had been in Eagle Mountain, plenty of people would have passed on the news that an FBI agent was staying at the Ranch Motel. They probably even knew she was investigating the murder of a woman at the Forest Service campground. A few of them might even have connected Zach to the woman. Everyone on Search and Rescue knew that last fact, and one or more of them might have talked.

"What was Agent Dryden doing here tonight?" Owen asked.

Besides kissing me senseless? Zach struggled to turn his thoughts toward a safer answer. "She had some more questions about what happened here last night," he said.

Shelby stood back as the wrecker hooked on to her car then slowly winched it onto the flatbed. She waved as the wrecker drove away, then rejoined Zach and Deputy Owen. "He thinks he has the right tires in stock and can get them on first thing in the morning," she said.

"That's good." Though he felt stupid as soon as the words were out of his mouth. Nothing about this situation was good.

She turned to the deputies. "Can I see those bullets you recovered?"

Owen took a small bag from the left breast pocket of his uniform shirt and passed it to her. She studied the two misshapen slugs in the bag. "Twenty-two long rifle," she said.

"Common as dirt," Owen said. "We'll check for prints, but I doubt we'll find anything." He returned the bag to his pocket. "Have you made any enemies lately, Agent Dryden?"

She shook her head. "I don't think this was about me."

All eyes focused on Zach. He held up both hands. "I don't know what's going on," he said. "I haven't done anything to anyone."

"We can give you a ride to the motel," Deputy Owen said.

"I'll take her," Zach said before Shelby could answer.

"I'll go with Zach," she said. "But thank you."

They waited until Deputy Owen had left before they went back inside the townhouse. The closeness of moments before had vanished, replaced by tension like a thick fog between them. Shelby collected her purse and slung it over her shoulder. "I apologize for my unprofessional behavior," she said, looking not at Zach, but at the space where only moments before they had clung to each other.

"I don't know. I thought you kissed pretty good for an amateur."

She glared at him. So much for trying to lighten the moment. "I don't think you did anything wrong," he said. He moved in closer to embrace her, but she sidestepped the move.

"I doubt my supervisors would agree."

"What say do they have over your personal life?"

"You're part of a case I'm working on."

"I'm not a witness or a victim," he said. "And I'm not a criminal." He didn't know why he was arguing with her. He wasn't in the habit of trying to persuade women who didn't want to be with him. Except that her reluctance didn't seem to be about him at all, but about some ideal she was holding herself to, or thought her bosses were holding her to. And that kiss had been pretty spectacular. He was reluctant to let go of the chance to repeat it, and take it further.

"We should go," she said, and turned her back on him and walked to the door.

He debated not going after her. She wasn't going to get very far without him. Then again, he wouldn't put it past her to walk all the way back to town. It wasn't an impossible distance, but the walk probably wouldn't endear her to him. So he pulled out his keys and followed her out.

He drove toward town but was reluctant to end the night this way. And he didn't necessarily want to be alone with his thoughts, either. He told himself having his apartment broken into and Shelby's tires shot out were only nuisances that should be ignored. No one had been hurt. But he couldn't make himself believe it. Sure, no one had been hurt *yet*. Tonight, some unknown assailant had shot out Shelby's tires. How much of a stretch was it for them to shoot a person instead of a car?

He smoothed his hands down the steering wheel. "I'm too wired to sleep," he said. "Do you want to get some coffee?"

She shifted in her seat. "Where?"

"The only place is the gas station." He glanced at her. Streetlights bathed half her face in a golden glow. "I don't promise it's good coffee."

"All right."

He drove to the station at the intersection leading into town and left the engine running while he ran inside and bought two cups of coffee from the machine at the back of the store. He grabbed a handful of sugar and creamer packets, paid, returned to the car and handed her everything. "Hold this until I find a place we can sit and talk."

He ended up parking on the street a block from the motel. It was after ten, and all the businesses in this part of town were closed, the sidewalks empty. The only streetlight was at the end of the block, so he and Shelby sat in deep shadow. He sipped his coffee and was reminded of the night he had sat on that Houston street, waiting for Camille to emerge from Britannia Pub.

"What are you thinking?" Shelby asked.

He could have lied and said he was thinking about her and the kiss they had shared. Or he might have tried to make a joke about how small towns really did roll up the sidewalks after dark. Instead, he opted for the truth. "I'm thinking about that night at the Britannia. The night Judge Hennessey was shot."

"Tell me about it," she said.

So many times over the years he had relived that evening, running through the events minute by minute, by turns berating himself for keeping silent and telling himself he had no choice. The words to describe what had happened ought to come easily, but he found himself faltering.

"Like you said, Camille's car was in the shop," he said. "She planned to ride the bus home, but I was free and decided to surprise her by picking her up. I parked across the street and waited for her."

"Could you see the pub from where you were parked?" Shelby asked.

"I could see the side of the building and the door that opened onto the alley that Camille would come out of. I couldn't see the front door or into the restaurant."

"Okay. Go on. I didn't mean to interrupt."

"Camille came out and said good-night to her coworkers. They left and she locked up, then started walking toward the bus stop. I pulled alongside her and said hello, and she got in the truck, and I drove away. But we hadn't gone very far before she remembered she had left her wallet behind. I circled back, parked in the same spot and she went back into the restaurant. I noticed she was taking a while, but thought maybe the wallet wasn't where she thought she had left it and she was looking around. Then I heard a loud popping—like firecrackers or a car backfiring. I thought that was what it was—someone shooting off firecrackers on the next street over. Then Camille came running out, dove into the truck and told me to get out of there. I drove away, and she told me what had happened—that Judge Hennessey had been killed, and the Chalk brothers did it. She had me drive her to the police station. She said she would go in and tell them what she had seen and I should go home and not tell anyone I had been there."

He set the half-full cup of bitter coffee in the cup holder and swiveled toward her. "I didn't want to leave her," he said. "I tried to convince her that we should go to the police together, but the suggestion made her frantic. She insisted there was no reason for me to risk coming to the Chalk brothers' attention. She had all the information the police would need. I needed to go home and be with our parents."

"So that's what you did."

He slid down in the seat. "That's what I did. The next day, police arrested the Chalk brothers, Camille went into protective custody and FBI agents showed up at my apartment and my parents' house."

"And you never said anything about being there that night?"

He blew out a breath. "Maybe I should have, but no one ever asked. Camille had it all under control. All the focus was on her, and I guess everyone believed her when she said she was at the restaurant by herself."

"But you were there," Shelby said. Clearly, she wasn't going to cut him any slack.

"Yes. I told you I was in my truck, parked across the street. I wasn't inside the restaurant."

"You heard the gunshot."

"Yes. Though I didn't know it was a gunshot."

She leaned toward him. "How many gunshots?"

"Two. Pop-pop." The sound had jolted him, but it hadn't frightened him. "It wasn't that loud, really."

"Did you see anyone near the restaurant before or after those shots?"

He hesitated. Shelby pounced on that hesitation. "What is it?" she demanded. "What did you see?"

"Right after the shots, a man ran into the intersection ahead of where I was parked."

The sharp intake of her breath told him she hadn't expected that. He braced himself for her to berate him for lying to her until now, but all she said was, "How long after?"

"A minute? Maybe a little less."

"Which direction did he run from?"

"From the direction of the restaurant. But I don't know that he came from the restaurant itself. He could have been walking down the street, heard the shots and they frightened him, so he ran."

"What did he look like?" she asked.

He closed his eyes, bringing the image in his memory into focus. "He was young—early twenties, maybe? He had kind of a large nose and a prominent chin. He was wearing dark pants and a white shirt."

"Would you recognize him if you saw him again?"

He had asked himself that question many times. "I don't know. Maybe."

"Did he see you?"

"No. He stopped in the middle of the intersection and looked my way, but I ducked down."

"Why did you do that?"

"I don't know." He shook his head. "I just reacted. I didn't think. When I raised my head again, he was gone."

"And you didn't think what you saw was important enough to mention?" Her voice was sharp, her words cutting.

"It was just a man in the street. I didn't think he had anything to do with the murder. Camille said the Chalk brothers killed the judge."

"That man could have been another potential witness. He could have even been the witness who guaranteed a conviction. The Chalk brothers might have gone free because you didn't say anything."

If she was trying to make him feel worse about his choice, she was wasting her breath. He had told himself all these things over the years. "I get it," he said. "I was a coward. I let my sister take the fall when I might have drawn some of the Chalk brothers' attention away from her. Don't think I'm proud of what happened, because

I'm not." He turned the key in the ignition. "I'll take you to the motel."

She put a hand on his arm. "This isn't over," she said. "You have to give a formal statement. We'll get a forensic artist to work with you and come up with a picture of the man you saw. We might still be able to find him."

"He was just some poor kid on the street that night. He probably didn't have anything to do with the judge's murder. And he didn't kill Camille. That's the only death I care about."

"I want to find this man and talk to him."

"What difference is that going to make?" he asked. "The Chalk brothers were acquitted."

"You never know. It might make a difference."

"And then what happens? The Chalk brothers find out who I am, and I have to go into witness protection, like Camille? Are you going to tell my parents I died, too? Because I'm not going to put them through that."

"No one has to know about this," she said. "Even if we find the man you saw, no one has to know unless there's a new trial."

"A trial for what?"

"I don't know. But you have to give your statement."

He checked his mirrors, then pulled into the street and drove down the block to the motel. "I'm not going to talk about this anymore tonight," he said.

He could feel her staring and sensed her wanting to say more, but he kept his gaze forward and his mouth shut until he heard the door of the truck open and the slide of fabric against the upholstery as she got out. "We're not done," she said, just before she slammed the door.

"Yeah, we are," he said softly. She could grill him about what he had seen that night, and he could give all the details to an FBI artist to reconstruct the image of the fleeing man. But none of that would bring back Camille or find the man who had killed her.

None of that would put Shelby back in his arms or have her kissing him again. Kissing him as if she never wanted to stop.

Chapter Fourteen

Zach was at his desk at the mine when he received a text from Eagle Mountain Search and Rescue. Injured hiker Cascade Trail near falls. The choice between continuing to transcribe the most recent assay figures or hiking a beautiful mountain trail to help someone wasn't a difficult one to make. Zach shut down his computer and walked down the hall to his supervisor's office. "I got a page about an injured hiker," he said. "I don't have anything pressing going on right now."

"Go." Devlin Shaw, chief metallurgical engineer, waved toward the door. "And be careful."

Zach wasn't surprised to see Eldon jogging across the parking lot ahead of him. Zach waved and followed Eldon's Jeep out of the lot to Search and Rescue headquarters.

"Danny's stuck at work," Ryan informed them when they, along with Caleb, Anna and Christine, assembled at headquarters. "I talked to Hannah. EMS has been in phone contact with the hiker, a sixty-year-old woman, Lynette Marx. She slipped on loose rock, and it sounds like she broke her ankle. We need to take a wheeled litter up the trail and get her down to the ambulance."

This kind of rescue wasn't as exciting or potentially dangerous as evacuating someone off the side of the mountain, but it still required the team to work together to make sure they had all the equipment they needed to get the patient to medical help safely. "There are some steep, rocky sections on that trail," Eldon said as he and Zach loaded the collapsible litter onto the team's rescue vehicle, dubbed the Beast. "It will take some muscle to get the loaded litter over those."

"Everybody watch your step," Ryan advised as he added a pack with medical supplies to the load. "The last thing we want is to have to evacuate one of you because you broke a bone, too."

Fifteen minutes later, they arrived at the Cascade trailhead to find a waiting ambulance and a handful of onlookers. Most appeared to be fellow hikers, identifiable by their daypacks and hiking boots. But a flash of blond hair made Zach do a double take. The woman had her back to him, but she was tall, and he was almost sure it was Janie. But that couldn't be right. Shelby had said the local deputies hadn't been able to locate her to question her after Zach's apartment was broken into.

"What's she doing here?" Eldon spoke over Zach's shoulder. He was also staring at the woman, who was walking away now. Almost as if she hadn't seen them.

"I don't know." Zach wanted to go after her, but he couldn't leave the team. Instead, he crouched to slide the straps of a pack onto his shoulders, then carefully straightened. One-half of the litter was strapped to Zach's pack. Caleb already had the pack with the other half of the litter, while Eldon would carry the mounting bracket and single wheel that would help them get the loaded litter down the trail. The rest of the team carried braces, splints, helmets and other medical and safety gear.

Hannah Richards, a Rayford County paramedic, waited for them at the trailhead. She would be in charge of the medical assessment and delivering any pain medication the patient might need. Ryan looked back over the assembled group. "All right," he said. "Let's go."

As Zach headed out, he took a last look at the hikers milling about the parking area. No sign of the blonde. Maybe his mind was playing tricks on him. Janie wouldn't have ignored him—although maybe she was upset that he had turned down her advances the other night. And Eldon had thought it was her, too.

He stumbled and Anna put out a hand to steady him. "Thanks," he muttered, and focused on the trail. The hike was a steep one, switchbacking up the side of the mountain on a path that was supposedly once used by mule teams to transport ore from the now defunct Simpson mine. The mine ruins were a popular draw for hikers, as was the view from the top of the trail into a wildflower-filled basin. Zach was soon breathing hard, but keeping up with the others. No one spoke much, focused on moving as quickly as possible toward a woman who was probably in pain.

Lynette Marx was pale but cheerful when they reached her. "I am so glad to see you all," she said as the volunteers surrounded her. She lay on the ground in a stand of aspen trees beside the trail, one foot, stripped of its hiking boot, propped on a fallen tree, her pack beneath her head. A young couple who had been hiking behind her had seen her slip and stopped to help, and the man had run down the trail until he had enough phone signal to call for help. Then he had returned to stay with Lynette and his wife until rescuers arrived.

While Eldon, Caleb and Zach assembled the litter, Hannah assessed Lynette's injuries, administered a painkiller and fitted her with a splint. "That feels better already," Lynette said as they prepared to load her onto the litter. Once she was tucked in securely, the team members arranged themselves around the litter and prepared for the trip down the mountain.

A little over an hour later, they were back at the trail-head, and Lynette was being loaded into the waiting ambulance. A few curious onlookers had gathered, but no tall blonde woman was among them. Zach helped pack up their gear and rode back to headquarters. "Good job, everybody," Ryan said. "It couldn't have gone any smoother."

At headquarters, they unloaded the Beast. Zach checked his watch, then decided to head back to the mine to finish his report. But first, he pulled out his phone.

"Hello?" Shelby answered right away.

"I was just on a Search and Rescue call near Cascade Falls," Zach said. "There was a woman in the crowd who might have been Janie. Her back was to me, so maybe I'm wrong, but Eldon was there, and he thought it was her, too. She moved away before I had a chance to speak to her."

"Did you see where she went?"

"No. I was busy with the rescue and couldn't keep an eye on her."

"Where is Cascade Falls?" she asked.

He gave her directions. "There were a lot of people there," he said. "It's a popular hiking area. It might not even have been her."

"If you and Eldon both recognized her, it was probably Janie," she said. "I'll see what I can find out."

Zach wondered if he should be more worried. But he couldn't see the overly flirtatious blonde as a real threat, no matter what Shelby said. Janie was just a woman who had a crush on him. Harmless.

Back at work, he realized the break had done him good—the figures weren't quite so boring, and by six he was happy with the job he had done.

He was less happy when he parked by his townhouse

and saw a familiar figure waiting by the door to his home. "What are you doing here?" he demanded when Todd Arniston straightened at his approach. Todd wore jeans and a T-shirt and a messenger bag slung over one shoulder.

"I was hoping we could talk," Todd said. "Just the two of us."

Zach stopped several feet away, wary. This guy didn't look like an assassin. Then again, what did an assassin look like? "I'm glad you weren't badly hurt in your accident, and I was happy to help," Zach said, "but I don't think we have anything else to say to each other." He needed to get inside and call Shelby. And maybe the sheriff, too. He tried to move past the other man to unlock his door, but Todd stepped in front of him.

"I want to be straight with you," Todd said. "I'm not just a hapless tourist. I'm a writer. I'm working on a book about the Chalk brothers."

Zach went very still. Was this guy telling the truth? "So you're not just here on vacation?"

Todd's face reddened. "I am, but I'm also here to see you. I've been researching this book ever since the Chalk brothers trial, and I've got lots of great material. I wanted to interview your sister, but she disappeared before I had a chance to talk to her. So I tracked you down to here and thought you could tell me about her. I mean, I really can't tell this story without including Camille."

Zach's new house key bit into his palm where he gripped it so tightly. "Why didn't you tell me you were at the Forest Service campground when it flooded?" he asked. "Were you following Camille? Were you the man someone saw around Camille's campsite the day she was killed?"

Todd's eyes widened. "I didn't know Camille was there! I thought she was dead. Everyone did. I was there camping, like everyone else. I was trying to figure out how to contact you. I didn't even know until later that you were part of the Search and Rescue team. I was too focused on getting out of there safely."

His expression transformed from fear to excitement. "There was a man at her campsite before she died? Seriously? Do the cops think he killed her? What can you tell me about that?" He pulled a pad of paper and a pen from his messenger bag.

"I can't tell you anything." Zach took a step forward, forcing Todd to move out of the way, and inserted the key in the lock.

"You can tell me about Camille," Todd said. "She's such an important part of the story. What she did—testifying against the Chalk brothers—that took a lot of guts. I see her as the real heroine of the story, you know. But I need that personal touch—a glimpse of her personality. You can show me that."

Zach turned away. His memories of Camille were personal and not something he cared to share with a stranger. Talking about her wouldn't bring her back, and doing so wouldn't help put the Chalk brothers behind bars. That was the worst thing about this whole sorry mess—Camille had given up everything, including her life, to try to bring justice to two killers who were never going to pay for their crimes. She could have still been alive, maybe with a partner and children, a career she loved, still with her friends and family. Instead, she was gone, and they had nothing.

"Talk to me, Zach," Todd prompted.

"I don't have anything to say." He shoved open the door. When Todd tried to follow, Zach slammed the door in his face.

Todd pounded on the door. "Let me in," he said. "I just want ten minutes."

"Go away, or I'll call the police."

That shut him up. Zach went into the kitchen and pulled out his phone. "Todd Arniston was here," he told Shelby as soon as she answered. "He says he's writing a book about the Chalk brothers, and he wants to interview me about Camille." He returned to the front window and watched Todd's white sedan pull out of the parking lot. "He's gone now."

"Why didn't you keep him there until the sheriff or I could get there?"

"Because I don't want to talk to the guy. And it's not like he threatened me or anything. Now you know for sure he's still in town, so you should be able to find him. I have to go now."

He sank onto the sofa, his good mood of earlier in the day vanished. Not for the first time, he told himself he never should have driven Camille to the police station the night the judge was killed. He should have taken her home and told her to keep her mouth shut. To stay safe.

Even as he thought this, a smile tugged at his mouth as he imagined Camille's reaction to this ploy. She would have lectured him, probably about justice but also about how no one was going to tell her what to do with her life, especially not her *little* brother. Never mind that Zach was almost a foot taller than her.

Then he should have gone into the police station with her and told his story about seeing a man running down the street near the pub right after the shots were fired.

Again, Camille's reply came to him—her actual words this time. "They don't need what you have to say." Only much later had he realized the subtext behind that message. Camille wanted to be the star of this show. She didn't want to share the spotlight with Zach, whose "evidence" probably didn't mean anything anyway. Camille was the eyewitness. She was the one who mattered.

Zach believed that, too. Shelby talked about police artists and trying to find that running man, but that wasn't going to convict the Chalk brothers. Whoever that guy was, he had simply been in the wrong place at the wrong time. Just like Zach.

The doorbell rang, and he blew out an exasperated breath, then heaved himself off the sofa and stalked to the door. "I told you to leave me alone!" he bellowed, and turned the dead bolt.

Shelby glared up at him. "You didn't say anything about leaving you alone, and even if you did, I wouldn't have listened," she said, and pushed past him into the living room.

"Sorry." He closed the door behind her. "I thought maybe Todd had come back."

"I called the sheriff's department after I talked to you, and they're looking for him. It would help if you could tell us what he was driving."

"A white sedan. Something small. A Chevy, I think. Probably a rental car."

"What did he say to you?"

Zach sat once more. "Apparently the real reason he's been following me around isn't because he's grateful Search and Rescue saved his bacon when he wrecked his ATV on the Jeep trails, but because he wants to interview me about Camille."

"Then why not come right out and ask you to talk to him?"

"Maybe because he knew I'd turn him down flat."

"What else did he say?"

"I asked him if he was the man seen at Camille's campsite before she was killed, and he got pretty excited," Zach said. "He swears he didn't know Camille was at the campground, or even that she was alive. For what it's worth, I believe him."

She sat in the chair across from him. Putting distance between them, he thought. Making sure there was no repeat of the other night. She didn't have to worry. He had gotten the message. No more kissing the fed. "Did you get your tires fixed?" he asked.

"Yes. But we have no idea who shot them. No one saw anything. I always thought small towns were full of nosy people, and that anyone who is a stranger would stand out."

"Word has probably gotten around that you work for the FBI."

"I'm not here undercover. But people don't need to worry about me. They need to pay more attention to everyone else." She hugged her arms across her chest. "Did Todd say where he's staying now that he's checked out of the Nugget Inn?"

"No. I didn't ask. Guess I wasted your time, even calling to tell you he was here."

"No, you didn't waste my time." She moved to sit next to him on the sofa. Her floral scent distracted him, so he almost didn't hear her next words. "I'm frustrated. But that's not your fault. And I was planning on stopping by to see you this afternoon, anyway."

"Checking up on me?"

She didn't really have the face for fierceness, no matter how much she tried to pull it off. "I let my boss know about the man you saw outside the pub the night Judge Hennessey was murdered. I informed the sheriff, too. The FBI artist will be here tomorrow. You need to come into the sheriff's department and give your statement, then work with the artist to come up with a sketch of the man you saw the night Judge Hennessey was killed."

"I have a job," he said.

"This is more important."

"I already took off half of today to go on a Search and Rescue call. I can't take off again tomorrow."

"Come after work, then."

He didn't say anything, merely took another drink of beer. She was wearing a blazer over her blouse, but he could see the silky black fabric of the top stretching over her breasts. He remembered how soft she had felt against him. How lithe and strong her body was. He didn't want to think about her that way, but he couldn't seem to stop himself.

"What was the Search and Rescue call?" she asked.

"A hiker broke her ankle. We had to hike up and bring her down on a litter."

"Was that hard?"

"Not really. Harder on her, I'm sure. As rescues go, it was pretty easy."

"What would she have done without you?"

"I'm not sure. It would have been about impossible to navigate that trail with a messed-up ankle."

She was looking at him differently now. That look made him uncomfortable "Do people realize how lucky they are to have volunteers like you who will drop everything and run to help them?" she asked.

"I'm not doing it to be anybody's hero," he said.

"There's no rule that says there's only one per family." She stood. "I'm starved. Have you eaten yet?"

What had she meant by the one-per-family remark? "My search and rescue work isn't about Camille," he said.

"Of course not. What do you have to eat?"

He followed her into the kitchen, where she opened the refrigerator and began pulling out produce and cheese. "If you have pasta, I can make a primavera," she said.

He opened a cabinet and took out a package of spaghetti. "Perfect."

He leaned back against the counter and watched as she

set water to boil and pulled out a cutting board. "You like to cook," he said.

"Don't sound so surprised. My guilty pleasure is watching cooking shows."

"I don't think I have a guilty pleasure."

"No guilt, or no pleasure?"

Funny how one lift of her eyebrow could send heat curling through him. "No comment," he said and turned away, before he risked finding out how much pleasure—and guilt—she could offer him.

Chapter Fifteen

"We tracked Todd Arniston down at the Cakewalk Café this morning," Sheriff Walker told Shelby when she and the FBI artist met him at the sheriff's department the next afternoon. "He agreed to come in and talk to us. He answered our questions willingly, and he appears to be exactly what he says he is—a writer working on a book about the Chalk brothers."

"You should have called me in," she said.

"I would have if I thought there was a need," Walker said. "You're welcome to listen to the recording of the interview and read the transcripts. Arniston's story checked out. He doesn't have a criminal record, not even a traffic violation."

"He admits he was at the campground when Camille Gregory was murdered," she said.

"So were a lot of other people."

"Why didn't you interview him when you talked to the other campers?"

"He says he left the campground before floodwaters cut off the road. No one else mentioned him to us, and he didn't fill out a registration form for the campsite he occupied. But he doesn't deny being there. He says he didn't know Camille was there. No one else places him at or near her campsite."

"What about the stuffed bear that was left at Zach's townhouse?"

"We don't know when it was left there," Walker said. "It could have been any time between when Zach left for work that morning at eight until he returned home a little after nine at night. Arniston admits he can't account for his whereabouts for the entire thirteen hours, but most people wouldn't be able to. We didn't recover any fingerprints from the scene. Unless someone says they saw him or his car near Zach's townhouse, we don't have any reason to think he was responsible."

"He's been following Zach around."

"Because he wants to interview him," Walker said.

"Except he never said that until yesterday."

"I'll admit that's odd, but odd doesn't equal guilty."

"So you took everything he said at face value?" She couldn't keep the accusation from her voice.

The sheriff remained as unreadable as ever. "We took his fingerprints and sent them to the state for analysis," he said. "We'll let you know if anything turns up." He glanced toward the artist, who was setting up a laptop on a table in the interview room across the hall. "Has it occurred to you that Zach might have staged that bear in his townhouse? We only have his word that he lost his key."

"Zach did not stage that bear or lie about losing his key."

"People do that sort of thing in a bid for attention. How well do you really know him?"

I know him, she wanted to protest. She knew all of Camille's stories about her brother—the quiet, thoughtful man who didn't go out of his way to seek attention. But stories weren't what counted with people like Sheriff Walker. "The FBI has a file on Zach Gregory that goes back more than four years," she said. "There are no signs of any tendency to lie or seek attention."

The sheriff glanced toward the FBI artist again. "He

never told anyone about seeing someone outside the restaurant the night that judge was murdered."

"Because he didn't think it was important, and he's not the type of man who likes to put himself forward."

Adelaide moved down the hallway toward them. "Zach Gregory is here," she said.

"I'll bring him back," Shelby said, and left before the sheriff could say anything else.

Zach stood at her approach. "What's wrong?" he asked.

"Nothing's wrong."

"You look angry about something."

She was tempted to tell him about the sheriff's ridiculous suggestion that he had made up the story about the bear, but decided against it. As much as she hated the idea of anyone suspecting Zach, she knew the sheriff was approaching the case as any good law enforcement officer would, looking at everyone as a possible suspect. No matter how compelling the evidence, it was never a good idea to focus on only one suspect, especially in the early stages of an investigation. "The artist is back here," she said. "You'll work with him first, then give your statement about what you saw that night at the restaurant. The artist will ask you questions about what you saw and use your answers to come up with a sketch, which you'll fine-tune together. The end result should be a drawing of the man you saw that night at the Britannia."

"What will you do while I'm doing that?" he asked.

"I have some calls to make. I'll check in with you soon."

She got Zach settled with the artist, an affable man named Fred who had driven over from Denver. "The most important thing is to relax and remember there are no wrong answers," he said as Shelby was leaving.

Though Sheriff Walker had offered her the use of an empty office in his department, she opted to walk outside to telephone Special Agent in Charge Lester. She told him about the sheriff's conclusions about Todd Arniston, and their inability to locate Janie.

"Neither of these people sound like very strong suspects to me," Lester said. "I don't think you're making enough progress in this case to justify keeping you in Eagle Mountain."

"Sir, I respectfully disagree. At least give me another day or two to follow some leads." She didn't have any leads to follow, but he didn't need to know that.

"I want you back in the office Monday morning, and that's final," he said.

"Yes, sir." She ended the call. Three days to find some kind of closure. Zach deserved that, even if it was the only thing she could give him.

ZACH SAT BACK and looked at the drawing on the artist's computer screen. A young man with a prominent nose and chiseled cheekbones looked out at him, fear haunting the man's dark eyes. For the space of a breath, Zach was back on that Houston street, the man silhouetted beneath the red glow of the traffic signal, his heart hammering in sympathy with the man's obvious terror.

"That's him," he said, back in the present now. "How did you do that?"

"You did it," Fred said. "I drew what you told me. I just knew the right questions to ask."

"Is it strange that I still remember him so well, after so much time has passed?"

"Not really. Trauma makes a strong impression. That, or a sense of connection with another person. You were afraid that night, and you saw that same feeling in him, even if you didn't acknowledge it." He started typing.

"What happens now?" Zach asked.

"I'll send this to my office, and from there it will be uploaded to various national databases. It will be up to the agents working the case, but sometimes these images are published in local media in the hopes that someone who recognizes the person will come forward." He closed the laptop. "You could help solve a crime. Or prevent another one."

He walked with Zach into the hallway, where Deputy Owen met him. "Come with me, and I'll take your statement," Owen said and led him into another interview room.

Telling the story yet again wasn't as difficult as Zach had anticipated. Declan Owen expressed no judgment or opinion, merely prompting Zach when he needed more detail or wanted to clarify the sequence of events. When Zach was done, he waited another quarter of an hour for a printed copy of his statement and signed it. "Thanks," Owen said. "You're free to go now."

He escorted Zach to the lobby, where he had expected to find Shelby waiting. Adelaide saw him looking around. "Agent Dryden said she would see you later," she said.

He hid his disappointment, but told himself he was being ridiculous. Hadn't he said he didn't want Shelby babysitting him? Maybe she felt the same way he did—that being together all the time was too frustrating, fighting this attraction between them, for reasons that still weren't clear to him. Though maybe she didn't want to start something she couldn't finish. He could understand that. She would need to go back to Houston sooner rather than later. The thought made him even more glum.

Rather than go home to mope, he stopped by Mo's, where he ordered nachos and a beer. He sat at a table by the window and watched groups of tourists on the sidewalk—couples and happy families laden with shopping bags, wearing souvenir T-shirts and stopping often to take pictures.

A flash of blond hair made him sit up straighter, and he leaned forward, studying a group of people across the street waiting to cross. Was that Janie in the back?

He shoved back his chair and rushed outside. But there was no tall blonde woman anywhere. He stood in the middle of the sidewalk, a boulder others had to move around, and stared in all directions.

Back in the restaurant, Kiki met him at the door. "Everything okay?" she asked.

"Yeah. I thought I saw someone I knew." He took out his wallet. "Let me settle up, and I'll get out of your hair."

He drove home, unable to relax. The tension didn't ease when he parked and saw someone by his door. He sat in the car, wondering if he should leave again, when Shelby moved into the light. He hurried to meet her. She didn't look happy to see him, fine lines of tension creasing her forehead. "We have to talk," she said.

As soon as the words were out of her mouth, Shelby silently cursed herself for being overly dramatic. Talk about a phrase that would send almost anyone running in the other direction. She rested a hand on his arm. "I just want to bring you up to date on some developments," she said.

"Sure." He unlocked the door, and she followed him in. They both stood just inside the door for a moment, looking around.

"Does everything look okay?" she asked.

"Sure. It's fine." He moved into the living room and sat on the sofa. "What's up?"

"I have to be back in Houston Monday."

Was that hurt or anger—or both—in his eyes? He didn't try to hide the emotions, merely shook his head. "I'm sorry to hear that," he said.

"The sheriff's department has agreed to run regular patrols, and if you see anything suspicious, they'll respond right away."

"I'm not sorry because I won't have a personal body-guard anymore. I'm sorry because somehow, as awful as the past couple of weeks have been, you've made them bearable. Some parts of them have been good, even."

The kiss they had shared was good. She sat on the edge of the sofa, close but not touching. "I won't forget you, Zach."

"Yeah, you will. You'll always have another case. Another witness."

"You're not just another witness." He was Zach. Camille's brother. The man she had fallen for before they even met.

He didn't look away, his gaze challenging.

"I care about you, is that what you want me to say?" she asked.

"If that's true, why are you holding back?" he asked.

The problem was she wasn't holding back. Not the way she was supposed to, not letting herself get involved with people who were part of the cases she worked. "My problem is I can never be what I'm supposed to be," she said. "I'm not supposed to become friends with the witnesses or victims I interview. I'm not supposed to let my emotions get in the way of my objectivity. I'm not supposed to care. But I always care." She clenched her hands into fists. "I cared about Camille. She was my friend, and I miss her. And now I care about you."

He pulled her close, arms wrapped around her. "I know." When he looked into her eyes, she was sure he didn't see the cold FBI agent her bosses wanted her to be, but the warm woman whose feelings dictated her actions every bit as much as the evidence in a case.

She was growing warmer by the minute. She touched

the tip of one finger to the corner of his mouth. "I'm not supposed to get involved with people who are part of my cases," she said. "I'm not supposed to be attracted to them."

He shifted, fitting her more firmly between his legs, the ridge of his erection pressed into her stomach. "You're not?" he asked, his voice gruff.

"I'm not." She raised up on her toes and replaced the finger on his mouth with her lips. "But I'm not a robot. I feel so much. I want you so much."

He moved his head just enough to cover her lips with his, his fingers buried in her hair, caressing the back of her neck, their bodies pressed together from chest to knee. He tasted of salt and beer, his lips so full and soft, his tongue warm and sensuous.

He broke the kiss and looked at her so long without speaking that her stomach fluttered with nerves. "What are you thinking?" she asked.

"That it's not wrong to care. And it isn't wrong to feel. And that professionalism is sometimes overrated."

Eyes still locked to hers, he slid one hand to her waist, then over the curve of her hip, down her thigh to the hem of her skirt. He pushed up the fabric, and she gasped at the heat of his palm on her bare skin. "Do you want me to stop?" he asked, lips close to her ear.

She shifted to look into his eyes again. "No."

He smiled, a lazy, sensuous expression that made her want to tear off his shirt. Instead, she settled for sliding her hand up under the fabric and across his taut stomach, his muscles contracting at her touch. "Do you want me to stop?" she asked, teasing.

"Not now. Not ever." He kissed her again, and she arched to him and hooked one leg around his thigh. He cupped her bottom, and she ground against him, while his mouth continued to prove that she only thought she had been kissed before. These were kisses she felt in every part of her. Was it possible, she wondered, to orgasm from a kiss?

"Let's go somewhere more comfortable," he said.

She nodded, and he led her to his bedroom. They were still moving toward the bed when he began to undress her, undoing buttons and lowering zippers with a minimum of fumbling. He peeled back her blouse and pressed his lips to the hollow of her shoulder, and she let out a sigh that was almost a purr and hooked one leg around his thigh to draw him closer.

He urged the blouse off her shoulders and down her arms, momentarily pinning her before she wriggled out. She popped the catch of her bra and cast it aside, then stepped back when he reached for her and took hold of the tab of his zipper. "You're still wearing too many clothes," she said.

For a big man, he moved quickly, and within seconds stood before her, naked in the glow of a single bedside lamp. He looked powerful, muscular and hairy chested. He might have been intimidating, but she felt safe with him. She wanted to touch every part of him and to feel him touch her.

"Do you have a condom?" she asked.

In answer, he opened the drawer of the bedside table and pulled out a foil packet. She smiled and moved into his arms.

He fell back on the bed and pulled her on top of him. He caressed her hip and smiled. "I was beginning to think this was never going to happen."

"Oh?" She straddled him, palms flat on his chest. "Have you been fantasizing about me?"

"All the time." He pulled her down and kissed her mouth, then began to work his way down her body.

She sighed again. "Do you like that?" he asked as he traced his tongue beneath her breasts.

"I do. And this." She moved his hand to cover her nipple.

"What about this?" she asked a few moments later, as she shifted against him.

"Oh, yeah," he said, and tucked her more securely against him. "And I like this view."

The men she had been with before hadn't talked much in bed. It wasn't that they ignored what she wanted—most were considerate lovers. But none took the time to check in with her the way Zach did. It surprised her, considering how quiet he was in everyday life. And it added another layer of connection she hadn't experienced before.

By the time he rolled on the condom and she welcomed him inside her, she felt tied to him more than physically. He held her gaze as the tension between them built, and when she felt herself on the edge, he kissed her with such tenderness tears stung her eyes, even as her body shuddered with passion. Then she felt his own release, moving through her, too.

Afterward, they lay curled together, silent, as if they had said everything that needed saying. She fought sleep, wanting this intense closeness to last as long as possible. But she must have drifted off anyway because the next thing she knew, Zach was shaking her. "Your phone is ringing," he said. "Do you need to answer it?"

She groaned, then sank back onto the pillows when the phone stopped ringing. But the message alert sounded almost immediately. "I'd better check," she said and struggled to a sitting position. She wrapped the sheet around her and made her way into the front room and retrieved her phone from her purse and carried it with her back into the bedroom.

Zach was sitting up now, too, blankets around his hips. She stared for a moment, struck by the thought that she would never get tired of looking at this man naked. "Who called?" he asked.

She came out of her daze and looked at the phone. "The sheriff." Her heart sped up as she tapped in the code to access her voicemail.

As usual, Sheriff Walker didn't mince words. "Call me," he said.

She returned his call and waited while the phone rang once, twice…on the third ring, he picked up. "Where are you?" he asked.

"Why do you need to know that?"

"We just found Todd Arniston."

"Where did you find him?" And why did she care? Hadn't the sheriff already dismissed Todd as a suspect?

"We found him in a car parked on the road near the Piñon Creek campground. He was shot in the back of the head. He's dead."

She gasped, and Zach leaned toward her. "What is it?" he asked.

"I'll be right there," she said to the sheriff.

"There's something else you should know," Walker said. "We just got a report on the fingerprints we sent in. Todd Arniston wasn't his real name. His real name was Thomas Chalk."

Chapter Sixteen

Zach insisted on going with Shelby to the sheriff's department. The sheriff, dressed in jeans and a T-shirt, met them at the back of the dark building. He frowned at Zach, but didn't say anything and allowed him to follow Shelby to a cramped office. Zach settled into one of the two chairs facing the desk. Walker sat behind the desk and tapped the keyboard to wake up his computer.

"Thomas Chalk is Charlie and Christopher Chalk's nephew, is that right?" Shelby asked. "I remember the name from our files, but I can't recall anything about him."

"Great nephew," Walker said. "He's the grandson of their older brother, Carter Chalk."

"Carter isn't involved in the family businesses," Shelby said. She turned to Zach. "Carter made a point of cutting himself off from the rest of the family as soon as he was out of college. He operates a ranch in Wyoming and, as far as we've been able to determine, has no involvement with any of their affairs."

"There's more," Walker said. "Thomas has an older brother, Martin." He angled the computer screen toward them to show a photograph of a dark-haired young man with a prominent nose.

Gooseflesh rose on Zach's arms. "That's the man I saw

outside the Britannia Pub the night the judge was killed," he said.

"You're sure?" Walker asked.

"Yes, I'm sure."

"Martin Chalk is dead," Shelby said. "I remember now. He drowned six months after Judge Hennessey was killed, before Charlie and Christopher's trial. It was ruled an accidental death."

Zach sat back, trying to sort out the thoughts spinning in his head. "Do you think Martin was killed to silence him about whatever he saw at the restaurant that night?"

"His death was never investigated as a possible murder," Shelby said. "I'd have to review the file, but the only mention I remember seeing was that he died in an accident when his boat was swamped on a lake where he was fishing, and that he had nothing to do with the Chalk brothers' crimes."

"Why was Thomas Chalk here?" Zach asked. "Did he kill Camille?"

"We sent his hair to the FBI lab to see if it matches the one you found at the campsite," Travis said. He turned the computer monitor back to face him and typed. "Now take a look at this photo." He turned the monitor again, this time to show a photo of a beautiful blonde.

"That's Janie!" Both Shelby and Zach spoke. He leaned closer, but there was no mistaking the woman in this photo for anyone other than the woman who had pursued him.

"Her name is Janelle Chalk," Travis said. "She's Thomas's twin sister."

ZACH TRIED TO focus on the road on this short drive to Shelby's hotel room, where she wanted to retrieve her laptop and files. But everything Travis and Shelby had told him kept pulling his thoughts away. "What were Janelle and her brother doing here?" he asked. "Did they kill Camille? Were they stalking me or something? And why?"

"Maybe they found out you saw their brother at the pub that night," Shelby said.

"But what difference does that make if their brother is dead?"

"I don't know." She stared at her phone, typing furiously. "I'm trying to log into my files at the Bureau, but the system isn't exactly set up to be read on a phone screen." She laid the phone in her lap. "I texted my boss with the news about the twins, though I don't know if he'll read the message tonight."

"You said they aren't involved in the Chalk brothers' crimes."

"Not that we know of. But maybe that's changed."

"Maybe Martin was at the pub that night to try to stop the killing," Zach said. "He got frightened and ran away."

"Or maybe he was the killer," Shelby said. "Maybe the Chalk brothers were right, and they didn't pull the trigger after all. Though that doesn't mean they didn't orchestrate the whole thing. Maybe Martin wanted in on the action, and killing the judge was the price of admission."

"Then why kill him six months later?"

"Maybe his death really was an accident. Or maybe he got cold feet and threatened to turn himself in. Or Charlie and Christopher were afraid he would cave under pressure and decided to eliminate the risk."

"So what were Thomas and Janelle doing in Eagle Mountain? Were they following Camille?"

"Or they were here to kill you," she said. "Maybe that's what led Camille here. I don't know. But we'll do our best to find out."

At the motel, Shelby fired up her laptop and scrolled through her files. Zach couldn't sit still, so he paced, mind and heart racing. "Where is Janelle now?" he wondered. "Is she hiding from whoever killed her brother? Or did she kill him?"

Shelby shook her head. "My files have almost nothing on those two. They're on a list of Chalk relatives, but as far as the FBI knows, they're both living quiet lives in Wyoming. This says that Thomas works on the ranch with his father and Janelle is a dental hygienist." She glanced up at him. "They both sound so ordinary."

"I wasn't really worried before," he said. "But now I feel like I'm waiting for the next terrible thing to happen. And I know the sheriff said he had contacted the police in Junction about protecting my parents, but maybe I should go to them."

"That wouldn't be a bad idea," she said. "It would get you away from here, someplace safer and with a law enforcement presence twenty-four hours a day."

"What will you do?" he asked. "Do you still have to be in Houston Monday?"

"I don't know. I would think this would change things." She closed the laptop. "Let's go back to your place. You can pack to go to your folks while I keep trying to get more information on the Chalk twins."

It probably would have been easier for her to stay at the motel and work alone, but he appreciated that they would be together a little while longer. He took her hand as they walked out to his car. "I'm going to miss you while I'm gone," he said.

"I'm going to miss you, too." She leaned against him. "But I promise, we'll talk every day."

And what about when this is all over? he wondered, but didn't dare ask out loud. What about when she went back to Houston, and he tried to settle in once more to life here in Eagle Mountain? Would they try to keep up a long-distance relationship, something that seemed to him doomed to fail? Or would they part as friends? The idea made his chest hurt. Better not to dwell on that uncertain future. He needed all his attention on now.

He parked in the lot in front of his townhouse and led the way down the path to his front door. But when he tried his key in the lock, it wouldn't go in.

"What's wrong?" Shelby asked.

"The key won't go in. It's like something is jamming the lock." He leaned down for a closer look but was unable to make out anything in the dim light.

A gasp from Shelby made him look up.

Janie—or rather Janelle Chalk—smiled at him. She held a pistol pressed to Shelby's side. "Don't try anything," Janelle said. "Or I'll kill her, then finish you off."

SHELBY TRIED TO remember the self-defense training she had received earlier in her career: How to overpower an opponent. How to evade capture. How to use your opponent's weaknesses against them. But none of those lessons applied here, with the barrel of a pistol pressed hard against her ribs and Zach standing across from her, his face bleached of color and eyes filled with horror.

Janelle patted her down and found Shelby's pistol and pocketed it. "Get back in your car," she ordered, grabbing Shelby's arm and marching her forward, the gun between them. She wore black pants and a black hoodie, the hood pulled up to hide her blond hair. She had a small black daypack on her back. Anyone seeing her would describe a tall, slim figure—the same description the camper had given the sheriff of the "man" he had seen running from Camille's campsite the day she died. "You drive, Zach," Janelle said. "But remember what will happen if you start thinking you're smarter than I am."

"Where are we going?" Zach asked as he opened the driver's door of his truck.

Janelle led Shelby to the passenger side and shoved her in. Shelby was grateful for Zach's bulk beside her, somehow comforting. Of course, it also meant that if Janelle decided to fire the pistol in these close quarters, both she and Zach were likely to be hurt. "Where do you want me to drive?" Zach asked again as Janelle shut the door behind her.

"Go to the Piñon Creek campground. I think it's fitting, don't you, that we end everything there."

The small town of Eagle Mountain was so much darker than Houston at night, without thousands of streetlights, traffic lights and the glow from homes and towering office buildings shutting out the night. But away from town, on the Forest Service road, they were plunged into a new kind of darkness. The headlights of Zach's truck cut a narrow wedge out of the inky blackness, revealing nothing but closely growing trees and the narrow strip of red dirt road directly in front of them.

Zach drove slowly, clutching the steering wheel in both hands as if he might rip it from the column. He stared straight ahead, and Shelby wondered what he was thinking. Her own mind raced, searching for some avenue of escape. But shaping a coherent thought was liking extracting bolts from a vat of molasses. The effort drained her, and nothing she could assemble made sense.

"What are you doing here in Eagle Mountain?" Zach asked, breaking the silence and making Shelby jump. "Did you come with your brother?"

"I followed him here because I knew he was going to screw up," Janelle said. "Not that he minded me being here. I've always been the only one of us with any real backbone.

He just went along with Uncle Charlie and Uncle Christopher because he was afraid of them."

"What was he doing here, then?" Zach asked. "Was he really writing a book about the Chalk brothers?"

Janelle laughed. "No, he wasn't writing a book! That was just a story he made up to get close to you. He had this idea that we should find out what you really knew about what happened that night at the pub before we killed you. I told him it didn't matter what you knew because the uncles wanted you dead, but Thomas felt he had to know if the killing was justified. He actually said that. As if it matters."

The casual way she spoke, as if murder was a mundane topic of conversation, sent an icy chill through Shelby. "I saw your brother, Martin, running away from the pub that night," Zach said.

"I knew it!" Janelle looked around Shelby to smile at him. "Martin told us there was a truck parked in front of the restaurant that night. He thought it was empty, but I was sure you were there, waiting on your sister. Of course, no one would listen to me for the longest time. After all, I'm just a girl." The smile turned to a sneer. "My uncles wasted so much time focused on Martin and Thomas, even though I was right there—the only one with guts enough to have a real role in the family organization. But because I'm female, I have to work so much harder to prove I'm capable. All my brothers had to do was stand around looking the part, when neither one of them had the nerve to actually do the work necessary."

"Martin looked really afraid the night I saw him," Zach asked. "What was he doing at the pub?"

"He was terrified," Janelle said. "All he had to do was show up, fire one shot into that worthless judge and Charlie and Christopher were going to hand over a whole chunk of their empire. Legitimate businesses, most of them. He would have been rich. Instead, as soon as he shot the judge, he fell apart. He ran away like the coward he was, all the way back to Wyoming. He told my uncles he had changed his mind and wanted to stay on the ranch. He promised not to say anything about what happened that night, but they couldn't trust him. How could they? He was liable to fall apart the first time anyone came to question him." She turned to Shelby. "But you never did. The FBI never figured out there was someone else in the pub that night, even when Charlie and Christopher's attorneys kept insisting my uncles never fired a shot. They told the truth."

"Why didn't your uncles tell the authorities that Martin killed the judge?" Zach said. "Especially if he wasn't around to implicate them?"

"Family loyalty and the family name are everything to them," Janelle said. "It's why they were so keen on getting my brothers involved. The two of them only have daughters. One of them has never married, and the other is a lesbian. They figured if they were going to find a man to run things when they decided to retire, my brothers were the best candidates. They couldn't see that I was the one they really needed."

Silence wrapped around them, broken only by the crunch of the truck's tires on the dirt road. Shelby watched Janelle out of the corner of her eye. The other woman was smiling slightly. She looked so pleased with herself.

"Who killed Thomas?" Zach asked after a moment.

"He couldn't follow through on the job he was sent here to do, and he was becoming a liability," Janelle said.

"So you shot him?" Shelby asked.

Janelle's look was withering. "I did what I had to do," she said.

"Did you kill Camille, too?" Zach asked.

"I did. But I promise, she didn't suffer. She wasn't even

supposed to be here, but she must have found out what Thomas and I had planned and came here to warn you. Under different circumstances, the two of us might have been friends. I always felt she was a strong woman, like me." She leaned forward a little. "Your turn should be coming up soon. The sign can be hard to see."

A few minutes later, the headlights illuminated the brown Forest Service sign that identified the campground. "Turn in and drive to the back," Janelle ordered. "Stop at number 47."

The campsite where Camille had been killed. "Is this where you killed Thomas, too?" Shelby asked.

"It is. The sheriff will have moved his car and his body by now. I like the symmetry of having everything take place here. I hope my uncles appreciate it."

Zach turned into the campground and bumped along the rutted road, past parked vans, RVs and tents set up next to stunted trees and stone fire rings.

Yellow crime-scene tape still fluttered from the last campsite on the road, and the broken tree still lay across the parking area. Zach pulled alongside the tree and cut the engine. The lights remained on, shining into the darkness. "If you shoot us here, the campers will hear," Zach said.

"There's no cell service here," she said. "By the time they call for help, I'll be long gone. I left my car in another campsite nearby. With a tent set up and everything. So the other campers probably think I'm sleeping. I hitchhiked to your place. It's not hard for a woman who looks like me to get a ride." She opened the passenger door. "Get out. We're going to take a little walk. And remember, if you try anything, I'm not going to miss at this range."

Zach squeezed Shelby's arm as she started to slide across the seat away from him. She glanced back at him, but couldn't read his expression in the darkness. "Go on," he whispered.

She wanted to tell him to run. She would distract Janelle and probably die in the process. But Zach could disappear into the darkness and would have a chance of getting away.

"Come out on this side, Zach," Janelle said. "I don't want you out of my sight."

He maneuvered his big frame awkwardly over the center console of the truck and joined them beside the vehicle. The headlights blinked off and darkness surrounded them. They could use the darkness to their advantage, Shelby thought. If they could get even a few feet away from Janelle, she wouldn't be able to see well enough to hit them.

And then what? They could try to get help from one of the campers, and possibly involve innocent bystanders in a firefight. They could run, but where? From what she remembered from her visits in the daytime, the area around the campground was a wooded mountainside along the river, full of uneven terrain, fallen trees, loose rock and other hazards. For all her law enforcement training, she had spent most of her career patrolling, interviewing, researching and compiling reports. She didn't feel prepared for a situation like this.

ZACH'S MIND RACED through all the possibilities in their situation. They were at the very back of the campground, away from most of the campers. In the darkness, he had only noticed a few sites occupied, and at this hour most people would be sleeping. He could hear the murmur of the river to their right. The terrain beyond the campground was rugged woods, scattered boulders and fallen trees from the recent storm ready to trip up anyone trying to flee in the darkness. If they did succeed in breaking free, they would have to run a long way before they got to a place where they could call for help.

They had darkness and numbers in their favor, but the pistol in Janelle's hand and her determination to use it evened the odds, or put them in her favor. He could try to distract her and allow Shelby to get away. He would probably be wounded or killed. And then what? Janelle would go after Shelby. Shelby was from the city. She didn't know the terrain around here. He didn't like her chances alone in this remote area with a killer after her.

He had to keep Janelle talking. As long as she was talking to them, they would still be alive. "Do your uncles know you're here, doing this for them?" he asked.

"They think I'm back home on the ranch where I belong." Bitterness colored her words. "When they find out I've accomplished what my brothers couldn't, they'll see me in a new light."

Zach eased one step back, moving as soundlessly as possible. Every foot away from her would make it harder for her to see him and easier for him to make a break if he got the chance.

"Come over here closer to me." She gestured with the pistol. "I don't trust you. You're probably thinking you're a big guy. You could overpower me. But I won't hesitate to shoot, and I'm a very good shot. There's not a lot for me to do on the ranch but practice."

Reluctantly, he did as she asked, moving not only closer to her, but to Shelby. He would do all he could to keep her safe. Keeping the gun aimed at him, she turned to Shelby. "Get some of the police tape that's around the campsite and tie up Zach," she said. "Ankles and wrists. And remember, if you try to run or scream or do anything suspicious, he dies."

Shelby turned toward the road. "How am I going to see

what I'm doing?" she asked. "Even with the moon, it's so dark."

Janelle shifted and slipped her pack off her back. "Look in there, and you'll find a flashlight."

Shelby opened the pack and, after a few seconds, drew out a small flashlight.

"Give it to Zach," Janelle said. "Zach, you keep the light on her. I'll keep the gun on you."

Shelby's fingers brushed his as she handed him the light. They were ice-cold. Then she moved away, toward the tape strung on the far side of the camp.

The light was small, not heavy enough to use as a club. He trained the beam on Shelby. A powerful blue-tinged glow cut through the blackness. There was another campsite directly across from this one, but it was empty.

Zach shifted his stance and the back of his heel struck something solid. The broken tree. He pictured it in his mind, five inches across and shattered into two pieces. Could he pick up one of the pieces and use it as a club? He thought he could do it. Could he knock Janelle off-balance before she shot him? At this range, one shot could be deadly.

"Do you have a knife or scissors?" Shelby asked, her voice sounding loud in the stillness. "I can't undo these knots, and this stuff is designed to not tear."

"Keep working at it," Janelle called. "I'm not going to hand you anything that could be used as a weapon."

Keep her talking, Zach thought. *Keep her distracted.*

Shelby grunted and tugged hard on the tape. "It's not coming loose," she called.

"That's because you're making the knots tighter," Janelle said. "If you keep being difficult, I'm just going to go ahead and shoot you." She was frowning in Shelby's direction, and though the pistol still pointed at Zach, the barrel had dropped slightly. He swung the light up, aiming for her eyes, the brilliant light blinding her.

Janelle swore and put up a hand to shield her eyes. Zach bent and hefted the log. The gun went off, the bullet striking the log in his hand, the impact forcing him to take a step back to regain his balance. But he recovered quickly and swung the log at Janelle, aiming for her head and shoulders.

The impact of the heavy wood striking flesh and bone shuddered through him. Janelle screamed, and the gun went off again, then she crumpled to the ground. He dropped the log and retrieved the flashlight from the ground.

Shelby ran to him and scooped up the gun Janelle had dropped. They stood for a moment, staring down at the woman on the ground. She was curled in a fetal position, moaning.

"Hey! What's going on over there!"

Zach directed the light toward the sound and saw a man in shorts and sandals standing in the road. Shelby moved toward him. "I'm with the FBI," she called. "Please drive until you get a cell signal and call 911. We're going to need the sheriff and an ambulance."

The man hesitated, staring. "Go!" Shelby urged. "Please. It's important."

He nodded and ran back down the road. Zach knelt beside Janelle and felt at her throat for a pulse. She opened her eyes. "I think you broke my shoulder," she said.

"It will heal," he said. "Lie still. The ambulance will be here soon."

She groaned and closed her eyes again.

Shelby came to stand beside him. "I can't believe I was wrong about everything," she said. "The Chalk brothers didn't kill the judge or your sister."

Zach put an arm around her and pulled her close. "They

orchestrated the judge's killing and ordered Camille killed, too," he said. "That makes them responsible."

She continued to stare at Janelle. "She killed her own brother. That's so horrible."

"It is. But it's over now."

She glanced at him. "Is it? The Chalk brothers will say they didn't know anything about this. They're very good at making people believe them."

He blew out a breath. Was she right? "Let's just focus on now," he said. "We're safe. We're together. That's all I want to think about." That was all that really mattered, wasn't it?

Chapter Seventeen

Shelby's eyelids felt as if they were lined with sandpaper, and her mouth tasted like old socks soaked in bad coffee. She sat in an interview room at the Rayford County Sheriff's Department, across from Special Agent in Charge Lester, who had arrived at dawn with a team of federal marshals who took custody of Janelle Chalk. She hadn't slept in more than twenty-four hours and wasn't sure what time it was now—probably before nine in the morning. All she wanted was a shower and to crawl into bed, preferably with Zach, whom she hadn't seen since they had arrived at the sheriff's department in separate vehicles hours ago.

She had spent most of the hours since then giving her statement to Sheriff Walker, then repeating the story for Lester. Her account of Janelle's statements about the judge's death, and the admission that Janelle had murdered both Camille and her brother, had sharpened his attention, and he had her repeat everything twice.

"Zach Gregory's sighting of Martin Chalk outside the pub that night confirms that Martin was at the scene," Lester said. "But Janelle is refusing to say anything now that she's in custody."

"Zach heard the same thing I did," Shelby said. "He'll confirm my story."

"And Charlie and Christopher will deny having anything to do with her and her brothers," Lester said.

"We can find more evidence," she said. "We can make a case against them. Especially if we can persuade Janelle to talk. She might do it if we promise her a deal."

"*We* will not be doing anything," he said. "I'm removing you from the case."

The shock of this statement cut through her fatigue. "Why?"

Lester's expression was grim. "For one thing, I understand you've become personally involved with Zach Gregory."

She opened her mouth to protest, but what could she say? She couldn't deny her feelings for Zach. "I know how to keep my personal and private lives separate," she said. "And it's not as if I'm involved with a member of the Chalk family."

"You're being reassigned. And you're booked on a one o'clock flight back to Houston." He checked his watch. "You should have just enough time to change clothes, gather your belongings and get to the airport."

"I'd like to see Zach before I leave."

"That isn't possible."

"Why not?" Alarm jolted through her. "Is something wrong? Is he all right?"

"Zach and his parents are going into witness security as of right now. Practically the first words out of Janelle Chalk's mouth when we spoke to her were that her uncles would wipe out the Gregory family in revenge for Zach hurting her."

"I'm not sure she's as valuable to her uncles as she believes she is," Shelby said.

"Nevertheless, we feel the danger to the Gregorys is real, and they have agreed to accept our help."

Zach was going away. Just like that. "I want to see him," she said. "I need to say goodbye."

"It would be better for everyone if you didn't." Lester stood. "Agent Crispin will drive you to your hotel to collect your things, then to the airport. We'll talk again next week."

He left the room without a backward glance. Agent Crispin, who had been standing by the door, walked over to her. He was a man in his late thirties, with short dark hair and chiseled features. The type of agent portrayed on recruiting posters, never a hair out of place or a move out of line. "Come on," he said. "You don't want to miss your plane."

She thought of telling him to get lost. She wasn't a prisoner. She could refuse to get on that plane, refuse to return to work.

And then what? She'd be out of a job, stuck miles from home and Zach would still be gone. She knew how witness security worked. Once the decision was made, few people looked back. The important thing was to keep Zach and his family safe. She couldn't do anything to compromise his safety. Even if it meant breaking her heart.

She waited until she was in the shower at the motel before she let herself cry. But she pulled herself together by the time she met up with Agent Crispin again. "You'll probably get a commendation for this, you know?" Crispin said as they headed to the airport. "What you did, capturing Janelle Chalk, took all kinds of guts."

Zach did it, she thought. He was the one who swung that log and hit Janelle, even as she was shooting at him. Without him, they might both be dead. But she didn't say that to Crispin. Talking about Zach hurt too much. She needed to find a way to lock that grief away so that she could still function. She had so much work to do.

Nine months later

MIKE CLAUDE DUG crampons into the ice coating the ledge on which he and fellow Search and Rescue volunteer Dave Mitchell stood. He clung to a rope with one hand and looked over his shoulder at the car that lay on its side on the edge of Cub Creek. A motorist had seen the dark gray sedan hit a patch of ice on the highway above and skid over the cliff and had called 911. Mike had just reported for work when he got the text and headed for Search and Rescue headquarters.

"From here, it's just a short drop to that clear section of gravel behind the vehicle." Dave pointed to a spot about fifteen feet below them. "We should be able to secure the vehicle to those trees over there."

"Looks good," Mike said. "I'm ready when you are."

Dave was right—the rappel down was short and easy. Mike was getting more comfortable with the rope work. He had spent a lot of hours these past nine months climbing, both in the gym and outdoors. It was a good way to let off steam and gave him time to process all the changes in his life. The new name, for instance. He was getting used to thinking of himself as Mike, not Zach. He was from the Midwest, newly relocated to northern California, working for a solar energy company. That was his reality now, and he was coming to accept it.

He and Dave secured the vehicle and determined it contained a lone woman driver. She was responsive, though in pain and frightened, trapped in the vehicle, on her back in the collapsed driver's seat, the powder from the exploded airbag coating her like frost. "We're going to take care of you, ma'am," Mike reassured her. "Just stay still, and we'll have you out in no time."

Darcy Yates, a paramedic, and Dr. Tim Westmoreland

arrived minutes later. Darcy, a petite woman with short, dark hair, climbed in through a busted window and began assessing the woman's injuries and keeping her as calm and as protected as possible while Mike and Dave began cutting apart the sedan.

Less than ten minutes later, the four of them worked together to transfer the woman—Marian—to a backboard and litter. They maneuvered her out of the vehicle to the ground, then prepared to haul her up. More volunteers arrived to help, and thirty minutes later, Marian was being loaded into a helicopter that had landed in the middle of the highway. The helicopter rose up and away. The volunteers watched it go, then turned away and began to clean up and gather equipment.

"Great job, Mike." Captain Ray Valdez clapped him on the back. "We're glad to have you with us."

"Glad I can help," he said. Being part of a Search and Rescue group helped him feel comfortable with this new life. That, and knowing his parents were safe.

His mom and dad—now Bill and Sally Claude—seemed to be enjoying their new life. "It's kind of nice, starting over," his mother had confided. "We're never going to forget Camille, but it's good to try to build a new life now. One that isn't connected to the Chalk brothers and everything that happened."

Except that Mike would always be connected to that.

In the early months, he had thought about little else, replaying that night over and over and over again. The last night he had seen Shelby. When he had asked to see her after his interviews with the sheriff and the FBI, he had been told she had already left to fly back to Houston. The news had stunned him. She hadn't even bothered to say goodbye? The FBI agent, a woman named Rochelle, must have seen his confusion. "She knows you're going into witness protection," she said, her voice gentle. "That's hard enough without prolonging the goodbyes."

They hadn't been together long. He told himself he would get over her soon enough. Except that hadn't happened. He was doing well, rebuilding his life into something better than ever. But there was still an ache when he thought of Shelby. She had meant something to him, and then she was simply gone.

He helped unload the gear at SAR headquarters, then went with Dave and the others for pizza and beer. He was trying to do that more, to be more social and part of the group. He had thought it would be difficult, remembering to give them the background story the Marshals Service had helped him compose to go with his new identity. But he had learned pretty quickly that almost no one asked about his past. They didn't really care.

As for the Chalk brothers, he hadn't heard anything from them. He checked the internet for news of them sometimes, but nothing came up. Janelle Chalk had been charged with the murder of Camille Gregory and Todd Chalk and was awaiting trial, but he hadn't been able to find out anything more. Rochelle had visited once and told him she didn't think he would have to testify in Janelle's trial. "We have enough evidence without exposing you," she had said.

He had asked her about Shelby, and she shut him down. "I can't tell you anything," she had said and turned away.

He tried to tell himself it didn't matter. He and his parents were safe. One day, he might even be happy again.

He left the pizza place and drove to the bungalow he was buying on a quiet street on the west side of town. He pulled into the driveway and cut the lights, then sat for a moment, studying the house with its little front porch and brick pillars.

Then a movement on the edge of the light made his heart stop. A woman stood there, silhouetted in the moonlight, a slight figure with hair around her shoulders. Not Janelle Chalk. This woman wasn't that tall. But Janelle might have cousins. Other Chalk women who saw themselves as assassins.

He started the car again, thinking he would drive away. He'd call his contact at the Marshals Service. Then the woman hurried down the steps toward him. "Zach, don't go," she said. "It's me. Shelby."

He didn't remember getting out of the car. He didn't remember running to her or pulling her close. But there they were, clinging to each other, both their faces wet with tears. He pulled her into the house and turned on the lights. "Let me look at you," he said. "I can't believe this is real." Maybe it was just another dream. One where he held her and loved her, only to wake to find her gone.

"It's real," she said, tightening her arms around him.

She was thinner than he remembered, her hair longer and a little darker. "I'm sorry it took me so long to get to you," she said. "I had to wait until you were settled in your new identity, and then it took some detective work to find you."

"My name is Mike now," he said. "Mike Claude."

"I know." She smiled, and he felt as if he'd stepped out of heavy metal armor that had been binding him for nine months.

"How did you find me?" he asked. "No one is supposed to be able to do that."

"I had help," she said. "Do you remember me talking about Phil?"

"Phil?" He shook his head. "I don't remember."

"The marshal Camille was in love with."

"The man who was ordered away and didn't come back?" He didn't have a lot of good thoughts about that man.

"He always regretted choosing his job over Camille. He agreed to help me find you, but he had to be careful. It took a while."

She caressed the side of his face. "It doesn't matter. I'm here now."

She leaned in as if to kiss him, but he turned his head to the side. "What happened? Why didn't I see you again the night we captured Janelle?"

"My boss wasn't happy about our relationship. He told me you were going into witness security and I would never see you again. Then he ordered me on a plane back to Houston. I started to refuse, but knew that would mean quitting my job and losing my best chance of finding you again."

He looked into her eyes, hers still glistening with tears.

"I was determined to see you again. I'm just sorry you had to wait so long."

"Are you still with the FBI?"

"No."

"What are you going to do?"

"I don't know. But I'll find a job. Somewhere close. That is, if you still want us to be together." Her arms around him loosened. "A lot can happen in nine months. Maybe you've changed your mind."

He pulled her against him once more. "I haven't changed my mind. I thought about looking for you, too, but I didn't know where to start. I looked online, but couldn't find anything."

"It's not a great idea for an FBI agent to have an online presence," she said. "And my address and phone number are confidential, too."

"I thought I'd lost you." His voice broke on the last word.

"You never lost me. And I'm here now."

He had always said he didn't believe in fate or destiny or

anything like that. Too much of what happened to people in life happened by accident. Camille always said she was at the pub the night Judge Hennessey was killed because she was meant to bring the Chalk brothers to justice. But that hadn't happened. She had merely been at the wrong place at the wrong time, and that hadn't worked out well for any of them. Their family had lost everything, even their names.

But he had found Shelby. Or rather, she had found him. He looked into her eyes. "I love you," he said.

"I love you, too. It's a little scary sometimes, how much. I think I fell in love with you listening to all the stories Camille told about you. I fell in love with the idea of you, then when we met, the reality was even better than the fantasy. How could I not love you?"

"I fell in love with you the night you brought over pizza," he said. "I was more than halfway there before then, but that night sealed the deal."

"Because of that kiss?" she asked.

"Because you put mushrooms on the pizza."

She looked puzzled. "But you don't like mushrooms."

"Exactly. You didn't feel like you had to leave them off the pizza just because I didn't want them. I liked that. I liked that you were sure of yourself that way. That you didn't try to make yourself over to please someone else. I felt like when I was with you, I was getting the real you, and that's who I fell in love with."

"Mike?"

"Mmm?"

"I've been practicing saying the name. I'm getting used to it."

"I'm still figuring out this new life."

"I hope you'll let me be a part of it."

"I never wanted to do it without you."

They kissed again, and for a long time neither said anything. It was enough to know that no matter what the future brought, they would face it together.

* * * * *

*Look for more books in Cindi Myers's
Eagle Mountain: Criminal History miniseries,
coming soon, only from Harlequin Intrigue!*

A Q&A with Cindi Myers

What or who inspired you to write?
Reading wonderful books as a child made me want to be a writer. I read all of Laura Ingalls Wilder's Little House books as a child and decided writing stories for others to read had to be the best job in the world.

Where do your story ideas come from?
I find stories everywhere—from observing other people, reading stories in the newspaper, listening to true crime podcasts, daydreaming. I'm fascinated by why people behave the way they do, and the many ways people find to overcome adversity.

Do you have a favorite travel destination?
The American Southwest—Utah, Arizona, New Mexico, and, of course, Colorado. I love the mountains and the deserts, the dramatic red rocks and arches. We love to camp and hike in these areas and find ourselves returning again and again.

What is your most treasured possession?
Photos of my mom and dad. They have been gone twenty years now, but I love seeing their faces smiling at me from the walls of my hallway.

What is your favorite movie?
Bull Durham. I love the baseball and the humor and the romance.

When did you read your first Harlequin romance? Do you remember its title?
I'm pretty sure my first Harlequin was a Temptation by Jennifer Crusie—*Getting Rid of Bradley.*

How did you meet your current love?
We met on a blind date, set up by my best friend, who was married to his former roommate. We were engaged six weeks later, married six months after that.

What characteristic do you most value in your friends?
Being a good listener. I find people who listen are naturally empathetic and interested in others.

Will you share your favorite reader response?
I had a Superromance titled *Child's Play* that featured a pregnant heroine. It had a small subplot with her brother and his husband adopting a child. I received a letter from a man who said he had picked up the book and read it on a flight to Europe. He and his husband were in the process of adopting and he said he cried to see characters who were going through the same thing he was, surrounded by a loving family. I still treasure that.

Other than author, what job would you like to have?
The Brown Palace Hotel in Denver has an on-site historian who conducts tours of the property and curates the many historical displays around the hotel. I always thought that would be the perfect job! And if I couldn't do that, maybe a naturalist at a botanical garden.